Antoni Story

*Coming of Age
on the Battlefields of WW II*

Linda Buzzeo Best

outskirts
press

Antonio's Story
Coming of Age on the Battlefields of WW II
All Rights Reserved.
Copyright © 2022 Linda Best
v4.0

This is a work of fiction. The events and characters described herein are imaginary and are not intended to refer to specific places or living persons. The opinions expressed in this manuscript are solely the opinions of the author and do not represent the opinions or thoughts of the publisher. The author has represented and warranted full ownership and/or legal right to publish all the materials in this book.

This book may not be reproduced, transmitted, or stored in whole or in part by any means, including graphic, electronic, or mechanical without the express written consent of the publisher except in the case of brief quotations embodied in critical articles and reviews.

Outskirts Press, Inc.
http://www.outskirtspress.com

ISBN: 978-1-9772-4993-7

Cover Photo © 2022 www.gettyimages.com. All rights reserved - used with permission.

Outskirts Press and the "OP" logo are trademarks belonging to Outskirts Press, Inc.

PRINTED IN THE UNITED STATES OF AMERICA

Dedication

In loving memory of my parents, Antonio and Helena
for achieving the American Dream
making my siblings and me their priority in life
and serving as models of social and cultural values

Written with regard for their contributions during World War II
Helena's work in a lock factory and care of her parents
and
Antonio's military service in the European Theatre
as a citizen of Italy and legal resident of the U.S.
who earned a Silver Star for valor in combat

Table of Contents

Part I: The Winds of War

Chapter 1: A Life Changing Decision 3
Chapter 2: Antonio's Departure 15
Chapter 3: All Aboard! 25
Chapter 4: Alone 33

Part II: The Crossing

Chapter 5: Goodbye Italy! 45
Chapter 6: First Day at Sea 51
Chapter 7: Finding His Place on the Ship 63
Chapter 8: Gibraltar and the Coast of Africa 73
Chapter 9: Storm at Sea 87
Chapter 10: After the Storm, Camaraderie on the Ship 95
Chapter 11: Lady Liberty 109

Part III: Land of the Free, Meeting the World in the U.S.

Chapter 12: A Country Boy in the Big City 117
Chapter 13: Little Italy 127
Chapter 14: His New Home 137
Chapter 15: Familiar Faces in His New World 149
Chapter 16: Becoming American 161
Chapter 17: The Beguiling Seamstress 171
Chapter 18: Antonio Becomes Tony 177
Chapter 19: Home of the Brave, Tony Enlists in the U.S. Army 183

Part IV: Tony Goes to War

Chapter 20: Combat Training 197
Chapter 21: An Island Assignment 215
Chapter 22: From Curaçao to the War Games 227
Chapter 23: San Diego to Gibraltar 237

Part V: The War Escalates, The Enemy is His Neighbor

Chapter 24: North African Campaign.. 251
Chapter 25: The Enemy Is My Neighbor, This Is No Way to
 Return Home 263
Chapter 26: A Bold Direction, Operation Overlord 271
Chapter 27: The Invasion of Normandy, The Race through
 France Begins 287
Chapter 28: Tony's War, The Stories of a War Hero 299

Part VI: Forging an Identity

Chapter 29: Leaving Europe.. 317
Chapter 30: Going Home 331
Chapter 31: Homecoming 341
Chapter 32: Post World War II, A New Day................................ 353
Chapter 33: Walking on Clouds 365
Chapter 34: There's No Going Back, Becoming American 375

Epilogue, Part I: Mama 393
Epilogue, Part 2: Antonio 397
Acknowledgements 401

Prologue

Frosinone, Italy
Summer 1933

The boys of the local paramilitary youth group of the Frosinone region of Italy arrived impeccably dressed for their annual training exercises. They were in full uniform, wearing Il Duce's trademark black shirts, Bermuda-styled shorts, dark knee socks, mountain boots, and fez-like caps. Cords embellished their clothing, marking achievements and rank. They carried their rifles and musical instruments.

The birth of Europe's paramilitary youth groups grew out of the social unrest caused by World War I. International Scouting, which debuted there in the 1910s, served as a model although its philosophy differed markedly. The founding of Italy's youth movement fulfilled Mussolini's mission to discipline boys and indoctrinate them in the principles of fascism. The groups operated year-long in schools, on weekends, and during summer camps, altering the boys' growing up experiences to the degree of stealing their youth. The mission of both school and field training centered on drill and order with emphasis on respect for authority—the police, God, Country, Il Duce and his family. The principal objective was to cultivate over time relentless and fierce warriors. Ironically, Scouting became a victim of the organization it had guided, collapsing after the youth groups formed.

Among the boys standing in formation that brilliant summer day was thirteen-year-old Antonio, who was moving on to his sixth year in Italy's paramilitary youth groups. Ordered to serve on his eighth birthday, he was now beginning to understand the program for what it was. Though young, he was aware of the world. After all, the war in which his father served had altered life in Italy for the worse. Preoccupied with his thoughts, Antonio mentally scanned the group of boys on the field without a hint of movement that might suggest distraction. In his thoughts, he located his cousins and friends, a mere arm's length away, comforted by their presence. He dared not turn toward them for reassurance. During that thinking time, when photos—the tools of Il Duce's propaganda—were taken, Antonio sensed a tingling along his spine. With it came an image hinting that he would walk out of those pictures one day to another life.

The eldest child in his family, Antonio was a mature, sensitive boy capable of remarkable analytic thought. He was also astute and realistic. He found peace in solitude and knew much about himself that others, even those close to him, did not. Curious by nature, he sought adventure beyond occasional travel toward the Adriatic with one of his brothers.

Antonio's greatest attribute was hidden, and it frightened him. He possessed a prescient sense of future images and scenes. From as early as he could remember, he foresaw events before they occurred with detail and clarity that disturbed him even as they served to protect him. As he braced for the next photograph, showing his grit, a thought flashed through his mind. At that moment he knew, with absolute certainty, he would never serve in Italian Forces to aid the raging tide in Europe.

And in the fullness of time, those visions and scenes came to be realized.

Part I
The Winds of War

Chapter 1
A Life Changing Decision

He stood amid the foothills of the Abruzzi Mountains, the atmosphere aromatic and filled with the scent of pine. Having reached the pinnacle, he scanned his homeland—the valley and its quaint villages—one last time, whispering the name of every town and committing images of each to memory.

The chapel bells tolled in the small mountain town, causing Antonio to stir. His brain murky after a night of revelry, he was not ready for the painful glare of a new sunrise. But his eyes suddenly snapped open as his torpor collided with a jarring reality—the day he and his family had discussed for months had come. Within twenty-four hours, he would be leaving his village for the Bay of Naples where he would board a ship to the United States of America.

An array of issues crowded his mind, wrestling with one another. Warm thoughts of his beloved Italy; his joy in working its fertile land; the cypress trees in the distance, signposts to guide travelers on the unmarked local roads. His family—Mama, Papa, his brothers Salvatore and Mario, and his sister Francesca—the sources of light and kindheartedness in his life. But there was the country's political environment, the factor that had steeled his will. Its power thrust wholesome thoughts aside, replacing them with the darkness and anxiety spurred by the toxic Youth Group. Given its impact on his future, he was convinced he could not better himself or live peacefully in Italy under the fascist regime. In fact, remaining would put him at risk, physically and intellectually.

There is no going back, he thought. His eighteenth birthday looming before him, Antonio needed to carry out the plan he and parents devised to guard his future. The sounds and scents surrounding him brought peace and soothed his fears as though affirming the decision. The fragrant atmosphere then blanketed him, protecting him for what lay ahead.

On that final day in his country, Antonio planned to slip out of his family's house in the quiet before dawn for a farewell walk through Settefrati, the medieval village where he lived, along the path he had strolled for close to eighteen years. He would weave through the hills in the direction of the Shrine of Saint Maria Di Val Canneto, a Catholic Church revered in the region and beyond. The venerated holy site commemorates the vision of Mother Mary that occurred there in the 1500s and brought vitality to the region with the miraculous appearance of water.

Antonio had planned for a leisurely walk to immerse himself in his surroundings and create memories for the months and years ahead. To outsiders, the sights along his path would appear ordinary, but to him they were the heart and soul of his identity. Antonio rose from his bed and within a half hour he was on his way. He exited his family's village house, strolling toward the piazza. He walked until he reached the medieval tower and fortifications that date to 991 A.D., as recorded in archives at the Abbey of Montecassino that's perched high above

Cassino, the most bustling local city in the region. The alley alongside the tower was one of Antonio's favorite spots in the village for its historic value and view of the three-tiered expanse surrounding and defining the village—Val di Camino, the deep valley that rolls down to Rome and up toward the village, the village itself, and the soaring Apennines above it, where Monte La Meta, the highest point in the region reigns. Antonio scanned the vastness paying homage to his village and the area, especially its fertile land, lush orchards of apples, peaches, and pears, and extensive olive and walnut groves. After fully savoring the rapturous view, Antonio moved on, walking in the direction of the town's chapel.

The medieval village of Settefrati, within the external protection area of Italy's Abruzzo National Park

Though his pace was unhurried, Antonio was hardly relaxed, his impending departure a weight clouding his mind and heart. *An ornate structure*, he thought, as he approached the small village chapel. Entering, Antonio admired the well-maintained narthex, the art, and the stained-glass windows. It was a time for prayer, so he genuflected, turned into the pew, knelt, and put his head in his hands, experiencing peace and emptiness simultaneously. Minutes passed before he rose from the pew and withdrew from the side door to the courtyard and village cemetery. The scents of the lush flowers adorning the churchyard were heady, intoxicating. He ambled along, examining each of the many headstones inscribed with his family name, Buzzco [pronounced BooTSAYoh], and the photos affixed to them, every grave expected but for the one where his sister Maria lay. Born two years after him, she succumbed to an infection at the age of two. She would be fifteen years old now if she had survived. He stood back scanning the faces in the photographs. They were beautiful, richly Italian, expressive, and vibrant. Peering into them, he connected with the souls of his forebears, experiencing an infusion of strength.

After visiting the cemetery, Antonio continued along the one road in his village. It turned upward sharply just beyond the chapel and then curved to the right. Positioned at that location, Antonio began his ascent toward the mountains. The refreshing walk, over four miles in length in one direction, was one Mama completed daily regardless of the weather. It allowed her to survey the family property as well as reach the pinnacle where the sacred shrine stood.

Weaving with the contour of the road, Antonio admired the land, his family's property—the fields, pastures, and orchards that date to the Middle Ages when the village was born. He soon came upon a familiar site, the statue of Saint Giovanni Bosco, popularly known as Don Bosco. A priest and educator, Father Bosco influenced schooling worldwide following his ordination in 1841 by rejecting corporal punishment, advocating for a nurturing learning environment, and visioning vocational education. The statue was imposing, much taller than any Italian in the region and Italians in general, which made Antonio

Mama with her mother and sister, Antonio in his Youth Group uniform, and two of Antonio's siblings

conclude the statue's proportions reflected the Saint's importance in the eyes of the villagers.

Antonio resumed his hike, reaching midpoint within the unique and varied topography of the Abruzzi Mountains, where rolling hills lead to the high peaks that in turn descend toward the Adriatic. That juncture offers magical views of the valley below the village and hints at what exists above. Antonio paused for a break where he usually did, sat on one of the rocks, emptied his mind, and breathed the fresh air. In time, a wistful thought touched his heart. It centered on Mama, whose telling actions belied the strength she hoped to exhibit as the family prepared for his departure. Her inner turmoil was transparent—the excessive cooking and cleaning, the massive pasta production earlier in the week when she "required" his assistance, her ways for finding time for the two of them. He was only too happy to indulge her—and himself. Antonio was also anxious and could not bear the thought of days, thousands of days perhaps, without Mama. But when they worked together, knowingly or unknowingly, she bolstered Antonio with decades of warmth to sustain him while demonstrating how important and soothing routines could be.

Together, they had rolled and cut the pasta that afternoon. They worked with a soothing rhythm that re-created the feeling of being rocked like a baby, and Antonio would draw from those moments often in the years ahead. Antonio admired the generations-old rolling pin Mama used, asking about its stories, and she repeated many of the age-old tales about the hands that had held the hefty tool. Antonio delighted in hearing again about the pin's origins. He visualized his grandfather carving the extra-large dowel from a sturdy Italian maple tree and his grandmother using the tool to roll dough for pastas and breads or stir large vats of food.

Mama's favorite story centered on her tiny mother, who used the huge pin to blend the heavy polenta meal that she smothered with sauce and meats before serving. There were, of course, many embroidered tales about the pin. It sometimes served as a multi-purpose household tool for loosening an item stored above or for chasing an interloper. From time to time, the dowel warned an unruly young one, and more than once an unmanageable child pulled the dowel out of the pantry with the goal of wreaking havoc. Antonio registered Mama's sense of pride and humor as she recounted those family stories and made a place for herself in them.

They continued their work, Mama lovingly preparing the pasta for Antonio's farewell dinner. Comfort and purpose flowed from their movements, and Antonio had to admit he had not felt so peaceful in days. They were ready to separate the strands of fettuccini pasta and place them on the drying racks when Papa walked in. He had to control his reaction when noticing the vast quantity of macaroni Mama and Antonio had produced. In his heart, he knew Mama's preoccupation was harmless since the beautiful strands would keep for a long time as would the peaceful feelings that emanated from both Mama and her son. That afternoon had been momentous for young Antonio. The beautiful scene of Mama and him was now etched in his mind as a lifelong memory.

Antonio rose from his resting place, sighing with serenity, and moved on to preserve more mental images of his native country. Slowly, he scanned the countryside, drilling down on details and framing what he saw. Below, beyond, and above lay the fertile land of Italy that sustained the local people. He heard the cows, their bells ringing, as they situated themselves to meet the rising sun. The orchards, olive groves, and wild horses dotted the scene. Antonio reached out and picked his favorite fruit, a luscious ripe peach.

The walk resumed. The road was no longer paved, and the grade was steep. Antonio ascended the hillside where silence surrounded him, the elevation providing a gentle breeze and the atmosphere conducive to thought. He absorbed the beauty of the setting as well as its warm embrace, which reinforced the protection he felt in the cemetery.

Eventually, he reached the pinnacle of his hike. He had ambled along for some time to reach it. At the peak, he was surrounded by jagged rocks that rose above him. One might expect the area to be stark and empty, but that was not the case. There were remarkable signs of life at the summit where the soaring Monte La Meta dominates the scene and draws attention for a natural formation on its face. That configuration depicts another face so smoothly laid that it appears etched. The marking is readily visible to anyone arriving and has become a point of interest for visitors who seek explanations for its existence and most often turn to religious themes for answers. Standing at the apex, Antonio stopped to admire Monte La Meta and ponder its lore while also taking in the appealing features at eye level—the entrance to a national park, the large Catholic Church and Shrine, and a cozy café consisting of a coffee bar and a dining area. The atmosphere was aromatic, filled with the scent of pine.

Then Antonio set his eyes on the vastness below. He stood and turned slowly, taking in the 360° panorama from the mountain top of the sweeping view of the Abruzzo region. He rotated slowly, whispering the name of every one of the twenty-four towns perched within and above the valley. *Breathtaking*, he thought. He continued to another site with sentimental value, the National Park of Abruzzo, the oldest park in the country and the greenest region in Europe at the time. Situated on the mountain's crest, the pine-scented recreation area is a destination for travelers from many points and is favored by Romans in the summer and skiers in the winter. The area developed as biodiverse, is protected land, and has remained uncontaminated through the decades to sustain the beautiful flora and fauna. For Antonio, visiting was frequent, within walking distance. On the grounds of the park, he discovered and observed wildlife native to the area—the brown bear, golden eagle, Apennine wolf, deer, otters, and chamois. The rich atmosphere of the park explains why it is home to seventy-five percent of the animal species of Europe.

Antonio's earliest memory of the park was still vivid. He recalled sitting by Lake Ladito and also swimming in it, the water cool and refreshing. He was young, his eyes wide open as he observed wildlife larger than he was. Those were peaceful and beautiful family days. Now, years older and more fond of the park than ever, Antonio stood at its entrance, ready for his good-bye promenade. To his surprise, he was chuckling rather than feeling melancholic. He could not ignore the welcome sign to his right that featured the face of the park's most noteworthy and notorious inhabitant, the wolf. Perceptions of the species have always varied worldwide, reflecting culture. In some areas, views of wolves are benign, depicting them as caretakers of humans and enemies of evil forces, but in the remote region where Antonio's lived, the wolf was and still is regarded as menacing, devilish, sneaky, and haunting, the characterization aligning with the concept of the "big bad wolf" that originated in Great Britain. Among Italians, that portrayal of the species led to a specialized form of humor, a physical slapstick style involving pranks and chases that amused children to no end but were not at all funny. In many respects the so-called fun was nothing more than a glorified version of hide and seek. The goal was to track a friend somewhere in the extensive and eerie fields of the village, act in the manner of the wolf, and scare the innocent youth to no end. That behavior was deemed hilarious during childhood, lost its luster by the late teen years, yet emerged again in other types of silly pranks among adults.

Although Antonio laughed and was warmed by his thoughts about the simplicity of Italian humor, his good cheer was short lived. Dark clouds invaded his playful musing, transporting him to the past. He was eight years old and in his first year of the Youth Group, already learning how to use weapons. It was understood that all boys from ages eight through eighteen would become active members of Mussolini's Groups. Now in his late teens looking back on those years, Antonio realized how disturbing its philosophy was.

The Youth Group's regimentation of young boys and mission imperative to annihilate the enemy during maneuvers had a profound impact on nearly every boy Antonio knew. The ten-year-long service robbed children not only of their childhoods but time with their families, the ability to concentrate on their studies, and the opportunity to envision a future other than the military. Over time, Antonio's family became increasingly concerned about the prescribed direction for his life, and well before he was of age, they began conversations about altering his future. For his brothers, who were quite a bit younger than he, there was no threat or issue yet. But for Antonio, each year brought him closer to mandatory service in the Italian Army and the transition from theoretical training to the implementation of Mussolini's plans. On his eighteenth birthday, Antonio would reach the point of no return for his future if he were not sailing to America.

Antonio was deep in thought about his past and his future as he continued to walk. He recollected a conversation with his brother Salvatore that enabled Antonio to feel comfortable about leaving his country. He could never deny loving it and the way of life in the village, but something within told Antonio he could achieve more in a place where opportunities other than farming existed. He explained his view about leaving to his brother Salvatore by pointing to a type of small bush that grew along the countryside.

"My brother, here in Italy, I feel like one of those low-lying bushes in the fields that grows out rather than up. They do not respond to the sun, they bear nothing, and they don't change much. What is their purpose? And I ask myself, what is my purpose? Some trees grow tall. Think of the beautiful fig trees in our orchards. They soar up and out, seeking the sun and soaking up its energy. The trees thrive in every way. They produce beautiful foliage, their deep emerald leaves broad and bright. They produce the succulent figs that fill our tables and provide our community with delicious cookies and biscuits, pastes and jellies, bruschetta, and fig bread. I want to be tall and productive as a fig tree is, taller and brighter than any tree around it."

Salvatore is moved by his brother's story. "Antonio, my brother and best friend, I have always known this ambitious side of you. I see it clearly, and it's something most people cannot ignore. You are someone everyone can count on. You have ideas and solutions. You are grander than this small village. It brings tears to my eyes that you are leaving, but you have *la grande forza, la volontà, e il coraggio* [the great strength, the will, and the courage] to travel to the United States on your own. I envy you. I don't know if I would have the courage to leave. You are the promise in our family, and you may well bring all of us to America in time."

Antonio's recollection of that day steadied him, and he felt strong. Then a distraction came his way. Someone was calling to him from a distance. Walking briskly up the hill were Salvatore, the middle of the three brothers, Antonio's youngest brother, Mario, and several cousins. Antonio could sense their energy and excitement. Unlike him, they were singularly focused on the upcoming celebration. While he walked and pondered, they were on their way to the orchards to pick fresh ripe fruit for the feast that would begin in a few hours. The event would not only serve as Antonio's send-off, but it would also celebrate his upcoming 18th birthday, which would occur on the ship.

Pulled back into the day by his brothers and cousins, Antonio picked up his pace. He walked briskly to town satisfied with the memories he was now carrying with him and fortified by the recollection of his conversation with Salvatore a few months ago. When the road curved, the village came into view and more signs of life were visible. The figures in the distance, the farmhands heading to the family's pastures, orchards, and groves created a beautiful tableau of his land and the farm's industry. He tucked that scene away in his memories, too.

Chapter 2
Antonio's Departure

Riding toward sea level from the picturesque hills of Italy, they feasted on the panoramic view of the city and its surroundings. They peered through the lens of time, viewing the historic Castel Nuovo, the famous Mount Vesuvius known for the destruction of Pompeii in 79 A.D., and the remarkable Bay of Naples that opens the west coast of Italy to the Mediterranean. A breathtaking slice of Italy's history lay before them.

The closer Antonio came to the center square in Settefrati, the livelier the activity. In that open space, the piazza, the necessities of life were set out, open market style—baked goods and meats, produce, and other agricultural products like cheese and milk. Italians shopped daily for fresh products since conveniences for storing food did not yet exist. One stall, the coffee bar, was particularly popular as much for the gossip as the coffee.

From a distance, Antonio could see his neighbors, friends, and family members gesturing broadly while speaking. He did not need to be close to them to know they were talking over each other for the most part. And he knew that the cacophony occasionally paused to focus on a single speaker who expressed an outrageous or exaggerated point and was then hit with a chorus of contradictions and questions. Accepting his countrymen's eccentricities, manner, and exuberance, Antonio smiled with gratitude for the simple good life in his village.

As he approached the perimeter of the piazza, many villagers waved or called out to him. Some of his friends ran toward him. With his departure fast approaching, he was the man of the hour. Acting worldly for the sake of others, he held his head high, taking on the role of a hero to heighten the group's excitement. His friends gathered around him, they made plans for the day, and they rehashed the fun and games of the previous night. As the hours passed, the feast moved slowly out of the background and into the foreground, reminding everyone that Antonio would leave the country soon. His life's path was taking a sharp turn.

In Antonio's village of approximately 400 people there were no strict rules as to who could or could not attend an event of such magnitude. It was generally understood that everyone in the town was invited to attend and encouraged to contribute a dish for the event. Only the immediate family would have seats of honor. Some villagers chose to make the distinction between those closest to the family and friends or acquaintances. The latter were more likely to visit the piazza later rather than arrive for dinner. As goods were delivered, the women arranged the banquet table while the men set up the wine barrels and accompanying supplies, including the colossal cheese rounds. When the meal ended, a designated group would organize and unveil the crowning touch for the evening, the lavish dessert table and rich coffee. By then, everyone in the town would either be present or on their way to express their regards and sample the confections.

In one small way, the gathering was no different from a typical day in the village, for the townspeople loved being outdoors and dining in each other's company. Many a day was spent outside in the open square, the elders seated, the women serving food, and the men playing bocce on the grounds outside the piazza. The young adults, teens, and children engaged in ball games or chased each other through the medieval town. The daily simple pleasures of life in the village offered startling images of youth and age that captured the energy and vitality of Italians across generations. Yet this day was not just another day in the town.

The community was now gathering to celebrate Antonio and provide a proper send off for an unusual occasion. Rarely did someone leave the peaceful yet sleepy town in the magnificent hills east of Rome at such a young age and on his own. In Antonio's case, there was no scandal associated with his departure. Rather, as witnesses to the winds of change in Europe, the townspeople, including Mama and Papa, were perceptive and realistic. The foreboding atmosphere on the continent along with the intentions of the Youth Group threatened the future of the young men in Italy, motivating Antonio's parents to act. They drew from their resources, family, and community to arrange for their eldest son to enter the U.S. legally under the sponsorship of Papa's sister Lucia who was an American citizen. Antonio would work in her laundry, providing much needed help to earn his keep. It was a drastic yet logical decision under the circumstances.

That evening Antonio's time was not his own. His obligations during dinner explained why he and his friends had celebrated and reminisced the evening prior. He circulated and visited with everyone in the piazza that evening and needed to set aside time to call on those who could not attend. Reasons existed for those expectations, the principal one the community's intense respect and love for the elderly. The village was a true interdependent community, one that exuded generosity of spirit. In some way, shape, or form, each person extended good wishes to Antonio and offered him modest gifts. The belief among Italians is that what one gives in life will be returned in a generous and meaningful way. In their words the saying is "Ottieni solo ciò che dai." [You only get what you give.] Equally important was the community's regard for the young gentle yet energetic Antonio. He was a favorite in the village for his resourcefulness and willingness to help others. He gave promise and hope to the aging villagers. Though they would miss him, they would be inspired by him, always.

So, on the evening of May 10, 1938, Antonio prepared for a major change in his life surrounded and overwhelmed by the good will and generosity of his friends and family. He would remember that night for the rest of his life, returning the munificence shown to him in multiple and unexpected ways in the years to come. While everyone present felt a weight in their hearts given Antonio's departure and the country's uncertain future, the evening passed with merriment, dance to traditional Italian folk music, stories, and jokes, to include the lore of the wolves and, of course, the consumption of good food and wine.

The festivities broke up earlier than usual to give Antonio time with his family. While they soaked in the warmth of togetherness on his final evening in his homeland, each knew they were not saying everything they wished to convey. There was fear of extreme emotion among them that could have been paralyzing when they needed to be strong and release him for his own safety.

On the morning of his departure, Antonio awoke earlier than expected. His parting imminent, he felt his stomach churning with anxiety. Consuming breakfast took effort on the part of everyone seated at the table. They were all subdued though his parents' steadiness was palpable and comforting. He understood the emotion they were holding within, for he was doing the same.

Antonio's Story 19

In an hour and a half, a family friend and his son would stop by to pick up Antonio and his father for the eighty-three-mile trip from the village to the Port of Naples. Antonio had already packed his belongings yet needed to change as did Papa. Before the two were fully prepared for their travel, Papa and Mama gifted Antonio several treasures. Knowing his parents' modest means, Antonio was surprised to receive additional funds from them. Since he had never traveled alone or lived on his own, his parents explained why he might need cash, immediately or over time, and why he should protect the funds he had. Mama presented him with his great-grandfather's Italian-made leather valise that had been handed down the generations to the eldest son. Usually, the valise held documents and business papers pertaining to the family property. The bag had weight to it, and Mama showed Antonio the family portraits tucked inside that included pictures of his grandparents along with his grandfathers' and father's war portraits. She also pointed to a leather journal in the valise that Antonio could use to write about memories of his homeland and his sailing to America.

Mama sent the photographs with Antonio to provide him with something tangible to hold on to if he struggled to adjust in America. She was also realistic about the darkness looming over their village. Every day she worried about their modest heirloom possessions and did not want to risk loss or damage to the precious family stories those mementos held. She sewed valuable coins and a few pieces of family jewelry in the inside pocket of the valise, telling Antonio he would return them to her one day when it was safe to do so. On the lighter and practical side, there were two hampers of refreshments for the journey. To everyone's surprise, Antonio told his family about a keepsake he had packed for himself. Earlier in the week, he dug around the hardiest fig tree in the orchard, the one he valued so much. He unearthed a slip of its root, hydrating and packaging it for the journey to America with him. That gesture brought tears to his parents' eyes. He could barely speak when he told them, "I want to hold on to my heritage and remember the beauty of our village with this piece of my beloved fig tree." The emotional scene that followed did not break until Mama steeled herself and urged Antonio and Papa to get ready.

Mama's eyes filled again when Antonio re-entered the kitchen dressed for his journey. Her veneer fractured with the reality of his leaving. *Quanto è bello il mio ragazzo*, she thought. [How handsome my boy is.] Like any other Italian setting out on a journey regardless of age, gender, or status, Antonio was impeccably attired, wearing dress clothing one would expect at a wedding or a funeral. His fine wool suit included a vest, a crisp shirt and tie, and a Stetson hat. He also carried his grandfather's leather valise. Antonio cut a fine figure. Given his stature and manner, he appeared regal. *My first born is now a man,* Mama thought. The family was of less than modest means, yet no one would guess that the clothing fitting Antonio as custom tailored was anything less than that. An onlooker would never fathom that every item of his apparel was handed down and altered, each piece gifted by a local resident as a sign of good will and regard.

Shortly, the family progressed to the piazza, one of the few spots in the village where vehicles could pass. The villagers were on hand for the farewell, but they gave the family space. Everyone could see Mama was beginning to fret, which was understandable. Papa tried with his eyes to remind her to remain calm, but she ignored him, clinging to Antonio and ensuring he had everything he needed. Everyone watched, unable to look away from Mama's pure love for her son. They noticed Antonio reaching to the neckline of his shirt and slowly pulling something out—his *Cornicello Portafortuna*, a curved golden horn. Centuries before, the talisman had established its roots in Italian culture as a sign of luck and the source of protection for the wearer from the pervasive evil in society. Mama was relieved to see Antonio wearing the amulet. It would supplement her prayers for her boy's safety in the time ahead.

Preoccupied with her fussing, Mama did not see their friends arrive. Friends and family started waving to Antonio as his belongings were placed in the trunk. Antonio turned to embrace his brothers and his sister fully and warmly, tears flowing freely. They could barely look at one another. *How could it be*, Antonio thought, *that I will no longer see them every day?* Mama pulled him to her, holding him tightly. For a moment her resolve about the decision nearly collapsed. Antonio turned to his neighbors and friends waving goodbye to all of them. Mama embraced him one more time, and then Papa put his arm over Antonio's shoulders and walked him toward the car. Thankful that he would have time in Naples to collect himself before Papa left, Antonio turned again to wave but gravitated to the scene that would be etched in his mind forever—his sister and brothers clinging to Mama and holding her up. In Antonio's mind, the scene he witnessed equaled the impact of Michelangelo's Renaissance sculpture *Pieta*. He held the word "compassion," the translation of *Pieta*, in his heart as he turned toward the car.

Papa patted Antonio's back as they approached the car. They both got in and settled, with the older men up front and the young in the back. A striking picture of Italian tradition, that image of the four men was something Mama would hold in her mind to her dying day. A wave of emotion overtook Antonio; with it came images of light, fire, and a premonition of an older version of himself returning with joy. The car rolled forward, ceremonially, turning out of the piazza. The spiraling road afforded the opportunity for one final look at the town, his family, and his friends. The word hero entered his mind; why, he wondered, brushing the thought away. It was not yet the time for him to claim that title.

There was little conversation during the drive to Naples, each man sitting with his thoughts, the fathers thinking about their children's generation. Much of the route followed narrow country roads, often unpaved and challenging. The atmosphere was intoxicating given the scents and deep green foliage of the season. Antonio scanned the countryside as he did his village during his walk the day before. He thought about the land in Connecticut, where he was headed, and wondered about the plants and trees common to it. Passing the orchards and groves, admiring the lush terrain, and paying special attention to his favorite image, rows and rows of fig trees, Antonio pondered the possible differences between land and agriculture in Italy and the U.S. He had no idea about what to expect. He was content to be carrying a cutting from his fig tree with him but paused with the realization that the climate in America might not be conducive to growing it. He was crestfallen to think that he might never see a fig tree again. Antonio could not hold himself back from mentioning his worries to Papa. In response Papa said, "My son, my cousin Domenico has traveled twice to the United States and found fig trees growing there, not as many as we have but enough to show your tree will survive if you take care of it." Antonio sighed with relief and hope.

Before arriving to the city, the roads improved, but the busy streets toward and into Naples pressured the village driver. The group knew the feel of an urban environment as they inched toward it. Roads were wider, more cars were on the streets, there was evidence of public transportation, and the buildings had some height to them.

Riding toward sea level from the picturesque hills, they feasted on the panoramic view of the city and its surroundings. They peered through the lens of time, viewing the historic Castel Nuovo, the famous Mount Vesuvius known for the destruction of Pompeii in 79 A.D., and the remarkable Bay of Naples that opens the west coast of Italy to the

Mediterranean. A breathtaking slice of Italy's history lay before them. The view offered a timeline of development, Italian architecture across centuries, leaving all four men deeply proud of their country despite the political culture of the times and the threat they felt on the continent. At that moment, none of them would have imagined or anticipated the bombardment Naples would undergo in the future.

The Port of Naples stood out in the spectacular scene, and the tall ships docked there served as their navigational guides. In time, they located the S.S. Roma of the Italia Lines, the vessel on which Antonio would sail. A sign of modernity and mobility, it served as a portal to his future. Their friend edged as close as he could to the ship to drop off Antonio, Papa, and a large steamer trunk and then left the area to park and have lunch. Antonio and his father took care of details at the pier.

Antonio examined the ship while waiting for the dockhands to take his trunk. He absorbed the vessel's size, how it rose out of the water, towering above the land. He admired its design and construction, thoughts of exploring it passing through his mind. Examining the vessel, a peculiar notion came to him and relieved his stress. *Perhaps,* he thought, *I've come to understand why it's typical to refer to a ship in feminine terms. Right now, I'm standing here looking the Roma over, observing her shape and beauty as I would a woman!* Antonio was simultaneously embarrassed and amused by the thoughts that crossed his mind. The steamer trunk collected and the ticket for it issued, father and son walked up the gangway to enter the ship.

Chapter 3
All Aboard!

Pointing to the map, Papa traced the Mediterranean Sea, showing Antonio how it connected to the Atlantic and was for the most part surrounded by land in the section he would traverse. Due to those conditions, the water would likely be calm for the initial part of the journey, Papa explained. Antonio observed his father's hand, a hand worn from years in the fields and orchards, as much as he listened to the point Papa was making. He committed the image to memory for the times when he needed to feel his father's presence and strength.

Antonio and his father stood in line on the gangway. Emotions tussled within Antonio as he formed the courage to acknowledge the sliver of excitement he felt about his impending departure. He had never admitted during the lengthy discussions with his family that the idea of going to the U.S. fed the imaginings of his young spirit. He was now realizing they would have understood his feelings since he was always first among his friends to try something new, wander and explore, or exceed the usual limits for young people his age. Antonio was thinking about how he might broach the topic with Papa just as Papa turned to him to say they were next in line.

The crew member who was registering Antonio seemed somewhat confused by the single ticket they displayed. He looked up at them as though searching for something. Papa explained the situation, and the crew member briefed Papa about the departure time and process for all visitors. All documents in order and Antonio's berth confirmed, he and his father moved from the entrance hall to a passageway with information about the ship's layout. The two could not resist viewing the beautiful scene at sea level. Antonio pondered the size of the world as he scanned the city and the sea. Papa sensed Antonio's enthusiasm about his travel and sighed because it eased his concerns about stepping off the ship and walking away from his son. Knowing Antonio would be distracted in a beautiful way during the ship's departure from the Bay, Papa felt reassured more than anyone would understand.

Papa had thought long and hard about how to handle the drop off and departure. He wanted to provide as much support as possible while also managing his own emotions about the separation. But Papa had to do even more—return to the village and assure Mama that Antonio had boarded safely and was settled before he and their friends left the port. Papa had to anticipate the questions Mama would have and be prepared to answer them to her satisfaction. He'd also have to admit to Mama and the children that the ship fascinated him. He had never traveled on the sea though he had heard so much about it from others.

Directions to the berths were clear, and father and son had little difficulty understanding where to go. Inside, the ship was not as large as its exterior suggested. The vessel's body was thick, consuming space, and many areas had sizable storage or service sections. Accustomed to open air and the breadth of the space available to him, Antonio felt uncomfortable until reached the beautiful open areas that spread light over the decks and into interior sections. Admiring the vessel's elegance, he was amazed to discover glass ceilings in several common areas. Etched and stained, they brought both light as well as color into the ship, and Antonio was mesmerized by the faceted effect. They reached the corridor where his berth was located, noticing the cluster of several cabins in that wing and more than one full-sized common bath. To Antonio and his father, whose village lacked running water, the amenity was luxurious though the mechanics and the logistics of the water system were something neither man could fathom. The concept and its practical use caused Antonio's mental wheels to turn, and Papa knew that one way or another his son would obtain answers to the questions that were forming. Papa exhaled a quiet sigh of relief over the space and privacy the area provided when they entered the room. Mama would be so pleased to know Antonio's room was not inferior.

At that point, Papa felt a lump in his throat. In four days, his son would turn eighteen. He had never been away from home but for the highly restrictive and regulated camps run by the Youth Group. Even then he was no more than three hours from his family. He was now leaving for another continent, far from his home, to a new country and a different language. He forced his mind not to dwell on their decision. In time, his anxiety as well as Mama's would ease. On that day, they would sigh with relief, feeling comfortable with the decision they guided Antonio to make. For now, Papa gathered himself, restoring his good disposition and sense of humor to explore the room with his son.

Both Antonio and his father knew the ship was not as large as other vessels. It accommodated only one hundred seventy-four passengers in berths, sixty in the large and luxurious first-class cabins and one hundred fourteen in varying levels of second class-cabins. Neither Papa nor Antonio could understand the need for lavish rooms. The modest berth was better than adequate for them. It was a homey, comfortable room, surprisingly equipped with a modern convenience, a sink.

Antonio had heard during family conversations about another class of accommodations, open steerage, and knew Mama was opposed to it for his purposes. From what he had heard, the space was communal. He imagined the number of passengers who traveled in that category was probably large given the economy, unrest in his country, and the widespread desire to flee.

While they were sitting on the bed, which was built into a wall, they were surprised by a knock on the door. Never did they think anyone would come to the door, but then they remembered that a porter was supposed to deliver Antonio's steamer trunk. The round-top treasure trunk brought life to the room with its ornate design and the stories it held, which Antonio and Papa re-lived for a short while as they sat together in the cabin. Papa started by telling how that type of chest was commonly used for sea voyages and travel to boarding schools. It was an exquisite piece of woodworking made of pine and stamped with its own identification number. Its sturdy brass handle dated to the early 1800s. The steamer spoke of a life dating back to Casablanca in the 1850s when it was owned by a middle-aged Moroccan merchant who traveled to Italy regularly for trade. The chest also brought Antonio's grandfather back to life with the story of his bartering with that merchant in Rome, trading wines and olive oil for spices, exotic oils, and the trunk.

Papa reminded Antonio about the trunk's modern-day stories, how it was one of a few communally owned chests in their village and the surrounding towns. It was shared across families, carted back and forth on various journeys, having been used by Papa during his service in World War I. The trunk traveled throughout Italy and to other countries and continents, the U.S., Austria-Hungary, Casablanca, and France. Among the Italians, there was always some level of movement in and out of the region by those seeking opportunities. Individuals left, sometimes returning and other times not, searching for success, fortune, exploration, or goods to buy and sell for a higher price. One way or another, no matter where the trunk traveled, it had the habit of returning to Settefrati. Migration between the village in Italy and Stamford, the city in the U.S. where Antonio would live, was common. Italians from Antonio's village gravitated there because a support system for getting them settled was in place. Given all the stories about migration, Antonio knew his trunk would be re-commissioned for another journey one day.

Antonio and Papa moved on to arrange the trunk while remembering and embellishing its story. They also discussed other village lore and gossip. The chest appeared to overtake the room, barely allowing the two to pass until Father saw the closet area where space for a trunk was carved into the wall. The two worked together to get the chest in place. They then checked its contents, locked it, and agreed to take some of their packed lunch to the deck and enjoy time together until Papa had to leave. In the process they would explore more of the ship.

Making their way out of the narrow corridors for second class berths, Antonio and his father re-traced their steps to reach the wide Promenade Deck. They detoured when one area was cordoned, and fortuitously their alternate route brought them directly to the ship's route map, which drew Antonio's attention. Given his training in the paramilitary Youth Group, he was familiar and facile with maps and map reading. In fact, Antonio loved immersing himself in maps. It was a favorite pastime, but only recently had he begun to extend his experience to other countries beyond Italy's immediate neighbors. He had used the large Atlas at his school to expand his knowledge of geography by matching events around the world with their exact geographical location. His method developed his geopolitical awareness, an interest that became a lifelong endeavor.

Examining the ship's map together, father and son learned surprising details about the route of the S.S. Roma. The sailing had originated in Villefrance, France, and proceeded to Genoa, Italy, before reaching the Port of Naples. There was a rush of excitement when they looked beyond Naples, for they discovered the ship would dock in Gibraltar a few days after it sailed. That location seemed exotic, causing Papa to burst with enthusiasm, "What an opportunity for you, Antonio! You will discover another world." They smiled at each other in acknowledgment of their shared interests in exploration and discovery.

Pointing to the map, Father began to trace the Mediterranean Sea and the ship's route. "Ahh, Antonio, an adventure lies ahead! Look at how our Mediterranean Sea leads to the Atlantic. Land will surround the ship as you sail from Italy to the tip of Europe. You will see beautiful coastlines and small islands. There will always be something to view. The sea will likely be calm during the initial part of the journey." Antonio observed his father's hand, a hand worn from years in the fields and orchards, as much as he listened to the point Papa was making. He committed the image to memory for the times when he needed to feel his father's presence and strength. "And here, Antonio, is a note about additional travel materials and maps as well as a timeline posted above the ship's map. It's waiting for the journey to begin as you are. The crew will mark the ship's progress and project plans for continuing. You will be able to anticipate sights of interest along the way, and according to the itinerary posted to the side of the map, you will travel three days to reach Gibraltar, part of a day visiting it, and an additional eight days to arrive in America." A lifetime, Antonio thought at first, but he reminded himself that time always seemed to pass too quickly.

Their discoveries raised all sorts of questions for Antonio. These rushed through his mind, and he knew he would be seeking answers along the way. At the same time, a satisfying feeling about the journey settled on Papa. He could sense Antonio's mental wheels spinning with all that he had learned so far. He could see his son consuming the books and materials available and monitoring the ship's course, using different approaches for doing so. They moved on, earnest about having lunch, and experienced a serendipitous moment when they located two deck chairs portside opposite the gangway. The location gave them a perfect view of Mount Vesuvius. What a beautiful setting for father and son to enjoy lunch and each other's company, talk a bit about the farm, and share their thoughts on what America was like. They sat on the deck, enjoyed the meal Mama prepared, relaxed, and chatted, while also communing in silence.

Restored by their lunch on the main deck, Antonio and his father agreed that it was time to move along. Soon all visitors to the ship had to disembark, and Papa knew their friends were likely waiting by the pier. They wove around the deck, the gangway in view, and stepped aside, giving themselves space. Father and son embraced, their eyes misting, each asking himself the same question: *When will we see each other again?* Neither dared to utter the words. Papa could not let go of Antonio after they embraced. His arm coiled around his son's shoulders. They stood like statues cemented to the floor.

Captain Donato Fabbri's announcement of the Roma's imminent departure and the call for all visitors to disembark echoed throughout the ship. Papa and Antonio embraced again, overcome by emotion, and gave their energy to keeping what they felt in their hearts. All that Papa could get out of his mouth was "I will look for you," reminding Antonio they would see each other again and again as Papa worked his way to the port's exit. They held hands until Papa could no longer do so. He exited the ship and immediately looked up. He smiled at Antonio and waved, receiving the same in return. He would take that moment to Mama, telling her that their eldest had boarded the ship which was secured for departure and Antonio had done well. And then Papa would backtrack and share every detail of the day starting with the drive to Naples and ending with his return to the village. He would tell everything he could remember about the ship, from the decks to the views, the berth, the steamer trunk, the map, the running water and sink, the light on the decks, and much more. With all that lay ahead, Papa knew it was the least he could do for Mama.

Papa proceeded toward their friends, who stood beyond the gangway. Father and friends turned, looking up at Antonio, Papa's hand on his heart. Antonio waved vigorously, also holding his heart. For a moment, Antonio felt pain like that experienced in the Youth Group boring into him again, bringing a sense of isolation, aloneness, and the feeling that he was going to drop to the deck. He willed himself to be brave, remain standing, and support Papa. One more wave and Papa turned away from the pier and into a side street with a heavy heart that Antonio could not see.

Chapter 4

Alone

He peered into the crystal-clear water, feeling a twinge of mind and heart. Burrowed shadows and swirling dust manifested in his mind, his eyes, and the water. Fleeting, they enveloped him, yet they did not trigger feelings of fear. Little did he know he would form a bond with the sea. It would figure considerably in his life story, bringing hardship, joy, and solace.

Standing alone against the deck rail, Antonio was surrounded by most of the ship's passengers, yet he was touched by loneliness. He felt frozen, unable to act or react. Bewildered, he had no idea about what to do or where to turn. His family, friends, and relatives in the village always referred to his migration as a meaningful life changing event, but he did not know what that meant. Well before Papa left the ship, he said, "In time you will understand the reason for your leaving." Antonio's reaction at that moment was mixed—a blend of fear, skepticism, and acceptance. Preoccupied by his thoughts and emotions, Antonio failed to notice other passengers who were behaving as he was. They, like him, were beginning to comprehend the magnitude of their dislocation and separation.

Antonio drew from his inner strength, willing himself to focus. He leaned on his practical side, telling himself to relax, look for a solution, or find something that would occupy his time or draw his attention. Having his mind wander was not an option for he feared where it would take him. He turned to the sea and found it mesmerizing and soothing. Feeling his anguish wane, he turned and peered into the ship where he noticed lost souls haphazardly roaming the vessel as though grieving. Their appearance triggered a strong response. Antonio had no reason to feel disoriented and refused to appear as lost as others did. It was not in his nature to come across as a victim. His observations prompted resolve and action, and he asked himself, *where is my sense of adventure?* That thought spurred him to get moving on the ship, return to his room briefly by way of a leisurely exploration, and then head out again to poke around the vessel to learn more about it and his fellow travelers.

Wandering since he was not yet familiar with the ship or its deck plans, Antonio examined something that stood out to him—the number of crew at work preparing for the ship's departure. He wasn't surprised that the crew's uniforms had attracted his attention. He had an aversion to uniforms having been tormented by uniformed Youth Group leaders, yet on the ship he was able to admire the crisp white naval attire. Clean and pressed, the professional look elicited a reaction much different from his memories of the fascist regalia he had recently shed. The contrast between the two sets of clothing evoked feelings of goodness and malice in his mind that nudged him to start shedding his personal darkness over fascism since it would no longer have a direct and deeply personal impact on him.

In that split second, a spark ignited, marking the first sign of Antonio's liberation from the Youth Group. Pausing to understand what had occurred, Antonio learned that a subtle shift in thinking changed his life in a big way. His aversion to uniforms was tied to the circumstances that forced him to wear them. But now he was uprooting to settle in a new environment where the mindset, according to Papa, was completely different from what he experienced in Italy. *A uniform is a uniform*, Antonio thought. *What defines a person is not what they wear. It's what the individual represents and how they conduct themselves that should determine how others react to them.*

Continuing his circuitous walk to his berth, Antonio noticed that activity on the ship had increased. More passengers were out and about on the main deck, and additional crew were on hand to serve them as well as prepare the ship for the sail away. He was beginning to perceive the vessel as densely populated, which really wasn't the case in view of the ship's capacity. For Antonio, being confined on the ship for an extended period would be a challenge. His life on board would not correlate in any way with the sprawling countryside he knew where crowds were not to be found, a bond connected humans and nature, and ample space was freeing and contemplative. Antonio thought again about the crowded open steerage area below, whose capacity could be hundreds of passengers for all he knew. Mama had never wanted that booking for him for fear of illness. As a young boy, Antonio had suffered with tuberculosis. He was now robust and well, but Mama still saw him as possibly vulnerable and the private room a necessity for that reason. He was deeply grateful for her loving care.

Antonio paused upon reaching his cabin to wonder whether he would feel his father's presence, but that thought did not prevent him from opening the door. He remembered Papa in the cabin and enjoyed the reverie about his presence. Antonio realized it would not bother him to sense the company of his father and all his family on the ship. He would feel content with a deep awareness of them. With the trunk tucked away, the cabin appeared even more comfortable for one person. His initial impression was reconfirmed. For a country boy from Italy, whose home lacked indoor plumbing, his cabin for the voyage appeared lavish. It contained manufactured furnishings, was finished with fine craftsmanship, well lit, and had a high ceiling. For a few moments the appealing features left him with a twinge of sorrow for his family. They lived without so much, yet he could not really focus on material items in his thoughts about them because their household was filled with joy and love for each other, the community, and the land.

Antonio wanted to remain true to his resolve and distracted himself by trying out everything in his room. He ran water in the sink, admiring the concept of running water, lay on the bed, and sat in the one chair provided. Everything was serviceable and pleasant. He would be comfortable in his windowless berth on a mid-ship deck. Antonio then spent time unpacking and setting up his personal space. He placed his journal on the table and pulled a book out to read when he wanted. He tried to remain active. He thought about the valise but convinced himself it was not a suitable time to look at family photographs.

Antonio soon realized he had little to do in his cabin. He paced, surveying his space, and leafed through a few papers laid out on a small table. Several words caught his eye, so he scanned the pages and found a treasure trove of information in his hands. It included an introduction to life at sea mentioning activities that would take place in addition to meals, such as bocce matches, shows, and card games. He learned about mealtimes, the location of the dining hall, and the ship's brig for imprisoning any violent or unruly passengers. He learned that luxury class passengers had a Dinner Salon, which was formal and sumptuous in contrast to the dining hall where all the passengers in second class quarters took their meals. Crew members would distribute daily schedules each morning following departure with recommendations on how to spend the day. The material also provided safety protocols and highlights of the ship's recreational activities and resources, such as the sports deck and the library. Antonio's prospects for staying busy on the ship suddenly improved, energizing him to explore the resources and activities highlighted.

Antonio was feeling good about having an agenda that would keep him busy for a while. He left his room, locking the door and checking to be sure. Strolling the corridors and climbing the stairs to the main deck, he was pleased to have navigated his way without difficulty. He walked across the deck toward the stern to take in the view from both sides of the ship and discovered that the Promenade Deck circled the vessel without obstruction. The ability to stroll freely and for a distance on board was in keeping with the Italian tradition for "*passeggiata quotidiana dopo cena*," the daily walk after dinner. Though not the proper time of day for the walk, Antonio joined the number of people strolling along the Promenade to establish their routines for days at sea. He walked nodding to and acknowledging others as was customary in Italy. He proceeded slowly on his course, observing the people, the public areas, the tiers of the ship, and the view of the Bay of Naples. Mount Vesuvius appeared before him again, which reminded him to secure a spot along the deck for viewing it during the ship's departure. As he strolled, questions about the vessel formed in Antonio's mind. The list increased with every step he took, yet there was no one he could pose them to. He froze with that thought, separating from everything around him and everything he knew as routine or familiar. Emptiness pierced him. His emotional rollercoaster had kicked in again, scaring him, but then the handsome journal Mama gifted him came to mind. If nothing else, he could pass time during the crossing in a meaningful way by writing his thoughts and questions as though he was sharing them with his friends and family.

One observation, the number of personally owned cameras on board, was close to Antonio's heart. He was fascinated by anything with moving parts. Taking mechanical items apart, studying how they worked and then re-assembling them was a pastime he enjoyed. His experiences for the most part centered on farm equipment, so it was not surprising that he would become excited about a tangible item that was relevant to life and lifestyle. Imagining family portraits and various poses on the deck of the ship, Antonio found the idea of having a camera tantalizing.

A sizable number of passengers busied themselves taking pictures of their groups, the ship, and the view of Naples Bay. One person had three cameras with him, all different styles and sizes, which forced Antonio to wonder about that man's story. He thought of the photos in his valise yet again and wanted more than anything to start documenting his new life with his own photos. That desire intensified days later when the ship began to enter the New York Harbor. The majesty before him as he looked out at Naples made him vow that he would earn the means to purchase his own camera.

Antonio proceeded to examine the ship by ambling along the deck. The vessel was in much better shape than he expected it to be, better than what his parents who were not familiar with sea travel thought it would be like. Based on the worst experiences they had heard, they prepared him with stories of drunkenness and brawls, theft, and cruelty. Then there was the Titanic, a shadow hovering over him during any discussion about his transatlantic journey. It made Mama fear for him. Though that ship, which differed immensely from his, had sunk twenty-five years earlier, it was a topic well-integrated in all conversations about transcontinental travel.

The S.S. Roma was not a new ship by any means and showed its age in contrast to others in port. Antonio concluded the Roma, with corrosion and rust here and there, was a seasoned vessel. That thought put his mind at ease. The moving parts of the ship left him with a different impression. They came to life, squeaking and moaning, raising doubt about all the words meant to assure him about a safe journey. Several other vessels in port were larger in comparison, more elegant in their design, and in better physical condition. As he continued to look out at the ships and evaluate them, Antonio found himself focusing on superficial features rather than quality or performance, which caused him to conclude he wasn't really qualified to evaluate a ship. Even though the vessel was seemingly modest and aging, Antonio had to admit everything he had seen so far was well appointed and especially generous in public areas. Every moving part and mechanical function intrigued him, and he wondered how or if he would have the opportunity to ask questions about the ship's operations and maintenance.

Antonio decided he had some work to do and set out to explore the ship further to obtain more information. He read every sign he passed while wandering along the Promenade, devouring the words yet not coming across anything worrisome. Most rules, such as where and when smoking was allowed, keeping exit doors closed, and not jumping overboard, made sense. Other rules like those referring to the game room and outdoor games offered detailed information.

The ship was scheduled to sail within the hour, and passengers were gathering along the rails on the deck. It was time to secure a good vantage point for viewing, so Antonio stepped toward the ship's stern to view Naples when they departed. Many passengers appeared to have the same idea as the area was crowded, but space for him and a few others remained.

The crowded deck afforded an unexpected means for becoming oriented. Antonio's proximity to others enabled him to catch tidbits of conversations. So far, he learned there were two priests on board and several religious sisters. The largest group of passengers, the count said to be in the hundreds, were headed to America for major federal construction projects like bridges and tunnels and were traveling in third class, the steerage section of the ship. He also overheard conversations elaborating on the ship's small library, its card room, and the daily bocce matches. "*A small world at sea,*" Antonio mused—*the Captain, two priests, nuns, a card room, bocce, and a prison. What would Mama say? Surely, she would love the idea of priests and religious sisters on board. I can imagine her monopolizing their time!*" Antonio was comforted by the presence of the people around him. As the ship prepared for departure, he committed himself to a peaceful journey to the U.S. To the best of his ability, he would attempt to resist dark moods and not brood over what might happen next.

The timing of his decision could not have been better. A few minutes later, the Roma's horn sounded one long blast announcing its imminent departure. Antonio regarded the timing of that signal as a sign, a message reaffirming his resolve about the voyage. Standing against the rail and viewing the City of Naples, Antonio felt a tap on his shoulder and turned to find a portly man speaking about the food trolley coming along. The gentleman told him to have something to eat, and Antonio was touched to know the man cared about him. When the trolley passed, he did indeed accept a panini sandwich, sparkling water, and a bag of cookies. The gentleman and his wife both smiled at Antonio, telling him to enjoy his lunch. Others turned to greet fellow passengers, everyone waving and saying, "*Salute*" while raising their beverages. Antonio joined in the tradition. Life on the ship seemed to be warming up, and he was pleased.

The ship took its time preparing to leave, and Antonio enjoyed the discussion around him, especially the fussing of those passengers wondering and worrying about the vessel's departure. Speculating about the same, Antonio reminded himself that Italians often lost track of time and were perennially late, except when going to Mass. That admission made him smile. Antonio finished his lunch, dropped his rubbish in the trash bin, and reclaimed his place at the rail. He looked down as he leaned over and glimpsed the sea, crystal clear and illuminated by the sun's rays. It glistened, bringing light to the soul. Mesmerized by the startling blue color and astonishing clarity, he peered into the crystal-clear water again with heightened perception. A twinge of mind and heart overtook him. Burrowed shadows and swirling sand manifested in his mind, his eyes, and the water. Fleeting, the feeling enveloped him but did not trigger fear. Instead, it exuded intense warmth. Little did Antonio he know that he would form a connection with the sea. It would figure considerably in his life in an encompassing manner, bringing hardship, joy, and solace over time.

Part II
The Crossing

Chapter 5
Goodbye Italy!

The world opened as his ship pulled from the port and turned. Briefly, the vessel rotated close to full circle. The movement was dance, a pirouette. He stood solidly on the deck as the Roma spun through scenes of Naples Bay, facets of Italy's history passing before the passengers' eyes.

Antonio settled in to watch the ship as it churned to release itself from the pier. He was captivated by what he considered an extraordinary event. The ship's progress toward the U.S., its navigation, and the vessel's operations would occupy his intellect and curiosity for the entire journey. The vessel's slow choreographed movement that teased and seduced interest was the beginning of Antonio's adventure. It allowed him to feast on and scrutinize the richness of the Italian landscape as it bowed to the waterway.

He admired the central urban plane dotted with parks. He was drawn to the hills for reminding him of his village and the fields. At the forefront of the scene before him was city life—buildings snugly aside one another and store fronts with rooms for rent on the floors above. For a second time that day, he savored the panoramic view of Naples's history, this time without Papa. While sad, Antonio was comforted knowing he and Papa would always remember their shared experience on the ship. Vesuvius stood boldly to his left as they departed, commanding the scene. The stratovolcano rose above the land, appearing mighty, bringing the artifacts of Pompeii to mind. Antonio stared at the colossus and imagined it erupting.

Once the ship steadied on its course, the beautiful panoramic view of the city receded, causing Antonio to shift his attention to what lay ahead, and he inhaled a magnificent portrait. The land, sea, and sky blanketed him with splendor. In his mind he held a memory born to last and be cherished over a lifetime. His surroundings sparkled on that brilliant day in May. *A heavenly image*, he thought, wishing he had a camera in his hand.

Modern Naples with Mount Vesuvius in the background

Still in range of Naples, Antonio used his book knowledge to establish his bearings, imagine places and locations, and visualize scenes. He knew the Isle of Capri was to his south in the Tyrrhenian Sea off the coast of the Amalfi Peninsula. His understanding was that Sorrento, from which someone could take a ferry to other points along Italy's Amalfi Coast, was perched on cliffs above the water. Photographs he had seen depicted a dramatic setting where precipices towered and dominated the sea. Sorrento was known for its foods and merchandise, from succulent seafood, luscious fruits, the renowned over-sized lemons, and vegetables to generations-old crafts, such as hand-tooled leather and carved-wood furnishings. The similar but more exotic Capri was a short boat ride away. The famous tourist village Ana Capri, a dot in the ocean, perched atop the island offering breathtaking views of the Mediterranean sea.

As afternoon moved into the evening, the ship sailed alone in the sea, the hues of sky and water melding to create an exotic, dreamy ambience. Antonio was lulled by the infusion of peace and tranquility. Every now and then a small island or two, specks in the sea, appeared, drawing his attention. The ship traveled at a generous clip since the sea was calm. For Antonio, the pace seemed slow. Surely, they would be approaching the channel between the islands of Corsica and Sardinia soon! But time passed, a pair of large islands did not appear, and Antonio realized he needed to study the scale of the ship's map more closely if he wanted to pinpoint key waypoints along the route.

Dusk began to settle and the crowd on the deck had diminished significantly. Antonio found himself nearly depleted emotionally yet physically famished. He weighed his options—whether to head to the dining area or take food from a trolley to his room. He chose the former to remain close to other people and made his way to the casual cafeteria-type setting for the first night on the ship. The room was neither crowded nor empty. No one table was free, so he needed to join a group and gave some thought to that while selecting his food.

His heart warmed when a gentleman older than he, perhaps in his 40s or so, reached out to introduce himself, point to his table, and invite Antonio to join him and his family. Antonio appreciated the generous gesture. He was not in the mood to sit alone.

The man, Giovanni, his wife, Sophia, and their two sons were sitting at the table, enjoying pasta that looked delicious. It was not difficult to fall into the moment with them because their children drove the conversation. There was intense excitement about the sailing. Giovanni's boys reminded Antonio of his brothers when they were younger, and Antonio himself felt like a child, sharing his fascination over the ship's departure.

Giovanni had traveled to the U.S. previously to visit family in Chicago and had stories to tell about it. In view of the political situation in Europe, he and Sophia were now contemplating immigration because they were apprehensive about their children's futures. Concerns about migrating connected Antonio and the family, which prompted Antonio to share more about his story than he intended. He spoke about his growing up, the family farm, and the youth groups, and was happy to know that someone on board was aware of him personally.

The group also enjoyed conversation about light topics. The family was impressed with Antonio's map skills and his knowledge about the itinerary, which led him to promise he'd show the map and route to the boys at a convenient time. Though the group enjoyed lively conversation, Antonio did not linger. He thanked them for the invitation as he left, telling them he appreciated the company, and they urged him to look for them on the ship. Giovanni expressed interest in discussing Antonio's emigration and paramilitary training as a child further. On returning to their quarters, the family remarked about how impressive the young man was. When Antonio returned to his berth, he thought about Giovanni and his family again and again. He felt he had met genuinely kind people who were interested in him.

Youthful, handsome, and unaccompanied, Antonio did not go unnoticed on the ship that evening. Many passengers found the attractive young man intriguing, especially the Italian mothers whose life's work was to find suitable husbands for their daughters. Why was he traveling alone? Where was his family? Did he have a family?

Chapter 6
First Day at Sea

From a distance, the ship appeared too large to pass through the strait. As it sailed the narrow path with little room to spare, it glided on a mirrored surface. Spectators lined the waterfront, which hugged the ship, creating an intimate moment, the marriage of the land and sea.

Early Morning

Unlike a spring morning in his village when Antonio awakened to the sounds of nature and a breeze entering the room through his open window, silence reigned in the cabin when he first stirred the next day. Darkness prevailed, the ship's rocking reminding Antonio he was at sea. He was alone and a single question dominated his thoughts. *Now what?* Panic accompanied his question, but a novel insight also bubbled to the surface. *At sea, it sounds exotic, dramatic.*

He settled in bed for a while, not ready to get up, and revisited the previous day. Pictorial images of his departure from his village came to mind, and he was pleasantly surprised to be able to look at the day with objectivity. He revisited different images but was unable to face the final emotional moments of his departure when the loving atmosphere in his village rode in tandem with the heartache of saying goodbye. Everything happening then and now cycled back to separation and confusion, which would not resolve until he began to adjust in America.

One special image from the previous day rested squarely in Antonio's thoughts. He would never forget Papa's gentle touch and twinkling eyes as they reviewed the map together. That interlude reassured Antonio, softening the emotion associated with their impending separation. As always, even in the worst of times, Papa's actions radiated compassion and provided the soothing touch of an angel. Paired with his bright sparkling eyes, his presence created comfort and safe space. Antonio felt good on the ship with his father beside him, and later as he viewed the breathtaking panorama before him by himself when the ship departed, he was able to smile with gratitude for his family, the beautiful day, and the people surrounding him.

It was impossible for Antonio to prevent his emotions from surging as he reflected. His eyes fell on his journal, which he picked up from the table and used to record his thoughts. Words streamed through his mind, and his pen raced to keep up. He felt good about expressing himself. A mix of impressions, insights, and drawings filled the pages, the most poignant entry his quick sketch of Mama and his siblings.

His mind rushing ahead of his pen, Antonio listed scenes he wanted to inscribe in his memories—family life in his village, sunrise in Italy, and the story of his memorable walk the day before he departed. Unable to keep up with the current of his words, he jotted down details to enhance later. Then a flood of questions flowed from this pen, most of them about the ship and his journey, fragmented thoughts of significance for him personally. A final rush of writing, for the time being that was, poured out the words and expressions he had heard yet not understood fully, some in Italian and some in English. He knew nothing about the correct spelling or gist of those words, but each intrigued him, and he hoped to learn to use them accurately.

Antonio's writing that morning was satisfying, reminding him he possessed an activity he could surely turn to any time on the ship. The release and relief he experienced by getting his thoughts on paper put a bounce in his step, and he was up and about to prepare for the day. Since the passage between the two islands was at least three hours away, getting out of his room for fresh air and checking on the ship's navigational position was the logical way to start the day. He walked up to the Promenade Deck for that purpose, and when he opened the door to step out, the brilliant morning sun fell upon him and the sea. The water was serene, a brilliant aquamarine blue. The gentle sea breeze was refreshing and enticing. He felt he could lose himself in thought standing there. He was surrounded by water with no land in sight. The beauty of the setting held him close, and he did not feel alone or stranded as he expected. *So far, so good*, he thought.

Mid-Morning

Antonio headed to the dining hall and chose to sit with a group of young men around his age for company. Like most young adults, the group came to the dining room to eat, and that they did. Conversation was limited to niceties and brief exchanges, which satisfied Antonio. When he finished eating, he moved on. Turning left to exit the room, he ran into Giovanni and his family, and they exchanged pleasantries. Since the children were hungry, the encounter was brief though there was sufficient time to make plans to meet for afternoon dinner.

Antonio had a few stops in mind. He wanted to learn about the evening bocce game since he played well and he could meet more people by participating. He assumed he could obtain the information he needed at the Reception Desk, so he walked up two decks and through the corridor to the open Hall. As he did, he heard music and turned to search for its source. To his surprise, an orchestra was performing a live symphony of Beethoven's Sonatas in a corner rearranged for the program. The sounds pleased him.

Antonio walked quietly to the desk, asked his question, and received an answer. Bocce games took place on the Sports Deck, an area he had not yet explored. Knowing he had an entire day before him, he proceeded toward the music and took a seat. He rested his eyes, allowing soothing sounds to bring peace. He was surprised at how quickly his tension ebbed and regretted the performance was not longer. He was beginning to realize the ship's programming occupied the passengers' time, not allowing a stray moment to cloud their minds. He concluded that activities on the ship were the best means for reducing his worry about how he would spend his time on board.

Ambling about the ship after the performance, Antonio realized he was disoriented for the obvious reason that traveling on a ship was well outside his realm of experience. He had left the structure of his days in the fields, orchards, and groves and entered something totally new that he was responsible for adapting to meet his needs. He thought of his time with Mama days before he left, reminding himself of the routine in her day-to-day life that made it satisfying. He paused, realizing the obvious—that he needed to create something similar to manage his time on the ship. And he was pleased to have started that process intuitively by pausing to listen to the Sonatas.

Lost in his thoughts earlier that morning, Antonio now had direction. He picked up his pace and proceeded with his plans by heading to the Sports Deck, which was conveniently located on the ship's highest level. There his mind was pleasantly occupied with the ingenuity of Italia Lines and all travel by ships, he guessed, for their attention to detail and emphasis on serving and entertaining passengers. He found the bocce playing surface, which was covered, and now knew where to go for the match later in the day. He also saw a notice about the hours for the ship's pool, a feature that seemed inconceivable to him. Though Antonio wanted to head to the library, where he hoped to find maps and other sources of information, the ship was within an hour of the passage. Interested in the approach to the islands, he retraced his steps to reach the Promenade Deck. There, he noticed something he had hoped for—food and beverage services.

Antonio stopped at the trolley for refreshments and then staked a place on the bow for a head-on view of the ship's passage. He looked out to the water, noticing land in the distance and how the sea mist added a dreamy texture to his view. He reveled in the ship's every movement as it sailed. Forty-five minutes prior to the passage, Captain Fabbri addressed passengers, orienting them to what they would see. He began with brief navigational details along with information about the Strait of Bonifacio between Corsica and Sardinia and the land on both sides of it. The Captain then explained the difference between a channel [*canale* in Italian] and strait [*stretto*]. He also cited the dimensions of both the ship and the strait, making a case for how snug the passage would be. At the end of his announcement, Captain Fabbri expressed all sorts of pleasantries reminiscent of the Old Country.

As the ship approached the islands, the separation between the two was obscured. In Antonio's eyes, the ship appeared on course to crash into the island, and that feeling was an uncanny foreshadowing of how he would react when the Roma arrived in the imposing Port of New York. As the vessel proceeded, though, perspective changed, and with little room to spare on each side, the ship entered the passage.

Spectators on the shores of Corsica and Sardinia lined the waterfront, twirling flags of Italy, waving, and cheering. The ship was so close to shore and the islands' inhabitants so close to the water's edge that Antonio could distinguish their faces. An intimate and dramatic moment, the marriage of land and sea, occurred. To the crowd, the ship must have appeared majestic and regal as it stretched toward the sky. An amazing feeling nudged Antonio at that time urging him to imagine victorious seacraft. He then felt chills along both arms that disappeared as quickly as they had come.

Antonio studied the scene from the perspective of the people on land, recalling how he felt when he arrived in Naples and admired the beauty of the seaport and waterfront. When the farthest ends of the islands were visible, Antonio took to the ship's stern to view their western sides. He noted the contour of the land as it differed from that along Mediterranean and wondered how the islands had formed over time. Anticipating and viewing the passage brought Antonio from late morning to what seemed like early afternoon. He glanced at the ship's clock and realized he would be meeting with Giovanni in less than two hours. With reluctance, he left his view of the sea and headed to the library before freshening up for dinner.

Afternoon

The late luncheon with the family of four was much like a traditional Sunday Italian dinner that ran from mid-afternoon into the evening. Antonio learned that afternoon dinners were a daily event on the ship, which provided only a light buffet late in the evening. There seemed to be flexibility in how passengers treated the dinner ritual. Some passengers left dinner early to return later for dessert and coffee. Others consumed their meals quickly, moving on to something else afterwards. The crew seemed committed to the traditional long and leisurely meal, which meant they paced the different courses. At the same time, they catered to passengers' needs as was the case when Sophia and the children stood up after the second course to leave the table for a while. The crew was at her side immediately with snacks and favors for the boys.

Antonio and Giovanni remained in the hall to enjoy the full meal. In that respect, the family adhered to the traditional roles of men and women in Italy, who tended to socialize separately during the latter part of Sunday dinner with the women leaving early to care for the children and sometimes returning toward the end for coffee. The comportment of Giovanni and his family caused Antonio to think about his own home life, where greater equality existed between Mama and Papa. Perhaps their joint involvement in the orchards and farmland factored into the difference between the two families.

If Giovanni was spending time with Antonio as a courtesy because he was traveling alone, Antonio would have been quite surprised. He sensed that Giovanni led a traditional Italian lifestyle and enjoyed discussions, especially over meals. He had a dynamic and magnetic personality—he was outgoing, expressive, demonstrative with his gestures, and generous with his time and opinions. But he did not appear to be stubborn or to perceive himself as better or more knowledgeable than others. He was interested—that was it. He never sought attention but was curious and concerned and therefore drew attention. In less than a day, he had made the acquaintance of numerous passengers, and regard for him was increasing rapidly. Antonio was a good judge of character—in social situations, he was able to identify individuals he could trust and those he could not. He saw Giovanni as the real thing—a sincere person, much like Papa, who exuded warmth and was personable.

In their conversation, Antonio and Giovanni covered a lot of territory—the districts where they were born and raised, interests, and how they would spend their time in America. Antonio was not surprised that Giovanni spoke English as he did, book English, they'd say, studied rather than used regularly and delivered with a thick Italian accent. Of course, they conversed in their native tongue because the words and the gestures worked better in Italian.

Course by course, the remaining dishes arrived at a leisurely pace during the lengthy dining period. The two men compared their thoughts about the ship, Giovanni adding insights from his first crossing and comparing the experiences. A businessman in the textile industry, Giovanni conveyed an air of competence and savoir-faire. Antonio valued Giovanni's views and decided to bring up his reaction to some of the ship's lavish appointments and his feeling about not fitting in. Giovanni took Antonio's words seriously, which Antonio appreciated, and had a great deal to say.

Giovanni stressed that he and his family did not live the type of lifestyle the ship promoted, and they, too, were unsettled by the grandeur and elegance during their first sailing. Observing the people on board, Giovanni concluded that they were no different from him and Sophia. The cruise line regarded itself as a service and travel industry, he said. There was the desire to create and market its product, a cruise, to involve passengers on the journey as a good business practice. Antonio was enthralled with the level of conversation and complexity of Giovanni's thinking. "In other words," Giovanni said, "the cruise industry is doing its best work to care for and entertain passengers in ways that make them feel they are in another world or special like royals for their comfort and enjoyment." It would be an understatement to say that Antonio found his time with Giovanni edifying.

Antonio's *Story* 59

The afternoon and the meal passed convivially with the addition of other passengers who stopped by the table from time to time, especially those from the same hometown as Giovanni. Antonio took advantage of Giovanni's knowledge when circumstances allowed. That enabled him to eventually ask Giovanni if knew anything about the man with three cameras. Antonio should not have been surprised to find Giovanni did indeed know the man. The person in question was a regionally known Italian journalist and reporter named Luca Bertucci. Giovanni knew the journalist's name in passing and had seen photographs of him in various media reports, but they had never met in person prior to the sailing. Giovanni took the opportunity the evening before to introduce himself, and the two conversed briefly during the sail away. In that conversation, Giovanni learned Luca was on assignment to write a series of articles about Italians immigrating to the U.S.—their journeys on the sea and both their short- and long-term adjustment to life in the New World.

Evening

The wait staff was setting up a lovely Venetian Dessert Table and coffee bar, which meant dinner was coming to its close though many passengers returned at that time, including Sophia and the boys. A beautiful display of confections was laid out and oh how people indulged. Antonio piled a generous number of sweets onto his plate. While treating himself to the luscious desserts, he reminded himself that the bocce game was a little over an hour away. Sooner than he wanted to, he excused himself from the table but not before asking Giovanni if he planned to play bocce and learning that he would be a spectator along with his family. Antonio left, saying he'd see them at the match and had enjoyed dining together.

Antonio had just enough time to change before heading to the Sports

Deck. There he found a few young men close to his age ready to play. He joined the group, and a crew member organized teams. While those formed, Antonio and the other players examined the bocce court, marveling over the crushed stone surface sized to specifications that had been covered earlier in the day.

The ingenuity of it all, Antonio mused. The Roma being an Italian liner, it was crafted to perfection to serve Italians. The match began, and Antonio reveled in the excitement of bocce at sea. In contrast to his unsettled feelings that morning, he was comfortable with the familiar pastime and not surprised to fit in so easily among people he hardly knew. Bocce had been part of Antonio's life since he was a toddler. The game held special meaning for him as a result, which made him grateful for the thought and care the cruise line put into activities for the passengers. He paused, realizing he was adapting to and understanding the company's practices, especially after hearing Giovanni comment on the topic.

The match over, there was the typical conversation among all Italians present during which everyone spoke at the same time to discuss the game in review. For Antonio, that enthusiasm was the greatest fun. The players decided to round up some beverages, and Antonio planned to join them after saying a few words to Giovanni and his family. The boys were excited to see Antonio walking toward them. He was good at bocce and now they admired him. Giovanni also acknowledged Antonio's athletic ability, and they all discussed the high points of various frames. They agreed to see each other the next day with Giovanni adding that he'd work on a meeting with Luca.

The post-match gathering offered a pleasant ending for what turned out to be a satisfying day for Antonio that passed much more quickly than he thought it would. The bocce players were not surprised to find they shared common interests. They were all fleeing Italy, some with their families, others on their own, and many from conditions more dire than Antonio's. They all looked forward to learning each other's stories and decided to meet for breakfast in the morning. Returning to his berth, Antonio realized how fortunate he was to have had a full day that warded off loneliness. He could not believe that fewer than forty-eight hours ago he had been in his village preparing for departure. With that, he whispered prayers of thanksgiving and prayers for his family. And then he turned to his journal, writing about his satisfying day at sea.

Chapter 7
Finding His Place on the Ship

> *Luca described the Strait of Gibraltar as a tempestuous passage due to its depth, the bodies of water that flowed into it, and the open sea. The Atlantic Ocean would be quite different from what they had experienced in the Mediterranean, a point reiterating what Papa had said. Surrounded by land but for the opening to the Strait, the Mediterranean most often offered a smooth sailing.*

Antonio woke up feeling fresh and enthusiastic about getting his third day at sea underway. He had slept soundly through the night, rocked gently in the darkness of his berth. Events of the previous day set the stage for this morning. Though Antonio had questioned himself and the tactics of the cruise line the day prior, he also sampled the goodness of his fellow passengers, tasted adventure as well as independence, and was waiting to see what would happen next. Obsessed with honoring his commitment to write in his journal, he jotted down notes about Giovanni's hospitality and the bocce match. He still could not believe the fine design of the ship's bocce square and never wanted to forget it. He also sketched a figure carrying three cameras to express his hope for an opportunity to meet Luca.

Though feeling better, Antonio would not fool himself into thinking his travels and immigration would be smooth in the short term. He realized he would have good days and bad as he adjusted to life in America and being separated from his family. Strolling through the ship, Antonio found the new day picking up where the previous one left off. He joined his bocce ball teammates for breakfast and enjoyed spirited conversations with them. The young men stood out among the passengers, who knew without asking that they had endured time in the paramilitary youth groups. As the men became acquainted with each other, they openly expressed their dismay and horror over the program's philosophy more strenuously than ever, and they experienced satisfaction for doing so.

Though Antonio continued to connect with different groups on the ship, he was reluctant about filling each day with group activities because he valued time on his own. He was independent, had personal interests, and also enjoyed spontaneous decisions. So, though Antonio's circle of acquaintances was growing, he planned to set aside time for himself to enjoy circling the Promenade Deck a few times each day, attending concerts, taking in the breezes and beauty of the sea, chasing down gossip, following the ship's route, and exploring. Antonio was shaping his independence.

Antonio liked routines, whether he was alone or in a group, so he headed to the Promenade Deck that morning to monitor the ship's progress as he usually did. The ship was now well beyond the Strait of Bonifacio and traveling west toward Spain. Antonio looked forward to seeing the country's jagged coastline in person as a point of interest. That interesting feature had caught his attention though it held no implications for the journey. As the ship sailed along approaching Spain, Antonio imagined figures and events from his studies. He thought of Christopher Columbus, Queen Isabella, the Spanish Inquisition, the

Spanish Reconquista, and Cervantes' *Don Quixote*. He yearned to see the country and understand its story. A love of travel was developing within him, but he would not have believed then that he would visit places of his imaginings much sooner than expected.

Eventually the ship turned south, cruising in the direction of Gibraltar. Antonio followed the course, carefully absorbing what he saw but also making a mental note to visit the library and learn more about the land slowly scrolling past the ship. Somewhat familiar now with the ship's schedule, Antonio left the deck and walked inside toward the Reception Area. He heard music well before he reached it. The musicians were performing again, this time playing the score of his favorite Italian Opera, the *Barber of Seville*. The lively music lifted his good spirits higher, ushering thoughts of his village and his family, where opera was commonplace in the piazza and sung by the villagers themselves. The music of Italy was handed down through performance for some time, but the invention of the victrola at the beginning of the twentieth century delivered it through a different and exciting medium. Antonio feasted on the familiar sounds, nostalgia transitioning to peace.

He had dressed casually for the morning though he knew he had to change for afternoon dinner. After the performance, there was a lull giving him enough time to visit the library and then return to his berth to change. The library was one deck above the Reception Area, and he used the stairs to get there. There was so much material available to review that he limited himself to the current leg of the route from the coast of Spain to Gibraltar and then out to the open sea. He turned to the globe first, the best way to get the lay of the land and the sea.

For Antonio, the sphere was an opulent work of art that he was afraid to handle at first. The ball itself was larger than the globe he used in his schoolhouse, but there was more to the object. An inlay of exquisite glistening semi-precious gems, an art form in Europe and the Middle East, covered the surface, presenting a precious tool for Antonio's use. He gently touched the cool surface first and then lightly traced the coast of Gibraltar with his finger as Papa had to highlight the transatlantic crossing. He turned to the Atlas beside the globe to read commentary on the country, only to discover his so-called knowledge about Gibraltar was incorrect. He had always thought of it as an island that was part of Spain though he did not know why. He now stood corrected that Gibraltar was a British territory, a small tip of land adjacent to Spain.

Antonio's breath caught as he continued to trace the ship's route. There lay the Strait of Gibraltar, their passage to the Ocean and America. On the map, the width of their crossing did not appear accommodating, but he was now better educated about scaling and calculations to gauge distance accurately. As he studied the itinerary, he absorbed the geography of one slice of the world. Consulting maps and the globe, he discovered a magnificent passage that could take place—if he and the globe were not mistaken, that was. Africa lay across the Strait, and all measures suggested it could be in range for viewing from any ship passing through the Strait to the Atlantic Ocean in the direction of the U.S. under certain conditions. On that side of the Strait lay exotic places he had heard of and read about that appeared other-worldly—Algiers, Casablanca, Morocco—names in history books that he never expected to be part of his life experience.

How extraordinary, he thought, *to skirt the coastlines of countries and continents during this journey.* His fascination increased his interest in the ship's passage into the sea, and he chose to read about Gibraltar and the Strait in the Atlas before getting ready for dinner. Photographs of Gibraltar showed desert ranges, a terrain unbeknown to him that he might see the next day. He also saw a distant view of the Rock of

Gibraltar and hoped they would be able to access it when visiting. He read about how sand dunes in the region and the confluence of major waterways churned the sea water, making it tumultuous in contrast to the Mediterranean. More informed than he thought he would become, Antonio left the library and returned to his berth. He took some time to jot down his findings about the region in his journal. He wrote as an explorer would commenting on how his world had enlarged in a few hours—through words on paper.

Giovanni and his family were already seated when Antonio arrived in the dining room. He noticed the empty seat in their area and was grateful they thought of them. After the morning's events, he looked forward to seeing them because he knew they would listen and he had so much on his mind from what he saw, heard, and read earlier. He would not rush, though. They had the afternoon and other days to catch up. Antonio took his seat, once again admiring the elegance of the dinner hour. He determined immediately that a traditional five course Italian dinner would likely be served because the "*Aperitivo*," a bubbly drink said to open the stomach prior to a meal, was placed at each table setting, along with plates of olives and nuts.

As the meal began, Giovanni's sons continued with their questions about the bocce match the evening before and that topic got the conversation going. The "*antipasti*," the next course, a starter consisting of Italian meats and cheeses, made the boys happy though the food did not stop them from asking about game rules, playing style, and strategies. Their interest amused Antonio, and he had to work hard to keep a straight face. They treated him like a star, and seeing the sparkle in their eyes, he was earnest about sharing details with them. Bocce was the country's pastime, and the least he could do was to share his insights and game strategies with them.

When *Primo piatto*, the first course, arrived, the boys were interested in the soup served, which meant the adult conversation could begin. Giovanni took the lead in telling everyone that Luca, the reporter, would be joining them for dinner at some point. The two had conversed after breakfast, Luca explaining his research and writing on migration from Italy and Giovanni telling Luca about Antonio's story. Luca was anxious to meet the young man simply because he was seeking serious and authentic conversations for his series on immigration. The information excited Antonio immensely. He was curious about Luca from the beginning, and his interest had expanded significantly when he learned Luca was a journalist. Immediately, Antonio's thoughts were churning, wondering not only about what they would discuss but also how open Luca might be to questions, given Antonio's inquisitive nature. From the few details Giovanni shared, Antonio concluded that Luca had crossed the Atlantic more than a few times, which was incredible.

Shortly after the *Primo Piatto* was served, Luca arrived, carrying his three cameras and a briefcase. He had been interviewing crew and passengers and taking pictures. The staff made room for him, adding a seat to the table, and serving him immediately. Antonio was pleased to the see the young journalist who was probably in his late thirties making good on his promise to stop by. Luca folded into the conversation, which had turned to the route from their present location to Gibraltar and then out to the Ocean. What Luca had to say enhanced what Antonio had learned. Together they chatted about places in the world that seemed exotic to them. Luca agreed with Antonio's assessment of the Strait in terms of the possible view of Africa and the churning waters, referring to his earlier travels and the unpredictable Strait as well as the force of the Atlantic. Luca described the Strait of Gibraltar as a tempestuous passage due to its depth, the bodies of water that flowed into it, and the open sea, which was what Papa had also concluded.

During his two previous voyages, Luca found the Atlantic to be more than unsettled. To reach New York, a ship traveled the northern route, which was affected by storms and winds from Africa and the characteristics of an open sea.

When *Secondo Course*, a steak, arrived accompanied by *Contorno*, a simple vegetable dish, the men were deeply involved in a discussion about immigration. Luca's assignment reflected the growing awareness and concern in Italy about the number of young men leaving the country. The pattern spoke to more than the separation of families. It forecasted a declining population, the loss of new talent in the country's work force, including the military, and a generational issue relative to the country's prosperity.

What Luca aimed to do with permission from the media company he represented was to better understand the scope of the situation by meeting with young men who already immigrated, were in the process of immigrating, or beginning to explore emigrating from Italy. Women were not discounted in his research, but they were scheduled for interviews at a later point because the model for couples and families immigrating showed men leaving the homeland first to establish themselves to some degree with family following later. The increase in the number of single men leaving Italy represented an alarming new trend, one linked to the country's politics as was the case for Antonio and his friends on board. When in the U.S., Luca studied the settlement of the Italians who left their homeland. He interviewed them some time after their arrival to learn about their living conditions, adjustment, livelihood, satisfaction, or concerns.

Since Luca was generally interested in Antonio's experience as possibly representative of many young men, he had a lot of questions and mentioned he hoped to discuss them with Antonio and his friends over the course of the journey. Antonio was agreeable. He was already aware of Luca's commitment to not publish the names of passengers who contributed to his research. Luca was supportive of the immigrants, understood their reasons for migrating, and did not want to put their futures in the U.S. at risk by naming them.

Dinner continued with the leisurely Dolce e Caffé [dessert and coffee], while the conversation turned to the cruising experience first but then returned to immigration. Luca was earnest about his research, which now involved the Captain, whose role in the immigrants' journey appeared vital to Luca's story. Luca reasoned that the person commanding the ship could speak to the habits and conduct of the immigrant passengers, whom Luca sensed were maligned in some stories about immigration. According to Luca, Captain Fabbri had already reported that during his seven years of transporting migrants thus far with a minimum of ten crossings per year, he could not remember an incident of disease, decadence, or debauchery among the immigrant passengers. In fact, he was impressed with their manner, courtesy, and hope. The Captain's impressions inspired Luca.

Antonio and Giovanni, one an immigrant now finding his way and the other considering migration, found Luca's insights comforting. Since Luca expected to visit with the Captain again during the trip, in fact dining with him sometime soon, he would ask about the possibility of touring the ship for the purposes of his research and writing with Giovanni and Antonio joining them as a courtesy. Antonio was overwhelmed by Luca's generous thinking.

Following the lengthy yet enjoyable dinner, the three men along with Giovanni's family went their separate ways for the early evening, most likely a siesta, with plans to see each other again during the evening bocce match. Between dinner and the game, Antonio kept busy by continuing his tour of the ship. He visited the library to spend more time learning about its resources, finding material of interest on Italy's history, that of the U.S., travel pages on Gibraltar, and a large book of maps. He also located the game room, which was furnished with card tables, a ping pong table, and stacks of boxed cards for anyone wanting to play to pass the time. Antonio walked leisurely through the ship on return to his room. He changed for bocce and headed to the Sports Deck, where numerous frames were played amid the rowdy Italian spectators. There was energy on the bocce court that night. The passengers were becoming familiar with the ship and each other, and the tension associated with their departure from Italy had tapered.

Following the matches and the post-game conversations, Antonio introduced his teammates to Luca, who described his project and interest in gathering information anonymously. Like Antonio, the group was generally receptive to the topic, feeling it pertained to them, and agreed to participate. They conversed a bit longer, Luca providing tips about Gibraltar. Soon the group broke up, intent on getting a good night's sleep and rising early the next day to experience the ship's dramatic entry to the port that everyone was talking about. Antonio ambled to his berth, thinking about how full the day had been. He had established a great blueprint for days at sea, his perceptions and emotions having changed 180° for the better.

Chapter 8

Gibraltar and the Coast of Africa

That afternoon, the ambience of the sea spoke to the passengers. Whether they realized the weight of their thoughts as they gazed at the African Coast or not, in their hearts they knew their lives would change irrevocably. Their silence was one of recognition. It pulsated with their awakening to the meaning of their journey.

Antonio and his new-found bocce playing friends were enthusiastic about going ashore in Gibraltar. Because of their ages and circumstances, they were cautious and had consulted Giovanni for advice the previous evening. "Big brother" that he was, Giovanni was all too happy to provide assistance. Having visited the territory previously, he talked about the area's natural beauty—the views and landforms, such as the dunes and barrier ridges. Giovanni added that they could access everything they wanted to see in the area surrounding the port, which meant there would be no difficulty with a timely return to the ship. It was not a matter of safety, he added, but one of practicality. He warned them again about getting back to the ship on time, and the young men took him seriously. Some captains were known for leaving passengers behind.

Antonio awoke early the next morning though work was not the force driving his energy. Enthusiasm was. His brief time at sea had already taught him to be ready for the unexpected, appreciate new-found interests, reach out to others, and treat the outdoors as scenery that would tell stories along the way. Everything he experienced so far was packed with discovery and insight—he had witnessed the Roma's departure from the Bay of Naples and received a life lesson about straits and canals when passing between the islands of Corsica and Sardinia. He was learning about the world by seeing it, and the more newness he experienced, the hungrier he was to learn more. He now approached each new day with anticipation, wondering how it would play out.

He refreshed himself and dressed quickly, heading to the Promenade Deck to get his bearings on the ship's path to Gibraltar. He knew the initial maneuvers were underway as soon as his eyes opened that morning, since the vessel's churning, his companion on the journey, was at full throttle. It was so early that darkness colored Antonio's view in shades of gray. Although a light mist hung in the air, he could distinguish the land mass ahead and the ship's movement toward it. Within several hours, he would experience both arriving to and sailing from the Port of Gibraltar.

Standing on the deck as the ship rocked a bit more vigorously than it had previously, the movement and the air invited him to sit for an early morning dream on the sea. He tasted the mist on his lips and sensed the gentle breeze brushing past his face. He was too awake to fall asleep, yet he dreamed, daydreamed that is, about different possibilities for his future. His imaginings played out against the backdrop of the ship's machinations as the Captain navigated into the narrow channel toward the port. Still, Antonio dreamed until he felt the advent of the day against his closed eyes. Opening them to check the ship's progress, he watched a stunning sight unfold—sunrise over the

Mediterranean Sea. The slowly rising orb began to color the horizon, shedding light on his day.

In time, Antonio extracted himself from the beautiful interlude on the deck. He relocated to the stern to follow the ship's approach to the port while still capturing the scenery on both sides of the vessel. The sun's arrival brought clarity to Antonio's eyes. The shadows that had previously lingered in the distance became distinct. The monolith Giovanni described emerged as a gray rock massif that jutted and soared from the land. The promontory was blanketed in green on all surfaces exposed to the sun. Antonio was drawn to the summit and felt a slight yearning for his village in the hills of Rome. He noticed how the mighty Rock of Gibraltar colored the sea, and his view led to an unexpected insight about Gibraltar's strategic importance as a natural fortress at the mouth of the Mediterranean. That location intrigued Antonio, giving him pause. His thoughts wandered to the protection and safety of Europe, and those tickled his mind, especially as he tallied a rough number of the ships in port and observed the territory's marine industry. Gibraltar suddenly seemed significant to him, and he would recall that observation on another day.

The ship had slowed to execute a wide turn toward the port. After taking a good look to understand the action, Antonio dashed off for a quick breakfast and to catch up with his friends for the disembarkation. The ship's procedures involved several protocols. Officials needed to inspect the ship and manifest, passengers departing for a stay in Gibraltar exited first, and then the passengers going ashore for a few hours were able to leave.

When they were eligible to exit, Antonio and his friends walked down the gangway, not as energetically as they expected because their legs felt like jelly. There was a residual feeling in their knees that matched the ship's movement and impaired their mobility. Their condition prompted lively discussion within the group, since they hadn't experienced instability on board, even when they were playing bocce! They slowed their pace, embarrassed that they might appear drunk. Yet their passing infirmity did not reduce their enthusiasm. Collectively, they had become enamored with the idea of "visiting" Gibraltar, even though they did not really know much about it. Without doubt, the massif above them was remarkable, its most incredible features its height and steep sides. Gibraltar's coastline was dramatic.

As they expected, services and shops filled the space surrounding the port, catering to newly arrived visitors. The group walked along window shopping at first, adjusting to the mix of accented British English, limited book English, Italian, Spanish, and French. Each hoped to purchase a small token to commemorate their brief visit, and they split up for a while in the shopping area to find something suitable.

Antonio took a liking to a small replica of the Europa Point Lighthouse because he had never seen anything like it and was drawn to what the shopkeeper told him about it. He learned the Lighthouse sat on the southeastern point of Gibraltar, and on a day as clear as it was then, anyone passing toward the Strait of Gibraltar could see the Lighthouse at the tip of the European continent. From that vantage point, Africa's coast was visible on a clear day as were Ceuta and the Rif Mountains of Morocco, the of Strait of Gibraltar, and Spanish towns along the shores. Mention of exotic places appealed to Antonio. He was enjoying a once in a lifetime chance to connect with another part of the world. On that day, if anyone were to tell Antonio he would return to the Strait of Gibraltar in the future, also set foot in Africa, and then remain there for an extended period, he would react with shock, wondering *how, why, when*.

From the shops, the group ventured toward the towering rock formations nearby, hoping to examine them closely and hike around or scale them for the 360° panoramic views possible. They found a suitable spot for ascending the incline safely and proceeded. It was not surprising that the trek took each of the men back to their paramilitary training, which had enabled them to develop superior skills in hiking and mountaineering. It came to light that they were using those skills for a completely different purpose, recreation, and they were satisfied that they had that acquired something useful during their arduous training.

Viewing the Rock of Gibraltar in all directions from their location, the men were unprepared for the dramatic beauty of the scenes above, below, and beyond. A few of them had cameras, which pleased Antonio, who was able to brush aside his desire for one and replace it with enthusiasm about the pictures friends would share with him. The breathtaking views from their vantage point encompassed not only natural beauty but signs of life too—the movement of ships in and out of the port, coastal services and recreation areas, the long-ridged monolith for which Gibraltar is known, and other formations both short and tall. The sweeping views introduced Antonio to a swath of life, industry, and nature he would never have known if not for his travel. He was moved by the experience, and its newness infused him with a boost of energy and the strength to not only follow but to carve his future.

The group lingered on the plateau, each man caught in his own thoughts, and all of them enjoying time ashore. Well before the ship's scheduled departure, they strolled back to the port, once again surveying the goods displayed at the different shops. Antonio decided to buy a few picture postcards even though he expected to receive photos. He wanted to remember the day until then. Reaching the ship, they walked the gangway, presenting their landing cards to enter, and then separated to return to their berths. Antonio's stop was brief. As soon as possible, he returned to the deck with his journal for a walk around and study of Gibraltar. The Promenade Deck had become an integral part of his life at sea. When he settled there that afternoon, he noticed the clouds had thickened and the water appeared choppier than it was earlier in the day. The churning tide tested the securely docked ships, creating an ominous tableau, and a foreboding veil covered his thoughts. He had the feeling the next few days would not be easy, but he kept that notion to himself.

The stop in Gibraltar altered the ship's schedule for the day. A walk-in buffet was set up in place of the traditional dinner hour. Passengers were invited to dine whenever they wished. Antonio figured he would likely see Giovanni and his family, hopefully Luca as well, in the dinner hall after the ship's departure. Until then, he remained on the Promenade Deck with his journal and a book enjoying the sail away. For reference, he wrote notes on some on his postcards about the pleasant day and the scenes featured on each card. He inserted the cards into the journal and then penned highlights of the visit—the spectacular views his central focus and the insight on the personal benefits of skills learned during paramilitary training an important and freeing second point.

That afternoon, the churning sea was garnering attention, and Antonio speculated that there would be more than rolling movement in the hours ahead. No information offered that insight, but Antonio had a feeling about a tumultuous sailing after leaving Gibraltar and believed it was beginning to play out. After a cacophony of sounds came together to announce the ship's departure, the vessel moved from the pier and out into the Mediterranean. From his vantage point Antonio could see every action initiated, both on land and in the ship, to move it back into the sea. And he was fascinated. The sights and sounds announcing the vessel's departure aligned with the ship's precise movements.

He could say everything was orchestrated or choreographed, but that would have been far too generous a statement. The efforts seemed arduous, taxing, and most frequently a response to the sea rather than an intended tactic. Following the Captain's final maneuvers, the ship departed the port and cruised toward the Strait.

The sea was not its placid self, which meant the ship's entry into the Strait was rough. Looking beyond to the water swirling and taking the ship's size into consideration, Antonio inferred that the vessel would proceed in broad rounded movements and was curious as to whether he was right or not. Moving to one of the ship's scopes, Antonio looked ahead to the waterway and his eyes popped open. From a distance, the water's movement and the tossing waves were clearly visible, leaving him to wonder what the next moments would bring. He glanced around, noticing few people on the deck. There were no notices indicating the area was closed, so he continued his watch for the points of interest, hoping to view either the Lighthouse or the African Coast.

As he expected, the ship did not veer from the coast of Gibraltar, which increased the possibility of seeing the Point. Antonio mentally reviewed the route he had seen on the map, remembering the maneuvers that would bring the ship into the Bay of Gibraltar and the Strait itself. The ship continued to hug the coast. Sailing was not entirely smooth yet no worse than moderate choppiness. While Antonio monitored the ship's progress, an onboard announcement indicated the Lighthouse was in range. The beacon came up quickly. Perched on a point over the sea and shedding its light in multiple ways, the Lighthouse was a dynamic presence at the water's edge. The ship paused in the sea, affording the view of a lifetime. As Captain Fabbri spoke, Antonio balanced a sensory load beyond anything he had ever experienced.

The Lighthouse, the breadth of the Gibraltar Coast, and the point where land and sea met all beckoned to him. Antonio did not know where to look first, but he listened. The skipper's historic perspective took the Lighthouse back to 1864, when restoration and development of the incredible crest was initiated, largely to utilize the potential of its sixteen-mile visibility. By 1894, several enhancements for guiding seafarers through the Strait's most perilous features were introduced. Antonio absorbed the historical facts that enhanced the shopkeeper's story, transforming the Lighthouse into a most worthy treasure. He listened carefully to the information about the instruments and signals developed for the beacon—the four wick burners needed to bring light to the Lighthouse, the mirrors and prisms that projected light, the flashing white lights, the foghorn that blew during their pause in the strait and nearly knocked Antonio into the sea, and the arc of red light that pulsated to mark a treacherous area of rocks and sediment.

At the end of his commentary, the Captain indicated the view of the African Coast would likely take place in thirty minutes or so. Something compelled Antonio's heart to take in that view, yet he could not understand why. The Coast of Africa seemed to appeal to many passengers as more and more people filed onto the Promenade Deck after the announcement, even though the weather was unstable. The ship moved away from the Point and toward Africa rolling with the movement of the sea. Gibraltar receded in the distance and was soon lost behind the ship. The departure was a beautiful sight, yet for Antonio, it paled in comparison to the majesty of Naples retreating.

Antonio was looking out to the sea when Giovanni and Luca showed up. They had been watching the same scene from the side of the deck rather than front and center and shifted to the stern, hoping to find him. Luca had a message for Antonio, who smiled broadly on learning Captain Fabbri welcomed their interest in the ship and invited Luca and a small group of friends to tour the vessel's underbelly and bridge. There was a complication, though—conditions over the next few days were going to be rough, and the Captain wanted to hold off on making plans until the situation improved.

It warmed Giovanni's and Luca's hearts to see Antonio light up over the news. His fresh enthusiasm was contagious! They were impressed with the earnest young man. Since he was traveling alone, they had joined forces to ensure he enjoyed the journey as much as possible. The three conversed a while longer before Giovanni left to check on his family and Luca was off to schedule an appointment with a professor on board.

Antonio turned his attention back to the ship. He was fascinated by the water's churning pattern and reasoned it resulted from the confluence of waterways he had read about in the library. Weaving forward, the ship dropped its speed, and Antonio did not know whether that action was required or at the Captain's discretion. He sensed the ship pausing before proceeding as a child might do if jumping into water from a high point. There had been so much precision in the ship's movements over the last few minutes. The ship having turned westward toward the Atlantic, Antonio shifted his position again, this time to stand port side, which would run parallel to the continent of Africa.

Having been told that he'd meet and spend time with Captain Fabbri, Antonio gave thought to questions he might want to ask, but not too many, since he did not want to impose. He stood in the breeze as he considered possibilities, his brain framing some queries when the public address system went live and another announcement began. The Captain's first comment indicated the chance of seeing the African Coast was strong due to their current location and the atmosphere. The second part of his message focused on the weather. It began with a warning about safety on board. Conditions were deteriorating since a massive storm lay ahead. They would encounter the tempest head on, timeframe unknown. That message conveyed, there was an undercurrent of quiet chatter on the ship, everyone reacting, many expressing fear. Traveling on his own, Antonio was touched by loneliness—he had forgotten that feeling for a while, but at least he now knew how to address it. He kept his questions for the Captain in mind and stood on watch for the African Coast. Despite the catch in his breath, he kept his focus and claimed a lounge chair on the deck a step away from one of the ship's scopes.

Watching and dreaming, Antonio was oblivious at first when Luca and Giovanni returned. The three men stood there, lost in thought. They contemplated their own reflections while also wondering what the others were feeling. The atmosphere at that moment was unique— the richness of the sea, an exotic region, a ship on the high waters, passengers journeying to their futures. For Antonio, the moment was other-worldly. He felt light years away from home and fathoms away from anything he knew. Drifting, that was the word for him—he was drifting with the sea—unattached but for the twenty or so people who knew him in some small way for who he was.

Antonio's eyes intertwined with the sea as he reflected, and in a split second, he was certain he had observed an image taking shape in the distance. Could it be the continent of Africa? The shape was more than a dot in the water, and Antonio was hopeful. He had promised himself before leaving home to make the most of his journey, to make it consequential in his life. Though he did not know why, seeing the African Coast had become part of that promise.

Anticipation was building and more evident in the expressions and movements of most passengers on the deck. Anticipation brought silence, breathless waiting. He stood with the hope that Africa would soon rise before their eyes. He leaned out from the rail as though trying to pull Africa toward him. Minutes passed and the formation Antonio thought he might have seen manifested in a flash. As was the case with the ship's approach to the Strait of Bonifacio, the optical allusion caused by distance suggested the ship and coast would collide. As the vessel plowed forward, though, perspective defined the distance between the two and the length of the Coast was unveiled.

What could be seen? Signs of life, settlement, and industry. Desert, sand, dots on the shoreline. Dreams of remarkable stories, explorations, and discoveries. Images of wild animals running freely. What each person saw that day as they peered at another continent was a combination of realism and the imaginings in their minds. With Africa appearing before his eyes, Antonio observed his view carefully, tilting his head to the right and to the left as though he was trying to understand or interpret a message. The scene was real, but also visioned in part, and felt.

Yes, he saw the dots along the shore and the desert. He could vision the animals. Who would ponder Africa without thinking of exotic wild animals? But Antonio also saw something else. It started with a feeling that in turn brought a shudder. His eyes focused on a picture though elements in it seemed foreign. He saw military apparatus—jeeps, weapons, tanks, and soldiers. Centering on the scene, his eyes encountered himself standing beside a tank in the heat of the day. He attempted to will the image away because it was so vivid and he could not tolerate it. Yet the image lingered, the memory of it becoming indelible. One day in the future, its narrative would resurface. Antonio found himself bewildered. He managed the incident by turning to a strategy he developed during training in the Youth Group. He detached himself from the source of fear. He tucked the image away, hiding it for another day.

Standing nearby, Giovanni and Luca felt the intensity of Antonio's thoughts and knew to leave him alone. In the end, he was a child, a very young man whose life story was undergoing changes moment by moment. Antonio had trusted his judgment about both men, and he was right to do so. Appearing close to a trance-like state, Antonio quickly released himself, shaking his head as though he was discharging the thoughts that had crossed his mind. Luca and Giovanni were pleased to see him adjust, wondering what he had been thinking about. Since Antonio traveled alone and did not have the benefit of conversation throughout each day, they saw reason for him to think and wonder. As Luca and Giovanni came to their personal conclusions, Antonio acknowledged the comfort of their presence and his need to put his experience into words to reconsider at another time. One day perhaps, he would discover an explanation for what had just happened along the Coast of Africa.

That afternoon, Antonio's thoughts may have exceeded time and space, but he was not the sole passenger on the Roma whose personal story, perceptions, dreams, and future intersected subconsciously as the ship sailed parallel to the African Coast. For those who had never traveled far beyond the villages and towns that were now part of their past, the experience was transformative as though it was literally lifting them and placing them somewhere else in the world. The incident opened the door to issues of identity at a crucial time in their lives, which many had muted until now—Who were they? Where were they going? Why had they left? What did they hope to find elsewhere? For others it was the discovery of the world, the realization that there was more to it than what they knew and that it is vast, complex, and diverse. For some, the unknown continent prompted them to acknowledge their fears.

The ambience—the water, the ship, a journey, a destination, and dreams captured the passengers' imaginations that afternoon unleashing their worries, not about the journey, but about what awaited them when it was over. Whether they realized the weight of the thoughts in their minds as they gazed at Africa or not, the exhaustion they experienced captured the intensity of what had occurred. In their hearts they knew their lives would change irrevocably in the time ahead. Their silence was one of recognition. It pulsated with their awakening to the fundamental meaning of their journey.

Chapter 9
Storm at Sea

By afternoon, the atmosphere had changed. Clouds rolled in from the southeast and increased steadily, becoming dark, dense, and low-lying. The ocean underwent a change, choppiness replacing serenity. As the ship entered the Atlantic, the waves announced their presence by crashing against its sides.

The passengers filed indoors intermittently during the scheduled time for the open dining that replaced the dinner hour that day. The adjustment accommodated the passengers who went ashore at various times while the ship was in port. At their tables, they began to speak quietly about their proximity to Africa and view of the coast, becoming animated as they continued. That dramatic interlude in their regular schedule altered the equilibrium on the ship. As the dining hour passed, everyone seemed more settled. They lingered, enjoying their bond as a group though their comfort diminished quickly when the crew came out in full force posting signs about the deteriorating weather and the impending storm. There were warnings to be cautious since the ship could jolt at any time. The newly posted signs announced limited light food service in the evening and distribution of in room food supplies from then on. Movement on the ship would be prohibited in due time. The tempest was now inevitable.

The ship began to rock, more so than at any other time so far, a sign of what was to come. Late afternoon gave way to early evening, and passengers for the most part were settling somewhere safe—in their rooms or protected common areas. The usual amenities, services, and programming —musical performances, food and beverage carts, and bocce—were all suspended. Quietly and efficiently, the ship's crew battened the hatches, a term new to Antonio's vocabulary. He did indeed observe the crew fastening all moving parts of the ship that could cause damage or injury. Crew moved methodically through the ship, securing items, stacking and then storing deck chairs, and removing furnishings on the decks that could not be secured.

Antonio, always curious, paid attention to the activity, impressed with the staff's organization and efficiency. During that period of watchfulness, he wasn't able to ignore the number of crew working on a platform located off the bow of the ship. He had not seen that platform previously. There was no reason for him to know about or look for it. The large item he scrutinized jutted out from the ship's side. It formed a floating basin and was currently holding ocean water. The crew hoisted, emptied, and pulled the unit out of the water. They folded the side panels into the platform and then fastened the entire unit to the ship's side. *What could that structure be*, Antonio wondered. He was so mystified that he called out to a crew member, asking what was going on below. "We're storing the ship's pool," the crewman said. *The pool? How could it be that the pool would be an appendix affixed to the side of the ship that would skirt over the sea? Who would dare get in that pool and risk falling into the open sea?* Watching the pool as it was disassembled and hearing the crewman's cavalier explanation, Antonio was left incredulous. He needed to learn about the pool, probably without getting in it, and made a mental note to do so when the sea was calm.

By early evening, the atmosphere began to change. Clouds rolled in from the southeast and increased steadily, becoming dark, dense, and low-lying. The ocean had undergone a change with choppiness replacing serenity. As the ship entered the Atlantic, the waves announced their presence by crashing against the ship's exterior from all points. Soon the turbulence was pronounced. The seamless mirror of seawater that allowed their ship to sail smoothly toward Gibraltar was gone.

Antonio had to admit that the imminent storm, its potential severity unknown, detracted from the comforting experiences that had occurred on the ship to that point. He had found safety and security in the daily rituals he was establishing. He had adjusted by creating a routine and carrying it out. With the ship's temporary suspension of all but the most essential services, he was feeling unbalanced and in the dark as to what the next hours, maybe even the next days, might bring. His feelings included the realization that what he had experienced so far, the ship cruising in waters sheltered by land, might differ considerably from a haul across the vast open ocean. There was no way for him to prepare but to listen to experienced voices and set his bearings. Antonio let his thoughts about the situation wander. They took him to his inner self, the two sides of his nature that were hardly complementary—the methodical cautious side that aligned with fear and the adventurous one that encouraged risk-taking. While fear of the unknown on a ship in the middle of a vast expanse of water during a storm initially evoked a reaction from Antonio's cautious side, in life he always ended up leaning toward exploration and adventure. Those were part of his spirit, and they led him to focus on the potential for the thrill and story of a lifetime.

As evening settled, he felt a wave of serenity against the backdrop of the lively sea. He took to his berth as directed, along with everyone else, learning a new phrase in the process—they would "ride out the storm." Antonio reached his room, stored the food supplies he received, prepared for the night, and then turned to his journal. On the light side, he recorded notes about the pool without limiting and probably exaggerating his own reaction. He summarized the highlights of the few hours spent in Gibraltar, yet he spent most of his time writing about the Point and the Coast of Africa, concentrating on the eerie vision of himself standing on the sands of the continent. *What was that incident? A dream, a premonition?* In his mind, what occurred was by no means understood or resolved, so he left a section in his journal blank for future notes.

Time passed. Antonio's berth did not undergo the thrashing and destruction he had envisioned when the dire announcement about storm conditions was broadcast. But the movement of the ship had increased. The Roma was rocking, tossing, and rolling. There was no straightforward pattern to its movement. The evening unwinding, Antonio had a snack, a drink of water, and prepared for the storm before going to bed. He placed the flashlight that came with his food supply on his bedside cabinet, pulled the bedpan from the closet, and placed it under the bed. Checking to ensure he did everything he could to prepare for the storm, Antonio got into bed. As he lay in there, his mind wandered to his view of the Lighthouse. Once again, the word "confluence" came to mind, and he recalled the flowing and dynamic movement of the waters in the Strait of Gibraltar. As his eyes were closing, he saw himself in Italy, walking in the orchard checking the apples, pears, and peaches.

The thrashing began in the early morning hours before daybreak. His location did not buffer the storm's pull at all. Antonio could hear and feel the wind howling but could not, of course, see or sense the deluge that was falling from the sky and striking the ship from all directions. Objects were not flying here and there as he had imagined, but for loose items, such as his chair and the papers on his desk. What was also unfastened was Antonio himself, who lay on the bed pitching and rolling with the movement of the sea. To his surprise, he did not feel ill but then realized the situation might be different if he stood. So, he decided not to try. Antonio had great curiosity about the water's appearance—the nature of its movements, the height of its waves, the foam at the crest, and the spray the waves emitted as they crashed into the ship. In his dark room, he invented scenes about what was going on outdoors.

With thoughts about the severe weather, the tumultuous sea, and his story filling his mind, Antonio fell asleep. Morning came, and he still slumbered in his berth. He awoke later in the day and was shocked to find himself still bouncing and rolling on the bed. How could it be that the storm continued? Little did he know that storms at sea could rage for days and that his own path on the ocean was now extremely dangerous. He sailed at a time when instrumentation for determining what lay ahead of a ship at sea did not exist.

Hours passed and a few mealtimes came and went since Antonio was first awakened by the severe turbulence. He had no idea about time as it slipped by and wondered how and why he was sleeping so much. What he did know as the ship rolled and dipped was that the storm was underway with tremendous strength. He had the most difficult time with body functions and struggled with illness as he groped his way to the small WC beyond his room. It was an effort to remain calm and not succumb to the movement of the sea. More than once the space around him spun. His mind yearned for his journal and books, yet he knew a glance at either would make him even more ill. As he lay in bed, he thought about the story he was crafting. His eyes were closing, and he submitted himself to sleep. Hours later, he could not say when, the public address system was activated and the Captain provided an update.

The report was not good—there was no indication that the storm would let up any time soon. The ship would offer minimal service in the dining hall and place all attention on emergencies and passenger services. Captain Fabbri explained how to contact the ship's reception, the points along the corridor where crew were regularly available, the location of the medical center and its operating hours, and the plan to continue food deliveries to each cabin. There was also a reminder to drink fluids, avoid excessive movement, and proceed with caution. The Captain discouraged passengers from leaving their quarters. While he underscored the severity of the situation, raising concern, he did not speak about imminent danger to the ship. He offered a status report, which Antonio regarded as routine. His interpretation of the message brought some peace. He lay back in bed, folding himself into the movement of the ship. It seemed that either the emotion and energy he had expended during his first few days at sea or the physical elements of the storm created insurmountable exhaustion.

It was early evening before Antonio woke again. The ship remained unstable, yet he thought there was a subtle change for the better in its movement. He could not say he felt good. His head throbbed, he was dizzy, and his body felt like lead. He was also thirsty. Now that was one problem he could solve! Fortunately, he had placed most of his supplies in the small cabinet alongside his bed and was able to reach for anything he needed. He leaned to his left toward the unit, snapping his flashlight on and grateful for its dim light. Anything bright would probably have exacerbated his pain. Pulling the bag out and seeing some bread and cheese, Antonio sensed his hunger. He drank his water slowly and approached the solid food gingerly. He could say he enjoyed what he ate.

Recalling the announcement earlier in the day about the delivery of additional food supplies, he braced himself to search for them when from the corner of his eye he sighted a blue object within reach. It was a crate packed with provisions that stood beside the cabinet. Luckily, he was able to lean over and pull it bedside. He couldn't help but look through the contents. His eyes rested on a seemingly fresh panini sandwich, and he gave it a try. He felt better having had bread, cheese, and water, so he tried to eat a bit more.

Searching through the additional food supply, Antonio realized that someone had delivered it to his room while he was sleeping. He could have felt uncomfortable about such an occurrence but decided it would be foolish to react to the matter during a crisis. He settled in bed preparing himself for a short walk outside the room to get to the lavatory. If he made it there without event, he would reward himself with a few more bites of the delicious sandwich. But before he attempted the short walk, he lay down to rest, light on, eyes open, yet he did not manage to stay awake.

The next time he awoke, Antonio braved the longer walk to the full restroom, his legs wobbly, returned as though heroic, and went back to bed immediately. In the process of accomplishing his mission, he learned he needed some time before heading to the ship's common areas. He had held on to handrails every step of the way, and completing his ablutions required utmost care. He could not imagine climbing the steps to the ship's central area, sitting up to eat, or watching the movement of the water. Thinking about those activities made him dizzy. He rested again, lamp on, eyes open, thinking, his mind wandering. More time passed than he thought, but he had nowhere to go and was feeling somewhat green. Eventually, he ate most of his sandwich, slowly, and found it satisfying. He rested awake, images and memories washing over him. He decided to surrender to the fatigue consuming him, turned the light out, and lay down giving in to the ship's movements.

Despite the turbulence, Antonio slept long and well, much better than he expected. His windowless berth was a gift, darkness enveloped and soothed him. Rather than having the nightmares he feared—worries about Italy or his own well-being and a disaster at sea, he dreamt of exotic places, love, and nature. Morning came, and he again woke up much later than usual. There was no indication that passengers were moving about. The ship was now rocking steadily, more than gently and still rolling but without the strong unexpected jolts. He imagined an announcement would come sometime soon. It came in time, and the news differed from what he expected. A stormy pattern lay ahead in the open sea, which would be turbulent and unpredictable until the vessel was closer to land again. The Captain indicated the ship would resume activities at some point but not yet.

Antonio was satisfied with the information provided. The situation had improved, and in time Antonio was able to relax comfortably in his cabin and work on his journal or read. By late morning, the instability continued but the atmosphere, the air pressure, had changed for the better. By noon, the ship's strong movements became predictable, and Antonio was able to move with them and felt steady. Something within told him to take it easy and he complied. Over fifty hours had passed, and for the most part he had lain in bed asleep on and off with little to eat or drink. He felt as though his body needed to be re-stitched. It took some time for him to remain standing without clutching to something. But he persisted, strengthening his melting legs and feeling optimistic that he would leave his cabin soon.

Chapter 10
After the Storm, Camaraderie on the Ship

The food trolley on its way, he resettled himself into a deck chair rather than a lounge. He saw some familiar faces but not anyone he interacted with regularly. Everyone was getting their bearings. That evening was not the time for bocce though he had the strong opinion that the next morning would be quite different. So, he folded himself into the evening, accepting a bowl of hearty minestrone, rolls, water, and a sweet biscuit. The waiter encouraged him to consume everything. "The food will settle your stomach to wake up fresh and alert the next day," the server said.

The atmosphere on the ship was eerie when Antonio finally felt strong enough to leave his cabin. There was no movement nor any sounds outside his berth, but for the ship's maneuvers against the strength of the sea, which had decreased but was not by any means normal. He made his way through the corridor assisted by the rails on both sides. Ascending the stairs was somewhat tricky because he felt dizzy—either the atmosphere or the narrow width of the stairway turned his stomach. As he reached the door that opened to the Promenade Deck, not yet having seen another passenger, Antonio felt he was in a different world. For some reason, *The Metamorphosis*, which had recently been translated into Italian, came to mind, making him shudder. While the short novel was highly regarded as imaginative and fantastical and he learned from it, it also frightened him then and even more now. He could not help but think he was living his own science fiction as the sole person on the ship.

Opening the door, he crossed into emptiness and continued toward the dining hall, moving slowly. He passed various stairways and corridors, all empty. When he was closer to the hall, he passed a service area, where two crew members were stationed. He was relieved when they nodded and smiled telling him the dining hall was open. He proceeded along the deck, seeing a few people out and about. Clearly, the ship was still asleep. If the passengers were going to be anywhere, he reasoned, they would be in the dining hall for water or coffee at least. He continued, nodding to those he saw, and seconds later he entered the room. There, an impressive figure, Giovanni, rose and waved him toward the breakfast table, where Luca also stood.

Antonio smiled broadly when he reached his friends and felt better already. "Giovanni and Luca, I'm so glad to see you this morning! During the storm, I thought the world was changing and would never be the same, but here we are meeting as usual. Nothing has changed." The men laughed, realizing they were all a bit giddy from the storm, causing Giovanni to comment. "Antonio, my friend, you have a wonderful imagination, and I think no matter how frightened you could have been, you treated the storm as a great adventure, a story that you will write." Antonio could not help but laugh and blush. "In a short time, you have come to know me well, Giovanni."

The three men enjoyed their reunion, genuinely pleased and relieved to see each other. They passed along the breakfast table, the light fare sending a clear message about pacing consumption while recovering from the storm. Though the men felt hungry and considered indulging, they went with the safe route of taking small servings. When seated, they shared their war stories about the storm. Giovanni and Luca praised Antonio for coping on his own, their generosity a perk after his long and restless isolation. The journalist surprised them with his sensational story about stepping out on different decks several times to photograph the storm. "All done in the interest of my profession," he said. Overcoming their initial reaction, Antonio and Giovanni listened carefully to his account, mesmerized by the details he shared and looking forward to seeing the prints. Giovanni's hands were full through the storm, his wife and children needing care. He was exhausted and straightforward about how pleasant it was to have his family sleeping so that he could step out into the fresh air.

Time seemed ample that day, and the unfolding from morning to night played out slowly. Antonio could not see much ambition among the passengers as was the case for him. The brilliant day was perfect for spending time outside and enjoying the ocean breeze even though the waves were lively and continued to break soundly. Following his late breakfast, he returned to his berth for his journal, a book, and his hat and then headed to the Promenade Deck, where he found a lounge in a quiet corner and started writing his dramatic account of the storm.

The cruise was now into the sixth evening at sea. Through the day, familiarity among the passengers resumed. Open hours for the typical multi-course dinner passed without service, yet appetites were beginning to return. Experienced with the mood of the sea and passengers, the ship's staff sensed the appropriate time for dinner. Just as Antonio was beginning to feel the pangs of hunger, a food trolley arrived on the deck, and that made him smile. Life on the sea was getting back to normal, he realized, but then again, what did he know about normality on the high seas?

Antonio preferred to eat outside, the atmosphere too appealing for him to go inside any sooner than he had to. The trolley approached, and he accepted a bowl of hearty minestrone, rolls, water, and a sweet biscuit. The waiter encouraged him to consume everything for a fresh start the next day. Antonio spent a quiet dinner hour on his own, enjoying the food and untroubled by the lively sea. He experienced peace by revisiting memories and was amazed when his thoughts reminded him that the ship's journey had passed mid-point.

The morning of day seven felt like a new day. It erased the alarm and isolation the storm had caused. The ship was back into its routine as though the tempest that pummeled the vessel had never existed and life had not missed a beat. He wrote about the sea for a while and then readied himself for the day. He was soon on his way because he was famished. No matter where he walked, the change in atmosphere was noticeable. The languor and infirmity of the day before had been obliterated. People were milling around happily though with caution due to the open sea. Notices about activities were posted. Approaching the dining area, the aroma of strong coffee wafted toward him as did heavenly scents of baked goods for a plentiful *colazione* [breakfast]. Crossing the threshold into the hall, he waved when he saw Giovanni and Luca enjoying coffee and many selections from the plentiful table.

Antonio headed to the banquet table first, greeting many passengers and glad to see his bocce friends, who invited him to play cards that afternoon and bocce in the evening. He agreed to both and moved along to fill his plate while thinking about the passage of time and the two additional guests who were sitting with Giovanni and Luca. All four men smiled and waved when Antonio approached, and introductions followed, better acquainting Antonio with two passengers he regularly saw on the ship.

Meeting the older of the two first, Professor Enrico Fermi, Antonio found himself in the presence of a distinguished Italian physicist and Professor at Sapienza University in Rome. Well-mannered and eloquent, Dr. Fermi was impressive, striking a chord with Antonio, who dreamed of becoming a professor. Alfredo, the second to be introduced was a very capable bocce player, who was also sailing on his own to flee Italy. His destination was Chicago, where he had relatives. Engaged with the Professor and others at the table, Antonio felt elevated by the depth of their conversation and the reality that he was seated in a cross-section of society that had seemed remote and unreachable to him until that very moment.

As seemed to be the case most days, Luca and Giovanni had news, which eventually explained the presence of the two additional men at the table. In rapid Italian, Giovanni brought Antonio up to date. Antonio listened with one ear, taking in all details, while simultaneously speculating about how between the preceding challenging days and that morning, Giovanni and Luca were able to scout out information, have a conversation with the Captain, and announce a tour of the ship at half past noon. Taking in the information, Antonio had to smile, respectful of Giovanni's and Luca's abilities to track down people and services, obtain information, and make things happen. Both men were connected, resourceful, and persuasive but not overbearing, and Giovanni had a unique way about him stemming from his imposing figure and his fine communication skills. Antonio admired the man and had begun to emulate his behavior.

Antonio felt fortunate to have woken up early. Though he spent some time in conversation at breakfast, he was still looking at a full day. He was surprisingly busy in a contemplative way through the morning, having enjoyed the symphony, and spent time recollecting the powerful discussion at breakfast. The word that caught his attention was "separation." Following the morning's discussion, Antonio was questioning his perceptions about leaving his country and his family. In view of others' thoughts, perhaps he was overstating the nature of his immigration by regarding it as a severance, which now seemed extreme. What prompted his thoughts was the luster with which the others spoke about an Italy that was alive and vital. In contrast, Antonio's view centered on the people of Italy, those close to him, and minimized attention to the country. Why? Perhaps he was trying to protect himself or thought it necessary to move away from the only life he recognized to adjust to the new. But now he was realizing separation was not as severe as he deemed it and possibly a subject he could not understand adequately at his age. He knew he was experiencing a confusing phenomenon that could only be grasped in time. As a result of the conversation that morning, though, he shifted his way of thinking about Italy, examining it through a new lens, one that kept his country vital and alive in his mind, and that step made him feel much better.

Insights Luca shared were also seared onto Antonio's mind. Luca spoke about the impact of immigration on identity, emphasizing how it differed across age groups for reasons of maturation and general psychological well-being. Antonio was not so worried about experiencing the phenomenon Luca described. Rather, he was interested in the concept of identity and how it could be altered or shaped by different factors. Antonio had no road map for how his life would play out in the U.S., but Luca's words opened his mind to the topic in real terms. During that period of introspection amid the strains of a beautiful symphonic performance, Antonio felt illuminated and moved by the insights he gleaned. As he walked from the performance to the meeting point for the tour, he looked around him and conjectured that many passengers were likely processing their circumstances as he was. Acknowledging that point reminded him of all the bocce players as a critical example.

Antonio's friends were standing at the meeting point on a lower deck when he arrived, and they greeted him with warmth and camaraderie. Captain Fabbri entered the room, receiving the group with good cheer and asking them to follow him. To the group's surprise, they plunged even deeper into the ship to the lowest accessible area where the vessel's mechanics were located. When each of them received hard hats before entering the engine room, Antonio wondered what his curiosity had gotten him into.

Consumed by the huge engine, the compartment was a hothouse. Seeing workers shoveling coal non-stop on shifts, upwards of a ton per day per worker, made Antonio thankful for his place in life. The Skipper told wonderful stories about life on the high seas while discussing the ship's features and operations. Antonio was startled by the account of a terrible problem with a sister ship. Through some error of judgement, the ship sailed without a sufficient supply of coal for the journey. The serious shortcoming was not noticed until the ship had sailed beyond islands and ports that could have provided assistance. To reach a location where help was available without taking a detour, the captain ordered the crew to burn some of the furnishings on board, which raised numerous health-related questions in his small tour group about fumes and the difference between burning coal and manufactured wood products.

The tour moved on to another room larger than the engine room. The two were clearly linked to one another. Multiple pipes matching those in the engine room lined that utility room. Antonio rightly conjectured that steam flowed through those pipes ship-wide to provide heat when needed. In an even larger open and unfinished area that was actually the frame of the ship, there was evidence of complex mechanisms for steering the vessel. Those functioned remotely through instrumentation that connected to the bridge on a higher deck. Each step of the tour was enlightening, and the group began to grasp the depth of Fabbri's technical know-how and responsibilities. From there, they climbed up the ship.

Their next stop was a quick view of the open steerage area, the lowest category of accommodations. The Captain indicated steerage on their journey was at capacity with 600 passengers, which shocked the group. Their brief exposure to the area conjured distressing images of passengers crammed together day and night throughout the sailing that upset the men, particularly Luca. Since that section lacked privacy and the services for passengers were few, steerage was profitable on the business side when booked to capacity. Contrary to what the general public believed, passengers traveling in steerage were not stowaways, and they paid for their passage though the fare was relatively low. Whereas the cost of Antonio's ticket was close to three hundred dollars, those in steerage paid around thirty dollars.

The group quickly exited the area and began a serious discussion about the lowest level of accommodations as they moved on. Their concerns were many—the lack of ventilation and privacy, sanitation, the cramped space, the spare meals, and limited movement. The Captain added that steerage was below the water line and consistently turbulent. The overview opened the group's eyes, troubling all of them.

Moving up another level, the tour moved on to the ship's galley and what a kitchen it was! Without hesitation, the five passengers were in awe, exclaiming "*mama mia*" over the galley's size, appliances, work area, and the quantity of food prepared. A dream kitchen for any serious Italian cook, the galley consumed the entire deck. They left it and continued their upward trek to a secure area that served multiple purposes. It carried stored luggage and cargo, housed the medical center and the brig, and also provided accommodations for some of the ship's crew. The group moved through that area quickly, climbing to the next level, where second class passengers and crew with certain levels of responsibility were accommodated. The crew resided in the narrow bow whereas passengers were allocated comfortable berths in the ship's wider mid-section. A quick step up to the next deck brought them to the officers' quarters and the luxury cabins, which varied in size but were all lavishly appointed. Their walk through that area was brief.

Certain that his tour group was familiar with the ship's common areas, the Captain proceeded to the area that interested people the most— the bridge, a term that originated with paddle steamers, whose controls were centered between the paddles on each side of a vessel to offer the best view of what lay ahead. On the top deck, the bridge spanned the ship's width, which provided a stunning 360° view of land and sea. Operations there were carried out by a full staff manning shifts twenty-four hours a day. The equipment on the bridge was enviable for the times. It included 20th Century forms of communications for technology and navigation such as radiophones and radar. The experience of being in the hallowed bridge generated numerous questions about operations and many stories of near disasters narrated energetically by the smart and jolly Captain Fabbri. Feeling they had taken up a great deal of his time, the group moved toward departure, not on their own accord but through meaningful eye contact from Luca.

While Luca and Giovanni had to leave the bridge immediately after the tour, Professor Fermi, Alfredo, and Antonio were not in a rush. They strolled along revisiting the tour and lamenting over the circumstances in Italy that were forcing many Italians to flee. They also expressed their horror over the conditions in steerage. It was painful for them to know their compatriots were traveling unsafely with the threat of illness on their journey. It was bad enough that they were fleeing, but doing so in squalor was probably humiliating. As they walked, Antonio had a fleeting question but did not feel comfortable asking it. *Why*, he wondered, *was Professor Fermi, a distinguished professor, not leaving Italy? Surely there would be a place for him in another country.*

Professor Fermi was grateful for the time with Alfredo and Antonio because the boys were traveling alone and had spoken so eloquently in the morning about their concerns as immigrants. Professor Fermi traveled frequently to the U.S. for professional reasons as he was on that sailing, and he wanted to put Alfredo and Antonio at ease. So, he told them about his travels, describing the aura of New York and its skyscrapers, the country's beautiful land, the friendly Americans, and the dynamic lifestyle in the cities. He also spoke about Chicago, where he was headed, on Alfredo's behalf, describing the beautiful downtown area where the city met the shore of one of the Great Lakes. A warm conversation flowed from Professor Fermi's kindness, with Antonio explaining how his perspective on immigration changed as a result of the morning conversation and the Professor citing important reasons for immigrating. In fact, he went so far as to mention his Jewish wife and the persecution she was now experiencing in Italy. Antonio and Alfredo were sickened by the thought. The Professor's way of speaking about the topic gave Antonio the impression that Professor Fermi was considering or may have wanted to consider migrating.

Before the group scattered, Professor Fermi felt he had to mention the Youth Groups. So grateful that they were instituted after his youth, he felt empathy for anyone who had to endure the programs. He advised the boys that the Youth Groups were behind them and they would be free in the U.S. to carve their paths. Antonio and Alfredo appreciated his counsel. Having discussed the youth groups in Gibraltar and benefitted from conversations with Giovanni, Luca, and now Professor Fermi, Antonio and Alfredo found a burden lifting and they were grateful. They thanked Professor Fermi for his time, enjoying his response, *È stato un piacere. Per favore, parliamo di nuovo. Ci vediamo questa sera.* [It was my pleasure. Please, let's talk again. I will see you this evening.]

The tour was a topic of discussion awhile later at dinner, which passed convivially and quickly largely because of the boys' interest in the ship and the Captain's visit to the table. Having missed the dinner hour during the storm, everyone stayed for the entire meal to restore the feeling of normalcy on the ship through company with others. After a splendid dessert table appeared and sweets were consumed, Giovanni and his family left, promising to attend the bocce match. With Luca and Antonio remaining, the dynamics at the table shifted, and the two discussed the tour, especially the steerage area. Though Luca traveled widely and wrote about immigration, he had never accessed the steerage level and was shocked by the conditions they witnessed. He had new-found regard for the strength of those who left one country to reside in another. He could see the potential for writing about the topic yet also realized a reporter had to be cautious about calling out the cruise industry.

Antonio's knowledge about steerage surprised Luca and was important even though none of it was firsthand. It was common for people from his region to travel to the U.S. for guaranteed construction work, their travel paid by the construction company, which meant the least expensive cost. Within his community, the thought of steerage instilled fear over illness, injury to or abuse of women in the open space, hunger, and severe seasickness. It was something everyone in his village avoided if they possibly could, as was the case with Antonio's current travels. To keep their son from traveling in the steerage compartment, Mama and Papa not only saved, but they took up contributions in their village to secure private accommodations for him. Luca hung on Antonio's every word, not knowing until now his background, modest means, and the sacrifice of many that made his departure from Italy possible. Their conversation so relaxed, Luca thought about shifting to an informal interview, sought Antonio's opining, and received permission to continue. To start, Luca wanted to hear Antonio's story in full, especially the events that led to his decision to migrate. He prompted Antonio along the way for information other than the basics of age and family life. There was interest in migration from the village and region, relatives in the U.S., if any, the paramilitary, the reason for his immigration, and the process by which it was arranged.

Antonio agreed to participate for several reasons. He wanted to help Luca because his reporting would serve immigrants and the countries welcoming them. He thought the process was beneficial to him. What he had learned about Luca since they met was that he advocated for immigrants and was quick to write whenever they were treated unfairly. Antonio regarded Luca's work as important as a result, and since Antonio wasn't certain about what constituted fair treatment in the U.S., talking with Luca might enlighten him about adjusting to the country and possible pitfalls. Antonio also thought the interview might provide an opportunity for him to express some of his feelings about immigration. While he socialized on the ship and spent time daily with Giovanni, he was not fully aware of the nuts and bolts of the immigration experience. He knew his purpose was not to share his woes, but he hoped that by sharing his thoughts for the benefit of Luca's research, he might clarify and better understand his own insights on immigration and the future.

They settled in, the interview a conversation. Antonio narrated his story and was comfortable when Luca probed topics for added information. Luca used a recording device, something Antonio had never seen, which generated an audio version of the conversation that Luca could review later. Articulate and capable of maintaining eye contact and expressing emotion, Antonio proved to be a superb interviewee. As soon as there was a break, Luca complimented Antonio on his vivid details and storytelling style. Hours passed, yet time was spent in the most pleasant and freeing manner for both men. That first interview led to two additional conversations before the ship arrived in port and a group interview with the bocce players before the end of their journey. Luca was not only gathering information, but he was giving young Antonio space to begin forming his own immigration story. Antonio felt that space and affirmation, telling Luca that evening, "I'm beginning to realize how my immigration will influence my identity," which was a concern Antonio had from the start. Luca's reflection on the evening picked up on Antonio's astuteness, *What a bright young man with a future ahead of him*, he thought, looking forward to their next meeting.

Chapter 11
Lady Liberty

Shadows of their destination were in sight, veiled by the morning mist. Tall dark shapes loomed ahead, gaining definition as the ship pressed forward. New York City! The anticipation was palpable. Shadows turned to images, images became tall buildings, people and vehicles took form.

An aura of expectancy cloaked the Roma on May 21, 1938, its final evening at sea. Preparations for arrival were underway by afternoon. Passengers attentively followed the ship's navigational maneuvers on its path to the United States of America. The general feeling on board spoke to the good will and resilience of human nature. Filled with hope from the first day, passengers had adjusted to and interacted with each other every day of their shared journey, making it special. Now with reality setting in, they were giddy with excitement, and the atmosphere at their American-style luncheon was festive and celebratory. On May 11th the prospect of eleven days at sea had seemed an eternity, but time had passed quickly.

The passengers' preoccupation with their arrival mirrored that of the crew. They, too, had business to organize for arrival. Most passengers traveled to America with the hope of establishing residency or for an extended stay. That meant a significant amount of luggage to organize, pack, and turn over for unloading. Having traveled lightly as a young single man on his own, Antonio was more free than others to enjoy his final day at sea. He had ample time to explore, remember, and register his memories as well as daydream about what would come next. In his reverie, he mused about the very famous New York City of the United States of America, what it was like and how it would compare to his Italian village. He expected an expansive low-lying city like Naples, which was the largest city he had ever seen. Within fourteen hours, every detail of his imaginings about the City would be crushed by its sheer magnitude. For the moment, though, Antonio dreamed, comfortable with and excited about his speculation.

The feelings of the afternoon carried into the evening, and the dining room that night was more alive with excitement than the luncheon had been. Passengers shared their plans for the next day, exchanged addresses, and wished each other well. Saying good-bye on the ship was a moving and emotional process. The passengers had become a family at sea, their Italian identities by region of birth having melded into a single group with a shared purpose.

For Antonio, leaving the ship represented an inevitable and irrevocable change. He would step out of a routine he had come to know and enjoy to a whole new setting that would require a different type of adjustment, a permanent change. He was grateful to all his friends and acquaintances and thanked them one by one, beginning with people he had come to know in passing and then moving on to stronger connections—the bocce players, Professor Fermi and Alfredo, and finally Giovanni and his family along with Luca. He exchanged addresses with many, yet the fondest farewell and expression of gratitude involved Giovanni and his family for saving him on the first day, and then Giovanni himself for his company and mentoring. Finally, there was Luca who educated and inspired Antonio and then surprised him with the gift of many photos from the journey that he had developed on route—photographs of the ship, passengers, Captain and crew, and Antonio, along with shots of Naples, Gibraltar, the Strait, the Point, and the Coast of Africa. Antonio could have wept when he opened the bulky package Luca handed him. The photographs fulfilled his fundamental desire for pictures as a testament of his travels to help him remember the journey and share it with others. The most emotional moment of Antonio's departure ended up being his most satisfying.

No passenger could admit to a restful night before the ship's arrival, and most arose before four a.m. on the 22nd, when the meticulous maneuvers for bringing the ship into the bay began. Among the many on deck to witness every aspect of the vessel's arrival was Antonio. He had vowed to not miss a moment.

For the most part, the ship's movement was slow, unbearably so, along the coast. Some passengers surmised that the pace was less a necessity than it was a desire to treat passengers to an amazing view of their destination in the beauty of the first light of day.

Before long, the morning sun shined on the Jersey coastline, highlighting beaches, towns, the oil industry, and New Jersey's gateway cities, Newark and Elizabeth. Turning to the right and pulling away from the coast, the vessel moved in the direction of the harbor and Manhattan Island. In that space, fog loomed, dropping a curtain over the bay crossing and the City itself. The circumstances were uncanny. Nature had decided to stage the City's unveiling and tease the passengers with ephemeral views of their New World.

The fog remained as the ship inched closer to its destination, uncovering landmarks as it progressed. The atmosphere was eerie, and sites of interest emerged suddenly, startling the passengers. Soon a remarkable and majestic sight appeared portside. A rush of emotion flowed, captured in gasps. A symbol known to all, especially those journeying to a new life—the revered Statue of Liberty—stood three hundred five feet atop its platform on an island of its own. Immense, captivating, inspirational, and soothing, the glorious monument elicited a reverential pause, a sacred moment. Passengers were silent, mesmerized. That moment stirred them, offering the strength to sustain them in the months and years ahead.

The Statue of Liberty in New York Harbor

Other spectacles awaited. Shadows of their destination were in sight, veiled by the morning mist. Tall dark shapes loomed ahead, gaining definition as the ship pressed forward. New York City! The anticipation was palpable. Shadows turned to images, images became tall buildings, people and vehicles took form. At the same time there was much to take in on the waterway. Suddenly, the vessel was surrounded by watercraft that ranged in size and served different purposes. That stunningly varied background overwhelmed passengers, who worked hard to interpret the scene. Police boats, freight vessels, fire boats, large ships, fishing boats, military might, bridges in the distance, all filling in the picture before them. Unbelievable!

The passengers felt small, alone, and intimidated.

Part III

Land of the Free, Meeting the World in the U.S.

Chapter 12
A Country Boy in the Big City

Antonio expected the Roma to glide into port, yet the aged Italian liner was forced to dance in the river's wake and wrestle its way to the berth. Tranquility reigned when the engines cut, freeing the senses to look beyond the ship and discover a canvas of the City's skyline.

The ship's destination gained definition as the vessel proceeded to the port. Buildings and bridges came into view, revealing a City much larger than anything the passengers could have imagined. A hazy sense of place was forming in their minds while their memories wanted to hold on to the past. Hearing the ship's announcements in two languages gave new meaning to their situation, creating a tug of war in their minds and hearts between the old and the new. Life was beginning to feel different as the ship, their cocoon and haven, prepared for their exit.

That busy process of setting up for disembarkation agitated many of the passengers on board, exposing the emotional tenor now that arrival was imminent. Though Antonio remained attentive to the commotion, he used the Roma's navigation toward Pier 59 as a distraction. While he expected the vessel to glide into port, the aged Italian liner was forced to dance in the river's wake and wrestle its way to the berth instead. Tranquility reigned when the engines cut, freeing the senses to look beyond the ship and discover a canvas of the City's skyline. America, land of the free and home of the brave, welcomed the predominantly émigré population.

The passengers' peaceful reveries were cut short by insistent reality. When the ship was secured at the dock and its arrival announced, the U.S. Government assumed responsibility for disembarkation and immigration. Rapid-fire public addresses in both English and Italian, spoken with clarity and urgency, directed passengers to the departure points, and explained procedures. Antonio had reviewed the protocols for the arrival of immigrants several times, and he carried a copy in his pocket. Even though he was arriving legally under his Aunt's sponsorship, he was no exception to the rigorous process the U.S. had in place for screening immigrants who wished to enter.

According to the announcement, a few groups were scheduled to disembark before Antonio could begin the process. Waiting patiently for his group to be called, he watched as others exited the ship. In time, he was in queue for departure, moving slowly along the outer deck, the atmosphere and happenings outside the ship drawing his attention. The vessel's location in the City itself made everything real. The pier, the crowds, the streets beyond, and the tall buildings were not images but real structures and people, and their essence and stature shocked Antonio. Though he had seen photographs of New York City in books and newspapers, nothing had adequately prepared him for the large and robust City.

Observing the differences between what he saw outside the ship and where he came from, Antonio found a comparison between his village and the City impossible. He had trouble registering the volume of people, vehicles, services, and processing stations that filled the pier's narrow space. The vessels in port—ships from other countries, their flags revealing their homelands, and the variety of linguistic sounds wafting into the ship—unexpectedly created a window to the world. The scene Antonio observed was something he could never have anticipated or imagined. In the area surrounding his village, his personal point of reference for the concept of urban living was the small city of Cassino, which was no match for the thriving city of Naples that was now eclipsed by New York City's skyscrapers, atmosphere, and density. His moment of discovery was by no means a negative reaction. In Antonio's eyes, the scene shined bright with newness and promise, but a glance toward the waiting crowds made him freeze. From his perspective as a country boy, the situation leaned toward chaos, and for a moment he wondered how—if— he would find his Aunt.

Urged to move along, he took a deep breath, looking at the queue of passengers ahead of him and noting that passengers moved smoothly and quickly through what was now the exit corridor, following the protocols for disembarkation. In time, passengers fanned out across several different check points. Immigrants snaked their way through the line only to be directed back into the body of the ship where the medical center was located. There, a physician asked each passenger for their medical papers and then physically examined the individual, thoroughly yet expediently, measuring vital signs and more. A person either passed through medical and continued or was held for further examination and possible deportation without ever stepping off the ship. Antonio felt insecure as he waited even though he had obtained a medical statement before leaving Italy. He also carried more detailed documentation from the Italian Armed Forces about his full recovery from tuberculosis, for the health matter had been as important in the Youth Group as it would be in America. Though Antonio agonized over the medical screening as he waited for his turn, the congenial Italian American doctor who examined him found Antonio's health robust.

Antonio followed the doctor's directions for reaching the Immigration desk, which was the next and hopefully final stage before he exited the ship. He turned his Passport and Landing Card listing his address in Stamford, Connecticut, over to the authorities. After careful scrutiny, those were approved and returned to him. He then moved on to the next station. There, an Italian-speaking Immigration Officer questioned him about his reasons for coming to the U.S. and his background, especially his politics. Antonio had not expected the latter yet realized why it was a topic of importance. He did the best he could to support his country while indicating he did not favor the current leadership. After reviewing all of Antonio's documents with care, the officer declared that everything was in order. He stamped and signed the Landing Card, stamped Antonio's passport, welcomed him to the U.S. with Italian gusto, and pointed to the corridor leading to the gangway, where he would disembark from the ship. The life changing event Antonio and his parents had discussed for some time was now in motion. He had not yet stitched together the full meaning of his immigration to America, but it was being woven with every step he took.

Looking beyond the ship, where many businesses and forms of transportation were located, Antonio realized a sizable portion of the ship's passengers and cargo had already spilled out onto the pier that was crowded and inching toward chaos. His knees felt wobbly. He no longer stared straight ahead as he did from the ship. Instead, he began to observe and take in details about the world enveloping him. He was breathlessly greeted by new sounds, smells, and images. They intoxicated him—overtaking his senses and allowing his imagination to run wild. Scanning the throngs, he absorbed the scene as he moved. A rush of unfamiliar swooshes confronted him as he reached the gangway and noticed seagulls above. Before stepping on American soil, he paused and listened to the sounds surrounding him—tonal and guttural voices, speech more rapid than Italian, the clothing of nations, a mix of races. The faces of the world in one place. He had studied that world, but he did not know it.

Commotion and clamor rushed toward Antonio as he stepped into the United States. Robust voices, food vendors. Stylish clothing, exotic textiles, short work trousers, elegant women's clothing. Women holding umbrellas despite the absence of rain. The contrast between beautiful pastel dresses and long dark skirts covered with aprons that tied across the waist, similar to but not quite like Mama's clothing, oriented him to class and culture. Men's hats of all shapes and colors—some like his fedora, others a cap tightly held at the top of the head, a tall red hat, a broad brimmed leather hat—framed the faces of the world.

The open path from the ship continued. Antonio took in the crowd while scanning those waiting, many bearing signs naming the passengers they sought. And in a glance, with enormous relief, he sighted his name on a placard and a family face resembling his father's—his Aunt Lucia, whom he had not seen in at least eight years. He made his way to her.

Aunt Lucia looked at her nephew with pride. He was ten years old, two years into his service in the Youth Group, when she left. He was an adorable boy then and a handsome one now. He had the distinguished Roman look and regal bearing, the latter likely the result of his disciplined paramilitary training. His sandy brown hair still curled, and from the distance she sensed yet could not see his clear magnetic green eyes that appeared capable of seeing into the soul. His manner matched his disposition—he was a typical Italian who could be boisterous and enjoyed socializing as was customary in his communal village. Now on his way to her, he was serious and determined. A fine figure, he was Italy's loss and a gain for the United States, Lucia thought. As he walked, she enjoyed watching him, how he balanced the clarity of his purpose while continuing to observe the richness surrounding him. She knew he was awed. She saw in him the same reaction she had experienced eight years before.

Lucia had to smile as she watched him, knowing the impact he would have on the Italian American community in Connecticut, especially the ladies. There were many lovely young Italian women available, and Lucia was already scheming to have him meet all of them. Wouldn't Aunt Lucia love to see her handsome nephew marry the prettiest and sweetest of all?

Lucia stayed put as Antonio found his way to her. She felt it wise for him to start dealing with his new environment right away. He needed to know he could fend for himself and gain confidence about his place in America. By time Antonio was close to where she stood, he had a sense of urgency about reaching her because he realized he was missing the touch of someone close to him. His upbringing loving and demonstrative, he could do with a hug from his Aunt, and that's what he received when he reached her. The reality was that she, a widow settled yet alone in the U.S., needed him as much as he needed her.

They walked along and talked about the journey. Lucia herself had questions for him, but she yielded the floor to him and let him talk. They made their way towards the baggage area, reached the pick-up point, and obtained his trunk. Then they looked for his Aunt's friends, restaurant owners who arranged their visit to the City to coincide with Antonio's arrival. Though the friends had no room for passengers, they were able to take his trunk and hamper and deliver them to Lucia's home. Antonio and Lucia were then freed of everything but for

Antonio's *Story*

her handbag and his valise. They were on their way to a special place she wanted him to see where they could refresh and relax before they set out for Connecticut.

Making their way out of the Pier, Antonio found the atmosphere at the waterfront intense. The crowd, sounds, and movement represented a different world, which was appealing but also overwhelming. Familiarity was limited, and he had little to hold on to as a result. He returned to the insight that came to him on arrival—he could make no comparisons between the life he was witnessing and the one he left behind. The divergences were numerous. They were deep and unfamiliar but not unpleasant. He felt a beat in the atmosphere in New York, an energy that enticed him.

Before leaving the area, Antonio turned for a final view of the Roma. He registered the ship in his mind, realizing his strong sentiment for it. Towering on the waterfront, the Roma symbolized a new life—for him and many others. He sighed, smiled at his Aunt, and walked with a strong positive feeling in his heart. New York would be part of his life story. How, when, or why, he did not know.

When Antonio and his Aunt exited the port, he was stunned by what lay before him. The road ahead, as it ran from left to right, was, he had to believe, larger than his village! The street appeared to go on forever as did the movement of people. Now walking along that road, the pair was fast approaching a transportation hub, the likes of which Antonio had never seen. First, unique sounds came to his attention. What stood out was a repetitive noise, the clanging he had already heard which, if his hearing was accurate, was not from one direction but several. He had expected conveyances like those in Italy, but the variety startled him. Cars, yes. Scooters, no. But there was much more. Carriages either motorized or horse drawn. Larger box-like cars that he'd never seen before, and then the trolleys, the source of the clanging, not one or two but dozens, traveling in different directions and carrying so many people that some passengers were hanging out of the windows. The trolleys navigated through the area, people entering and leaving them. *A people mover*, he declared to himself. He was so absorbed by the scene that he paid little attention to his Aunt, who had given up on trying to communicate with him anyway, his fascination so intense.

The pair continued, weaving their way through the traffic. Looking at her nephew, Lucia felt a pull in her heart. She considered Antonio's arrival and adjustment in the U.S. in view of her own. She was fortunate that her husband had made his way to the U.S. alone to establish himself, relying on help from relatives already settled in the country. Doing so, he carved a place for his wife, Aunt Lucia. He suffered first, overcoming the obstacles that impeded him—language, culture, awkwardness, isolation, and lack of focus—to spare her from experiencing the same. He prepared for her arrival with clothing that would not make her feel out of place, a group of friends with whom she could relate, and a friendship with the local priest who would welcome her. Her husband had been her guide, and she learned quickly from him, returning his generosity of spirit by welcoming newcomers again and again, befriending them and helping them adjust. Aunt Lucia would do the same for Antonio. She understood what the first few months in the U.S. were like for immigrants whose knowledge about their futures was non-existent. After arriving, despite the support she had, Lucia felt she was on trial and had to prove she could forge a new and prosperous life. Though she detected a stronger will within Antonio to create his future, she imagined there would be pitfalls along the way.

While Lucia reminisced, Antonio's eyes were riveted on the movements of the trolleys as they passed or crossed over each other or travelled in an unexpected direction. Everything about the cars fascinated him—the tracks on the roads, the number of cars, the multiple directions in which they traveled, and the different color-coded routes. He observed people moving along, not as individuals but as a group. They progressed at a rapid pace with clarity and focus, fanning out in all directions and never missing a beat. He was mesmerized by their "landscape"—the dense population, the buildings and construction materials, the height of structures, and people living up and across chains of buildings. The general traffic patterns of people on foot and those in some sort of conveyance told of a pace and lifestyle much different from everything he knew. As he sorted through his observations, he found himself building a new reality in his mind.

Antonio and his Aunt approached a one-story building that stood in the center of the large road they were crossing. Watching his Aunt's actions and looking at pictures on that structure, he realized they were going to board a trolley. He was still uncertain as to where they were going, though he had no complaint about how he was spending his time and what he was discovering.

Following his Aunt, Antonio stepped into the trolley, excited about riding in it. On that brilliant day in May 1938, the trolley provided a refreshing experience, both physically with the cool breezes entering the cars and intellectually for the newness, sense of freedom, and innovation. After a loud clang, the trolley started moving, smoothly and quickly. Antonio continued his observations, not knowing what would come next.

Chapter 13
Little Italy

Passengers darted across the terminal, disappearing into tunnels. An accompanying cacophony surged—the movement of trains, rapid announcements, conductors blowing whistles, and vendors promoting their wares. The New World encircled Antonio. Would he run from it or step into it?

The movement and rhythm of life on the streets of New York made for a dynamic environment that drew Antonio in but also terrorized him. The City was so expansive and densely populated that he felt it might devour him if he was not careful. He would never be seen again! The mix of cultures, swirling scents and aromas, manner of dress, the wide streets, modes of transportation, and modern conveniences tantalized him. "*Innovazione*" [innovation]—that was the word he sought for describing everything he saw. Evidence of the know-how and ingenuity to fashion a New World manifested everywhere he looked. His mind raced about the how and why of everything he saw though he had few words for speaking about them.

As the trolley rolled along in the direction of the site Lucia planned to visit, they passed an even larger trolley station. If Antonio thought that station was the central station, he was seriously mistaken. In time, they viewed what could only be called a large depot. Countless trolleys passed through or stopped at that station, snaking in and around places to transport passengers to their destinations. To his surprise, his Aunt nudged him, saying they needed to transfer to the larger station. They stepped from the first trolley they had taken, walked with the crowd for a few steps, and then crossed an impressive network of rails. Never before had Antonio stood within such a large mass of people. He wondered about their lifestyles and where they were going. He also noticed that everyone was walking quickly. He asked himself, *Why are the people rushing?* Lucia and Antonio walked a bit farther and then stationed themselves by the depot to wait. Lulls in the trolley traffic occurred from time to time, which made Antonio believe the trams followed a schedule that cleared the depot periodically before other throngs of people arrived. The breaks also reduced the noise level from time to time, which made conversation possible at regular intervals.

Eventually, their trolley arrived, and the journey continued. Antonio was vigilant and wide awake. The City itself did not allow him to sleep. From afar, he saw something unusual—a train coming out of nowhere and then rambling over a bridge. He had barely gotten over that incident when another train ran alongside a second bridge. The trolley system was a maze! Yet another discovery followed. It occurred below rather than on or above land. A trolley traveling in the same direction as theirs dipped downward moving into a tunnel. The different modes of transportation and how they intertwined with each other and then separated fascinated Antonio. There was no way during his first day in the United States that Antonio could have fathomed the City's vast transit systems. It would take many excursions to New York to become familiar with them, especially the complex network of the renowned subway system.

Antonio's *Story*

A place they passed along their route, a colorful outdoor market, caught Antonio's eye. Rows of tents lined a wide intersection and all streets connected to it. The canopy-covered tables displayed goods for sale. Colorful banners and signs decorated the open market area though Antonio found their presence puzzling. If he wasn't mistaken, numerous flags of Italy festooned the tables and flapped in the breeze. Lucia and Antonio, now two of the few people on board, continued to their destination. When they passed a second open market decorated like the other, Antonio wasn't surprised to see his Aunt pull the cord to alert the conductor. No doubt their destination was in range and there was a tie to Italy in the area. But what was it? The building they reached was Our Lady of Pompeii Roman Catholic Church. Founded in 1892, the religious community served the growing Italian American population in the U.S. Its location in the heart of New York City's "Little Italy" was not an accident.

A visit to the church was a welcome gesture and devotional practice for Italians arriving in America and passing through New York or settling in the region. The visit was both prayerful and celebratory. The ministry sought to show evidence of Italian culture in the U.S. to newcomers, provide rest and temporary housing when needed, sponsor a luncheon when ships arrived to promote fellowship, and establish local contacts for individuals who requested them. Since leaving the ship, Antonio had focused on features of the City, his thoughts about immigration having drifted to the back of his mind. Now, at the church, his eyes and ears took in everything his fellow migrants had to say. He could learn from them.

Antonio's world was about to change for the third time that day when he and his Aunt boarded the local trolley to reach the center of town, which lay north of the piers. It went directly to a station with out-of-state train service since their destination was Connecticut, where

Lucia lived. She told him the name of the New York station that would take them home, "*Grande Centrale*" she said, pronouncing English with an Italian accent, which was common in the region. Her words incorporated the flow and sounds of Italian, and that made Antonio smile.

The trolley to Grand Central expanded Antonio's perspective of the City. Along the route, he viewed different districts or areas characterized by distinct buildings and businesses. In the areas between Bleecker Street, where they boarded the trolley, and the start of midtown, buildings were low, many constructed of brick. Some had glass fronts and appeared to be small service companies or shops of different types. Others were restaurants, delicatessens, or coffee bars, and outdoor vendors with decorative stationary wagons filled with souvenirs, necessities, and food. The types of services Antonio noticed were not unfamiliar. It was the abundance of what the City had to offer that amazed him.

Antonio was a farm boy from Italy, whose village had one church, one café, one grocery, and one restaurant on the pinnacle of the hills. The variety and volume of services that now surrounded him excited and overwhelmed him at the same time. Watching crowds passing through and those waiting in line to be served made Antonio want to hide. Life in the U.S. seemed complicated. In a few minutes curiosity buffered his reaction. On the roadway, he saw something unfamiliar — bicycles with carts attached to the backside and an umbrella overhead. He followed those vehicles with his eyes as they darted in and out of traffic competing with much larger conveyances and sometimes getting struck by them. Antonio waited to see what purposes the vehicles served and determined they were mobile food vendors who set up on street corners or were flagged down by potential customers. There were similarities between the vending cars and the food trolleys on the ship, which Antonio should have realized sooner.

Midway through their ride, Antonio noticed the buildings gaining height and the number of vehicles on the road increasing. He learned that when there seemed to be too many vehicles on the road, they encountered traffic, and forward movement was slow as a result. By time they reached the station, the trolley was surrounded by very tall buildings, so tall that Antonio would have to move back quite a distance to estimate their height. He was fascinated by the towering buildings and made a mental note to return to the City one day to view its layout from different angles.

New York City exuded a sense of importance, an impression Antonio could not put into words or explain adequately in either language. The people around him differed from the workers at the pier and the lifestyles he observed on his way to Bleecker Street. In his present setting, he observed yet another change. People in the City were well-dressed and transported in elegant vehicles rather than traveling in packed trolleys. They exuded culture and class. While such lifestyles existed in Italy as well, they were not as pronounced there as they were in New York. There was a sense of grandeur, as would be expected in the largest city in the U.S. at the time.

Antonio recalled his arrival earlier that morning, realizing the port was a mere dot in the panoramic skyline that welcomed the ship as it entered the sea terminal. With that thought came a dose of reality. The weight of Antonio's journey suddenly fell upon him physically and emotionally. He was standing on the soil of the United States of America uncountable miles from his homeland and his family. He had arrived in a completely new place where he would be lost without his Aunt.

Antonio had not intended to have his thoughts travel a dark path, and he was relieved when his Aunt tapped his shoulder, telling him it was time to leave the trolley. They crossed the tracks and walked in the direction of a double door, the building nondescript on the exterior, matching surrounding structures, and at eye level not providing any hint as to what was to come. From the exterior, muted among the side-by-side buildings, Grand Central Terminal appeared plain and functional. Excepting its location and size, Antonio believed it to be no different from the trolley stops and stations that fulfilled the singular purpose of moving people. But when he crossed the threshold and entered, Antonio found himself in a dazzling world. The first word that came to mind was "art." He attempted to take in the entire scene yet failed miserably. The structure was so rich that it blinded his mind yet not his eyes.

Antonio noticed the building's depth right away, understanding that the spacious area consumed street after street of New York City. What he saw did not even include the entire rail apparatus for trains traveling in the City or beyond its borders. To his surprise, that sprawling system remained hidden. He wondered where the trains and the rails were, knowing he would learn in time. Mesmerized by the building's interior, he looked at the whole, finding himself unable to imagine the capacity and significance of the magnificent building. He changed his tack as a result, focusing on the building's opulence. Thoughts invaded his mind, and Antonio struggled to keep up with Lucia as she forged through the building's vestibule to its Grand Hall. The whole of the interior was an assault on Antonio's senses.

Once again, Antonio intended to scan the entire space and place it in his memory, but his eyes feasted on one masterpiece—a clock that rested in the atrium for all to see, its size comparable to a tall monument. Its ornamentation was vivid gold with gems adorning the golden crevices. With four faces total, one on each side, the oversized timepiece greeted every traveler, granting them the ability to check the hour from any vantage point without impediment. Antonio looked at the clock, and Lucia looked up at him, enjoying his interest. He had succumbed to the chronometer's presence as most people did and stepped away from Lucia, so engrossed in the timepiece that he didn't realize he was "on his own" in New York City. He circled the clock, moving toward and away from it to take in every detail and element.

When he returned to his Aunt's side, she explained the clock's lore. "For all New Yorkers, there is only one clock, this one" she said. "It's regarded as a meeting place, and there's great romance associated with it. One person is likely to tell another, 'I will meet you by the clock.' There would no confusion about which clock the person meant, and they would find each other right here at the agreed upon time." Antonio detected traces of the Old World in Lucia's story, and everything she said appealed to his prescient self. He remained glued to the clock and watched it because he felt it had a message for him. Lucia looked at him expectantly, asking directly and boldly, "Do you see or sense something?" Without pause, he shared a message he did not yet understand, "Today's one of two special days when I will stand by this clock. I have no details about the other, but I know it will happen." Time stopped, they paused. Then Lucia smiled at her nephew, telling him they needed to buy their tickets to Stamford.

The Grand Central clock in the center of the famous New York City train terminal

While waiting for Lucia, Antonio studied the terminal. His world expanded with every breath he took. The moment amplified his experience at the dock, seeing the newness from yet another perspective, one different from the waterfront, the trolley system, Bleecker Street, and the distant view of the Empire State Building. Being indoors added a layer to his experience. It magnified the dynamics of City life. So many people, different groups clustered by language and dress, many well attired for travel as he was. Noting some personal similarities to the crowd, such as his hat and overcoat, Antonio was overcome by a feeling of belonging. But then, he saw many others who also belonged—men, women, laborers, the poor, clergy and religious, vendors, and beggars, along with languages galore. He could not adequately describe what he witnessed. He sensed words he did not yet know and accepted the experience for the awakening it was.

Though the activity in the station was non-stop, Antonio detected a sense of order in the building, and that was something he could respect. Within the pulsating crowd and non-stop movement, patterns and direction existed. He found beauty in those and the stylish people. A comparison entered his mind, momentary embarrassment followed, and then came the shame for permitting the idea to enter his thoughts. *Mama in her peasant dress in contrast to the showy women. Would Mama fit in here? Would the presence of someone from the terminal cause a scandal in his village?*

Antonio acquired weeks of knowledge while his Aunt purchased their rail tickets. His learning continued as they sat and waited for their train to be announced. Amid the noise, it was impossible to chat, and Antonio was grateful. Having observed the people and the terminal's atmosphere, he wanted nothing more than to sit and take in the characteristics of the building that seemed simple on the outside but was grand on the inside.

Initially, Antonio found his gaze moving rapidly back and forth, his mind attempting to conquer images and information. His inefficient observation stopped soon enough, though, shifting to a deliberate and thoughtful mode. What amazed him was the building's architecture. The newness of the United States was something he could not dispute. There was a futuristic look to what he saw—the high ceilings, the sharp lines, the geometric designs, and the oversized windows of cut glass that filtered in the sunlight, casting an array of bright colors over the hall.

Along with those modern features, there were others familiar to him— the walkways that led to different services. Embedded in those architectural mazes were arches reminiscent of Italy that Antonio did not expect to see in the U.S. He had no words for the multiple services tucked beyond them—places for dining, the novel food take-away service; the variety of shops, some selling trinkets and others exotic or elegant gifts; shoe-shine stations, another service he'd never seen before whereby men wearing aprons stood by large elevated and elegant chairs marketing a shine. Antonio was amazed by the popularity of the service and wondered who would spend money on a shoeshine rather than doing it himself.

Restrooms with running water dotted corners of the building. Not having experienced indoor plumbing but for visits to places like Naples and the ship, Antonio marveled at the conveniences that existed in the United States. Studying the services, committing everything to memory, he mapped the building's architectural design in his mind. The main hall was, he realized, the pulse of the rail network. Services like shops and restaurants were on the periphery. The hall was reserved for anything that had to do with rail services—ticket windows, the corridor leading to the trains, an information booth, and a striking feature—a huge board that posted and regularly updated a schedule for all trains, both arrivals and departures, in chronological order. The hall was the terminal's business center.

In time, their train to Connecticut posted on the board, and it was Antonio and Lucia's turn to disappear into a tunnel. He had been waiting for that moment for over an hour. He wanted to pass through the archway in the direction of the trains to know the building as a train station. How could it be that he had not yet seen a train in the railroad terminal? He had seen smaller conveyances but nothing as large as he was now anticipating given the size of the station and the number of passengers scurrying through it to their trains. As they entered and proceeded through the tunnel, his frame of reference for what he imagined travel by rail in the U.S. to be like imploded and needed to be reconstructed.

They began to walk as quickly as those around them. People filed in and out of the area, darting to get to their trains. They could both feel and hear a rumbling roar below and around them with every step they took. They were being sucked into a tunnel as though they would never see the light of day again. They were descending. Before long, natural light appeared suggesting an opening to the outdoors. The tunnel became a path, a concourse they called it, and the scope of what occurred in that one area where the tentacles of many concourses stretched toward different numbered tracks was surreal.

A cacophony of tunnel sounds surged—the movement of trains, whistles blown by uniformed attendants, vendors promoting their wares, ticket sales, the announcement from somewhere, and conversations in a variety of languages. A field of tracks and trains, and as they walked, fresh air delivered a breeze. The coming and going was a sight to behold. Antonio and Lucia reached their track and then walked a short distance until they found a car with seats available. They boarded the train and took their seats.

Chapter 14
His New Home

Antonio pressed his head to the window. He examined building after building in the town where he would live, not seeing anything as tall as what he had seen in New York City, yet something different from what he knew. A society, a collection of houses, churches, businesses, and schools tightly held together and sprawling along the road. He sat at his window, watching his new world and could not pull himself away.

Antonio now rode in his third mode of transportation since arriving in the U.S. Unbeknown to him, there would be one more after the train ride. Though he arrived in the United States as dawn broke close to ten hours ago, he was awake and alert, studying every detail of his first day in the country. As he settled into his seat beside Lucia, he heard the final commotion marking the train's departure. People were running toward the train, racing to enter it before the conductors gave the all-clear signal. Within minutes, the train began to roll forward to exit the terminal. Its movement was gentle and graceful. The light of day beamed ahead as though teasing the train from the underground. Antonio was glued to his window, waiting for his view to appear. The train found its place on the landscape of the

City, presenting Antonio with a new perspective on it. His encounters with New York that day told different stories. The first centered on the approach to land when he saw the City from afar. The second was his arrival to the port and Bleecker Street, where immigrants were the focal point. City Center, where he experienced New York City's dynamic nature and opulence, followed; and the City fading from view as the train pushed forward was the fourth.

Their train skirted past the business district and into the residential areas, where the signs of life centered on families, community, small shops, and services. The train rolled through neighborhoods where multi-storied buildings were nowhere near the height of midtown. They passed many rail stations without stopping, and Antonio learned interstate travel was one train line and local another, both traveling on the same tracks with different stops along the route. Compared to the trolleys, the trains were luxurious and quiet with comfortable seating, sizeable windows, and a refreshment bar.

Eventually the broad swath of the City ended, giving him a view of other ways of living in America. The change was dramatic. Attached houses were a few stories tall rather than towering, and some were detached stand-alone homes. Nothing was lavish, but there was space between the buildings, open land, a scattering of cars, playgrounds, community buildings such as churches and schools, and a variety of window front services. Antonio sensed peace in the areas he was passing through. They appeared warm and quiet.

Everything fascinated Antonio. Though he left his village believing it was the most stunning place in the world, he was beginning to understand there was beauty in other locations and among other people. Papa's words about how Antonio would come to realize the purpose and meaning of his immigration came to mind. Antonio still had no idea about the significance of the monumental change in his life or the path it would take, but he admitted to himself that so far the day had been pleasant. He questioned nothing and did not feel fearful in any way. To the contrary, he engaged and was captivated by his new world.

As the train rumbled along toward Connecticut, Antonio marveled at the changing landscape and the combination of old towns and development, like the lights that regulated traffic. From point to point there were changes in trees, structures, and the complexity of roadways. Antonio interpreted what he saw as the movement from city to country, but there were some surprises along the way. Mid-point on their route, they entered a small city with the look of New York but with a different atmosphere, one that was neither elegant nor opulent. The preponderance of smokestacks identified it as an industrial city, a sight unfamiliar to Antonio. There were broad streets in the center of town that fanned out toward the wide and deep manufacturing plants. One of those caught his eye. There atop the four storied building were five huge display-sized plastic candies in different colors, all in a row. They were circular and thick with an open center. There was no way Antonio could miss the building and no mystery about it. It was a candy factory whose display introduced him to the concepts of advertising and marketing in America.

The well-marked border between New York and Connecticut came next. Antonio was getting closer and closer to his new home. At that juncture he saw no difference between the two sides. As time passed, though, Antonio did come to understand the major differences in size, topography, culture, and industry that distinguished one state from the other. Before long, he observed a dramatic change in scenery. The rolling land steeped downward to the west where lush foliage was expansive. The train was perched above the drop, a charming town running the length from the tracks to the bottom of the slope. That town differed from all the others he had seen thus far because of its distinct features in addition to the landscape—tall trees, the absence of soaring buildings, single-family shingled houses, and a main boulevard. Minutes later, the view opened to a wide body of water where boats were anchored or moored and seagulls hovered. The scene brought a restorative moment. During his long journey, Antonio had become fond of the sea and welcomed its presence as he anticipated arriving "home."

Lucia turned to tell Antonio the Stamford Station was the next stop, and his stomach felt as unsettled as it did when he departed Italy and when he arrived in New York that morning. He peered through the window for a view and saw a city much larger than any town in Connecticut they had passed through. There was a combination of manufacturing and housing. He felt they were close to the waterfront because the land went downhill. The train was now moving slowly, and his view of the station was clear. Antonio had begun to feel a bit drowsy, yet his new home piqued his curiosity. He perked up and peered out of the window with interest. What happened next was an unforgettable surprise.

Antonio's heart stirs when he sees the sign "Stamford" as the train enters the station. He is nervous about what comes next yet quietly excited about being in Connecticut. Suddenly, Antonio's eyes open wide. He sees his Cousin Rocco on the platform! Rocco is pacing back and forth filled with excitement in anticipation of his cousin's arrival. Antonio's Aunt is joyfully amused by Antonio's expression, which breaks into a broad smile on his sleepy face as he hurriedly makes his way to the exit door in intense excitement about greeting his cousin for the first time in five years.

As Antonio dashes out the door of the train he exclaims, "AYYYYYYY ROCCO!!!!" with wide-eyed delight. "AYYYYY ANTON!!!!," Rocco happily cries out to greet his cousin. "Come stai? Welcome to America, my cousin! We are so happy to have you here!"

The two cousins shake hands vigorously and give each other several slaps on the back following the customary salutation between Italian men even though they are in America. And they walk arm in arm toward the parking lot, the gulls flying above, reminding them of the sea, Rocco now familiar with it and Antonio waiting to greet it.

Rocco led the way to the parking lot and stopped by one of the cars. To Antonio's surprise and delight, Rocco would drive them home. *So, this is the New World*, Antonio thought. He admired the car, large, strong, and well designed. It was huge compared to the small and light vehicles Italians drove to navigate the narrow village roads and turns that he knew. A magnificent machine, classy. It hadn't taken long after arriving in the country for Antonio to glimpse the concept of opportunity in the New World. He cautioned himself to not be sold on the place at first sight, but he did allow himself the promise that all would be fine. As they exited, each man thought about the other, how well they looked and how great it was to re-unite. Antonio could not hide his astonishment over how at ease Rocco seemed in the United States. He appeared comfortable and confident, leaving Antonio to wonder what it took to adjust in a new country and whether he would experience the same.

Antonio was again in the position of not knowing where he was going. He was with trusted family, so he sat back to enjoy the ride, liking what he saw and conversing with them about the city, its services, the population, and where people generally worked. The city was more than a village or a town yet nowhere near the size of New York City.

It had extensive roadways for the times. Most houses were shingled, something he liked more than brick. It was impossible to have any expectations as to what would come next because he had no reference point. In a way, acknowledging that reality abated tension. He surrendered to the ride and the sights along the way.

On the way to his new home, Antonio noticed the many traffic circles that cars navigated in full or part to access another road. Unlike New York City, Stamford had few traffic lights, and courtesies were needed for cars to progress when more than one automobile was passing through. Occasionally, two or more cars approached the same point, and he noticed that there seemed to be an understanding as to who should pass first. He thought about Italy and imagined grand conversations at such crossroads, whereby traffic would halt for some time until the matter of how to advance was resolved. He smiled at the thought, feeling a small amount of shame for ridiculing his fellow Italians.

Antonio pressed his face to the window, absorbing details about his new home. He examined building after building in Stamford, not seeing anything as tall as what he had seen in New York City. He observed the sprawling society, a collection of houses, churches, businesses, and schools tightly held together and sprawling along the road, unable to pull himself away. Although Rocco and Lucia continued to talk, they did not expect much from Antonio. They, too, had fallen into that newness at one time, not knowing what to think of it. For several reasons, they both thought Antonio seemed better engaged than they had been. Perhaps his parents had prepared him, or it was his nature. They both knew him as a boy who loved adventure, and they realized the venture of his lifetime rested before him. It seemed likely that he would seize it.

The New World invited Antonio in, and he was mesmerized by it. Much of what he saw remained unnamed in his mind. He had no experience with his environment and thus no words. Thinking in Italian, he had some working phrases—*the walking path* for a sidewalk, *the top* for the roadways, and *the building with many doors* as a reference to the multistory apartment buildings he saw. His surroundings, thoughts, and feelings were larger than his words. But that would change.

Rocco and Lucia started pointing out certain sites as though they were useful for him to know, and he concluded they would be "home" soon. He was pleased to see trolleys along their route. He wondered at first why they were not the same color as those in New York but then realized the variation was probably nothing more than a random decision on the part of a town. He also studied the trolleys symbolically for what they meant for him personally. Mobility, he thought—they would provide the means for him to move from one place to another and explore his immediate area as well as everything beyond it. Comparing the density in the heart of the city with the country surrounding it, his opportunities for exploration seemed more varied and accessible than anything in Italy. That observation had to do with the types of transportation available. He wondered when he would have time to explore, what he would explore, and whether anyone would accompany him. He hoped to find answers to those questions in time, sooner rather than later.

In the past three hours or so, Antonio had traveled between two different places in the U.S. through different modes of transportation. One day he'd have to measure the distance between the various stops along the way and also learn the names of all the towns and attractions he rode by while on the train. Then he thought he should look at the bigger picture, calculating the distances between the major points of his entire journey—from his village to the City of Naples, from Naples to New York City, and on to Stamford. He felt powerful, as though he was at the wheel of the one of the vehicles he'd seen earlier in the day rather than as someone who rode in them.

Rocco deftly executed a few turns in the road that led to a hilltop. Along the way, they drove by homes, open land, small businesses, and a field. They passed a large brick building which he identified as a hospital because the spelling of that word was similar in the two languages. Then they drifted toward tree-lined streets and the largest homes he had ever seen. The pinnacle offered a striking bird's eye view of the city. It did not compare in any way with the highest point in his Italian village, but Antonio found it appealing for capturing the marriage of city and countryside. With the water in range, Antonio could see why the Italians who left their country flocked to this pleasant area.

After they reached the top of the hill they slowly descended to the city. The road they traveled led to rows of buildings that vaguely resembled the small shops in his village because they were specialized stores. To his far right he saw a church, realizing it was the most easily recognizable structure he'd seen. Looking ahead, he could see the town center that served the same purpose as the piazza in his village though this city center offered the vitality his hometown lacked. The area was large and busy. In town, they passed through a circle riding toward the area they had just driven through. Antonio looked ahead and behind studying the scene, Rocco pulled the car up to a building, and Lucia welcomed Antonio home.

Hearing the word home, Antonio experienced a twinge in his heart, feeling like a traitor or an interloper. Yet he was drawn to look at what she was pointing out for many reasons—respect, curiosity, interest, and because the experience everyone described as his dream was beginning to unfold. Any reservation that might have held him back, the questions and insecurities that traveled from Italy with him, had been shed the minute he saw Rocco, his cousin and good friend. Rocco's comfort eased Antonio's mind, and he followed his Aunt with an open heart. Rocco said his good-byes, indicating he was in an apartment nearby and would see Antonio the next day.

The building Lucia moved toward was more than he expected, and Antonio could not believe he would call it home. The first floor had a windowed front and door, along with words on the glass that he could not fully translate. They paused by the door but did not enter. Lucia identified the area as her business, a laundry she and her husband had operated together for some time until he died suddenly. His Aunt went on to describe the shop, telling how she he took in clothing to dry clean, wash, press, or mend. The business was successful, she added, largely due to her deceased husband's efforts. He had established major accounts with important organizations, such as the police force and local hospital, to launder batches of uniforms every week. With her husband gone, she desperately needed steady help since the business continued to grow. Peering into the glass front, Antonio saw a clean facility, his work area, and the equipment he would use. He liked the well-lit store front, the view outdoors, and the likelihood he would see and meet many people in passing. He would miss working with the land, but the laundry offered honorable work and an opportunity to help family.

They reached the entry to the house and found Antonio's luggage by the door, entered, settled their belongings, and then Lucia showed Antonio around the common areas of her house and another section opposite the corridor where his room was. She called that section the Boarding House, a term he did not know. Lucia went on to explain that she often housed newly arrived immigrants, usually those without families in the United States, until they were able to set themselves up in the town or another location. For a modest fee or by providing help in the laundry, they could stay with her and receive meals until they found an apartment to get started. The guests provided company, and she had the pleasure of getting them started in America. Lucia mentioned the boarding area so that Antonio understood that others might live in the house with them from time to time.

Lucia wanted Antonio to know he would be treated like all workers. She spoke in Italian, quoting his hourly pay in Italian Lira so he would understand the value of his work. Antonio was astonished to learn he'd be paid, in currency no less. In his poor Italian community, work was performed for goods. As she spoke, Antonio gained insight into the matters that worried him most. Looking at the vibrant activity in his new town, he wondered how and when he would become part of it. He guessed many doors would open to him because he had a job and income.

Evening was upon them, and Antonio and his Aunt sat down for a simple dinner. Lucia wanted to learn all about the family, and Antonio reported on each person in detail. He could tell she was hungry for information. He also showed her the letters he had carried with him, and she indicated she would see to them. Then he pulled the family photographs from his valise. Lucia's hands shook as she began to leaf through the collection, the portraits so large and beautiful that her family members came alive. They were vivid, joyful as usual, and seemed to occupy space on the sofa alongside her. She and Antonio poured over them, recounting stories and memories. For Lucia the photos demanded the careful study of every face to see how each person had changed since her departure. For Antonio, there was the prescient realization that someday he would be looking at photographs discerning the changes in Mama, Papa, his sister, and his brothers since they last visited with each other. An hour of reminiscence about family events, ceremonies, festivals, and the National Park followed, reinforcing the bond between the two to soften the sting of separation.

Since Antonio did not want the day to end yet, he decided to describe the walk he took before leaving Italy. He talked about visiting the cemetery, his 360° view of the valley from the crest, and his walk through the National Park. Whereas he thought his words would seem trivial, Lucia hung on every one of them to revisit her native land. Occasionally during their exchange, she looked at her nephew, appreciating his earnest nature and the strength of his perceptions. As his narration of the walk came to an end, she said she wanted to hear him tell that story again and again. His words had transported her to Italy, rekindling her memories, and she was grateful. He paused, then, because something else came to mind. He overcame his hesitation and told Lucia about Luca and the photographs he gifted Antonio the night before their arrival in New York. Antonio had been moved by her generous reaction to his story and thought she would enjoy the pictures, especially since the initial ones were taken in a familiar and momentous place, Naples. Lucia was amazed by Luca's lavish gift and beautiful photographs of Antonio's journey. She saw his story and remembered her own, tears filling her eyes.

Feeling the hour, they talked a bit more before retiring for the night. Lucia asked Antonio to be ready to leave for Mass at 9:30 a.m. and said they'd enjoy a traditional Sunday dinner afterwards. He brought up the root of the fig tree, which pleased her, asking if there was a place to plant it. There was plenty of room, she said, and they would set it after dinner tomorrow. Antonio wondered if there was space for a garden too, so he asked, and Lucia lit up when she heard the question. She said she'd welcome a lovely garden. There was a sizable plot he could use, and she promised to buy everything he needed to get it started in her sunny backyard.

They cleaned up after dinner. The hectic day now catching up with Antonio, he asked to be excused, but did not leave until he was folded into his Aunt's arms for an Italian-style hug. Feeling exhausted, he readied himself for bed while also looking back not only on the day but the entire journey. His thoughts formed in short bursts, and he grabbed his journal so that he could jot them down and return to them another day.

Antonio had entered a New World. He believed his time on the ship, the company of other passengers, the routine he created, and the activities that engaged him had created a foundation for his adjustment to America, which included coping with his separation from his family and native country. He learned a lot about himself over the past twelve days and was beginning to understand Papa's comment about how his reasons for immigrating would be realized in time.

Chapter 15
Familiar Faces in His New World

His subtle glances at the young ladies were no match for their open interest in him. During siesta when the old folks' watchful eyes were closed, the girls circled him. If Mama were watching, she would say, "si lanciavano contro di lui." [They were throwing themselves at him.]

Antonio had no trouble waking up the next day since the ship had slowly adjusted to the local time zone during the crossing. The stillness surprised him. Bells did not toll, roosters did not crow, and the cows' bells were not clanging, nor were waves slapping the side of a ship or a vessel's engine churning. Silence. Given the early hour and quiet, he spent some time thinking about the previous day to catch up with his own life.

Antonio regarded his arrival to the U.S. as the most consequential event in his life thus far. It called for a whole new way of living, yet there was no way he could prepare for his adjustment. From time to time through the years he had heard the expression "sink or swim" in discussions about immigration. The point was that people who sought to live in another country either succeeded and remained there or were unable to adjust and returned to their homeland or tried another country. He had already glimpsed the challenge on the ship in a minor way when he needed to create a routine for his days to keep himself busy and satisfy his interests. Though there were similarities between the two, he had to admit that establishing himself in the U.S. was a monumental undertaking and managing himself on the ship paled in comparison.

Antonio had plenty of time on his hands before getting ready for church, so he went back to what he wrote the evening before, fleshing out the details and completing his perception of the main highlights of the day. He retraced his itinerary in words, recalling the sequence of events, from the ship's arrival to the surprise of Rocco welcoming him to the United States! Having surpassed what he expected to write, he was more cognizant of the journal's value. As he leafed through a few pages, it occurred to him that Mama, Papa, and his siblings would enjoy reading details about his travels and life in America. Didn't he owe them that information? How could they otherwise continue to know him as their child and brother?

Uplifted by his early morning reflection, Antonio started preparing for the day. When early morning reached a respectful hour, he opened his door and called out to his Aunt, telling her he would be ready on time. Before closing his door, he breathed the fragrance of a simmering marinara and the welcome aroma of freshly baked bread. Aunt Lucia had already begun preparing for Sunday dinner at home. The scents he inhaled transported him to a typical Sunday in Italy that would start with morning Mass followed by coffee and socializing in the piazza. From the square, everyone would return home to continue with the dishes they started to prepare before going to church. When the food was simmering or baking, the early siesta would follow.

The traditional leisurely multi-course dinner would typically begin any time between one o'clock and three p.m., depending on the season and whether other events, like a Baptism, were taking place. Usually, the dinners accommodated large numbers because extended families lived in the village or nearby and followed the tradition of gathering every Sunday. Everyone contributed food for a large-scale meal. Sunday dinner in Italy played out as an event. It involved much more than the consumption of food and was always celebratory. It was also artful because the creations flowing from the kitchens were masterpieces of pasta and homemade sausages, artisan breads, unimaginable towering confections, homemade sweets, and vegetables from the fields prepared with aromatic oils and herbs.

To say there was spirited discussion during Sunday dinner is an understatement. The tradition was a time for families to catch up with one another, sort through matters important to all, such as wedding dates, events like baby showers, needs or illnesses in the larger family, issues with the weather or the health of the crops, and, of course, politics and current events, which presently generated heated discussion. Antonio always relished the conversations at Sunday dinner because they were dynamic and he learned a lot. He also enjoyed the outdoor activities and entertainment, from bocce or soccer to parades in the piazza, music and songs, theater, and opera. The fun and games would run through early evening before the dessert table and coffees were set up. He did not know any other way to spend a Sunday, yet over the course of his life Antonio became comfortable with departing from the tradition every now and then.

The ship had spoiled Antonio by incorporating the Italian lifestyle and customs at sea in a formal setting, but there was nothing better than a family and neighborhood dinner, especially one in the square. Since it was the month of May and most likely a gorgeous day in Italy, a feast was probably underway in the piazza at that very moment. Antonio imagined the banquet table, wine and beverage set-up, and the faces of his family and friends. He drew from a notion among Italians resulting from their experiences with the challenges and consequences of migration. The custom centered on the desire of parties separated from one another to feel the presence of each other.

According to tradition, if an individual or group in one place looked toward heaven when thinking of a party or individual elsewhere, the two groups would connect and feel the presence of each other, regardless of the distance between them. Never wanting to disrespect the mores of his country and faith, Antonio looked up toward heaven with his family and village friends in mind and was certain he felt the aura of everyone in the square that Sunday. He could visualize the scene in the piazza and evoked the villagers' good wishes for him. His departure a mere week and a half ago, he *knew* he was on their minds and in their hearts as they were inscribed on his heart. In that time of change, Antonio often turned to the past for comfort. That coping mechanism enabled him to regard his second day in America as a new start. He committed himself to stepping into life in America with his Aunt's guidance, and he prepared for Mass.

Antonio met his Aunt in the parlor, and they departed. As they walked, Lucia pointed out the different shops and offices he would likely explore and use. She gestured to the east to point out where he would find Long Island Sound and its beautiful beaches. They turned left, which brought the city's main boulevard into view from a better angle than the previous afternoon when he arrived. There he could see a well-maintained city square with a statue, a fountain, and gardens. A picturesque snapshot formed in Antonio's mind and became an indelible memory. To reach the church, they eventually turned right.

Walking toward the church, Antonio spotted Rocco in a large group of people and waved. For a reason not yet clear to him, Antonio felt a rush of emotion. Was he nervous? Was he expected to join the group? Was he experiencing the phenomenon of homesickness that many passengers on the ship discussed? He pressed on, looking at the people and noticing their European attire. A flash of recognition occurred, and Antonio attempted to hold back his tears as he approached the group without any prompt to do so. Familiar faces, recognizable in either of two ways. Some were individuals he knew personally, and others had the distinctive Italian countenance that paired them with the country and its culture.

The faces of cousins, a friend, the butcher from his village, and other Italians who had come to the U.S. for a better life some time ago. Everyone embraced and welcomed him, and finally he felt like himself. Antonio sighed with relief. He had found Italy in America. Until that moment Antonio hadn't given much thought to the possibility of seeing so many Italians in Stamford, except for Lucia and some of her friends. As inspired as he had been the day before when experiencing a taste of New York City and enjoying the innovation, Antonio could not fool himself into thinking that he would readily melt into that society. Entering the church cushioned by the presence of his compatriots, strains of Antonio's conversations with Luca about the Italian communities that formed in the U.S. and went on to ease the adjustment of newcomers came to mind.

Antonio did not see any measurable difference between his church in Italy and the one he was entering in the United States. Family and friends proceeded as a group, reverent, filling the pews to sit together as one family. It pleased Antonio that they could freely manifest their faith and culture in America. That was another affirming moment for him. There was no need for him to be something other than who he was.

Antonio stayed close to his Aunt in church, feeling he had a responsibility to her, and he noticed how she lit up in a different way among her Italian friends. The day before, she was capable and helpful yet watchful. Now though she was her lively self. He admired how she could cross over two social contexts and realized she would be a true model for him as he adjusted to the country. Mass began and to Antonio's surprise the opening greeting was delivered in Italian as were other parts of the service, including some hymns. He did not dare look around, but he thought it was safe to say that the congregation at Mass was predominantly Italian immigrants.

After Mass there was yet another gathering outdoors on that lovely spring day for chatter about the service, the announcements, who attended, and new faces. Antonio noticed the group moved and reconfigured constantly as they talked. They sauntered in the direction of the laundry but stopped short of it to enter a large Italian-style café offering tasty cookies, pastries, espresso, and cappuccino. The group of at least forty people split up between outdoor and indoor space, conversing with enthusiasm. Having gained a bit of objectivity about practices among Italians during his travel to the U.S., Antonio was amused at how the different groups within the Italian community were consistent across continents as to how they congregated. The "old folks" and children always sat together for playful time though the seniors' watchful eyes simultaneously monitored blooming romances and possible transgressions among the young adults. The latter group always split into groups by gender. The early teens were the easiest group. They were more interested in sports and games rather than relationships. In the café after Mass, Antonio witnessed the strength of Italian traditions in America.

Antonio would admit he was doing some monitoring of his own while conversing with young men his age, who were sharing their stories about coming to the United States and wanted to learn about his experience. A large family on the periphery of the group piqued his curiosity. From the looks of it, the parents were traditional Old World Italians. Their children, however, exhibited gestures, nuanced behavior, and attire that leaned toward American culture. Why was he interested in that group? The couple had seven children, three males and four females, one of whom sparkled. Antonio could not help but sneak a glance at her glowing face every now and then. "Who is that one?" he asked his friends. "Ah, that's Helena" [the H in her name silent] was the reply.

Their time at the bakery was ending, leaving Antonio with a warm and comfortable feeling about his first day in town. The group began to disperse, moving in the direction of the laundry. As they strolled, Lucia told Antonio everyone would be arriving at the house within the hour for Sunday Dinner. That news was a most welcome and pleasant surprise. It made the prospect of his second day in the U.S. as enjoyable as the first, and he thanked his Aunt for generously planning a day that would make him feel at home.

Antonio and Lucia got to work shortly after they returned home. Friends were arriving non-stop, carrying dishes and ready to help set up the tables outside. There was much more to Lucia's beautiful house than he had seen the night before. Her sizeable backyard rivaled the square in his village. The way everyone worked to get the area ready for dinner showed a level of familiarity and intimacy within the group and the depth of their sense of community.

Noticing all the supplies for the large dinner stored in the backyard, Antonio realized why Lucia had not shown him the area sooner—she wanted Sunday Dinner to be a surprise. Guests were pulling tables and chairs out from the side of the house. Long tables were set, many created with boards. The area easily accommodated fifty people or so. A feast of wonderful Italian dishes materialized, a beverage table was set up, and dinner was almost ready. No food was consumed, though, until two rites took place, first a prayer and then a toast. The prayer was offered by the priest who performed the Mass they attended, and the toast provided by the butcher who, as the senior male from Settefrati, welcomed Antonio to America and wished him well. There were cheers and excitement. Antonio felt like a celebrity!

Like any activity involving Italians the event was lively and boisterous. Discussion and eating went hand in hand. The meal was a banquet of foods meant to satisfy everyone and get the week off to a good start. For Antonio, the event was emotional and memorable. Looking at the people who came to welcome him, his heart filled with joy, and the good will he felt chipped away at the fear and uncertainty he experienced from time to time during his travel. Though his surroundings did not look like Italy, everything felt like Italy. Mama would be grateful when she learned about how warmly Antonio's compatriots welcomed him to the U.S. Thinking of her, he remembered his manners about how a young boy his age should conduct himself at a reception in his honor.

As the lovely repast in Lucia's backyard got underway and continued in the Italian tradition, Antonio engaged with everyone there as a courtesy for their presence and contributions to the dinner. In the process, he learned about the impressive accomplishments of his countrymen and women. Even though most hadn't been in the country more than a few years, their successes with the English language and in education, employment, and their personal lives surpassed his expectations. What Antonio noticed left him optimistic about his own path.

While circulating to meet every guest, which was something Antonio did with ease and enjoyment, he kept his eye on Helena, the young lady he had noticed at the café. As Antonio interacted with everyone, Rosa, the formidable mother of the attractive four sisters, kept her eye on him. She and her husband grew up in Sora, a city about twenty miles east of Settefrati. Antonio's family was well known in a wide area for their olive oil and dairy products and highly regarded for the swath of property they owned and cultivated. With daughters of marrying age, Rosa knew she could not neglect any opportunity to befriend the young man, who appeared courageous, congenial, and well-mannered. Did she notice how Antonio's eyes dwelt on Helena?

One of the Italians' pastimes, the siesta, had greater importance on the weekends when they could be more generous with their time to rest. What that meant for the welcome dinner was a break in activities for about two hours primarily for the older guests to digest, take a nap, or continue their conversations. For the youngest in the group, there was quiet play, walks, or naps. The spirited late teens and young adults took advantage of the siesta to spend time together in town. For Antonio, being welcomed into the group and invited to accompany them to the city center represented hospitality beyond what he expected, and he was deeply grateful for the gesture. They took off on their own, women and men by gender but only until they were beyond the watchful eyes of the old folks. When the groups intertwined, the young women underwent a transformation, and Antonio discovered his subtle (and for Helena, not so subtle) observation of them during dinner was no match for the girls' open interest in him. Having broken the charade of separating by gender, the girls circled Antonio. If Mama were to see this, Antonio thought, she would say, "*si lanciavano contro di lui.*" [They were throwing themselves at him.] He smiled within and let the girls pay attention to him.

For Antonio, walking through town with his young friends fulfilled a longing he had not satisfied since leaving Italy. He enjoyed the closeness in the group, the stories shared, and their sincere effort to orient him to the ins and outs of the city. They returned to the house radiating warmth from their time together and their exciting plans to head to the beach together the following weekend.

Before preparing for dessert and coffee, a special event took place. Lucia remembered something important that Antonio himself seemed to have forgotten. She went into the house, returning with the slip of the fig root he carried with him from Italy. She gently lifted the planting, showing it to everyone. There were gasps about how clever he was to bring the cutting with him. Everyone wanted to know exactly where the host tree had stood so they could place it in their minds. Lucia pulled out her two shovels, asking others who lived nearby to get theirs so that they could plant the tree before having dessert. There was great emotion when the tree was dropped into the soil, and from then on all the fig trees propagated from Antonio's' root became symbols of Italian American roots in the U.S.

Antonio worked diligently, getting the root deep into the ground, building the soil around it, and then watering it. Everyone walked up to get a close look and began to think of the tree's future—fig cookies, fig bread, and more trees. Antonio made promises that he was able to keep because the tree thrived under his care and is still alive today. Before getting to dessert, Lucia, who paid meticulous attention to rituals and ceremony, wanted to pray to St. Rose of Lima, Patron Saint of Gardens, for the tree to flourish in the years ahead. The crowd was jubilant following the planting, all saying they would celebrate by having *dolce* [dessert]. The table was set, the sweets and coffee served though the day was hardly over. They spent a few additional hours together listening to Italian music, singing, and dancing. But for the absence of a bride and a groom, the afternoon strongly resembled a reception at a big Italian wedding.

As the festivities concluded, everyone began to clean up, and then partake in the long, emotional farewells characteristic of Italian culture. Antonio was heartened by the day and grateful for the guests coming to welcome him, many bringing small gifts. He thanked each person, especially Lucia, whom he recognized publicly, which impressed everyone. The gathering and the people inspired him. They offered an example of the good life in the United States without cutting bonds to the past, bringing clarity and reason to Antonio's early misperception of immigration as a change that would sever him from his country. As he and his Aunt stored the last of her supplies, Antonio told her the day was the best second day in the country he could imagine. It left him with a good feeling about his future.

Chapter 16

Becoming American

Antonio liked to help Luigi with home repair, canning vegetables, and projects that required more than one person. During one visit, he learned Luigi brought his father's wine press to the U.S. when he immigrated. How he managed to ship the heavy equipment was a great mystery to Antonio, though he was more interested in making wine. A huge project that pleased Luigi and the whole family grew out of Antonio's ambitious thinking.

In the months following his arrival to the U.S., Antonio dedicated himself to his work while also spending time with his friends, both Italians and Americans. There was a curious practice of leisure time in America for enjoyment and pleasure that he needed to adjust to. He knew of no such practice in agrarian Italy, where farming consumed time day and night, weekdays and weekends. Whether at work or enjoying leisure time, Antonio was immersed in American culture and deliberately worked on his language skills. He found his basic study of English in Italy helpful as a foundation now that he had reason to speak English. He listened carefully to any source of English, picking up words and phrases from anyone crossing his path. He also read the papers and listened to the radio. Month by month, Antonio's English improved in all modes—reading, writing, listening, and speaking. One morning about seven months after his arrival in America, he experienced the success of learning something new on his own by reading the news.

That morning, when Antonio looked at the papers before leaving for work, he was surprised to find a photograph of Professor Fermi alongside an article about him. If ever there was a day when Antonio worked his hardest to understand English, that day was the one. Reading with care, Antonio learned that a few weeks prior in late 1938, the Professor received the Nobel Prize for Physics at a ceremony in Stockholm. Antonio was overwhelmed by Professor Fermi's great success, joyful for him, and overcome by his own honor of having been in the presence of such a dignified and distinguished individual.

There was more to the story. Professor Fermi and his family did not return to Italy after the award ceremony as expected. Rather, they fled to America, seeking a better life, and made their way to Chicago where Fermi secured a professorial position at the University of Chicago. Antonio recalled the question he did not think he could pose to the Professor about immigration and was speechless while genuinely happy for Professor Fermi and his family. Reading the article that morning, though there were challenges with doing so, Antonio discovered the power of language as a tool for learning, and he doubled his efforts to achieve fluency in English.

Early on, Antonio's job consisted of labor only and work in the back room until his language improved, yet before the start of his second year in the U.S., he had acquired English conversation skills that were more than adequate for working in the laundry. His role and responsibilities in the business increased as a result—he took orders in person or over the phone and made deliveries. Antonio had an excellent relationship with Lucia's long-time clients. When they learned that young Antonio had full responsibility for their regular orders, they praised him for the quality of his work, which pleased and embarrassed him at the same time.

Antonio's contact with the public was illuminating about life in the U.S. He learned about occupations and how Americans spent their leisure time. He became acquainted with words like *hobbies*, *pastimes*, and *vacations* and discovered so many options for leisure time that he was overwhelmed by the opportunities. They filled his mind with thoughts about an exodus of people to beaches, parks, museums, sports events, major cities, and recreation areas for swimming, water sports, and fishing. Antonio was close to exhausted thinking about activity when one could indulge in a siesta. But then he realized he was looking at life through the lens of the Old World rather than that of America. Free time was now part of his lifestyle. The shop closed daily and did not open until the next day. In time, he realized the benefits of and uses for leisure time, while acknowledging it was taking him a while to adjust to the luxury of it.

By time Antonio's second year in the U.S. was underway, he had reason to feel satisfied. He had the experience of a full year in the country, during which he participated in civic, religious, and national holidays the Italian Americans celebrated. He was awed by their attention to both countries and how they adopted traditions like the Fourth of July and Thanksgiving while continuing those they brought to the U.S. like the Banquet of Seven Fishes on Christmas Eve and Ferragosto, which honors the Emperor Augustus and also coincides with the religious Feast of the Assumption.

He had a social life with the young people and particularly the sparking young woman he had met on his first day in Stamford as well as the many Americans he had met since then. As a group they headed to beaches, amusement parks, and New York City, always using public transportation. In time Antonio was falling in love with Helena though he did not exactly know that was happening. His regular letters to Mama and Papa regaled them with stories of his adventures and details about American culture and his New World. He often copied excerpts from his journal into his letters. He made ordinary matters like growing his fig tree and special places like the beach seem extraordinary. His life excited them. The way he wrote conveyed additional information that Mama and Papa scrutinized. They savored the maturation they detected in his words and his blossoming personality, shedding tears of joy over his adjustment. Antonio was a good son for writing regularly and easing their worry, yet he was always cautious about what he disclosed. Mama was perceptive, formidable, and fiercely protective of her eldest son. A word about a woman in his life would have him married within the month should the young lady meet Mama's high standards. If she learned about his recent excursion to New York City, he would be on the first boat back to Italy.

Though Antonio was active, he felt the Italian Americans he lived among and socialized with lived a simple life as he did. None of them were of high financial standing. They did not really see wealth and status as personal goals. Rather they dreamed of modest homes, families, and health. Antonio was now in the middle of his second year in the country, and he was beginning to understand and enjoy the idea of leisure. It brought more meaning to events with family and friends on the weekend, and it offered rest in an enriching way. He discovered the beaches of Connecticut with his friends and the lovely Helena, and they went to the shore most weekends from early spring to the beginning of November. There she introduced him to clams and how to dig for them. At the shore, he sketched images of her and the Sound through the seasons. She was frequently mentioned in his journal because she warmed his heart. One day, when the time was right, he would create a story about her to share with Mama and Papa.

Antonio was beginning to spend time with Helena and her family, and he especially enjoyed time with her parents. Helena's mother was a traditional peasant woman from the countryside, and it was comforting to talk with her about the Old Country. Like all women of her time, she was a fabulous cook. Helena's father, Luigi, was a large-boned man with a distinguished look, who was resourceful, earnest, civic-minded, and attached to Old World traditions. He wore a suit every day and kept a pocket watch on a chain in his vest pocket. Antonio liked that sophisticated look, often thought about his own image, and concluded he would aim for sophistication that blended Italian and American styles. Luigi was a knowledgeable, well-read man who followed the geopolitical situation in Europe. That practice forged a lifetime bond between the two men because Antonio always thought about his country and his family. As the war ramped up, he was preoccupied with events that could affect his family's well-being and their land. Luigi was sympathetic about Antonio's concerns and always kept himself informed, one way or another, about the conditions where Antonio's family lived. Together, the two men discussed their homeland every time they met. They were alike in several ways, their gentle manner and warmth the strongest similarities.

Antonio liked to help Luigi with home repair, canning vegetables, and projects that required more than one person. During one visit, he learned Luigi brought his father's wine press to the U.S. when he immigrated. How he managed to transport the heavy equipment was a great mystery to Antonio, though he was more interested in making wine. A huge project that pleased Luigi and the whole family grew out of Antonio's ambitious thinking.

To the side of Luigi's house beyond the garage was a large plot where he and Rosa cultivated a small garden and a sapling from Antonio's fig tree that was now growing steadily. That touch of Italy in the backyard warmed the hearts of family members and neighbors who always reminisced about the past. With the wine press in mind, Antonio suggested the family grow grapes in the portions of the lot that remained unused. The sprawling vines would beautify the property and rekindle memories of the homeland and all their immigrant dreams. By then, everyone knew Antonio had a miraculous green thumb and a way with creating beautiful gardens. They would be foolish to turn down his generous offer. Luigi's older fig tree, another spawn from Antonio's cutting, was growing beautifully in the front garden. It served as a testament to his abilities.

Not willing to wait until the first crop yielded fruit, Luigi and Antonio decided to chip in and buy grapes from suppliers in upstate New York. While awaiting the grape harvest and delivery of their order by train, they cleaned and set up the wine press and then planted their own vines. By then the grapes had arrived, and they were soon in the business of crushing grapes and making wine. They all had some experience with the process in the Old Country and had little trouble remembering the stages of winemaking from crushing the grapes to racking and fermentation. Everything was in place for decades of wine production on a small scale at home though they knew their first vintage would not be ready for some time.

Antonio was a family man, whose devotion to others, especially his Aunt, kept him busy. His role in the laundry continued to expand, and he now had working knowledge of the financials and began to participate in business decisions. Sometimes his job presented him with adventures. One day Lucia asked him to go to New York City to evaluate a clothing press new to the market and decide whether to buy it or not. What an honor for Antonio to receive that level of regard and responsibility! The thought of a solo trip to New York appealed to him, not because he preferred to be alone but because he wanted to revisit his memories of arriving in New York, something others might find tedious. Antonio remembered details of that day, so he wasn't interested in reconstructing it. Rather, he wanted to retrace his steps to reminisce about the day he arrived when he was so overwhelmed by the atmosphere that he could not adequately appreciate his surroundings.

On the day of the excursion, Antonio left the house early in the morning. He walked the streets of Stamford with confidence, chatting with shop owners on his way to the trolley stop. He conversed with them in well-articulated English that left them appreciative of his efforts to adjust to the country. Through his courteous manner and words, his warm Italian nature, humor, and know-how manifested. Antonio's comfort level was not bound by his local neighborhood. He was sure of himself no matter where he went and never hesitated to converse with people he met or ask questions. As he continued to the trolley stop, he gave thought to the day and his itinerary until mid-afternoon, when he would head to the Garment District to examine the press. How far along he had come in feeling safe, capable, and independent in the country! He no longer over-planned for fear of making a mistake or getting lost. He was completely comfortable with heading to New York City without specific plans in place. He wanted to go with the flow of life, moving against traffic so he would not lose time in the delays rush hour tended to cause. He expected to navigate the City with ease, utilizing the massive transit system.

Antonio's extraordinary day began with his arrival to Grand Central Station, where the ornate surroundings left him breathless for the sixth time in his life. From there, he headed to the Empire State Building, whose striking silhouette was the very image of American vision and ingenuity in his eyes. He was fascinated with the island, boroughs, and waterways, so much so that he added a ferry ride to the day's agenda to view the City from the water. What excited Antonio most was the perspective of the entire City that he managed to see by walking along bridges and taking the elevated subway as well as the Staten Island Ferry.

Later, Antonio picked up lunch from a vendor, reminded about the first time he saw the vending carts in the City, and then made his way to the Garment District to examine the press. He arrived at the shop before three in the afternoon. The owners, an Italian family, were expecting him and invited him in. The three sat together briefly to enjoy coffee and cookies in the Old World style. Antonio was at ease with the couple though they had never met previously because the three of them were all raised in the same sociocultural milieu of respect. Lucia was acquainted with the couple and that connection was a signal for him to follow the mores of small towns and villages in Italy that had been carried over to the U.S.

After their respite, the equivalent to afternoon tea or coffee in Europe, they moved on to business. Antonio examined the press, learned how it worked, and considered its place in Lucia's shop. The couple urged him to use the press, which he found lighter than expected. He deemed the steam heat strong and effective and found the press's board a brilliant idea for avoiding kinks and folds in a fabric. He agreed to the sale, paid for the item, and found it easy to carry on his return trip. Most people on the streets of New York would have regarded Antonio's adventure as commonplace, but for him it was the escapade of a lifetime that made him grateful for the vast inviting world in which he lived.

As the country settled into a new decade, Antonio continued to be educated by the world because people from points worldwide lived in the same coastal region as he did. The immigrant population in his town had increased since his arrival, with more people arriving from Europe, Italian, Greek, and Polish families the most common. Italians remained the dominant immigrant population there, and collectively they were settling in comfortably by that time. All financial indicators suggested the U.S. was moving out of the Great Depression, yet geopolitical matters and the likelihood of a war caused worry.

Antonio had now been in the U.S. for two and a half years and he felt a sense of security. He enjoyed speaking English, handled money well, and managed to live comfortably while saving modest funds. Overall, he was feeling good about his place in local society. As is always the case with life, achieving goals begs for new directions and growth. Feeling successful and financially stable, Antonio found himself ready for the two forces that would define his life as the country moved into the 1940s: a woman and a war.

Chapter 17
The Beguiling Seamstress

Helena's parents were born in Italy and migrated to America before having children. They spoke English with an accent whereas their children did not. Helena's English was beautiful, something Antonio admired. Early on, Antonio felt awkward speaking to her. He considered his accented broken English inferior, thinking he was not good enough for her. Helena did not look at people in that way, though. Accented English was part of her family's identity.

One morning, Antonio awoke with a sense of expectancy about something wonderful happening. He paused, reminding himself of the date and considering whether there was something special about it. To his knowledge, the answer was no. He remembered Lucia was taking care of errands that morning, but that was neither unusual nor exciting. There was no explanation for what he sensed, yet something told him to take special care, to be ready, so he chose his clothes carefully, buffed his shoes, and passed on having morning coffee with his friends. He intended to get started in the laundry early and stand ready for whatever the day brought. He could not shake the idea that he was on the cusp of something special.

As was usually the case, business was brisk shortly after opening. Many customers picked up or dropped off their laundry and that kept Antonio busy. Close to mid-morning the neighborhood police on watch stopped in, and that meant great conversations about sports and topics in the news. By time the officers left, the laundry was quiet, and Antonio moved on to packing and organizing finished orders. He liked those tasks for the satisfaction of "a job well done," as his customers would say. Antonio also found the work straightforward yet not tedious, which gave him some space for thinking and daydreaming. As he collected the bundles he needed to pack, he reviewed the morning's events, still wondering about the day's importance. No surprises yet, but the feeling remained alive.

Antonio cleared his workspace to accommodate the large number of orders he had to tally that day. He positioned himself at the end of the counter where he could work while also monitor the entrance and even wave to passersby. When he turned to pull another order, he was thinking about the upcoming Italian picnic to celebrate the Feast of the Assumption and wondered how he and Helena might spend time together in public that day without infringing on the family's strict code for the girls. His mind circled his dilemma and he stopped to think of a few possibilities, holding his head up and staring at nothing as he always did when contemplating concerns. As he ruminated on matters of the heart, he happened to tilt his head in such a way that he caught sight of a figure through a beveled section of the glass store front. The image was distorted, but he could see a woman proceeding along the sidewalk. Since she was carrying a stack of coats, he expected her to enter the laundry.

He could not determine whether he knew the woman because of the bundle in her arms. She seemed to be peering out from her far side, and that left her face outside his field of vision unless he did something ridiculous, like stand on the counter, to see her. A thought came to him, and it made him flush from his neck to the top of his head. Helena worked in a coat factory nearby along with all her cousins. He often yearned to walk in the direction of that shop with the hope of seeing her.

Antonio wondered if this was the day when just the two of them would connect outside the watchful eyes of family and friends. He could see dark hair, which resembled hers, and his heart thumped faster. But then most of the women he knew had dark hair. His optimism plummeted. He interrupted his musings and did the right thing by running out to meet the woman and take the bundle from her. For a few seconds he and the young lady were lost in the tangle of the coat transfer. But the moment came when he secured enough coats that Helena's smiling face appeared and made his heart flip.

Helena was a talented seamstress who had taken work into her family's home to make ends meet until she obtained a job at the coat factory. She remained the same sparkling young woman Antonio was drawn to from the start on his second day in America. He knew her family well and often had his morning coffee at the deli with two of her brothers and other friends. He was on good terms with her parents, who had been kind to him since the day they met. He had seen Helena at every Italian American activity he attended and had conversations with her on all those occasions, always under her parents' watchful eyes. When she arrived in the shop with Antonio, she opened and held the door for him because he was carrying the coats. They both laughed over their shifting roles, and his mind spun. Her angelic glow and full, hearty, yet feminine laugh nearly brought him to his knees. Her creamy Italian skin and gentle disposition made her beautiful inside and out. When she smiled, she lit the room with warmth.

That morning, their conversation picked up spontaneously as though they had known each other for a long time. That perspective on their relationship was actually true though their connection was so natural and pure that they themselves did not always understand how close they had become. Finding kindheartedness in her company and not wanting her to leave any sooner than she had to, Antonio took his time recording her order. They had so much to talk about—their mutual interests, the recent Fourth of July picnic, the beach where it was held, the fireworks, her family, and the war. They chatted as he created the ticket for her order. At that moment, he felt calm and peaceful.

Antonio

Helena

Helena's parents were born in Italy and migrated to America before having children. They spoke English with an accent whereas their children did not. Helena's unaccented English was beautiful, something Antonio admired. Early on, he felt awkward speaking to her.

He considered his accented broken English inferior, thinking he was not good enough for her. Helena did not look at people in that way, though. As he came to know her, he realized accented English was a characteristic of her household that did not figure in her opinion of others. In fact, he had never met a person as kind and loving as she. If Helena had known what Antonio was thinking, tears would have filled her eyes. She was a generous person and the least judgmental person he had ever met. She had her eyes on Antonio from the start as he also gravitated toward her. But she was not the type of woman to chase a man. She was fun yet quiet, always well-dressed but never showy. She was a fabulous cook, he heard, and a devoted daughter.

In contrast to Antonio, who seemed so worldly to her, Helena felt common. She did not think she could match his style and courage. She would have been heartbroken if she had to leave her family for another country. But Antonio prevailed in adjusting to the U.S. In fact, he did more than that, he succeeded. He had already turned heads in the Italian American community as being bright and resourceful. He was respected by many and often found himself advising others simply because he had common sense and reasoning skills. Time would eventually present Antonio as a leader in his community in a way that reflected his upbringing and values.

Helena knew Antonio was devoted to her. He worked to please her and brought her something special every time they met. He was also kind to her parents and generous in helping them maintain their home. Helena enjoyed conversing with Antonio and wished they lived in a different time and culture where the eyes of the community were less observant. The stars seemed to align that day, bringing the two together. Warm, friendly though shy, Helena was moved by Antonio's enthusiasm, his soulful green eyes, the curiosity that prompted his learning, and his storytelling. She could listen to him tell stories for the rest of her life, and she loved his stories about Italy, especially the sentimental ones about leaving for the United States. He was earnest, Helena thought, as she listened to and followed his animated story.

Antonio was besotted with the lovely Helena. When describing her to his friends, he'd get nudged and kidded for saying, "She has the smile of the Mona Lisa—a closed-mouthed smile and warmth in her eyes as though she is holding on to a secret." Her black hair was lustrous, and her large dark eyes conveyed her every feeling, exposing her kind heart and generous spirit. "A Madonna," he deemed every time he looked at her.

Their time together that morning led to a revelation about each of them as individuals and the two of them together, the perfect complements to each another. Their conversation and the writing up of her order seemed an eternity yet also felt too brief. They always reminisced about that day and the many that followed. They could not refer to it as the day they met because that was not an accurate statement, but they regarded it as the day they began to share love.

What Antonio and Helena never knew about that occasion and others like it was that Lucia's hand played a role in the seemingly serendipitous meeting. She was a matchmaker, a great one at that. Helena had been Lucia's first choice for Antonio even before he arrived in the United States. She was elated when she saw the sparkle in his and Helena's eyes whenever they were together, and she wanted the best for her nephew. A modern woman, Lucia cast old-fashioned views aside, took time off from the laundry, and talked her cousin Lenny, the owner of the coat factory, into giving Helena the responsibility for bringing coats to the laundry every week to be pressed. One other person knew of Lucia's scheme, Mama. She had been apprised regularly from afar about the budding romance, and she approved.

Chapter 18

Antonio Becomes Tony

Johnnie, the oldest in the group and the one most likely to lighten or diffuse a tense moment, tried a mix of humor, diplomacy, and emotion as he usually did to alleviate the pressure the men were experiencing. He spoke from the heart when he turned to Antonio, slapping him on the back, to address a topic he'd been meaning to broach for some time.

Early one morning, Antonio and his friends were sitting in George's Luncheonette and Grocery enjoying coffee and rolls before getting to work. Their morning ritual was an important one. It was a time to catch up, especially about current events. By mid-week it was also a time to make plans for the weekend, for Saturday afternoons and evenings that is because many of the men, including Antonio, often worked on Saturday mornings. Most of the men were also Italian, which meant Sunday was reserved for church and family. No matter what they talked about, the discussion always made its way to the war and events underway in Europe. Anyone hearing the young men would appreciate the caliber of their conversations. They all met or exceeded the minimum age requirement for enlisting, so serving in the military was a key topic in their discussions. Should they or should they not sign up?

Events in 1940 complicated the men's perspectives on going to war. Initially, their motivations varied, with some having a strong inclination to sign up and others driven by personal reasons, such as seeing the world or solving employment problems. Those intentions belonged to their daydreams of the past when the thought of U.S. involvement seemed unlikely or distant. As the likelihood of the U.S. becoming involved in global affairs increased, the young men became impatient and even more interested in serving on the side of America. They were not eager to place themselves at risk, yet they were zealous about saving the world. A definitive turning point occurred, and it pushed them further.

In July 1940, Italy entered the War as a member of the Axis powers. A few months later, it became part of the Tripartite Pact with Germany and Japan to create the Axis Alliance. For the Italian immigrants, the possibility of Italy and the United States, the two countries in their life stories, opposing one another was unfathomable. Italy's actions were unforgivable. They subjected young immigrants like Antonio and his friends to a test of loyalty and morality and placed them at a crossroads for decision-making about enlisting, yet some of their options were not tenable.

It was unthinkable to return to Italy to serve in the Italian military. The men did not support the position Italy had chosen. That path was not only unthinkable but impossible for the increasing number of Italians in America who had sought an exemption by the Italian Consulate in the U.S. as Antonio had on the advice of his Aunt, who was familiar with such matters. Since Italy was not engaged in an active war when Antonio arrived in the U.S., he qualified for exemption during peace time [in temp de pace] according to Italian law. His application was approved, and he received documentation indicating he would not be called up to serve in Italy for the remainder of his life even if he maintained Italian citizenship, provided he did not reside in his homeland. Since then, Antonio recommended the same for all his friends. In 1940 that documentation protected them from being recalled to Italy to be part of the Axis Alliance as many men were.

While they were conversing at the Luncheonette that morning debating the most important decision in their lives following Italy's actions, their friend Paul, an American, or Paolo as they called him, walked in. Paul was a great buddy who steered many men in the group through their adjustment in the United States. A work friend of Rocco's at the power company, Paul genuinely enjoyed the spirit of Italian culture. He was dating one of Antonio's cousins, which meant he wanted to feel comfortable with Italian traditions and lifestyle.

Paul knew the men would talk about the war that morning and was concerned about how they were feeling. He hoped they wouldn't do anything rash before thinking through the consequences, and he had a relevant question to pose to the group, "Are citizens of another country who reside in the U.S. eligible to serve in U.S. Forces?" When he asked the question, his friends looked at him with shock. They had never considered that angle in their deliberations and were astonished by how their spirits plummeted at the thought of not being eligible to serve. The air felt thick with the sighs they expired and the disappointment they felt. For Paul, their reaction spoke volumes. Then and there, he knew the group of friends he cherished would choose to enlist if the option to do so existed. He could see it in their eyes.

The atmosphere in the Luncheonette became tense and filled with discontent over the question of whether immigrants who were not yet U.S. citizens were eligible to serve. The conversation shifted to identity and related topics, which seemed to depress everyone further. Johnnie, the oldest in the group and the one most likely to lighten or diffuse a moment, tried a mix of humor, diplomacy, and emotion as he usually did to alleviate the pressure the men were experiencing. He spoke from the heart when he turned to Antonio, slapping him on the back, to address a topic he'd been meaning to broach for some time. "Antonio," Johnnie said, "I know you're seriously considering signing up and you'll want to fit in. Look at me, Johnnie. Giovanni, my birth name, always made me feel like an outsider. Now I feel as though I fit in everywhere I go." Friends readily nodded in agreement. Neither argument nor dissension followed Johnnie's assertion.

Antonio experienced a rush of warmth, looking down at the table for a few minutes to catch his breath. Knowing the guys well, he realized what had come about—acceptance. He was regarded as part of the Italian American brotherhood. He had always known he belonged with them yet sometimes felt he sat along the fringe. In part, his own hesitation delayed his full acceptance into the group. Was he Italian or Italian American? Until that day, he could not be sure. He looked up and smiled broadly, saying, "Call me Tony! Thank you, Johnnie, I've been thinking of doing this for a long time." "Tony it is," Paul said. "It will matter in time. You'll want to become a citizen one day and rise in the community. Tony is less formal and warmer. We need to thank Johnnie, who always knows what's right." Noticing the hour and the need to get to work soon, they all quieted, with contentment, finishing the last of their coffee.

A while later, Tony left the deli to return to the laundry, but not before stopping at the counter for a brief conversation with George to ask if he knew whether immigrants could serve in U.S. Forces. "Immigrants with U.S. citizenship, definitely," George said, "but I'm not sure about non-citizens. I'll ask around." As Tony strolled across the small city, he thought through what had just occurred, realizing there was more to it than the obvious. Something deep that reflected the opinions he formed over the past few years was taking place. As early as his first week in the country, he devoted time and thought to cultivating himself to succeed in his new country. That meant improving his English and presenting himself well in the urban community where he lived and worked. The matter involved appearance, manner of dress, habits, and gestures. He was well on his way in those areas because his Aunt emphasized them too. Her business served everyone in the city. Over a decade ago, she experienced the same realization and worked to fit in. Following her husband's death, she had to re-fashion herself yet again to adhere to both Italian and American expectations about what was and was not appropriate for a widow running a business on her own.

What occurred earlier that morning supported Tony's adjustment to the U.S. He had undergone a transformation since his arrival. He felt validated by his friends at the deli that day. He had gained something he needed and wanted, even though he had not put a name to it until now. He had been longing for a sense of affiliation in the Italian American community since arriving in the country. He paused, realizing he had abandoned the long-time hesitation about seeing himself for what he was becoming. And he then wondered what Mama would say. In his heart, he knew she would be proud of him just as Papa would be, yet he vowed to always be Antonio to her, which was the case for the remainder of her life.

Over time, Tony was well served by his new nickname. It felt casual and carefree, youthful. In serious matters, that minor change was of consequence. It related to culture, specifically his immigrant status, at a time when the U.S. was fraught with anti-Italian sentiment. The migration of people streaming out of Italy and into the U.S. did not appeal to the many nativists in the United States put off by the enclaves Italians were forming and thriving in, confident about their colorful and lively ways and work ethic. To their jaundiced eyes, Italians in America disrupted society. Yet, expectations that the Italians would fail did not play out, and early bigoted stereotypes of them as greasy and dirty continuously lost traction in American society as Italian Americans became stitched into the fabric of the United States. They were skilled in many areas from construction, masonry, and plumbing to baking and cooking, sewing, winemaking, gardening and landscaping. It took no time at all for them to find work and prosper.

Since arriving, Tony had monitored the reaction to Italians, never feeling any direct affront against him but sensing judgment in the air. He was aware of the legislation against immigrants, especially Italians in California, who were surveilled, arrested, and deported. He could not feel any animus about what was taking place. In essence, what Americans felt about Italy, their distaste for Mussolini's ways, was no different from what Tony felt and had led to his departure from Italy. Amid that backdrop of unfounded animosity, he walked a thin line, demonstrating he had the good sense to avoid being misunderstood in his host country.

Antonio's thoughts drifted to his journey to the U.S. when he began to examine his situation through the eyes of another person, the journalist Luca, whose writing appeared in the New York papers from time to time. Luca had his eye on the topic when Tony had been naïve about what he might experience in America. Tony was fortunate to have had those small doses of learning on the ship that made him more personally and socially responsible in the present. While there were no immediate solutions to the misunderstanding about immigrants, Tony aimed to move forward. The powerful moment he experienced early that morning marked the beginning of a new way of existing and finding a place in American society.

Chapter 19
Home of the Brave, Tony Enlists in the U.S. Army

Immigrants from the same region in Italy lived on ten or so lengthy streets that ran parallel to one another in a quaint urban neighborhood. Traces of Italian traditions were visible. Small gardens, trellised grape vines, and fig trees reproduced the ambience and charm of the "Old Country," and there Tony conjured his clearest memories of Mama, Papa, his brothers, and his sister.

In late fall 1940, households in the U.S. reverberated with non-stop chatter and worry about the expanding war. Everyone wondered exactly what recent developments in the Axis Alliance meant for America as the holiday season approached. The war was very much on the minds of the young Italian immigrants who wished to serve, but they had the wisdom to slow down the pace of their deliberations in respect for the religious holidays and what they meant to everyone, especially their older family members who made many sacrifices to reach the United States. Through the cooperation of all, the holidays were as warm and memorable as they were every other year.

Slowly after the New Year however, the war once again made its way to the forefront of all discussions. No one dared ask what would come next because they knew in their hearts what the answer would be. Conversations occurred in minds only, as was the case with the young women, who waited and wondered what their men would decide to do. They were engrossed in a nagging question. *Would he sign up or would he not?* They had reason to believe some men would say "yes" though it was possible some could say "no." The topic was debated for some time but could not be resolved by anyone other than the men themselves. Quiet conversations occurred among the men in hidden places so as not to upset others until they knew what they planned to do. Deliberations about the war and enlisting became earnest, causing a mantle of fear to descend on the Italian American households in Stamford and other local towns where immigrants lived. A funereal atmosphere hung in the air as more and more young men answered the call to enlist. Parents fretted over the matter, fearing the outcome, and wanted to intervene and dissuade their adult children from enlisting.

Rosa herself lamented the situation, praying. The issue was a conundrum. There were many reasons to serve—the interests of both the United States and Italy. Compelling reasons for not serving, family and personal safety, also existed. So much had occurred during the last few months that war was no longer perceived as an adventure. The men took it seriously, knew the burdens and benefits, and acknowledged the risks.

Rosa was distraught. In one sweep she could have her two sons Jerry and Anthony, her son-in-law Rocco, Tony, cousins Patrick, Antonio, and Johnnie, and family friend Paul off to war within a month. She was a surrogate mother to many young immigrant men, the pride of their region in Italy, who had come to the U.S. for a better life. *What was better,* she thought, *than building a life in America and thriving?* Luigi's opinion differed from hers. As surrogate father to many young male immigrants who flocked to America to escape Mussolini's Army, he regarded enlisting as an opportunity for them to earn their place in American society by serving the country they had come to love. In many respects, Luigi's response reflected his personal lamentation for not assimilating fully in American society.

Lucia understood the opinions of both Rosa and Luigi. Never having had children, she could not speak from the perspective of a parent, but she had a strong opinion about Tony. As much as she wanted him safe and sound, she saw success in him and felt he could elevate himself in society by serving in the U.S. Army, which differed markedly from the heavy-handedness of Italy's current regime and military. He needed a push. Confident about the strength of the U.S. Army, she saw the benefits of serving on the side of morality.

Darkness and tension gripped the community, and Tony had to talk with someone, but not Helena nor his pals at first. He turned to Luigi out of respect and to discuss the decision he was leaning toward. Luigi heard Tony's case and was pleased with his balanced discernment.

"My dear friend and advisor," Tony says, "I grieve for my family and all our compatriots in Italy. I cannot see anything but darkness on the horizon for them and all Europeans. The people live in fear, knowing they are on the path of war."

"Ay, Antonio, I feel the same," Luigi said. "The continent is on a path to war and its darkest hours lie ahead."

"Si, si, Luigi. What you say reinforces how I feel. I regard the present as an extraordinary moment for Europeans in the United States to gather their bearings and enlist in what is clearly the ramping up of the U.S. Military. Papa always told me I was coming to the U.S. for a reason. Remembering my premonition during the crossing, I feel that I'm being called to serve."

"The emotional weight will be heavy, my son," yet Tony replied in turn "I understand. But I've developed an attachment to the U.S. and its values. The Youth Group filled my growing up years with tyranny, forced service, and the demand for blind loyalty. I breath freely here, and I wish the same for the countries of the world. Serving in the war, if that's where enlisting takes me, is my choice, Luigi." Luigi commends Tony for his courage, guides him on how to present his views to others, and reminds Tony to send a telegram to his parents when he makes his final decision. He goes on to assure Tony that his parents are aware of the crossroads where the young Italian immigrants stand.

Like Tony, each man in that close-knit group searched within to reach their decisions, and eventually each said "yes" to the call to serve even before soldiers were being drafted. Their next step was to discuss the matter with the women in their lives, asking their views, and then sharing the reasons for their desire to enlist. The conversations were not easy, nor were they overly difficult. The women were strong, practical, supportive, and realistic. They looked toward the future but admitted they had never been tested in this manner. They showed their strength by accepting arguments about courage and a path for success for the U.S.

A few days later, Tony and one of his cousins visited the local Armed Forces Recruiting Center to ask a few questions and learn about the process for enlisting. At the top of their list was the question about eligibility as non-citizens. The answer they received left them buoyant about the opportunity before them but not without some weight in their hearts about the reality of their next step. The elements of enlisting aside, they listened to recruiters, who painted a compelling yet realistic picture of the developing war plan, the skilled training they would receive, and their chance to contribute to America's efforts to support European causes. The benefits attracted them, satisfying questions about how they could advance in American society. What the recruiters knew for sure was that young Italian immigrants were well prepared for warfare and would be an asset in the U.S. Military.

On Tuesday, February 18, Tony returned to the Recruiting Center with his family and friends who were ready to sign up and initiate the process. The atmosphere in each household turned to darkness and mourning that day. Older family members were stricken by the prospect of the mass departure of dozens of young Italian American men. The recruits, however, were filled with conviction about their decisions. They would head to war as much for the United States as they would for Italy and Europe.

Tony had now placed himself in a position where for the second time in his life he would leave his home, in this case his home in his New World with his newfound Italian American family. The confluence of forces in his life that brought him to that point drove the next few weeks for him. In the short term, he planned for special time with Helena. He wanted to take her to New York City one day for dinner, a show, and a walk down memory lane. He also wanted beach days as the weather improved, lovely walks along the shore to dream and reminisce. Long-term involved two paths. The easiest was the path of falling in love with Helena, which he now saw clearly and forever. The other focused on preparing for active duty, following the calendar the Recruitment Center provided, which carried good news, relatively speaking that is. The scheduled estimate for their processing placed their timeframe prior to departure at six weeks minimum. Everyone had assumed departure would be imminent, but that was not so.

Tony calculated six weeks to two months in Stamford before departing sometime between early April and mid-May. For a few weeks after signing up, Tony experienced little change in his life. He reduced his work hours in the laundry to manage and complete scheduled enlistment requirements and to increase his free time. He and Helena had plenty of time to meet, and life returned to normal as much as possible for a while. During that time, a letter from Italy arrived. It was a message from Mama and Papa about his impending departure for Europe—not to see them, but to serve in the war.

My dearest son,

Mama and I pray for God's watchful eye as you set out on your journey. We mourn the events in Europe, and we fear for our country. I know war. I remember my companion Gustavo, the loyal horse I rode in Austria-Hungary, and how he and I fought vigorously against the enemy. No one realized how hard the horses worked. I thought of our own ponies and stallions here at home and how lovingly we cared for them.

You will fight in a different war, my son, [figlia mia], because the world has changed. We follow the path of the U.S. Army and read how it's preparing for a vast war on the ground. New machines will replace the horses. They say it's a new day in the world of warfare.

You will learn so much my son, and you will fight for the two countries you know and love. Antonio, we are proud of you. Do not fear the war as I returned from one. God bless you and bring you home safely too.

Be strong, be well, my son.
We will continue to pray for you always.

Tutto il nostro amore,
Mama e Papa

Tony wept over his parents' words but was also enlightened and bolstered by Papa's insights. He cherished his parents' good wishes from afar, their words a treasure that would keep him. The letter made Tony's enlistment more real. He had no doubt that the note would comfort him and serve as a connection with his family throughout the war.

Sometime after signing their enlistment paperwork and handling other logistical matters, the process of preparing for service became more rigorous. The group spent more time meeting requirements, which one day included basic aptitude tests and other measures. Those robust evaluations were comprehensive and left the group humble about their language skills and grateful that they each had focused on improving their English over the past few years. The other requirements they had to fulfill challenged them at different levels, and some were daunting. They had their personal physicals, which in and of themselves could have eliminated any one of the men from serving, but that did not happen. Mental health was as important as physical health in the services, so psychiatric testing and evaluation as well as in-person mental health assessments were required. Enlistment also involved a personal appearance before a board of community leaders for an intense interview and evaluation of lifestyle, habits, and background, which could have been a critical issue with the wrong type of board, and personal information, such as interests, finances, skills, and work history. The boards attempted to confirm or challenge a recruit's readiness and ability to contribute to the war effort.

In their discussions about the different requirements they had to fulfill, Tony and his buddies were astounded by the attention paid to individuals' readiness and the quality of the review process. Engaging in such revealing exercises about themselves frightened them, but they also realized the screening was for their benefit and that of all the men and women who wanted to serve. The soldiers feared the battlefield, hoped for their safety, and did not want conflict among the troops to interfere with their ability to serve and survive. For all the Italians in Tony's group, which were all but one of the eight, the enlistment process was an eyeopener in contrast to Italy's youth groups, which demonstrated no regard for the "selves" of the boys aged eight through eighteen. Throughout the haunting paramilitary maneuvers required by the youth groups, the mental and physical development of the boys was not a consideration. On hearing about the men's recruitment exercises, the immediate family sighed with relief about the measures taken to ensure recruits were of sound mind, health, and substance.

As the countdown to departure continued, Tony was classified as 1A as were his family and friends. That classification enabled them to conclude the enlistment process. Most of the final steps for enlistment were formalities about follow-up, like receiving vaccines or checking in with the armory. The group of eight—Helena's two brothers, four cousins, their American friend Paul, and Tony were able to handle their final requirements at the same time. That brought them to an induction ceremony in Hartford, the state's capital, which was seventy-seven miles away and accessible by train. There they were fingerprinted, signed their induction paperwork, received their serial numbers, and took their oaths. Only a few errands and loose paperwork remained to be done. Otherwise, they were on furlough for more time than they had thought.

During the reprieve, Tony received an enthusiastic response from Lucia when he asked if she would accompany him to the Italian-owned jewelry shop to find an engagement ring and band for Helena for the future. Together, unbeknown to anyone in town, which was a miracle among the close-knit Italians, they visited the in-home shop three times before selecting rings. Between the first visit and the third, they were attentive to Helena's jewelry styles and reactions to other rings purchased and given by soldiers leaving for war. There was an air of excitement, limited to Tony and Lucia only, the day they procured the rings. They lovingly admired them as the perfect choice. When Lucia locked the rings in the laundry's safe, Tony watched the unit close, reminding his Aunt about his feeling that he would propose to Helena before the war was over and he returned to the U.S. for good. As he spoke, his mind held an image of the clock at Grand Central. As Lucia listened to him, shock pummeled her. She hoped his insight was not a premonition that he would return early for the wrong reasons.

Having completed their enlistment obligations, the inductees looked reality in the eye while taking comfort in knowing they would journey together to Fort Dix, New Jersey, one of their waypoints to Fort Benning, Georgia, where they would all be stationed for Basic Training. They hoped seeing familiar faces from time to time would aid their adjustment and decrease feelings of loneliness and separation, the latter something they had already experienced when settling into life in America. Within their group, the seven immigrant recruits represented a small subset of the growing Italian American community forming in Southeastern Connecticut. The larger vibrant group was leaving its mark on American society as small business owners offering Old World skills as tailors, bakers, cooks, and butchers.

The Italians who lived in that special city and those who continued to arrive succeeded in replicating what they had left behind in Italy and became family to each other. They followed the Italian tradition for making every day count and celebrated all milestones in their community. With respect to the men's departure, custom called for a huge farewell gathering to lift dark thoughts and toast the young recruits with send-off messages of love, devotion, and prayer.

The early April weather made it possible for Helena and her family to host the farewell feast of over sixty people both inside and outside the home where they lived along with Rosa's brother and his wife and their niece. Immigrants from the same region in Italy lived on the ten or so streets that ran parallel to one another in the quaint urban neighborhood, creating Tony's Italy in America. Traces of Italian traditions were visible. The gardens, trellised grape vines, and fig trees reproduced the ambience and charm of the "Old Country." There, Tony conjured his clearest memories of Mama, Papa, his brothers, and his sister as he prepared to leave and drew from the warmth of his Italian American neighbors and friends to sustain him.

The families spared nothing for the event. Others beside family came to wish the recruits well. The Italian priest, neighbors, and friends passed through from afternoon to evening to express their regard, good wishes, and prayers. The undercurrent created by words unsaid did not detract from the event because the group, all immigrants from one period or another, understood the reality of life. They had weathered the peaks and valleys of life, experiencing love, loss, separation, war, disease, and heartbreak. They also knew not to ruin the day for all the young couples who would be so personally and emotionally affected by the men's departure.

There was a lovely well, with the authentic look of a wishing well, along the front walk to the house, where couples usually met to talk beyond the range of the senior adults. Throughout the day, all the young couples made their way to the well, sometimes reminiscing as a group and other times having couples-only conversations. Helena, one of her sisters, her sister-in-law, and her cousin's wife had been preparing themselves for the departure and vowed to stay close to and support one another while the men were away. Through the day, in that spot by the well, they shared their feelings with each other and with the men, husbands, fiancés, or boyfriends who were going off to war. Though emotions were palpable, good will and good hearts stood up to sentimentality, making for a lovely day and setting the tone for the remaining day prior to departure. After that, when the men were gone, memorable places were visited and whispered promises remembered.

At six-thirty a.m. on the day Tony reported to the Armory for active duty, Helena awoke early, dressed with an elegant touch, placed small photos of herself in her pocketbook, and when ready drove her uncle's car to the laundry, where she picked up Tony and proceeded to the Armory. On the short twenty-minute ride, they shared their dreams for a life together even though they were not engaged. They sat side by side quietly for a short time after arriving, feeling peace run through them. Helena sniffled, trying to keep her tears in check. She pulled a handkerchief from her bag and dabbed at her eyes while Tony held her other hand and whispered sweet words to her. Each experienced a rush of warmth, a sign of life in the future. With that, they embraced and embraced. Tony walked toward the entrance to the armory, turning many times to wave to Helena, who waved and smiled but then cried and prayed as she drove home.

Part IV
Tony Goes to War

Chapter 20
Combat Training

The considerably long ride south engraved images in their minds. No matter where they traveled, main routes or country roads, the convoys drew attention and fanfare. The adulation resulted in a heady experience that was not quite understood by the young soldiers. It was a bold American gesture, unlike anything they had experienced in the past, one that spoke to Tony in a cultural way. The attention peaked when they approached the military post, the sprawling Fort Benning, which dominated the culture and lifeblood of the region.

The void the Italian American community felt after the soldiers left began the night before when friends and neighbors wished the soldiers well. The next morning the most difficult goodbyes were said, and listlessness and loss of focus seeped into the atmosphere. In most households, adjustments to day-to-day activities needed to occur after the men left, yet no one was willing to address those yet. Superstition and an Old World mentality skewed their thinking. They feared that talk about reassigning a soldier's chores or responsibilities would create a bad omen. As malaise at home deepened, the roll call and inspection at the Armory were completed, and the men were now climbing into the vehicles of their convoy. Family and friends knew the schedule, could sense the convoy getting underway, and were paralyzed by their awareness.

The small group from Stamford constituted a minute fraction of the state-wide convoy. Hundreds of newly enlisted soldiers were joining that caravan from all corners of Connecticut. It was one of many movements that would form over time in the unprecedented expansion of the U.S. Army that would eventually grow to over eight million service men and women. Now on their way to the military reception center and then the training camp, the soldiers were stricken with the paralysis of separation—from their families and eventually from each other. Leaving home along with friends and family had softened the blow of departure. In the back of their minds, though, the soldiers realized they would soon split up in the training center and then around the world. They would lose contact with one another, in some cases until the end of the war. But, for now, if they could do so, they had to push the future aside and stay with the present. Their induction and deployment were likely the most they could handle.

In the convoy, the mood was worse than subdued, and many men displayed expressions of bewilderment, knowing where they were going—to Fort Dix, New Jersey—but not really understanding where they were headed. The only fact they could put their minds around was that the reception center was approximately three and a half hours away. That alone was a novelty for many of the soldiers. Most of them had never been farther than their hometowns, let alone the state or country. They were on the road, covering distance, and traveled through three states to reach the base. Somewhat nervous about the unfamiliar and not knowing what lay ahead, they rode with apprehension. Along the way, they became acquainted with the space beyond their homes. As beautiful as the scenery was, it was new and representative of change. The open-air atmosphere of the convoy soothed some, yet most soldiers felt out of place and unsettled.

What the young recruits were experiencing brought them closer together. They did not realize they were beginning to bond by virtue of circumstance. Their shared experience pulled them together, establishing a foundation for the camaraderie that would form over time among soldiers who knew nothing about each other. The situation moved them to converse with one another, perhaps with shyness at first, yet the experience served them well along the way, especially when they approached the installation, a massive reception facility whose size shocked them. There, they bunked for two nights, experiencing a glimpse of military life.

Fort Dix was one of two waypoints along the route to the training facility. There, they completed their personal records, attended an orientation on the fundamentals of conduct in the military, and became acquainted with the ways of the Army, such as bunking in the barracks and eating in a mess hall. The post provided facilities and conveniences during the soldiers' brief stay, but the reality of the times—the absence of telephone service across state lines because it did not yet exist—extinguished the soldiers' hope for a phone call with family members. In time, the troops would consider their inability to reach their loved ones and hear their voices a deficiency detrimental to all soldiers serving in WW II for the long haul.

Following their short stay at Fort Dix, the soldiers departed for Fort Benning, Georgia, by way of Fort Lee, Virginia, on the outskirts of Washington D. C., where they camped in a rustic setting for two nights. Distance explained the need to stop, yet basic organization of the troops also took place for logistical reasons and to increase readiness with formation drills. The small cluster of troops from Stamford feared they would be separated then, but that did not occur. Organizing was merely a matter of forming groups and staging them for both departure and an orderly arrival to the training center. During their two nights at the facility, the newly enlisted soldiers camped in primitive surroundings, their experience an introduction to the concept of being in the field.

In three days, the troops were on their way to Fort Benning, Georgia, the home of Army Basic Training. The trek to the post was another considerably long ride south that engraved images in the soldiers' minds. No matter where they traveled, main routes or country roads, the convoy drew attention and fanfare. The adulation resulted in a heady experience that was not quite understood by the young soldiers. It was a bold American gesture, unlike anything they had experienced in the past, one that spoke to Tony in a cultural way.

The charm of being in a convoy and cheered by local communities diminished as they entered the sprawling installation that was the lifeblood of the region. The facility accommodated thousands of troops at a time. On arrival, the seemingly large group from Connecticut appeared miniscule and was quickly absorbed into a much larger assembly. New recruits continued to spill into the reservation throughout the day to be lost in a regimented sea of people. The next day, the troops were organized into platoons, and Tony no longer had the company of his friends.

The training environment compelled the soldiers to immerse themselves in the intensive six-week program they were all required to take and pass. What motivated most of them was their fierce patriotism and willingness to fight for their country. During orientation, they learned what was expected of them—to work together and become fighting teams that achieved the objectives assigned to them. To create a fighting force of that nature, Basic Training guided soldiers to think less of themselves as warriors acting on their own and to regard themselves instead as integral forces within their platoons. Emphasis was placed on uniformity rather than differences. Symbolically, the first step in their transformation began that day with the distribution of uniforms and the shaving of heads. The troops' appearance reinforced the Army's basic message and mission.

That emblematic event was only the beginning. To become a team, the troops had to perform as a team within their respective platoons. To facilitate team development, platoons were housed together, they took all meals together, they learned together, and became accustomed to helping each other. They were taught to respond to commands completely and uniformly. They practiced fundamental skills such as marching, loading, unloading, and cleaning their weapons, conditioning, financials, a mission-first attitude, and code of conduct tested under the watchful eyes and incessant challenges of their drill instructors. But those activities were not enough to take them to the seamless goal of performing as one.

As their regimen expanded to incorporate discipline and knowledge in basic exercises, maneuvers, and fitness, they learned they needed to go deeper to develop as one. They helped those who faltered and cleaned up training exercises that were ragged. Fear drove them to some degree. All mistakes were harshly called out, and if anything, the recruits did not want to risk the ridicule of a humiliating penalty, such as cleaning toilets, isolation, or public performances of harsh physical punishments. Time blurred as they took on the rigor and demands of training. They knew they were not sufficiently in sync with each other to perform with uniformity, and on grueling days they had difficulty conjuring the glorified images society painted of a modern-day warrior.

Their situation changed dramatically during their second week of training. Why? Because in a subsequent briefing they learned that they were being molded for duty, their behavior would be modified, and they would reach the ideal of uniformity. There were models to follow and leaders to guide them. What they learned facilitated conversations and problem solving, which were critical for extrapolating and taking on the core message of the briefing. With guidance from their platoon sergeants, they sorted through the skills and strengths within the group, talked through the exercises they were performing, and began to strategize. In the collective, they found strength and friendship. The more they spoke to one another, the better they got to know each other, and that process cultivated the camaraderie and friendships that would help them coalesce.

First friendships in the military formed. The soldiers gravitated toward others according to interests, hobbies, geographical regions, talents, backgrounds—any number of variables. For Tony there was the remarkable discovery of two soldiers he could relate to though their backgrounds differed to some degree.

First, there was Joseph [Yosef], a young Jewish soldier whose family made their way to the United States from Central Europe in the early 1930s to flee hardships and persecution with the hope of a better life in America. Joseph enlisted in memory of the grandparents he left behind and to fight the oppression and torment of Jewish families in Europe, should the U.S. become involved in the war. Their European roots and accented English drew Tony and Joseph to one another. They shared a keen awareness of the conditions in Europe, including the Youth Groups throughout the continent that were grooming and training boys to oppose Allied Forces.

Jack, the other friend, was a young American soldier who recently met the minimum age for enlisting. A farm boy from the Midwest, he was patriotic and felt an obligation to fight on the side of the U.S. though he was not fully aware of the reasons for doing so. Jack was earnest and sincere, had a wonderful sense of humor, and he was a grand storyteller. Jack stood out in the group for his height and red hair. It intrigued and liberated Tony to know he could become friends with two people who were so different from each other and bring them together into his group of friends.

All three men were mild-mannered with contemplative natures, they valued family, they found peace in nature, and most important, they learned from each other. Their friendship marked the coming together of the old and the new. Jack regaled Tony and Joseph with stories about cowboys, the plains of the U.S., the farming of wheat, and the impact of climate. In contrast, Tony and Joseph were urbanites. Joseph was born and raised in a city, immigrated to Western Pennsylvania, and became a bookkeeper. Together, Tony and Joseph introduced Jack to Europe, providing some history and explaining the underpinnings of the conflict that placed the world at war. The concept of the Youth Groups shocked Jack as did his growing understanding about the persecution of Jewish people. The men enjoyed lively conversations, family stories, playing cards, and the mutual support that took them through Basic.

When Tony stepped back and thought about the camaraderie among the three, his was reminded of his friendship with Giovanni, whose kindness and knowledge during the crossing made the voyage a maturing and enlightening experience. Now in combat training, Tony thought he and Joseph were providing the same for Jack, who was younger than they were, a good man and a quick learner. The friendship was by no means one-sided. Tony and Joseph being somewhat somber men, Jack made their days lively with his innovative ideas, mechanical know-how, and willingness to take risks. The young American soldier exemplified the American spirit. In contrast to Tony and Joseph, Jack was malleable about change, spontaneous about deployment, and an eager trainee. Both Tony and Joseph admired Jack's strength and bravado. His manner was representative of most American soldiers, and it was helpful in getting Tony and Joseph to lighten up.

The connection with Joseph and Jack enabled Tony to settle into training. With them he felt a bond like the one he shared with his cousins and friends from Stamford. No day at Benning passed without Tony wondering about about how they were doing. He saw them less than he expected because of the installation's size, yet he was grateful when he caught up with one or more of them and could reminisce about Settefrati or Stamford. They couldn't help but talk about their experiences in the Youth Group when they were eight years old and shooting guns whereas many American soldiers picked up a gun for the first time in their lives during Basic. Tony and his friends from Italy had learned in paramilitary training that drill and performance were the benchmarks of success. By that standard, they regarded themselves as well prepared for training. Now that they were adults, what stood out most for the Italian American soldiers was the difference in the underlying philosophies that drove military training the U.S. and Italy. The teamwork emphasized in the U.S. Army was not an element in Italy's Youth Group training, and that made all the difference in the world to them.

Well before the end of training, the soldiers realized Basic was a beginning rather than an end point. As the program continued, it expanded to inform the trainees about options for developing specialized skills. Through hands-on experience and observation, the soldiers discovered areas of expertise, such as radio operations, armor, medical support, and combat engineering, and they had the option to continue training in any one of those areas and many more.

Training was now unwinding, and it was time for the current cohort to move on. The men had matured during the training program, honed their skills, and were immersed in the culture of military life. They learned about themselves during the experience and were able to consider their futures in the Army based on self-awareness, their skills, and the impact of the training program. Their futures lay ahead of them, and for the most part, they charted their own courses. When Basic ended, Tony remained at Fort Benning for the armor specialty, Rosa's son-in-law went to Kansas for combat engineer training, and Paul went to Texas to become a medic. Jack went to Kansas, close to home, for artillery, and Joseph also headed to Texas for the medical specialty. The remaining five from Stamford, a mix of friends and family members, became part of the infantry and headed to the Philippine Islands via Hawaii. It was time for the soldiers to separate. Saying goodbye was difficult despite the training talks emphasizing the rotation of troops that had some friends moving along and new ones coming their way. In the emotion of their good-byes, they wondered when and if they would see each other again.

Tony found armor an appealing direction for enhancing his skills. Mechanical equipment had always fascinated him, and during Basic his trainers emphasized the potential for mechanized vehicles to alter the landscape of war. The program brought Tony to an unknown quadrant of the Benning complex with individuals who appreciated mechanization as he did. The hands-on approach to training complemented formal studies about machines and the variety of vehicles the program involved suited his way of learning. It did not hurt that Tony had acquired knowledge about and experience with the precursors to the armored vehicles during his paramilitary training in Italy as an extension of traditional cavalry.

The course opened with a history of armor, including present-day armored cavalry. The classroom experience included anecdotes from well-trained tank drivers and gunners as well as field experiences with the tanks. Tony found it all fascinating, but the field work was nothing less than exhilarating! On a continuous basis, trainees were in the field on simulated maneuvers designed to challenge the vehicles and assess their performance under various conditions. In those situations, Tony and his fellow classmates rode in tanks, serving as observers who examined operations from a learner's perspective.

Tony was so excited about those maneuvers that he quickly sketched some scenes for reference. Drawing appealed to Tony as an easy means for creating memories when little time was available to do more. Other class sessions focused on vehicle maintenance, routine or unplanned. Tony was fascinated whenever he had the opportunity to complete a repair or diagnose a problem under the supervision of his platoon sergeant. His knowledge of the metric system surfaced as one of his strong points. Over the six-week period, he immersed himself in the science, and the art he thought, of mechanized warfare. He was transfixed by the subject matter.

During his lengthy stay at Benning, Tony became increasingly aware of a novel training program that was reconceptualizing warfare with the aid of mechanization for the scale of combat expected in Europe. It remained clear at the highest levels in the U.S. Military that even specialty training was insufficient for what needed to be accomplished in Europe. Dubbed the Louisiana Maneuvers, the exercises generated numerous stories at Benning, where Tony first heard of Generals Eisenhower and Patton, the great military minds who developed the program and would play key roles in the war effort. With military brass on the ground for the exercises, the implementation of bold and novel ideas for deploying forces came to be. The realistic on-the-ground training aimed not only to rival but surpass known strategies.

Having heard the buzz about Louisiana, Tony was not surprised to be part of a large contingent heading there after his special training. The massive convoy took the troops through the lush southern states, offering an opportunity to see a unique swath of the country. They traveled from Benning to Montgomery, Alabama, to Mobile where they set up camp for the night. Moving on the next day, they reached their destination, Camp Claiborne, Louisiana, one of a few new or re-purposed military training camps in Louisiana. The camps and their surroundings were perfect for what the military envisioned for advanced training. Purposing the land included carving out or restoring facilities in national forests and bringing three existing installations, Fort Polk, Camp Clairborne, and Camp Livingstone, back to life. Along with the restored Camp Beauregard, the four reservations sprang into action to support the logistics and activities of the 500,000 or so troops who would become combat ready there.

Since the camps' leadership was intent on the efficacy of America's armored forces in view of what was unfolding in Europe, the maneuvers centered on the M2 and M3 tanks.[1] That focus and how it played out during training further enamored Tony with the armor specialty and motivated him to excel in the upcoming exercises

A full range of military capabilities supported the maneuvers' mechanized equipment, including infantry, artillery, paratroopers, and cavalry troopers. The philosophy and design of the drills moved training from isolated and often one-sided to true military scenarios. Training

---

1   The M2 and M3 tanks were medium light tanks used for the sole purpose of training soldiers for WW II. They carried a 30 caliber gun and several machine guns and informed development of the heavier equipment desired for the scope of the field experience expected in Europe.

advanced to adversarial exercises and drills designed to replicate realistic large-scale experiences on the battlefield, and the troops acknowledged the professionalism of that acceleration.

In addition to ingenuity, the development of the maneuvers reflected common sense. Logistics and support worked on re-creating the sounds of war, which meant using blank rounds and playing recorded battle sounds. Some actions needed to be simulated, such as airstrikes and the destruction of bridges. Admittedly, equipment shortages sometimes hindered realism as was the case with antitank guns, which were often made of logs. The terrain was central to the Camps' successes. The land available appeared limitless and could handle the tens of thousands of soldiers who needed space to spar during a single training cycle. Uncharted swamps were numerous. Scarred rural land and the surrounding areas became sludge generators. Rain was frequent, exacerbating the problem. Together, those elements tested the mechanized equipment and the teams that operated them beyond their wildest expectations.

The maneuvers operated on a four-week cycle from mid-1940 until late September 1941. Training began when cohorts of 50,000 descended on the camps, formed into units, and were in the fields that same day getting the lay of the land where operations would take place. Their formal exercises were underway the next day with the combination of classes and hands-on training in the field on tactics, maneuvers, and strategies. On that day, they also learned that "hostiles" existed in the area. The troops did not know how, when, or where a strike would occur and had to be ready around the clock. They were assigned duty schedules to ensure rapid response, and their commander then separated them into A and B teams that would oppose each other in the first maneuvers.

Developing the war games occurred while training was in progress, and it grew out of ongoing observations of training and analysis of data collected. While the elements of the maneuvers were closely intertwined and would therefore support soldiers during *the* hostile mock wars, great care was taken keep the nature and design of the mock wars under wraps to avoid compromising the element of surprise.

Until a mock war played out, a cohort of soldiers trained seven days a week to become accustomed to the terrain, master use of the vehicles, and conceptualize the scope of a field experience in Europe. Development of *the* war game they would participate in was quietly underway in the capable hands of distinguished World War I heroes. Their blueprint for the battle was modeled on their professional knowledge about the ground war in Europe, including the narrow war fronts. Their plan was influenced by the U.S. strategy for defeating the Germans. Within that context, the concept of a tank destroyer as key to limiting the heavy losses expected emerged. The maneuvers examined a variety of tactics from the high-speed hit and run of tank destroyers, tanks against tanks with highly mobile guns, and the forward placement of antitank guns that infantry regiments usually towed. Critical to the program was the ongoing collection of data that would further shape the war effort. No maneuver became a model in and of itself. Rather, collectively, the maneuvers formed soldiers' judgment and unified response.[2]

Methods of warfare evolved through the maneuvers. Major changes to the program based on observation and data enhanced the exercises, making each rotation more refined than the one before it. In the end, the final maneuvers reflected critical changes introduced by Omar Bradley, who concluded that the 50,000 soldiers involved in each

---

2   Louisiana Maneuvers (1940-1941). https://www.historynet.com/louisiana-maneuvers-1940-41.htm.

cohort of training was not adequate for the battlefields they expected to encounter in Europe. Further, the program would conclude with a full and decisive evaluation about the nature of warfare regarding the future of the U.S. military in terms of mechanization and the introduction of more modern approaches. The effort to implement those insights was underway prior to the start of the final maneuvers as Tony was packing his gear and preparing to depart Louisiana to participate in them.

Like the cohort before him, Tony participated in exercises until hostiles were identified and "war" began. What differed was the total number of troops who "fought" in the final maneuvers: 470,000 soldiers, which was close to ten times the size of any other cohort that had participated previously. The first maneuver reflecting changes in size and strategy took place on September 15, 1941, without flash or fanfare. Weather played a role in the success of that first war game not because conditions were great but because they were so poor. On the day of the assault, a tropical storm hovered over the area and the rain was relentless. The surface was wet and muddy, providing the mucky torn battlefields desired for the maneuvers. While dismal and grim, the situation could not have been better for studying the performance of the equipment and the teams under the new guidelines. That morning, the daily routine was unfolding when the war game commenced. Night guards had been relieved a few minutes before, and the troops began to awaken as dawn broke. They followed their readiness protocols as they moved toward daylight, thinking the present day would be no different from others with training of non-stop assaults and rotating responsibilities to test focus, skills, and performance. They had not yet worked their way through breakfast when radios throughout the installation came to life and the call to arms followed.

The soldiers raced to the battlefield while learning that Team A attacked Team B's forces to the south along the Red River on the flatland between Lake Charles and Lafayette. Team A attempted an armored sweep around Team B's left flank, but the counter was not fast enough to blunt the counterattack and reposition. The teams sparred, showcasing facility with their equipment. The exercise was not so much to determine who won the battle but to observe the soldiers' competence and decision making in the simulation. Adhering to the discipline they were taught, the soldiers could not help a minor transgression in gaping at a notable distraction, the presence of U.S. Army General George S. Patton, who was on hand to observe and evaluate the maneuvers.

A second unannounced exercise, the Battle of the Bridges, took place on September 24th. The fields were once again soaked from heavy rain throughout the day. In that situation, Team A defended Shreveport from Team B's forces attacking from the south. Team A carried out the simulated destruction of bridges and retreated northwest up the Red River Valley. Those actions forced B's engineers to construct hundreds of pontoon bridges alongside those already declared destroyed. The most dramatic event involved Patton, who participated with Team B. He conducted an armored sweep through East Texas. That strategic approach allowed him to get behind Team A and approach Shreveport from the north.[3]

Though the battles were simulated, the movement of heavy equipment was real, and casualties occurred as a result. On the first day of the second maneuver, a pilot died in a mid-air collision. In another incident, two soldiers drowned trying to cross the swollen Cane River. But there were also moments of levity. "According to one oft-told

---

3 The Home Front: The Experience of Soldiers and Civilians in the Louisiana Maneuvers of 1940 and 1941. John G. D'Antoni. Spring 5-18-2018. University of New Orleans Theses and Dissertations, https://scholarworks.uno.edu. Accessed January 14, 2021.

story, maneuver umpires declared a bridge wrecked, only to see soldiers walking across it. 'Can't you see that bridge is destroyed,' yelled the umpire. 'Of course,' one soldier responded. 'Can't you see we're swimming?'"[4]

Altered to address the war's mission, the final battles of the Louisiana Maneuvers generated significant results, and they became a game-changer for the U.S. military. By all measures, they succeeded in recreating the scale and spontaneity of war that would likely occur in Europe. The two events also set the parameters and tone for future training and specifications for the U.S. Army's strategic war plan.

From the trainees' perspective, the maneuvers felt loose at first, like a team organizing to play without having a playbook or guidelines. The exercises encouraged rigorous experimentation with tactics from the ground up. Only in retrospect would the soldiers understand which strategies worked, which did not, and the reasons for the outcomes they saw. The maneuvers aimed to develop soldiers' responsiveness on the ground and the learning of lessons on the field. Military leaders benefited from the program as well. They came to understand that wars are won not only in the battlefield but in a headquarters tent as well.

The systematic collection and analysis of data about the maneuvers paved the way for much-needed changes in the art of war. It was indisputable that the U.S. Army had reached a crossroads, one path focused on the past and the other pointed to new directions for the future. In the final maneuvers, horse troopers were pitted against armored units. World-War-I-era "square" divisions were tested against their newly organized "triangular" counterparts. The new clearly outperformed the old. Mechanization *would* replace the horse. In the course of World

---

4   History.net, https://www.historynet.com/travel-louisiana-maneuvers.htm, retrieved October 29, 2020.

War II, the U.S. Army would re-brand warfare, and that transition made Tony and the soldiers with whom he trained witness to a deliberate change to military conflict.[5] The visioning of the conditions for engagement, the emergence of mechanization and technology, and the unique environment of camaraderie that developed cultivated some of the greatest figures in U.S. military history—Eisenhower, Patton, and Bradley, to name a few.

As the final round of the maneuvers ended, Tony reflected on his experience thus far in the U.S. Army, comparing it to his ten years in the Youth Group. Four years separated the two experiences, and a world of difference distinguished them from each other. The maneuvers in Italy had been extreme, especially for the age group. With Italy's paramilitary training, each man was on his own, isolated though managed within the group. Interplay among the members was not fostered as a social or community element. Rather, the organizational structure was rigid and unforgiving. As a soldier in the U.S. Forces, Tony was experiencing something completely different and surprising. Performance and competence were expected, not in isolation, but as an outcome of teamwork. Camaraderie was palpable, enjoyable, and a life saver on the field. Training in Louisiana centered soldiers, fulfilling their individual assignments to meet the responsibilities of a team as a single entity. Soldiers worked together, helped each other, and protected one another. A military tradition of fraternal loyalty had taken seed and would flourish later on the battlefields, guiding the troops and holding them together when World War II was fully underway.

Well before the maneuvers concluded, Tony received orders for his next deployment. Based on his training in Louisiana and its mission to

---

5   Horse Tales of the US Cavalry in Louisiana - 1941 (May 2014). Stephen F. Austin State University. https://www.sfasu.edu/heritagecenter/9246.asp. Accessed August 6, 2021.

prepare soldiers for combat in Europe, he expected an assignment on the continent, but his thinking was off course. Instead, he was headed to the Dutch Island of Curaçao to serve on a security detail, and the news left him bewildered. What did a tiny island in the recesses of the Caribbean Sea have to do with World War II military operations in Europe, Africa, and the Japanese peninsula?

Chapter 21

An Island Assignment

There was not a native Southerner in the group, so they never learned the names of the exotic trees and plants that unknowingly offered peace to a group of soldiers heading to war. That afternoon, despite the warmth of the sun and the beauty of their surroundings, Tony felt the chill of death. The harbinger shook him to the core, yet he kept it to himself.

Tony was enjoying a brief respite from training and the maneuvers as he sat comfortably in a convoy to New Orleans, enjoying the fresh air and freedom from anything regimented. A winding three-hour drive, south by southwest, through the verdant Louisiana landscape carried the soldiers to New Orleans. That route led to a special area in the state, the heart of the Louisiana Forests. Traveling through scenic territory where the canopy towered above them was a memorable indulgence. For the length of their travel, shadows attempted to darken their passage, but the sun shined intermittently through the foliage. Their route carried them along narrow picturesque lanes, the fruity and floral scent of magnolias filling the air. The dense beauty of the preservations was not unfamiliar. During the maneuvers, the soldiers had frequently trekked through the woodlands whenever free time allowed.

At the time, the soldiers did not know they were riding through a prehistoric landscape shaped by the wind and sand dunes. Gusts and grit had worked the surface creating a hardwood base that remained dry unless flooding occurred. The vegetation that grew on that platform gave birth to the magnificent tiered display of deciduous trees the soldiers saw along the countryside. The assortment included the live oak tree, sweet gum, green ash, and tupelo, along with southern broad-leaved evergreens. The blend of native and migratory plants as well as ornamentals like azaleas and roses rounded out the exotic display. Touched by the sun and warm air in that fine setting, the soldiers experienced the indolence of youth.

The idyllic ride was all too short. The landscape began to change, gulls flew above, and the Gulf of Mexico lay ahead. Unfamiliar with the region, the troops had no orientation as to what was to come. As the convoy approached the outer city limits, the first signs of life in New Orleans emerged, introducing the troops to a new world. A welcoming community—people on the ground, whether at home or on the job—waited to greet and celebrate the troops. Within ten minutes, life changed dramatically, relegating the maneuvers to the past and replacing them with lively music, dance, and the pungent aroma of seafood and Cajun cuisine.

With New Orleans style warmth, the spectators lavished attention on the troops. An impromptu parade honoring them magically appeared. Lovely women ran into the streets throwing beads to the soldiers or jumping into the jeeps and trucks to slide beaded necklaces over their heads. The youngest of the soldiers succumbed to the city's allure without hesitation while the slightly older men moved with the music, enjoying themselves without losing their composure. Tony had to admit the party-like atmosphere was exuberant, unlike anything he'd seen before. He laughed and appreciated the attention but did not turn himself loose.

The convoy proceeded towards the center of the city slowly, the spirited welcome pacing its progress. By time the line of Army vehicles reached downtown, a mob scene had formed, and the convoy became a pageant showcasing French and Cajun influences in architecture, music, dance, foods, and customs. Vendors and restaurateurs joined the festivities and presented free offers and trinkets. Stores advertised all sorts of services and care, from fortune telling to voodoo and massages. The blend of so many people, practices, and cultures brought a special word to mind, taking Tony back a few years. His thoughts wandered to Gibraltar, where different bodies of water intersected, and he had learned the word confluence. Tony decided the word applied to life and culture too, as exemplified by New Orleans. The city was a confluence of differences that melded to form an electrifying tableau in America.

The dynamics of the cross-town show provided a lens into the lives and traditions of the city and its people. The adulation did not let up even after the convoy left the downtown area. It in fact continued non-stop to the Port, where a gate prevented the partying group from going farther. As the convoy was cleared to enter the docks, Tony checked the time and realized their two-mile trek from downtown to the waterfront had taken twenty-two minutes.

Arriving and unloading at the port went quickly. The organized system for directing soldiers whether arriving or departing guided them to train stations, ships, or convoys depending on their destination. Each step a soldier took brought them closer to others traveling to the same location. Lines of soldiers filed through the port that morning, and those traveling to Curaçao found themselves converging toward their ship. When they checked in, they learned they would not be sailing until the next day. Like others whose travel was delayed, they were dismissed and gifted several hours to explore

New Orleans after they signed in, claimed a hammock, and stored their belongings.

Groups heading into town formed naturally after arrival, and Tony set out with soldiers from his convoy and others who had arrived and caught up with them. Together, they exited the port and walked to the trolley stop they had seen on the way in. While waiting for a car to the French Quarter, which appeared to be the heart of city life, they read signs and studied maps. According to what everyone at the port was saying, the first order of business was to top their breakfasts with New Orleans's famous beignets and chicory coffee while getting their bearings.

The Quarter was alive and going strong, maybe too strong, for the hour of the day. In their uniforms, the soldiers had no choice but to act dignified, and they quickly learned the benefit of being in uniform. No matter where they stopped or what they purchased, they received discounts if not gifts, and they were warmly welcomed at Café Beignet where they each consumed the hot fried dough. South of Jackson Square, they hopped on the Saint Charles Line for a refreshing ride through the Garden District that took them past a park whose majestic entrance was lined with live oak trees. Late fall in New Orleans remained lush and beautiful with trees and plants in bloom, the earthiness a balm for the soldiers. They decided to stroll back to the Quarter and have their lunch there. During that free time, they refrained from discussing anything military. They talked about the city, what surprised them, each comparing it to their hometowns, which represented an impressive slice of life in the U.S. with Tony as an exception. As was always the case, there was interest in his views and experiences, for his fellow soldiers saw him as a man of two worlds, and they had many questions about life in Italy since it seemed exotic to them.

Returning to the French Quarter, they searched for a restaurant, all agreeing on a seafood feast. U.S. Forces filled the streets of the city, giving it an unusual look, a field of khaki incongruous with the vibrant atmosphere. They strolled by restaurants, feeling the goodwill Americans conveyed to their soldiers. They decided on a quaint courtyard restaurant where they spent an idyllic afternoon in the restaurant's enclosed space enjoying a great feast of the shrimp, lobsters, and oysters the Gulf of Mexico offered. They were unfamiliar with some of the dishes but enjoyed the meal immensely.

After lunch, on the recommendation of the restaurant owner, they boarded a different trolley line to reach a beautiful lake where they rented rowboats, exercised in turn, and enjoyed the lush and peaceful setting embracing them. There was not a native southerner in the group, so they never learned the names of the exotic trees and plants that unknowingly offered peace to a group of soldiers heading to war. That afternoon, despite the warmth of the sun and the beauty of their surroundings, Tony felt the chill of death. The harbinger shook him to the core, yet he kept it to himself.

The next morning, when the ship was ready to depart, Tony found himself reminiscing about his journey to the United States, his thoughts gravitating to the time he spent with his father before his ship sailed from Naples. He wished someone was in port right now waving goodbye to him. The presence of a loved one standing by would account for him, making visible the fact that he existed and was watched over. He took a deep breath and observed his surroundings as the ship cast off from the port. As they sailed ahead, he had to admire the beautiful spot on the southern coast of the U.S., the city standing majestically behind them. Its appearance was completely different from the towering images of New York City he remembered, and he was once again captivated by the variation in weather, land, and industries across the states.

The relatively brief travel time to Curaçao, a mere three days, was neither too short nor too long. The harbinger hovered over Tony though not in a disturbing or destructive manner. Since the ship's sole mission was to transport American Forces, organized military activities did not exist, and the atmosphere was relaxed as a result. Under the circumstances, there seemed to be an understanding among the soldiers about personal time and social interaction. As much as the soldiers spent time together playing cards and telling stories, they also valued the rare opportunity to rest and relax.

Tony appreciated the atmosphere on the ship. He regretted having shed so much of his daily routine since signing up. All he wanted was the time and space to resume activities that were important to him but dormant due to lack of time. What he missed most were writing or jotting down his experiences and creating drawings. Both activities took him back to his transatlantic sailing, when his writing and drawing enabled him to adjust and understand how to conduct himself on the ship. He remembered the questions he had written and the drawings he created, finding some of his work immature now but realistic then. For good reason, the journal was a meaningful endeavor. It now served two purposes, chronicling his travels and military service and reducing stress. The ship's gentle movement was conducive to his purpose, and he settled in to write.

Memories filled his mind, and he wrote them out to hold them in his thoughts and remember. He had questions about his next assignment, and he listed those, thinking he might try to find answers before they arrived in Curaçao. He reflected on his distance from both his current home and homeland, admitting his loneliness and the feeling that he was untethered and floating aimlessly without direction or destination. He had no anchor or roots and needed to learn to ground himself as he traveled farther from what he knew. He then backtracked to

Basic, where his service started, and the most instructive period of his life began. He went on to sort through his deployment to Curaçao, a place and region unfamiliar to him. Where was it? Why was he going there? He was humiliated by his ignorance.

Tony's writing inspired him to find answers to some of the questions he posed, and that led him to pursue another activity he enjoyed. He searched for and found the ship's itinerary, which was posted alongside a remarkable map of the world. This time he stood alone before the map, but that did not deter him from continuing to study it. The islands piqued his curiosity, and as he studied them and the seas along the way, he could visualize his father's hand on the map in Naples. The case where the map was posted also included a shelf with travel and navigational materials, including an atlas, charts, and books. Tony gathered information from everything available to him, starting with the Island's location, which fascinated him. He located the three dots in the sea between North and South America where the ABC Islands—Aruba, Bonaire, and Curaçao—lay. The islands and the thought of living on an island were not within Tony's sphere of reference, and that gave him pause. He knew Sicily was an island, and he recalled sailing through the strait separating the islands of Sardinia and Corsica. Those land masses all appeared close to and protected by a mainland whereas the ABC Islands loomed on their own.

In the Atlas, he found brief points about Curaçao's history, which created a link between the Island and the underpinnings of the war. Tony was putting together the pieces of the Curacao mystery and found his knowledge boosted tenfold by time his ship entered the channels between the islands. Thinking what he gathered was sufficient, Tony turned to another practice that was now a tradition for him—tracing the distance between his next deployment and the important people and places in his life. After orienting himself to the location of his next assignment, Tony settled into the short sea voyage, which went by quickly. The few days passed with soldiers enjoying their usual pastimes surrounded by beauty and warmed by the brilliant sun.

The passage of time, the ship's map, and the appearance of the Caribbean eventually indicated land was nearby. That discovery drove the soldiers outside, especially the curious and those interested in navigation as Tony was. As the ship sailed across the calm Caribbean toward the island, the vessel's scopes detected military build-up in the distance. Most obvious were the submarine conning towers that bobbled above the water's surface. Details became clearer as the ship pushed forward. To Tony's surprise, among the vessels were several Italian craft, all flying the country's flag, and German ships as well. Planes flew above a small stretch of the sea constantly. The soldiers inferred so much from what they saw—the lines of war, a reiteration of who was allied with whom, and a novel battlefield they had never seen before. As they scanned the panorama, they sighted oil refineries in the line of submarine fire, and they realized they would be dealing with torpedoes. As frightening as the land and seascape were, Tony experienced the added shock of knowing his compatriots as the enemy.

Their ship navigated the sea made turbulent by ongoing movement in the water. Approaching the port was tedious and tentative as several sharp maneuvers were needed to maintain distance from the warships while attempting to dock. Their arrival to the island lacked elegance, and disembarkation felt like an evacuation. To their relief, there was no evidence of the opposition on land. The troops entering Curaçao as opposed to those going on to Bonaire or Aruba arrived at their barracks, received their unit assignment, and went about the business of organizing for a briefing in ninety minutes.

An announcement during the session preempted standard procedures for orienting new troops to the installation. The news of the hour was that the defense and security of the strategic islands in the Caribbean would shift from Britain to the U.S. in mid-February 1942. This was a heady responsibility that resulted in a change of mission for U.S. Forces as well as enhanced training. They learned about the strategic importance of the islands and their charge to defend the Royal Dutch Refinery in Curaçao, which was the largest oil facility in the world at the time. It processed eleven million barrels a month and was the principal supplier for the Allies along with a refinery in Trinidad, known to be the largest plant in the British Empire, and another large one on the island of Aruba. As such the refineries were standing targets for the enemy. But there was more to the role of American Forces. The protection the U.S. would provide extended further to include the Panama Canal, Puerto Rico, and the U.S. coastline along the Gulf of Mexico, home of the country's petroleum facilities and trade.[6] Offensively through the region and beyond, U.S. Forces would safeguard the production and shipment of oil.

A detailed overview of a sequenced training program for ensuring a smooth transition followed. It highlighted orientation in the field, daily training, drills, distribution of arms, and rotating observation at all security stations. In time another phase would commence—shadowing British counterparts and then pairing with them prior to the turnover. The final stage of training accounted for all of the above with the addition of surveillance, reporting, and ground to air communications that would commence in late December.

An eerie feeling blanketed the outdoors orientation session. As the staff highlighted additional key information such as the perils of the assignment and protocols, the submarines were visible, and the U.S.

---

6   U.S. Consulate General in Curacao, History of the U.S. Mission on Curacao. https://cw.usconsulate.gov/our-relationship/policy-history/current-issues/. Accessed December 8, 2020.

Air Force hovered above them, non-stop, as they monitored for signs of a potential attack against the Allies' oil reserves. Since knowledge about the Island was important to the mission, training included a tour of Curaçao. For practical purposes, exploration of the Island began with its layout. The Island's culture and dynamics brought luster to the otherwise arid landscape. While the beaches were spectacular, the land and vegetation surrounding them were unappealing. Orientation skimmed over the Island's appearance, focusing on core issues that were discussed within the restricted area. Those concentrated on security issues, especially the points of entry and those that were most vulnerable.

One day while on duty near a primary line of fire facing the refinery, Tony spotted the Italian submarines positioned on the Atlantic side of the island. Their names, *Morosini*, *Oscilla*, *Enrico Tazzoli*, *Giuseppe Finzi*, and *Leonardo da Vinci*, evoked familiar sounds in his mind that were, unfortunately, accompanied by a dark jolt. That he was defending his adoptive country against his homeland was an ache that had begun to reverberate within Tony. It pained him to see the Italians' attempts to threaten the refineries and petroleum storage tanks. If his life's path had taken a different course, he could have been serving on the side of the Axis Alliance that day. He was disheartened by what he saw but could not condemn his brothers because he himself had been subjected to the propaganda of Italy's government.

When final training for the transition was underway, the war escalated, and its complexion changed dramatically. Following the bombing of Pearl Harbor on December 7, 1941, the U.S. declared war on Japan on December 8th, which caused Germany to declare war on the U.S. on December 11th, and the U.S. to declare war against Germany the same day. Those occurrences shocked everyone stationed on Curaçao and led to massive reviews, the addition of enhanced security measures, and an increase in the number U.S. troops prior to the transfer of security that would take place over a forty-eight-hour period on February 13th and 14th. Danger was palpable day and night, every single day. And though they were on land, the refineries, oil reserves, and ships transporting oil were targets, and they were nearby on land too. None of the soldiers could deny the potential ongoing risk for each of them. Two days after the mission was transferred to the U.S., the potential danger was realized. German U-boats succeeded in attacking the refinery and oil tankers in the waters surrounding both Curaçao and Aruba.

On a moment-to-moment basis, day to day for the length of his tour, Tony saw danger in the skies above, felt endangered no matter where he was on the Island, and heard the sounds of war twenty-four hours a day. The threat to all personnel and the precious oil needed to fuel the Allied Forces was real, unremitting. Tony learned the importance of vigilance and how to remain watchful no matter how tired or stressed he was. Due to the nature of that assignment, he found life on the island, which would otherwise have been considered exotic, to be restrictive. He and his fellow soldiers were able to leave the controlled area to enjoy their surroundings and the beaches, yet the size of the island limited their range, and the stress of being off the base without arms interfered with their ability to enjoy themselves and relax. The soldiers came to understand why their assignments were limited to several months.

Well before the detail ended, Tony received orders for his next deployment. He was headed first to the Desert Training Center in California and Arizona. There, he would follow a unique and significantly new training program created by Major General Patton to prepare troops for the battlefields, climate, and conditions in Africa. From the desert, Tony would travel to Africa as part of the North African Campaign.

Having trained in the Louisiana Maneuvers to serve in the European theatre, Tony experienced disappointment at first for not being involved in the heart of what was at stake. In time, though, he realized that he was always fighting for both his countries regardless of his location. From the start, Allied Forces organized worldwide, aiming to open transportation routes for the eventual invasion of Europe. With that awareness and his own discomfort about returning to his country as an enemy combatant, Tony was able to admit his relief about putting Europe aside for a while. He was not yet ready to fight in or close to his native country.

The danger Tony had faced on the Island of Curaçao was a harbinger of things to come. His education about the world was underway but not in the way he expected. He *had* begun to realize the scope and impact of the war, and the formation of his global view of it *was* underway. Yet his learning involved ongoing efforts to understand the war regarding Italy and how it was affecting his family's daily lives and livelihood. The latter was a critical matter since he as well as his Aunt rarely received information from or about them. Censoring interfered with the flow of mail in both directions. As modes of communication on the continent continued to deteriorate, Tony was fraught with worry about his parents and his siblings.

Chapter 22
From Curaçao to the War Games

For some time, they navigated the single rugged road that led them out of the desert in the direction of San Diego. While the terrain was barren, it was beautiful at the same time for the gorgeous earthy hues and the magnificent open sky. Little vegetation existed but for the occasional cacti that dotted the land. The scene caused Tony to think of Mama because she would regard the beautiful untouched land as a gift from God.

On yet another brilliant day when the ocean of opposing forces continued to churn with fury, Tony departed Curaçao. He looked back as his ship skirted warships and submarines, the dramatic tableau falling into the past. In the end, the least of its victims was the sea, the swath of the emerald green Atlantic blanketed with oil and debris. Alone on the ship's main deck after departure, Tony gave thought to the torpedoes that sliced through the waters toward land, marveling at how chance or maybe something more prevented him from being in the line of fire. Fear and distress lingered in his mind. In time he would learn those feelings never pertained to his departure from Curaçao. Rather, they were relevant at another time, on another beach, where the stakes were even higher.

Now on his way to Arizona and California to prepare for Africa, Tony revisited his Army story to date, noting what seemed to be an excessive amount of transience and adjustment. Sometimes he felt he was standing outside that story, looking at a scene he couldn't imagine in real life. In less than one year, he had traveled from Connecticut to New Jersey to Georgia, the marshlands of Louisiana, New Orleans, and Curaçao in that order. He had no sooner adjusted to his position in Curaçao when his rotation was over, and he separated from soldiers he had just begun to know. The intervals between assignments were always unsettling with times of loneliness when traveling and disquiet about fitting in a new group as well as a new location. Though he had already covered a lot of territory in his career to date and had more time in service than the new recruits who continued to pour into U.S. Forces worldwide, Tony was not yet accustomed to life in the service.

The sailing from Curaçao was brief and uneventful. The ship arrived in New Orleans mid-morning, which was unusually late for a military vessel but a necessity given the volume of craft in port. On disembarkation, the soldiers fanned out to information booths serving different destinations or deployments. Within minutes of reaching the location for The Desert Training Center, the soldiers heading there had orders in hand for departing New Orleans on a Southern Pacific Railroad train at 12:45 p.m. for a three-and-a-half-day journey along the Sunset Route from New Orleans to Phoenix. They kept moving toward the port's exit and joined the line of soldiers waiting for transportation to the station.

When they arrived, there was time to spare, which made the station a busy zone. Any soldier passing through was heartened by the messages posted throughout the area supporting the troops and wishing them well. There were also colorful and alluring posters and billboards in the downtown area advertising the rail line and its exotic destinations.

The photos were quite appealing, and in time all the traveling soldiers had a clearer idea of where they were heading. Those standing by signs for the train to Phoenix learned about the stops along their route—Houston, San Antonio, El Paso, and Tucson. The locations sounded exotic, conjuring images of the wild west and causing the men to feel they were worlds away from home.

New Orleans was a hub for military travel in the south, and most soldiers knew how to spend their time while waiting. The train arrived early, and the soldiers were surprised (though they should not have been) to learn the U.S. Military had requisitioned a number of trains for its sole use to facilitate the movement of troops. When they entered their coach, they were flabbergasted by its elegance and services. They were booked in private quarters that elevated their lifestyle during the few days they traveled by rail. They never expected card rooms, a classy dining room, a bar, and dozens of free amenities. When the train pulled from the station, they were living the good life, mesmerized by their panoramic views of the Gulf. Their route exposed them to stunning hues that showcased new images of America. They were enjoying a few of the chances of a lifetime U.S. soldiers experienced during their service.

The sweeping views of the marshlands in Louisiana, progress through farmlands and ranches to the west, and their taste of the markedly different cities emerging throughout the region enlightened the soldiers and made them feel worldly. Continuing west, they cut their way through humidity and were captivated by the sprawling Houston area and the surprising hills to the west. The closer they got to El Paso, the more the atmosphere and landscape changed. Cactus plants replaced greenery, the land was arid, and the temperatures extreme. They knew that environment presaged their next deployment, yet none of them had ever been in the heat of the desert, and they were beginning to understand the reason for the Center's location and one of its goals for training. They were, after all, assigned to the Desert Training Center that Major General George S. Patton had organized to prepare them to live and serve in Africa.

The buzz at Benning was that the War Games at the Desert Training Center were legend, and the troops were eager to understand what that meant. Thoughts about the hands-on training they expected to receive colored the soldiers' reveries for the duration of their train ride to Phoenix and convoy to the training facility's southern entrance. Competition and energy were in the air when they arrived, challenging the dust and grit as military contests played out in the area surrounding the convoy's route. Their hazy preview of what would take place at the camp was exhilarating.

Roads and paths did not carve a single route to the camp's administrative offices. The convoy loosened, and the vehicles traveled on open land, the wind whipping across and around the soldiers as they rode along. The air was arid, the land uneven and varied, lacking colorful foliage though native trees dotted the terrain. Ghost-like apparitions swirled with the wind and sand. They seemed to hover above the ground yet often charged forward or suddenly changed direction. There was substance to those images. They were military vehicles engaged in field maneuvers on a simulated battlefield. Colors distinguished teams from each another and the realistic movements revealed serious intentions. The training exercise in progress teased soldiers with a first look at what combat in a desert might be like.

The relatively new Desert Training Center (DTC) was a World War II facility for preparing troops to seize ports in Northern Africa and keep the Mediterranean open for Allied movement of personnel and supplies. Located in the Mojave and Sonoran Deserts in Southern

California and Western Arizona, the Center's mission primed U.S. Army personnel to test equipment and develop tactical principles, techniques, and training methods for fighting in the desert. A simulated theater of operation and the largest military training ground in the history of military maneuvers, DCT was created to meet—and surpass—its mission. Every detail of the extensive camp, from the design of team installations to challenging roads and the construction of foxholes and other defensive structures reflected the labor, ingenuity, and fighting mentality of Major General George S. Patton Jr., the Center's first commanding general.

Training began with an orientation to the Center's mission and structure. The soldiers appreciated the practicality of their hands-on exercises. Those realistic circumstances called for on-the-spot combat decision-making that by nature demanded teamwork and professionalism. Looking back at his preparation in Georgia and Louisiana, Tony could see the consistency in training over time—with teamwork the overarching thread and the war games a culminating exercise affirming the soldiers' readiness.

The swath of land the Center occupied showed Patton's influence, know-how, and philosophy about military training. Over a dozen battalions set up camps in situ, independent and distant from each other. Airfields, hospitals, supply depots, and sites for other support services completed DCT's capability, creating a self-contained installation for each team. There, each division or major unit would train in its own area to cultivate spirit and develop a sustained focus for competing in spontaneous battles. They would live and train as a collective, understanding their interdependence and capitalizing on the skills of each to function as one. Through the course of the program, they were expected to coalesce and develop camaraderie as "esprit de corps," fulfilling the concepts of pride and loyalty introduced on day one of Basic Training.

During orientation, the soldiers could not help commenting on the similarity between the maneuvers in Louisiana and the simulated warfare that took place at the Desert Training Center. Without doubt, the latter was superior to the former, but that difference did not explain the hoopla over the war games, which had earned the accolade "The War Games are Epic." When the first phase of training in the fourteen-week program began, the soldiers discovered the primary focus for training. Having grown up in southern California and served in the Mojave Desert, Patton understood the desert as a unique environment for warfare. His intimate knowledge of it influenced the training program, whose principal interest was to prepare the troops to manage and adapt to the extreme environment, understand the performance of mechanized vehicles in that environment, and become familiar with the scale of the ground war needed to subdue Axis Forces.

Well before reaching the Center, the soldiers had begun to feel the heat and humidity of the desert. Once they were on the installation and physically involved in setting up camp and beginning their exercise regimen, they encountered the challenges of working in temperatures hovering at 120° F or more. They stood witness to soldiers who collapsed and a number who died attempting to perform their duties. Dehydration came suddenly because sweat evaporated. To address the problem, Patton instituted a training requirement for acclimating the troops. Each soldier needed to qualify for the program while immersed in it by slowly developing the ability to run a mile in ten minutes during their first month at the camp. As orientation expanded to include exercises during that month, a rigorous program of fitness and military exercises evolved to support the soldiers' success.

Knowing they would face other teams in the final maneuvers, soldiers treated their work as competitive every single day and never let up. DTC's protocols allowed for only three days off per month.

The Center was isolated, and there was very little the soldiers could do other than train. They divided into different sub-teams regularly to increase versatility and to vision the role most suitable for each soldier in the team. They revered the state-of-the-art equipment available to them—mechanized armor, extensive weaponry, and effective communication tools. They benefited from the capacity of their units. There was access to support troops from different branches such as engineers who could construct or destroy structures and adjust resources like water and forward observers to call in long range artillery fire. The tools stimulated thought and teamwork in the creation of inventive war game scenarios for the maneuvers that would mark the end of training. The exercises were not about winning and healthy in a competitive way. They examined strategy, decision making, and learning.

Upon completion of the program and final exercises, troops received deployment orders to Africa. Tony's cohort was to be deployed to North Africa, where along with soldiers from a few Allied countries, U.S. troops would constitute the Western Task Force of the North African Campaign for the Allied Invasion. They would train further while traveling to Africa, honing the skills and knowledge they acquired for fighting the real war.

The soldiers' culminating experience at the Desert Training Center was meaningful and life-changing yet eclipsed by the logistics for their departure. During training, the troops had navigated their way from western Arizona to southern California. They were literally in the middle of nowhere when it was time for them to depart and start making their way to Africa. They wondered how they would get from the middle of nowhere to Gibraltar, their staging location for Operation Torch. What they learned was that their present location was not an accident or a problem.

They were not leaving the Desert Training Center by returning to the camp's southern entrance. Because they were now far west and well into California, they would instead proceed to San Diego, where, unbeknown to most of them, a sizable naval base was located. Putting their heads together, the soldiers explored notions as to how a journey from San Diego to Northern Africa might transpire, pinpointing one possibility that would be the journey of a lifetime. Many holes existed in the itinerary they conceived, yet they knew the gaps could be filled.

As an open conveyance, a convoy made conversation among the troops difficult. The challenges with communication coupled with the fresh air and the aftermath of rigorous desert training caused many of the soldiers to fall asleep as soon as the convoy began to move. While most soldiers rolled with the convoy, enjoying their rest, Tony's wheels were still spinning about their route to Africa. Visualizing a map, the possibility that seemed most likely to him was also one that appeared unfathomable. And then there was the thought of Africa. His memories of viewing the continent's coastline in 1938 returned, along with the vision it had triggered of seeing himself there in the sands and dust of Casablanca. He could not underplay the significance of his itinerary. He was now on the path to learning the meaning of that unusual occurrence, but he did not dwell on it.

Instead, Tony attended to their unusual route out of the desert, which offered a unique landscape to study. Their itinerary had them driving northwest. For some time, they navigated the single rugged road that led them out of the desert in the direction of San Diego. The terrain remained barren along the route. It retained its initial appeal on their arrival to the region, the earthy hues gorgeous and the big sky ready to consume them. Little vegetation existed but for the occasional cacti that dotted the land. The scene caused Tony to think of Mama, who would regard the beautiful untouched land as a gift from God.

Within the hour, Tony thought of Mama again, for he was viewing something he regarded as miraculous. At the time, they were still pulling out of the desert though the end seemed to be in sight. How did they sense the impending change? Elevation was the first clue. The convoy was riding uphill, and as the vehicles moved forward, the soldiers caught sight of the canopies of green leaves atop the towering trees, the most vegetation they had seen in some time. There was something reverent and regal about the moment though the transformation of their setting was not yet complete. The road rose out of the desert as they drove, and they experienced the uncanny feeling of being lifted from the wasteland rather than driven out of it. The experience elicited something divine that Tony would feel for the rest of his life and call to mind when his spirit was low. That memory would elevate his mood, allowing him to find the will to continue.

Their desert road morphed into something new—a better roadway, an elevated path that continued to rise, and a fresh, breathable atmosphere. Along the route, their surroundings changed. At first, the differences were subtle. In time, they became pronounced. The changes were staged, with barren land shifting to fertile turf that suddenly changed to lushness. The clear air and fresh scent raised consciousness and awoke the senses. The transition complete, the soldiers felt that someone had turned a switch to effect a transformation.

No one knew what to expect, for they were on uncharted territory physically and mentally. They were alert, expecting more change. They reached what felt like a summit—vehicles ahead were no longer visible, suggesting they had peaked and were proceeding downhill. Anticipation built about what lay ahead, but nothing could prepare them for the scene that appeared. Tony gasped, shaken by a personal awakening. In the beautiful swath of land before him lay lush rolling terrain, fields in the distance, a valley, and houses with colorful terra cotta tiled roofs. Tony gave pause seeing the hills of Italy before him. The resemblance but for the oceanfront was uncanny. His knees felt weak, his heart palpitated—the scene played with his mind. For a few moments, he thought he was daydreaming. He pushed aside some not-so-minor details, like his U.S. Army uniform, and saw himself walking down the summit of the National Park that rose above the village where he had lived. Influenced by the scene, he sensed the taste and texture of a fresh ripe peach from his family's orchards in Italy.

Chapter 23
San Diego to Gibraltar

In minutes, the African coastline was in sight, distant though visible. Tony experienced an eerie aura followed by a sense of déjà vu. His ship heading to Gibraltar for final training and maneuvers, he was positioned on a vector where past, present, and the future converged.

The spectacular scene at the summit seized each soldier in a personal way. Warships filled the port; lush greenery lined the roads and interior. Land and sea manifested beautifully, one rugged and the other lively, as though a canvas on display. The panoramic view gripped them, as did the approach to the port, a winding descent toward the shoreline that allowed an inviting gradual unfolding of the full scene. The soldiers felt the restorative impact of the ocean breeze, slowly coming to appreciate the opportunity resting before them.

The drop to the shore was dramatic. Several parks surrounded the base, making the area pleasant to view. The aquatic life along the shoreline was a surprise. Dozens of seals lay sunning on an extensive rock formation, ignoring the presence of the humans watching them. Occasionally, they rolled playfully on the surface, offering a brief show for their audience. The scene added a light touch to the day, the seals a wonderful distraction for the soldiers.

The sloping road spiraled downward and reached sea level. The convoy navigated toward the base, entered it, and pulled alongside the designated warship. When the convoy stopped, the soldiers spilled out of the different vehicles, systematically unloading all personal belongings and cargo to complete their work as quickly as possible. San Diego appeared inviting, and they hoped for time on land prior to their departure.

There was not much to do on the ship aside from finding their quarters, which involved claiming a hammock in the appropriate area, and participating in periodic roll calls. U.S. Forces permanently assigned to the base handled loading and inventory, leaving the newly arrived soldiers with a full day to enjoy San Diego. Tony and a few pals from his team at The Desert Training Center were on their way out within the hour. A few additional soldiers from the Center who were standing around looking for something to do joined them. The group planned to make the most of their day and started by traveling south on a comprehensive trolley tour to view stunning agricultural vistas and then turned to head north to mountains reminiscent of Italy. Tony was surprised to see the trolley reach some of the minor summits. One stop positioned them above the port and the breathtaking view of the bay, the barrier island, Coronado Beach, and the Pacific Ocean. The view was one of the most beautiful Tony had seen since leaving Italy.

Their tour continued, taking them to the San Diego Zoo. The exquisite permanent reserve and park surpassed the soldiers' expectations as they marveled at the extensive gardens, the beautiful and humane habitats for the animals, the lavish appointments from lamps to landscaping, and the delightful pathways and trails for visitors. Tony surveyed his surroundings with wonderment, for he had never visited a zoo though he was accustomed to animals on the farm and in the wilderness. He lamented again about not having a camera, but his spirits lifted when they saw a small shop alongside the exit. There, he found flyers, cards, and photos for purchase. He bought several to send to others or insert into his journal.

The day was still young and the soliders caught a trolley in the direction of the port though it followed a scenic route. Riding along, they found the atmosphere so refreshing that they decided to stop along the way to enjoy a meal by the sea. The driver recommended the Historic Gaslamp Quarter not only for its restaurants but for its architecture, shops, art, and clubs. The group was dazzled when they stepped out of the trolley and into the Quarter. The bold colors were arresting, the carnival atmosphere unexpected on a scale so large. They devoured a delicious lunch at a Mexican Restaurant, authentic dishes with fresh local avocados and California wines that were a treat for all of them. When Tony picked up his wine glass to take a sip, he smiled thinking about Luigi and how the two of them had started their own home winery. Tony was comforted by the thought, realizing home was always with him. After lunch, they walked around enjoying the atmosphere and feeling free without worry. It was a gorgeous day, and they did not want it to end.

The Gaslamp Quarter was reasonably close to the San Diego Naval Base, so they chose to walk in the direction of the ship and explore along the way. What struck them was the feeling that they were in a bowl, at least on one side. To the east, the hills and mountains rose majestically from the land that appeared protective yet foreboding in its dark corners. The formations left Tony wondering about the weather patterns at the highest point. The configuration and elevation there were not exactly what Tony knew at home in Italy, but they were similar and remarkable.

In the distance, the soldiers noticed a group of large buildings, one topped with a massive glass sphere. They learned from a local vendor that the structure was an observatory for oceanic and sea life studies. They stopped in the building, where they were greeted warmly and entered without cost. The exhibits beautifully depicted sea life in the Pacific Ocean. The artistic bubble amazed them, not only for its design and construction but for what it contained. The cylinder ran from the ground floor to the top. In it was something none of the men had seen before, a richly colored sea habitat filled with leopard sharks, cormorant, seals, sea lions, gray whales, mahi mahi, rockfish, and many other species from the region. Maps from around the world lined the walls throughout the multilevel building, and the soldiers browsed through those, bringing to mind the deployments of the past and those to come.

Walking toward the shipyard, the men agreed that time seemed to stand still during their short furlough. As they conversed about the passage of time in a military environment as moving too quicky or not fast enough, they heard someone behind them calling out loudly. Tony was uncertain, but he thought someone was calling his name, his birth name, Antonio. He paused thinking there was something wrong with him though his friends turned, which meant something *was* going on behind them. His mind raced. *Could someone be calling out to me*, he wondered. *Who? Why? To my knowledge there is only one person in the military who has called me Antonio, and that's Jack. Could Jack be here? Why? Or am I so tired and spent that I am imagining this moment?* Tony turned around and saw a flash of red hair that he knew well. Jack was running to catch up with Tony and his friends.

Tony and Jack enjoyed an emotional reunion while Tony introduced Jack to friends and acquaintances from The Desert Training Center and the ship. They all walked together until they reached the vessel.

The others entered, but Tony and Jack stayed outside to catch up. They were excited to see one another, each was trying to figure out why the other was there. The short of it was that Tony was part of the amphibious invasion while Jack would serve in an artillery battalion and be deployed as needed in the operation as a whole. They would travel to Gibraltar together and separate there though their paths could cross from time to time as the war continued. Through the first few days of the sailing, they would each be relatively free like all others soldiers aboard, and they vowed to make the most of that time, playing cards, telling stories, talking about their past deployments, and exchanging farming tips.

Back on the ship, Tony and Jack caught up for dinner, both bringing friends with them. Their idyllic time in San Diego had relegated discussion about their itinerary to Africa to the background, but it was now one of the two most talked about topics on the ship. The mess deck at dinner time created the perfect venue for conversations about the significant waypoint on their itinerary, the Panama Canal. A historic engineering feat known worldwide, the Canal had altered trade routes considerably when it opened.

Within days the troops traveling to Africa from California would sail toward Panama, traverse the Canal, and pass from the Pacific Ocean to the Atlantic. Everyone on the vessel knew they were on the cusp of a once in a lifetime event. If ever there was a reason to trace the ship's route, the passage through the Panama Canal would be at the top of the list. Jack smiled when Tony brought up the itinerary and maps. At Basic Tony had shown himself a master of map reading, which both fascinated and instructed Jack. He was honored to immerse himself in their itinerary and enjoy the route with Tony and their mutual friends.

Later in the evening, the troops learned of an additional grand and unusual plan for their itinerary. Their ship would be part of a convoy of 102 vessels assembling country-wide over several days to carry over 60,000 troops to Africa. Formation of the sea convoy was a staged build-up with fleets forming and merging port by port. At intervals during its movement south, then east, and eventually north, the troopship transporting the soldiers from San Diego would initiate the marshalling for a subsequent multi-phase rendezvous in the Atlantic and Mediterranean, which would in turn form the flotilla to Gibraltar, the staging point for Operation Torch, the Allied invasion of Africa.

Since the first rendezvous would not occur for a few days, the soldiers concentrated on the beautiful scenery along the Pacific coast, passing Southern California to sail along the coast of Mexico. They were treated to more sea life and studied the towering cliffs. They continued south following the western coast of Central America in the direction of the Canal. The area's unique land formations piqued their curiosity, and they later learned the noticeable peaks that dotted the coastline and interior were caused by volcanos.

The voyage introduced Tony to regions, landscapes, and countries that were beyond his knowledge of the world. In his journal, he jotted down every country within range of their itinerary, promising himself that he would research them one day to learn about the places and peoples the ship passed. Over his lifetime, Tony held to that promise. The war itself had opened his mind to the world, but his experience of getting from one point to the other introduced him to the people of the world. If he passed their territory, he felt he owed them the respect of knowing who they were, what their lifestyle was, their cultural practices, and how they fit in the world regarding their economy, society, politics, and educational systems. Sometimes when researching such information, Tony was sad to learn about the plight of many of the world's inhabitants. He had been naïve during his youth to believe the war would solve problems around the world.

At the same time, Tony's war-time travels introduced him to innovations that did indeed change the world. Those were not limited to ingenuity in the military. Rather, they stretched across areas of thought and industry, from construction to mechanization and transportation. And within hours, Tony would enjoy the rare opportunity to view a lasting symbol of ingenuity—the Panama Canal. The ship was approaching the channel, and there was not a person who chose to sleep rather than awaken during the middle of the night to be part of an historic moment. From afar as they sailed toward the Canal in the dark of morning, everyone on board saw the lighted ships in queue ahead of them waiting to pass through the seaway.

That queuing and staging of large vessels created an eerie atmosphere for the soldiers on the warship who would participate in the amphibious attacks. In broad strokes the image served as a precursor those soldiers were traveling toward—the thousands of ships that would support the staging of the largest amphibious landings in military history. Tony could see the two images as parallel—the one that lay ahead and the other that lived in his mind. Unfortunately, his mind could not stop looking ahead. Tony shivered, with good reason, feeling he was not ready for his future and the planned attack in Africa. His mind and words were not ready for the image of soldiers in landing craft staging dangerous launches into the North Atlantic Ocean. As the warship closed in on the Canal, the pictures in his mind tracked with its movements and he could see his future. Visioning an assault of extraordinary proportions, he cried within, but was rescued from his emotion by Jack, who was aware of Tony's prescient nature though he did not understand it fully. Jack called to Tony, addressing him as Antonio and pointed to the cog that would pull the ship through the canal. When

Tony's eyes locked on the mechanism, fascination overtaking premonition and revealing the essence of his self. He was transfixed by the mechanics of the ship's passage through the Canal as Jack was. They were enthralled not only over the passage but for the ship's entry into the Atlantic, which was like a piece of home.

Sadly, the crossing marked the end of a respite at sea as well as Tony's and Jack's time together. There were hours of work ahead of them that day and those that followed. The leisure of the Pacific sailing behind them, rigorous training and duties commenced immediately. The troops had their vehicles, sidearms, and the supplies needed for the assaults. While they lacked the space and freedom for large-scale maneuvers, they trained through fitness, sparring, map study, creating scenarios and strategies, and small-scale simulated maneuvers. They followed a rigorous exercise regimen to remain toned and strong for what lay ahead, but Tony and Jack did not say farewell. They reasoned they were on the same ship together, and one way or another they would likely see one another more than once before separating in Gibraltar.

No matter what they were doing on any given day, the troops remained attentive to their itinerary as best they could and watched startling sights sometimes from afar through a scope. The southern border of the U.S., which evoked memories of New Orleans, stood out as the most common departure point for soldiers traveling to the Desert Training Center. They lingered along the Gulf Coast that day, waiting for three warships that would create the beginnings of the armada from the U.S. to Gibraltar and on to Africa. As they watched the maneuvers play out, the troops were afforded a grand and unforgettable view in the Gulf. The three warships reached the troopship and slid in front of it to take the lead.

The presence of the warships relieved the aloneness of the vast waters traveled to that point. The convoy's formation quickly became a fascination for Tony. The process—communications and precision with latitude and longitude—created a new pastime for him. When the convoy passed the Florida peninsula, a feature familiar to most, tears clouded Tony's eyes. There was no need to ask himself what was happening. A revelation had come to him—Not only did he love Helena, her family, and her friends, he loved the United States of America. He loved it for what it represented, its innovation, and the opportunities it offered, including his current mission.

When the ship passed Florida and turned north, it began a south to north crossing of the Atlantic that aligned with the addition of more ships from the east coast of the United States. In sequence, three ships from Norfolk, four from Philadelphia, six from Brooklyn, and five from Boston joined the convoy. With each addition to the caravan, the formation became more regal. The U.S. flag flying on each of the twenty-one ships offered a compelling image of country and strength. No scene could have conveyed more aptly the message that the U.S. was war-bound. Tony's passionate appraisal of the procession did not offset the ache he felt as they sailed northeast, close to his friends, family, and precious Helena. He yearned to divert the ship to the port of New York for a few days.

The convoy complete, the ships pulled away from the U.S., the path now reminiscent of Tony's initial crossing in 1938. He paused in anticipation as the ship veered east, on a course for the Strait of Gibraltar. He saw his past reflected in the water. Memories of Naples, the Strait of Bonifacio, Gibraltar, Giovanni, Luca, and Professor Fermi brushed his thoughts. He was hypnotized by the ocean, seeing his story in it. Days later in the morning haze, the view was veiled but he sensed land ahead. In no more than ten minutes, the African coastline was in sight, distant though visible. It was not by chance that Jack also stood on the same deck a short distance from Tony that day. While he was not aware of Tony's vision, he knew there was a sensitivity about Africa that was perhaps tied to the impending amphibious attacks. Whatever the issue, Jack wanted to be there for his friend who had guided him through Basic. Jack stood quietly watching the emotion in Tony, who was experiencing an eerie aura followed by a sense of déjà vu. He re-lived his vision in the same region years ago, when he saw himself on the continent in the uniform of the United States Army standing beside the jeep. He had always known he would return.

In a gripping confluence of factors, Tony's past, present, and future converged. Knowing the ship was heading to Gibraltar for final training and maneuvers, he was positioned on a vector that represented all three. The experience transported him to a higher plane where he felt elevated, whole, and knowing. A collage appeared in his mind, placing him in Italy. He saw himself in France and then visioned his soldier self on a train leading to his hometown in the U.S. Overwhelmed with tears in his eyes, he thought of his survival and, dare he say—his return one day. He saw his life ahead of him and felt strong and capable, infused with energy, because he was hopeful. Reveling in what he saw, he drew from one of Mama's strongest admonitions, "Metti le tue visioni nel tuo cuore. Lascia quindi lì dove nessuno può giocarci o provarli. Questi segni sono per te e per te solo per proteggerti." [Place your visions in your heart. Leave them there where no one can toy with or test them. These signs are for you and you only to protect you.] Tony turned and saw Jack, who waved and said, "I wanted to be here, Antonio, because I know that Africa is a sensitive topic for you, and I did not want you to be alone. It does not matter what the concern is. I just wanted to provide company. Come, let's go to the mess deck and get some coffee." Tony was moved and appreciative. "Jack," Tony said, "you stand with my brothers as the best friends I have ever had."

Africa (left, on horizon) and Europe (right), as seen from Gibraltar

Their upcoming mission, Operation Torch, *the* first offensive of amphibious landings originating at several beachheads in the general area of Casablanca, set forth his future, completing the intersection of time in his story. The ship proceeded on its journey, delivering the troops to Gibraltar for final training. Their ship had traversed 6,162 miles, consuming eighteen days at sea and three additional days on the shores of Gibraltar. That they would position for the onslaught and likely become visible to the enemy in the process caused Tony to dwell on the element of time and its role in the war. Acts of war during his time did not seem as spontaneous as one might think. Troops traveled unexpected distances to reach battlefields, and war activity was held at bay until the troops who would participate in it arrived. Communications were somewhat similar. They were effective but nowhere near the quality and speed that came about later in the century. Perhaps the combination of unsophisticated communication and an unpredictable sea made impending assaults less transparent than Tony thought. He wondered what that meant for him and his fellow soldiers.

Traveling by sea had eased the soldiers' adjustment to changes in climate and time zone. As they sailed through the choppy Strait of Gibraltar to their destination, they experienced the raging force of the Atlantic meeting the Mediterranean, which Tony remembered well. They stood on the decks watching it slap the ship with fury. They regarded the sea as an adversary, and their mental wheels began to spin with strategies for battling it. They began to look forward to the Gibraltar training maneuvers, and that was a good start in positioning themselves to surrender to warfare and succeed.

With Gibraltar looming ahead, the soldiers looked back on their sailing as edifying in several ways. There was something glorious about eighteen days at sea, calm seas until the end, watching the sun rise and set, a feeling of infinity. They had skimmed the world on their journey, passing exotic points and stunning land formations. They imagined life on the lands surrounding them, learned about the sea, and built friendships. The memories, the good will, and the enchantment of the sea enabled them to see themselves differently. They recalibrated their perceptions and deemed themselves ready to take on the sea and the events that would unfold.

Part V
The War Escalates, The Enemy is His Neighbor

Chapter 24
North African Campaign

Tony understood the risk soldiers faced as the tenders approached the port, thrusting against the beat of the sea. Troops lined up by the gate, waiting for the command to "move on." The movement of the waves, accentuated by the wake of the vessels themselves, eclipsed their progress. The soldiers fought the sea, a prelude to the real war. The sea's wrath was more strongly felt in the smaller craft, which tossed in the waters, lifting bodies and dropping them unpredictably on the decks of the craft.

The winds were fierce and the water furious as the ships docked in Gibraltar for a few days to acclimate to the environment in preparation for the staging and roll out of the amphibious assault. Within hours of their arrival, maneuvers to train for the landings were underway for the remainder of the day. Training for assaults at dawn was emphasized. The Navy released the landing craft loaded with troops from the warships. The craft moved from the port into the churning waters where the Atlantic, the Strait, and the Mediterranean converged. There, the soldiers trained to exit from the craft into the water and make their way ashore.

They first entered the water without equipment to experience its force and turbulence. They then moved on to round after round of maneuvers bearing their equipment, starting with a limited load, knowing the sea could easily take them, and then increasing their gear to the full weight of what they were required to carry. They entered the water again and again, each time carrying more gear to manage the water's assault and their own reaction to it. They experienced and overcame the panicked sinking, breathless feeling that naturally came with each plunge into the sea. Day after day they practiced, increasing their confidence about overcoming the challenges they faced.

Late in the evenings, they studied the war plan, present situation, and the historical events that brought the Allied Troops to Africa. Few soldiers realized that the North American Campaign had been underway since June 1940 or that its beginnings dated to 1882 and involved Libya, an Italian colony for several decades, and British forces in neighboring Egypt. In 1940, Italy invaded Egypt, declaring war on the Allied Nations. In a counterattack, British and Indian forces captured some 130,000 Italians. Tony had lived through that event vicariously by reading Italian newspapers available in the states. It was the first of many war-time experiences that accentuated geopolitical events and the complexity of his life as an Italian immigrant and citizen of Italy fighting for America. He was not alone. He stood among the estimated 700,000 to 1.5 million soldiers of Italian heritage who weathered the critical issues of country and allegiance that emerged during the war.

The situation in North Africa developed further when Hitler responded to Axis losses by deploying the newly formed "Afrika Korps" led by General Erwin Rommel to the area. Several long, brutal slogs back and forth across Libya and Egypt reached a turning point in the Second battle of El Alamein, when Montgomery's British Eighth Army broke out and drove Axis Forces all the way from Egypt to Tunisia. At the same time, German and Italian intelligence detected the build-up of Allied shipping around Gibraltar. There were mixed reactions as to what was occurring, the Germans brushing off the activity as the innocent delivery of supplies to Malta while the Italians deemed it suspicious. By then, the Germans had begun to marginalize the role of the Italians in the war, their opinions no longer welcome. The intelligence reports about what was happening in the area surrounding Gibraltar were accurate. The build-up was in fact a component of the Allies' logistical plan for the ensuing invasion of French North Africa that Tony was training for.

Learning about the raid and awaiting their ship's departure from Gibraltar, Tony watched history in the making when the final build-up for the campaign in Africa was delayed due to disagreements between the United States and Britain on how to carry it out. It wasn't until President Franklin D. Roosevelt intervened, contradicting his own military leadership, that the original plan moved forward. With Roosevelt's decision came the roll out of the largest amphibious attacks in history, an awe-inspiring plan to position troops along the Moroccan and Algerian coasts with support from 670 vessels and heavy air cover. A dramatic choreographed assault was about to begin.

The final preparations for the operation included the reorganization of military leadership to correspond with the change in mission from training to combat and the staging of troops in the armada. For the second time in his war experience, Tony found himself serving under the elite leadership of two significant figures and brilliant war strategists, Lieutenant General Dwight D. Eisenhower and Major General George Patton. The soldiers who converged in Gibraltar to serve under the two Generals' command arrived in the sea convoy under Eisenhower's leadership. That operation delivered 102 warships and an additional 65,000 Allied troops to support Operation Torch. The assault aimed to invade French North African enclaves at Casablanca, Oran, and Algiers. Three task forces would execute those orders—two conducted by British forces, the Eastern and Central Task Forces. U.S. soldiers comprised the third, the Western Task force under Patton, who led the 2nd Armored Division and the 3rd and 9th Infantry Divisions with a total of 35,000 troops. Naval support came from a separate American Task Force of one aircraft carrier, four escort carriers, three battleships, and seven cruisers. Along with British troops, the total number of soldiers in the joint Task Forces reached 100,000.

In early November 1942, the joint forces departed on their mission in a sea convoy with air coverage. The ships plowed through the water, sailing from the mouth of the Mediterranean into the Strait of Gibraltar and toward the French North African colonies. Eventually, the joint forces separated into three convoys, one for each Task Force. The convoys' journeys to their staging locations were perilous not only for the turbulent waters but for the likelihood of German submarines.

The goal of the Western Task Force of American soldiers was to seize Casablanca, which lay 190 miles south of Gibraltar on the Atlantic coast. Due to the strong presence of the opposition, their staging and access to the continent took place northeast of Casablanca where the water was turbulent and unrestrained. The Task Force landed before daybreak on November 8, 1942, at three points in Morocco—Safi, Fedala with 19,000 men and the largest landing, and Mehdiya-Port Lyautey. The craft bobbled in the sea, making the landings hazardous, but the soldiers moved out. Under the withering fire, bodies of American soldiers floated in the broader staging area. Unfortunately, U.S. Forces committed a serious act of misjudgment that day. Prior to the assaults, they failed to question intelligence reports indicating the French would not resist and did not carry out the pre-emptive strikes that would have been expected. That mistake was costly, its victims the U.S. landing troops who were subdued, injured, or killed in action as they approached land or were advancing to the interior. Loss of life cast a cloud over the American troops of the Western Task Force, squelching their bravado.

There was a story behind the inaccurate intelligence report Allied troops received. It reflected the last-minute efforts of General Antoine Béthouart in Morocco, who attempted a *coup d'etat* against the French command in Morocco the night before the attack with the intention to surrender to the Allies the next day. His forces surrounded the villa of General Charles Noguès, the Vichy-loyal high commissioner, but Noguès did not capitulate. Instead, he telephoned loyal forces and stopped the coup. Thus, the General's good intentions played their role in undermining the forces he wanted to support. News of what had occurred spread rapidly, causing the French opposition to bolster all coastal defenses. In the end, the French Vichy opposition awaiting the Allies' arrival numbered 125,000 forces who were aided with infantry, artillery, armor, and air capabilities. Those numbers did not bode well for Allied troops, but the growing apparent disarray within the Axis strengthened the Allies' hopes despite their rough start.[7]

At Safi, the objective was to capture the port's facilities so that medium-sized tanks could enter, and the landings were mostly successful in the end. They began without cover fire, believing there would be no resistance. But the French opened fire, forcing Allied warships to withdraw. By time the 2nd Armored Division arrived, U.S. assault troops, many experiencing their first battle, were held captive on Safi's beaches. As the operation continued, the situation worsened. Landings fell behind schedule, critical manpower was not in place, and the team was unable to advance. It was not until air support from U.S. carriers

---

7 Anderson, Charles, U.S. Army Center of Military History. Algeria-French Morocco: The U.S. Army Campaigns of World War II. Defense Department, Last Update: August 19, 2012, https://bookstore.gpo.gov/products/algeria-french-morocco-us-army-campaigns-world-war-ii-pamphlet.

destroyed a French convoy that the offensive began to turn around. By afternoon on the 8th Safi surrendered, by November 10th the remaining opposition forces were routed, and the 2nd Armor division moved on to Casablanca.

Landings at other locations also faced challenges. Confusion over landing coordinates at Port-Lyautey postponed the second wave of landings. That delay gave the French defenders time to organize a counterattack, and the remaining landings were conducted under intense artillery bombardment. With carriers providing air support, U.S. troops were able to push ahead and capture the opposition.

Tony was among the soldiers heading to Fedala, where the disruptive weather made the maneuvers treacherous nearly to the point of failure. Like most troops on the tenders, he was contending with his combat assignment. Scheduled to land on the beachhead in the final wave of the assault, he was presented with the gut-wrenching experience of watching the war, raw and live, at its worst. He remained helpless to intervene in any way. As he viewed the action firsthand, Tony understood the peril the soldiers faced as the landing craft approached the port, thrusting to the beat of the sea. The soldiers lined up by the gate, waiting for the command to "move on." The movement of the sea, accentuated by the wake of the vessels themselves, eclipsed their progress. The soldiers fought the sea, a prelude to the ground war. The sea's anguish was more strongly felt in the smaller craft, which tossed in the waters, lifting bodies and forcing them to drop unpredictably onto the decks. From his vantage point, Tony followed his fellow soldiers' movements with his eyes, swaying with them, being pulled as they were, and prizing his life as they were grasping for their own. He watched the first release of the three landing craft in the initial wave, trying to remain attentive to his own safety. The precarious conditions faced by the landing craft as they launched and then navigated to the beachhead were daunting. The boats appeared light and unstable, not fully adequate for the mission.

Able to view the landings preceding his, Tony had the unusual feeling that he was watching a war movie, a story of challenges, pain, and loss. In that movie, Tony witnessed the disappearance of fifty-five landing craft and heavy human loss. The unexpected defense of the French Vichy forces nearly wiped out the first wave though artillery and air cover arrived quickly enough to protect the remaining landings.

Tony's first direct contact with loss of life during the war, the loss of his team members, was far worse than anything he had imagined. He sensed and was correct in thinking he would see more of the same in the years to come. Other craft carrying engineers and medics were on the scene for rescue and recovery, and Tony found himself engrossed in the operations of both groups. The second wave proceeded, their entry equally perilous. Tony re-watched the real-life movie of his team invading North Africa, deploring the cost of victory in human terms. During that second wave, he saw five additional landing craft disappear, which left the unit with two operable boats for transporting all remaining troops and supplies to the beachhead.

Even before the third wave began, Tony prepared mentally for his landing and his first face-to-face encounter with the enemy. As he did so, his inner strength coalesced, yet his thoughts drifted briefly to the odd, unsettling feeling that overcame him six years ago when he traveled from Italy to the U.S. That day, as his ship passed along the coast of Africa and he glanced toward the continent, he saw himself in the distance dressed in the uniform of the U.S. Army. Four years after viewing the coast of Africa, Tony was positioned to know the premonition for what it was. Before he moved on, he scanned the sea and sky, the vastness reminding him of the stakes.

The wind and the water uprooted Tony as he positioned himself to drop into the sea. He felt pressure across his shoulder as though something was bracing him. He turned, thinking yet not believing one of his fellow soldiers would clutch him and disrupt the landing. Seeing nothing in his way, for a split second he had no idea what was happening. But then he recognized the weight as familiar, something he had experienced previously on the ship in Naples as Papa prepared to leave the vessel. Though there was no physical explanation for the contact Tony felt, he chose to believe that Papa was as aware of him as he was aware of his father. The strength of the connection forged enabled Papa to reach and touch his son, protecting him as he plunged into the frigid sea. Tony felt his body descend below the dead on the surface, and he prayed he would not join them. Drawing from the strength he suddenly found, he commanded his body to ascend. He powered himself up from the water to be met by the debris—human, natural, and man-made—scattered on the water's surface. His nightmare had occurred. *Will this get even worse,* he wondered.

Dodging fire, Tony continued to the shore, fixed his bayonet, and faced the enemy. Like the soldiers who preceded them, Tony's group encountered considerable opposition on land. That morning all beachheads ended up under fire though the tide turned after Patton arrived. Hours later, all beachheads were secure though the assault in Algiers continued.

The scenes Tony witnessed in that brief offensive on the shoreline seemed days longer than their hours. Facets of those moments became emblazoned on his mind as lasting images and issues for another day. No preparation could have adequately primed him for the brutal reality of the situation, from the thrashing water to the debris and human loss. Nothing, other than raw footage of battles, could have captured the nature of hand-to-hand combat. Fighting with a bayonet felt primitive, and the human familiarity in those face-to-face encounters went to the soul to be stored within him for the rest of his life.

Following the landings in Safi, Mehdiya-Port Lyautey and Fedala, U.S. troops re-organized in Fedala for the assault in Casablanca. They secured their landing craft and tenders and shifted to a field operation. Their equipment and supplies included jeeps, light armored vehicles, bayonets, and ammunition for their journey south. For the mission, Tony served on a tank team as gunner, realizing he was fulfilling the scene he visioned six years ago. Proceeding toward Casablanca, U.S. soldiers endured enemy fire non-stop along the route. They stood within the frame of that moment, a fraction of the full picture of war, each forming their personal war stories. For Tony, his assignment to the tank team marked a pivotal turn that would define his career for the remainder of the war, and he began to rely on his prescient sense more than he ever thought he would.

By November 10th, U.S. troops had surrounded the port of Casablanca, and within an hour of the final planned assault, the city surrendered. As the principal French Atlantic naval base following the German occupation of the European coast, the port of Casablanca was of critical importance. The primary purpose of Operation Torch was to secure it, and that objective led to the Naval Battle of Casablanca, during which a sortie of French cruisers, destroyers, and submarines opposed U.S. troops. In response, American gunfire and aircraft annihilated a cruiser, six destroyers, and six submarines. An incomplete French battleship—the *Jean Bart*, which was docked and immobile—fired on American landing forces with its single working gun turret until it was disabled by the 16-inch U.S. naval gunfire from the *Massachusetts*. For the U.S., that success represented the noteworthy achievement of having fired the first heavy-caliber shells of WW II. During the engagement, two U.S. destroyers sustained damage. While a sense of victory existed for having seized the port of Casablanca, the conquest would not be complete until there was resolution in Algiers.

Like other teams in Operation Torch, the landing forces along the Algerian coast encountered stiff resistance from the enemy. Forces of nature also plagued the overall roll-out. The surf interfered with landing operations, causing their cancellation for the entire day. The landings then took place the next day, but the element of surprise had been lost, and that worked against both sides, altering all expectations for what might occur. The French prepared to launch a counterattack on the second day, but they were stymied by Allied air attacks and naval gunfire. By the evening of November 8th, the 1st Infantry Division had accomplished its objectives but for one area. The see-sawing effect of gains and losses after the landings tested the strength and ingenuity of American soldiers.

Though resistance on the Algerian coast was tenacious, Brigadier General Theodore Roosevelt, Jr., son of the former President, emerged as an inspiring and effective combat leader. Under his command, U.S. Forces battled their way to the Port of Algiers, the operation's target. The French were prepared with substantial ground forces as well as fifty-two fighter aircraft and thirty-nine bombers. Strong coastal artillery positions protected the port. Consequently, Allied attacks had to approach the city from the east and west. British Commandos and Regular infantry along with the U.S. Army's 168th Regimental Combat Team landed to the west, and the American 39th Combat Team, supported by Commandos, came ashore east of the port. The eastern landings succeeded against mild resistance. By midmorning, American troops had secured the airfield, and Royal Air Force Hawker Hurricanes were flying over the city. By night, Allied Forces from the west were on the outskirts of the city as were those from the east. Their locations placed French defenders in an untenable position, which led their commanders to agree to a cease-fire.[8]

Operation Torch was widely recognized for its success. Although the lessons learned in the invasion caused the landing in France to be postponed, the adjustment gave the U.S. time to complete the mobilization of its industrial and human resources for the vast air and ground battles envisioned for the Allied campaigns of 1944. In both a direct and an indirect sense, Operation Torch figured considerably in British and American strategies for the remainder of the war. The Allies' decision on the timing of Operation Torch may have been the most important one they made.

---

[8] ---. Algeria-French Morocco: The U.S. Army Campaigns of World War II.

Chapter 25
The Enemy Is My Neighbor, This Is No Way to Return Home

With reluctance and a heavy heart, he bayoneted a soldier in the name of a higher duty. Seeing the imperative as one to subdue rather than kill the enemy, the wound was merciful, fleshy, and far from major organs. He continued to plow through the Italian line. Imagined or real, one will never know, he sensed the "enemies" who fell by his hand looking him straight in the eye, saying, "I know you."

The victory in the North Africa Campaign freed the massive Allied contingent in the southern Mediterranean to expand their reach militarily. The decision on how to proceed was in the hands of American and British strategists who relied on their current positions to determine where they would head next. Their analysis identified two paths for getting a handle on the scope of Axis control. One would move Mediterranean forces to the north in anticipation of the Allied troops invading Europe from the English Channel at some point. The other would have soldiers remain in the area to prepare for and undertake a campaign in Italy. Dissension existed among the Allies about how to proceed. At the Casablanca Conference in 1943, both countries finally agreed that bearing down on Italy following the success of Operation Torch would establish the foundation for a large-scale invasion of Europe involving several countries. There was also the benefit that Malta could provide air cover for activity in Italy, especially if a campaign began in Sicily.

For Tony, the inevitable was about to occur. The assignments that had conveniently buffered him from a painful and haunting experience had expired. The recent agreement between the United States and Britain on war strategy triggered the beginning of the European Theatre in earnest. Tony was headed to his homeland as an enemy of the people, forced to confront his personal war on morality and loyalty.

For the assault, ships equipped with landing craft arrived from the United States and Mediterranean ports from Beirut to Algiers and converged on Malta, where the underground operations room for Operation Husky, the Allied invasion of Sicily, was located. Arriving in Malta from Africa, Tony sailed within 500 miles of his beleaguered village, the closest he would be to it for decades, though he would see his family sooner than then. His situation created a scenario both real and surreal, yet victory in Sicily would lessen Axis strength, which would constitute a major step toward ending the occupation. In his heart Tony knew he was fighting for Italy when other Italians could not.

The convoy from Malta approached land, and the invasion of Italy was imminent. Similar to operations in Africa, several contingents dispersed strategically to take the Island of Sicily by disrupting Axis forces not only with a land invasion but through calculated hits to key sites such as airports and bridges, to curtail movement to and from the island. Allied Forces entered Sicily at four points—the southeast coast, the southernmost tip, the western side, and the west/north coast. Operations in each vector commenced simultaneously. Since the number of Allied troops continued to increase, the readiness and skills of the soldiers engaged in the operation were uneven at times.

When the gates of the landing craft dropped for the first round, many young soldiers were momentarily frozen, and Tony could sympathize with them. The reality of their mission, close combat, was a staggering thought. When the command to "move along" was reiterated, the soldiers filed out and stepped into the warmth of the calm Central Mediterranean Sea. They made their way to the shore and immediately fell into marching columns. The invasion was underway.

When Tony's craft was in position, he moved forward, his heart pulsating. *This is not how I envisioned my return to Italy*, he thought. He prayed and walked into the waters he had gazed upon during his journey from Italy. A cloud now hung over him and the sea. The serenity of the Mediterranean as he had known it was broken. He passed through the water to his beloved country, which he had not seen in over five years, and stepped on to it, tears in his eyes. Many of his brothers squeezed his shoulder as they fell into formation. They could only imagine the confusion and pain he felt, the duality of his identity sundered by invasion. Duty and country. *But which country*, his heart cried!

On that consequential day, Lieutenant General George S. Patton led American ground forces with Field Marshall Bernard L. Montgomery directing the British. By the afternoon of July 10, 1943, 150,000 Allied troops reached the shores of Sicily supported by naval and aerial bombardment of enemy positions and 600 tanks. The troops advanced onto the island with bayonets fixed, fanning out toward the wall of Italian soldiers protecting *their* homeland. Tony was surrounded by the Italian language, its familiar melodic strains flooding and dizzying his mind. He girded himself to confront the ultimate distraction for a soldier at war, an emotional attachment to the enemy. Tony found his focus fading, and he needed to re-calibrate his moral and emotional compass. The situation was far more unusual and serious than anything he had ever encountered in his paramilitary training. Following his instincts, Tony summoned the strength of his mental capacities and called for his father. *Aiutami, Papa!* [Help me, Papa], he silently appealed. His spirit lifted, he maximized his stride, running in tandem with and bolstered by a squad of American soldiers. Together, they dodged incoming fire, snaking inward, outward, up, and down to continue the assault while avoiding injury.

The soldiers scattered and charged toward the enemy. Tony's first face-to-face encounter with one of his countrymen was unnerving, not that it ever became routine for him at any time during the war. Shaken, he acted with a reluctant and heavy heart, bayoneting a soldier in the name of a higher duty. Seeking to subdue rather than slay the enemy, the blow was merciful, fleshy. Tony continued to plow through the Italian line following his combat training. Imagined or real, the "enemies" who fell by his hand appeared to look him straight in the eye, saying, "I know you." He stumbled over bodies during the rampage, when in fact he wanted to give them his hand and pull them up. And then American soldiers were ordered to seize the wounded as prisoners of war and escort them to the temporary enclosures, where once disarmed they were reclassified as Disarmed Enemy Forces. The war played with Tony's mind, causing his past, present, and future to conduct their own battle.

The landings and combat engagements that initiated the invasion took place in the cities of Gela and Licata along the southern coast of Sicily. The images from those confrontations formed snapshots in Tony's mind that were unforgettable as were the thirty-eight days of combat that followed, each day a reiteration of the one before. Collectively, the scenes of war added to the movie forming in his mind, and it continued to replay constantly. By July 21st, the 82nd Airborne Division became part of the operation as the troops progressed to the more populous cities of Butera, Campobello, and Palermo, the island's capital. Tony's unit advanced into and took each city in turn, covered by air and his division's tank unit. In the line of duty, Tony witnessed the defeat of his countrymen and the bombing of his homeland that reduced thriving cities and villages to rubble. The movie in his mind expanded with the accompaniment of the relentless explosive sounds of warfare.

Throughout the offensive, resistance was lighter than it could have been. As history tells, the Allies benefited from a deception that had Hitler believing Corsica and Sardinia rather than Sicily were the targets. Hitler remained convinced about the ruse for some time, and he continued to warn his officers that the main landings were likely to occur in the two locations. In Tony's eyes, the Axis defense of Italy appeared weak. Having recently served in Northern Africa, where several hundred thousand Axis troops were captured, Tony was not surprised by the ineffective defense. But he also wondered if the young Italians in the Axis Forces lacked the will and allegiance necessary to fight the U.S. and British troops more aggressively. Tony's insights came from his heart. It took him back to the Youth Group and the mindset of its leaders, who imposed opinions on the young boys, suppressing their thought processes and decision-making. Italy was fighting for that way of thinking, but Tony's heart would never have allowed him to fight that mission. Had he not immigrated to the U.S. and was instead fighting in Sicily that day, his performance on the field might have lacked the vigor that he was demonstrating as a member of the U.S. Military.

The invasion of Sicily had not concluded, by any means. The next five weeks involved the entire 2nd Army. Led by Patton, the divisions of the 2nd Army moved toward the northwestern shore of Sicily, then east to Messina, protecting the flank of Montgomery's veteran forces as they moved up the east coast of the island. The operation was initially a majestic march, one that met with light opposition that encouraged American troops. They functioned like machines, and they were probably better off for that. The strength of the Allied assault brought about a thrilling outcome, an emotional one that Tony welcomed yet found hard to believe. As they had hoped, the Allied invasion destabilized and demoralized Axis Forces. Concurrently, the Italian fascist regime declined rapidly, and on July 24, 1943, to Tony's astonishment, Prime Minister Benito Mussolini was deposed and arrested. Equally providential for Italy and the world was the new provisional government set up under Marshal Pietro Badoglio, who had opposed Italy's alliance with Nazi Germany from the start and immediately began secret discussions with the Allies about an armistice. Tony was overcome with emotion by what was achieved, and he acquired greater understanding about why Mama believed he was destined to leave their country.

The nature of the operation changed radically, with Italian Forces withdrawing but Hitler's soldiers continuing to fight fiercely against the Allied advance. The latter took U.S. troops into the mountainous Sicilian terrain where the Germans had dug in. The Americans were unprepared though they prevailed, pushing Hitler's soldiers back to the point of trapping them in the northeast corner of the Island. For Tony, the stress of that final stand was offset by the beauty of Sicily's mountain region, which was reminiscent of his village perched in the countryside beyond Rome. He scanned the landscape rising to the crest and experienced the pleasure of viewing the beautiful trees of his country, among them numerous majestic fig trees whose height had always inspired his ambition and dreams. He took in the heady scents of home, a tear in his eye. When the soldiers were told to ease down for a while, an elderly Italian couple befriended Tony. They recognized the Italian features of the man in an American uniform and their kindness prompted them to greet him. During their conversation, they mourned the loss and destruction but celebrated the outcome. The gentlemen assured Tony by saying, "*stai facendo la cosa giusta*" [You are doing the right thing] and that moment was redemptive. Much later in the evening, the story seemed blurred in the distance, and Tony was afraid of losing it. He pulled his journal out of his pack and wrote his recollection of the chance encounter as a talisman to pair with his Italian gold horn.

While U.S. and British troops anticipated a fierce fight after the German soldiers were cornered, they found all Axis troops and their supplies gone by morning. The invasion of Sicily was over though the Allies' failure to capture the troops was an embarrassment that undermined their victory, especially for LTG Patton. Since German losses had not been severe but for the loss of Italian Army Forces, which caused a considerable reduction in the overall size of Axis forces, the United States now considered the impending invasion of the mainland more complicated and costly than initially thought. As operations in Sicily ended, U.S. troops were reorganized with some soldiers deploying to England to prepare for the Invasion of Normandy and others going on to mainland Italy. Once again, Tony faced a crossroads with no say on which path he would be taking. He was tested in Sicily, overcame the challenges confronting him, yet knew images of his countrymen as well as the destruction of his country were likely to stay with him for the rest of his life.

Chapter 26
A Bold Direction, Operation Overlord

Each soldier received their personal copy of a letter from General Dwight D. Eisenhower. For the troops, most of whom were in their third year of service in the war as Tony was, an eternal battle raged between their grim fatigue and optimism about being on the path to victory. Their spirits were buoyant when they received Eisenhower's address, which opened with "Soldiers, Sailors and Airmen of the Allied Expeditionary Force!" His words presented them with a call to arms, an invitation to save the world.

A strategic success, Operation Husky created options in the Mediterranean for expanding Allied operations in both Africa and Europe. With its conclusion came the reconfiguration of troops and the formation of the largest fighting force in the history of the United States. Tony couldn't help but think about the two possible paths that lay ahead. One would position him on the Italian mainland in penetrating battles against his countrymen and German forces. If he received orders to that end, he would likely arrive as part of a military assault against the city of Naples, which was a mere eighty-three miles from his birthplace. There was a haunting element to such an assignment. The possibility of having his family nearby raised conflicting issues that could place a deep emotional burden on him or threaten his family. Fate intervened. Tony was assigned to an armored division in the re-organized 3rd Army led by General Patton. He was bound for England where he would remain until July 1944, when he became part of the bold and massive campaign known as Patton's Race Across France to Germany.

The central mission of Patton's 3rd Army was to spearhead a cross-Channel invasion. Units training for that offensive reported to the elite U.S. Assault Training Center in the coastal area of Devon, England. There, both Americans and their British counterparts trained vigorously over a year's time, integrating the amphibious, mechanized, and field components of the anticipated battle plan. In conjunction with the build-up for that campaign, Tony received a new classification, that of an armored infantry soldier, a transition designed to make him versatile with the capacity to serve on a tank team as either a driver or a gunner. As time would tell, his role was flexible and challenging, often stretching beyond his training and capacity. The assignment boosted Tony's morale, enabling him to re-commit to the mission after witnessing the grim and personally wrenching strains of war.

As he trained for the largest operation of his career, Tony's thoughts often drifted to circumstances in Italy. He worried about his family and was grateful one day to receive an unexpected letter from Jack who unbeknown to Tony until then was part of the Italian Campaign. Tony smiled when he started reading the letter. He was not surprised by the way Jack began it, based on something that had happened in Basic. One evening when there was a chance to congregate, soldiers sang to entertain each other. Tony chose to participate and rendered a remarkably moving performance of "O Sole Mio" [My Sun] that startled the audience. Jack was enamored with the language and begged Tony to teach him some Italian words and phrases. It was clear from the letter that Jack was comfortable in the ambience of Italy, which was good for him, Tony thought, as a means for handling stress. Tony read Jack's letter again to bring himself close to his beloved homeland, and he was smiling afterward. *Cara Antonio,* Jack wrote, *I am now in Italia and want you to know your homeland is molto bello [very beautiful]. The people are so kind, and they are happy to see us here! There is damage but not in the hearts of the people, which is what matters, my mother says. I will write from time to time. Tuo fratello [your brother], Giovanni.*

Amid the turmoil about his family, Tony was thankful for Jack's letter and his new classification for gifting him extended and novel training that engaged and therefore distracted him. His assignment in a small tank detail provided intimacy along with camaraderie. Even though it was impossible to hear anything when the tanks were in motion, the steady company with his tank crew was a favorable change. The maneuvers themselves served as the ultimate diversion. The training protocols and intensity were familiar to him, reflecting his cumulative training. For him personally, re-organizing with familiar leadership was a huge boost that brought stability, the most important element being the consistency in military strategies.

During that rigorous year of training, soldiers were on duty non-stop, seven days a week. The idea of weekends was non-existent in Tony's war and continued in that vein indefinitely, as he had anticipated. He realized the stakes of war had increased, making the continent more dangerous and the tasks of the military all the more important. Europe was now under siege, and in September 1943, the unthinkable happened—the Germans occupied Italy, which caused Tony's family to flee, their whereabouts unknown for some time. The war continued to escalate, the Allies' mission was refined in the process, and the troops ratcheted up the intensity of their training. But several months later, Tony would look back on the training period as relatively easy compared to what he would endure on the ground in Europe.

On a typically arduous day in November, around midpoint in the year-long training period, Tony experienced an unbelievable stroke of luck. The story began three weeks before when he entered his name in a lottery to staff a security detail for the transport of supplies and equipment between the U.S. and Britain. The flights were scheduled to leave Britain for the Brooklyn Navy Yard in a land and air convoy roughly around December 16th and return on December 24th. The positions to fill were for escorting and protecting cargo during transit. For Tony, the compelling detail was that the assignment had no obligations in New York after permanent staff assumed responsibility for the shipments shortly after arrival. And the expectation for return travel merely required his presence no later than early morning the day of departure.

Though the trip sounded like a crazy idea, given the brief stay and the logistics with transportation, Tony had the dream of winning and making his way to Connecticut. After close to three long years, nothing would soothe him more than time in the U.S., no matter how brief. A visit with family and friends would serve as a balm for his soul, especially since everything about Operation Overload told him the worst was yet to come. After registering with the lottery, which many soldiers did, Tony put the idea out of his mind, since the odds of securing a seat were low.

The drawing took place before the Thanksgiving holiday and the "winners" were then posted. Tony dreaded looking at the random list of names but owed it to himself to check. It was hard to do so as he was not looking to be disappointed. The jolt he experienced as he scanned the posting nearly knocked him over. What timing! As of late he had been troubled by spontaneous recollections of the day in New Orleans two years ago when he felt the chill of death on his return to the naval yard. Since then, he experienced visions and dreams depicting bodies strewn on battlefields. Some would say he was experiencing fear or trauma, yet Tony would disagree. There was a sense of foreboding and realism in what he perceived. Amid that darkness, a trip to the U.S., no matter how limited it was, would grant time with his loved ones, the gift of a lifetime. His thoughts of Helena always counterbalanced the trials of war, and he regarded the outcome of the lottery as a providential invitation for him to propose to her. What greater purpose could there be as Operation Overload loomed ahead than to offset the war with a brief interlude of joy to sustain him?

Tony was busier than usual with training and preparing for his trip. He sent a telegram immediately after the drawing about his plans with scant details—the purpose and tentative dates for his travel, emphasizing time in Connecticut. He intended to follow up with more specific information before he left. Letters soon began to arrive in response to his communication since mail delivery between the U.S. and Britain was faster than locations in Europe. It pained Tony that he could not telegraph his parents and family. How excited they would be to know he had an opportunity to return to the states briefly and escape the war for even the smallest amount of time.

Across the Atlantic, Lucia bore the emotional weight of Tony's travel plans because she stood in place of Mama in America. She had no doubt about how Mama would feel about Tony's return and took on the burden of that worry. At first, Mama would be shocked by the news, her emotions out of balance for the joy Tony would experience by returning to the U.S. Yet the risk of traveling in and out of war-torn

Europe would trouble her deeply. Mama received news about the war on the other side. Due to her experiences on the continent, she knew well the animus against the United States and the threat to Allied Forces worldwide. The submarines that prowled the Atlantic Ocean stood ready to attack. Lucia thought about Mama because she, herself, feared for Tony and sought solace in Mama's heart.

As word spread about Tony's impending return, so did the speculation about his proposing to Helena. She shied away from such conversations, not wanting to wish for their engagement and then be disappointed. Of course, Lucia also wondered about an engagement. She was the instigator along with Mama who had shepherded the couple along. Their engagement was her dream too, but she didn't see it as her place to get involved with the family's conjecture and pressure. In England, Tony was doing his own planning, and what the family hoped for was no different from what he wanted. What Helena wanted was never discussed because everyone knew what was in her heart, and no one believed she would turn down a proposal from Tony. Thankfully, absent from the minds of everyone were the rather parochial views and superstition of traditional Italians about not becoming engaged to a man at war until he returned.

Tony's plans for visiting Connecticut were complicated because he had to work within the logistics of his trip and his responsibilities. He had a plan in mind, and he hoped to make it happen. In the meantime, he learned additional details about his travel. He would travel by plane for the first time in his life, which seemed long overdue given the distance he had covered thus far in the war. Information Tony acquired from the administrative offices laid out the itinerary and the flight time, which helped him plan beyond the logistics of the flight itself. He was familiar with the flying boats that would "ferry" the convoy across the Atlantic, stopping at different points to refuel, which pushed total travel time to approximately twenty-five hours. With that information, he calculated four to six days total with his family in Connecticut, which gave leeway on both ends for delays. Knowing the intended mission—to become engaged—planning for the journey was an exciting endeavor.

Shortly before his departure, Tony sent a brief telegram asking Lucia and Helena to meet him at "The Clock." Previously, he had told Lucia that he would make his way to Grand Central and asked her to take care of the details for meeting there. Lucia read deeply into the words in his message, realizing he might not have stated everything he wished to convey since Helena would probably read the telegram herself. Lucia had a feeling, and she was going to run with it, hoping she and Tony were on the same wavelength. With battles to prepare for, there was only so much time Tony could put into the logistics of his trip. Planning and training took place every day of the week, leaving little time for anything other than his duties. He was relying heavily on Lucia to interpret his plan by reading between the lines in his telegrams, and he was confident she would do so. After all, the two had shared the lore of the Clock in Grand Central Station, and Lucia was the one person who knew about the engagement ring and had access to it.

In the weeks prior to Tony's departure, the rigor of training intensified. In addition to the strategizing, re-organization, and field work that laid the framework for the invasion, there was special attention to the elements, terrain, and atmosphere for staging and initiating the assault. The build-up of supplies was also ongoing and was in fact related to Tony's upcoming travel. It was hard for Tony to imagine that he would be leaving during such a critical time, but his platoon sergeant indicated he was doing something equally valuable for the war effort by taking on a security role in the upcoming cargo shipments.

Days before the flight was due to depart, Tony left the Assault Training Center in a land convoy larger than he expected due to the cargo they were carrying. The first leg of the trip was a four-hour ride from Devon to Poole Harbor in Dorset, where the flying boats departed after loading. That process consumed three full days. Tony's responsibilities were light as an escort because permanent transportation staff were directly responsible for passengers and cargo on the ground. His work placed him among flight personnel, and he could not help but learn some pointers about aircraft and air travel, especially the weight and size of cargo relative to each plane's capacity. He was fascinated by the process of distributing the load on each plane, which explained why there was so much time on the ground in Dorset.

On the water and in the air, the planes themselves were in a convoy formation with a squadron for cover and safety. They were returning equipment and supplies from many points in Europe to the U.S., and on return, the convoy would transport fresh and much needed supplies for Operation Overlord. The staff were primarily American soldiers though they flew under the auspices of Britain's Royal Air Force. The flight path followed a northern route that passed through the Azores, Iceland, and Greenland, shifting to water travel when fuel was running short until they were able to acquire more. There was a dramatic element to the flight, for the altitude reached modest heights and the views were extraordinary. Never before had Tony experienced an aerial view, and at times the details of what he saw astonished him. As their path swept over Europe, restricted in a number of ways, he could distinguish towns and major buildings such as cathedrals. War had afflicted segments of the continent, cities in some places and the countryside in others, creating shameful desolation and legacy. When populated areas gave way to untouched bucolic landscapes, the natural beauty of Europe, including the gorgeous winding waterways, continued to shine for the most part. The same held true for Greenland, which was pristine and, yes, so very green.

Flying over large bodies of water was unnerving as Tony could think of the plane taking a nosedive into the sea at any time. Looking down, he re-evaluated his family's shock over his plans to fly from Europe and viewed them in a new light. Traveling for twenty-five hours, he had the remarkable opportunity to experience night flight, which was eerie and replicated the feeling of a ship passing in the dark of night that he had witnessed twice. He was thankful for the opportunity to sleep on board since he wanted and hoped to arrive rested to reach Connecticut as quickly as possible after completing his required sign-off.

Tony's idyllic flight was uneven, often bumpier than the ship he sailed from Italy, except for the storm, as it made its way toward the Brooklyn Naval Yard. Watching the scenery as the boat descended offered a fascinating lesson on perspective. Tony had his camera with him and took pictures, hoping to document his unexpected journey. He knew what his naked eye saw as the seaplane descended and hoped he had sufficiently adjusted the camera to capture it. The final approach for landing afforded an exquisite view of New York Harbor, the Statue of Liberty, and the City itself. With tears in his eyes, Tony remembered his arrival in America, this time with painful thoughts of his scattered family who were on the run. He felt the plane settle on the water and turn toward land. Tony was back in the U.S., and he was able to breathe easily for the first time in a few years.

Tony would never forget the tantalizing experience of traveling to the U.S. through the air and on the sea. He would dissect the event for weeks, but for now he tucked the story away and focused on his personal reason for making the trip. If everything fell into place over the next several hours, Tony would experience a very special day with his path for the future clearer than ever. He rose, gathered his belongings, worked with the team to re-inventory every item, and then signed off on the crew's list. From there he entered the administrative office to sign in while also requesting a temporary area to rest briefly, shower, and dress. He did so without delay and left, expecting to arrive at Grand Central Station before the appointed time. Knowing his Aunt, she and some of Helena's friends would arrive early too. Tony wore his uniform, a case woolen taupe long sleeve shirt and trousers with a black tie.

Lucia, Helena, and her friends had already arrived and were waiting. All eyes were watchful, the women gathered loosely around the clock within view of the entrances to the station. Helena and Tony's connection to each other was so strong that she sensed his presence the minute he entered the building. Without doubt he was there, the tingle down her arm and the flush that rose toward her face told her so. Lucia knew he was there too, her link to him also powerful and her memories transporting her to the day he had arrived in the country. As she smiled through images of that day, she saw him from the corner of her eye. Lean yet muscular, a much more mature look. Dashing, she thought. What would Mama say? Lucia assessed Tony through Mama's eyes and concluded she would be so pleased though she would deem him too thin. Tony noticed Lucia and merely nodded to her. She did not miss a beat by tapping the side of her pocketbook where she had secured the ring. Tony smiled, and Aunt Lucia bloomed with excitement.

Everything was in place though Helena had not yet seen Tony. Suddenly she knew exactly where he was and turned to her right. Simultaneously, Tony turned slightly from his Aunt and toward Helena. When their eyes met, the connection was a bolt of lightning. Her face lit up and her tears began to spill. They rushed toward each other, and he took her hand while everyone converged on him. As the reunion played out, he deftly held out the camera in the hope that someone would know how to use it. He held Helena tightly as the women greeted him. He received more Italian double kisses than ever in one day. Cousin Palma knew how to use the camera and started taking photographs, not knowing what was meant to happen. Lucia had slipped the box into Tony's hand when she hugged him. Tony then dropped to his knee still holding Helena's hand. The girls all squealed. Palma took pictures, Tony posed his question, and Helena said "Yes!" in response.

More photos were taken and then the two groups split, promising to see more of each other in Connecticut during Tony's stay. Tony and Helena went directly to the famous Oyster Bar restaurant, a favorite of theirs for both memories and the food, and started planning their lives together. As they sat side by side in the restaurant booth, laughing and catching up, Helena looked down at her ring many times, not believing their engagement though she had felt from the start it was the reason why Tony registered for the lottery. While they looked over the menu, the same thought crossed their minds. If Tony had to turn around and leave immediately to return to his assignment, they would both be satisfied with the day and what had occurred until they met again.

Tony's visit was a whirlwind, and they did not mind that at all. Their first obligation was to see Luigi and Rosa, who always felt the engagement was imminent, for their congratulations and approval. It didn't take long for everyone to realize what being engaged meant in terms of their wedding day. Had Tony not returned for that brief visit, their engagement would not occur for more than another year and a half when Tony returned, which would have pushed the wedding date even farther in the future. Their five days together were heavenly; many times they simply sat together, Tony often resting, given his travels and the demands of his deployment. They also visited their favorite spots, spent time with family, set the date for their wedding, and met with the priest. Tony, Helena, and others also discussed difficult topics, the most pressing at the time Germany's occupation of Italy, which had emptied Tony's village of its native inhabitants.

The reunion established the conviction among family and friends that Tony's visit represented the promise of each soldier's return. There was so much hope in the community that Tony decided he could not and would not share his war-time fears. There was profound emptiness in the vibrant neighborhood with the men off to war, and he could not take his friends and family down any lower than they were before his visit. Every woman he saw seemed hollow without the man in her life. Every mother or father he conversed with appeared distracted if not lost due to the absence of their son. Such were the circumstances for the families at home, and that realization pierced Tony. No matter how tired he was or how haunted he felt, he did as Mama taught. He spread good will and kindness to help his family feel better about the war after he left than they did before he arrived.

While tears were shed the day he left, Tony had inspired strength and vitality in both himself and his neighbors. He left the U.S. with a warm heart and a sense of renewal even though he saw pain that added to his war-time burden. He enjoyed his return flight as much as his flight to the U.S. The views stirred him, making him cognizant of the world and his reason for serving in the war. When he returned to the Center, he caught up with developments quickly and moved on to a new level of training. In view of the drills and briefings, Operation Overlord was ramping up. As a result of his travels, Tony more clearly understood the assault's strategy and build-up. The massive supplies the U.S. delivered regularly to Europe to support the war effort were now tucked away in the small towns of Britain. The stockpile tallied an approximate total of 7,000,000 tons, and the flood of supplies continued to amass everything the Allies needed for the scope of war they expected under the code name Operation Overlord.

Better known as D-Day, the Invasion of Normandy, Operation Overlord represented the largest amphibious assault in the history of combat world-wide. Multifaceted, it served as a prologue for war on a scale never seen or imagined. It was the Allies' vision and response to the type of war the Axis Alliance was undertaking.

Overlord began with strategic deceptions for misleading Germany about the operation's actual target. Spun over a full year, the plan pointed to a northerly location in France for the main landings. Deep and flawlessly executed, the deception aimed for success and included several compelling distractors to attract the Germans' attention—a phantom army commanded by Patton, double agents, parachutes with dummies, fraudulent radio transmissions, and fake equipment, all of which suggested an assault was imminent in Calais rather than Normandy. At the same time, preparation for the invasion of Normandy continued.

The dates for mobilizing the troops and stationing them in the channel were fast approaching and would continue for over a month. The operations to deceive the enemy proved effective in protecting the true objective until the actual invasion began. The final marshalling pulled together an unprecedented military presence of 156,000 troops, 11,590 Allied aircraft, and an armada of 6,939 combat vessels consisting of 1,213 combat ships, 4,126 landing ships/craft, 736 support ships, and 864 merchant vessels. An endless number of vehicles and machinery as well as the 7,000,000 tons of supplies, including ammunition, constituted the build-up, which had assembled on Britain's coast and many of its seaside towns and villages. And on the appointed day, everything mobilized. Vehicles were loaded, convoys were formed, ships were loaded, and the staging protocols were executed.

Ships carrying hundreds of thousands of troops with gear, fighting machines and all modes of transportation (including trains) assembled in the Channel to launch phase two, the crossing and invasion. Another massive undertaking would eventually release cargo and then drop personnel. The scope defied anything any man or woman had ever seen in military strategy and warfare. When all vessels had reached their positions in the area spanning the Channel, the distribution of a personal letter from General Dwight D. Eisenhower to every soldier took place and continued with every flotilla of ships that joined the month-long invasion.

For the troops, an eternal battle existed between their grim fatigue and optimism about *the* path to victory. Their spirits were buoyed when they received Eisenhower's address, which opened with "Soldiers, Sailors and Airmen of the Allied Expeditionary Force!" His words presented them with a call to arms, an invitation to save the world, "In company with our brave Allies and brothers-in-arms on other Fronts, you will bring about the destruction of the German war machine, the elimination of Nazi tyranny over the oppressed peoples of Europe, and security for ourselves in a free world." And it closed to encourage the troops, "Your task will not be an easy one. Your enemy is well trained, well equipped and battle-hardened. He will fight savagely."[9]

> But this is the year 1944! Much has happened
> since the Nazi triumphs of 1940-41.... Our air

---

9   D-day statement to soldiers, sailors, and airmen of the Allied Expeditionary Force, 6/44, Collection DDEEPRE: Eisenhower, Dwight D: Papers, Pre-Presidential, 1916-1952; Dwight D. Eisenhower Library; National Archives and Records Administration.

offensive has seriously reduced their strength in the air and their capacity to wage war on the ground. Our Home Fronts have given us an overwhelming superiority in weapons and munitions of war, and placed at our disposal great reserves of trained fighting men.

The tide has turned! The free men of the world are marching together to Victory!

I have full confidence in your courage, devotion to duty and skill in battle.

We will accept nothing less than full Victory!"

From the time the war began, Tony followed the major figures in the U.S. Army and had become familiar with their tactics and strategies. He admired their brilliance, competence, and doggedness. They trained the troops hard for strength and passion, teams against teams, bringing training and performance to levels that exceeded those achieved in the Louisiana Maneuvers and at The Desert Training Center. He experienced fascinating enlightenment as he learned to crew a tank and calibrate his senses and perceptions to guide its movement. His appreciation for both the atmosphere of teamwork and the expectations for standards grew day by day. Those led to results, for the division not only trained with their equipment, but they also created realistic scenarios of conflict and warfare, working in the vast area allocated to them to experience the environment, create natural obstacles, and then take the conflict on, one team against the other building defensive and offensive strategies, dealing with the elements, and honing their skills. They were transformed by the scale, integrated forces, sophisticated tools, and strategic angle of their training. They became an Army much stronger than that of Operation Husky, capable and savvy in contrast to the first amphibious assault in Morocco. They developed know-how in the waters of the English Channel, engaging in maneuvers with multiple battles, the swelling, churning sea presenting unique and everchanging challenges given the unpredictable winds, high humidity, and chilly sea. That day, the entire campaign, a growing corps of soldiers that now included international forces, answered the call to arms. The largest amphibious invasion in military history was positioned to strike.

Chapter 27

The Invasion of Normandy, The Race through France Begins

> *When the time came to assemble in the staging area prior to landing, the pristine beaches were already saturated with the blood of war. Gone was the crystal-clear water that gushed, unobstructed, to the shore. Sunken landing craft and jagged metal shards rose out of the Channel defiling the curvature of its life and flow.*

On June 6, 1944, the Allied Invasion of Nazi-occupied France commenced on the Normandy Coast against the setting of the chalk cliffs of England, the Channel, and the Atlantic Wall—the 2,400-mile line of bunkers, landmines, and water obstacles along the French coast designed to repel Allied Forces. The massive campaign to liberate North-Western Europe was underway. From Day 1 of the build-up, the operation was regarded as the beginning of the end of the war. And for the 3rd Army, it served as the prelude to D-Day 3 in July, when landing troops with reinforcements arrived and proceeded to sectors on the front, marking the beginning of The Race through France to Germany.

The break of dawn on D-Day 3 had Tony wavering between reservation and courage about the greatest military endeavor in history. Awaiting the drop onto Omaha Beach, there was no man in an open landing craft who could miss the magnificent 360° view of the land and seascape surrounding them—the chalk cliffs as the armada set sail and the French coast as their ships arrived off the Normandy coast. Poised between the cliffs and the coast was the awe-inspiring panorama of the military build-up, the majesty and power of the Allied Forces that stirred the mind and heart. For the troops who arrived for D-Day 1 in June, the initial scene represented the calm before the storm of war. But by D-Day 3 in July, the shoreline of Omaha Beach had changed forever, physically yet also in hearts and minds worldwide. Tony never had the opportunity to appreciate its pristine state.

The landing craft moved away from the staging area in turn amid the natural mist of the channel and the grime of war. As they moved closer to the coast, Tony could taste and smell the struggle. He tracked military action on land in the form of incoming enemy artillery fire and crossfire in the distance. He completed a different type of 360° turn, witnessing the nature and signs of war. He viewed sunken battleships and burned-out tanks against the backdrop of the sea and sky. Barrage balloons floated in the atmosphere, watching for German craft as the troops moved. He took in the rocky cliffs and the German blockhouses. The perspective on war, the impact of war, was unrivaled. Straight ahead, he watched the first of the landing forces in his contingent drop from their craft and proceed to the shoreline, the waves lashing against them and their gear hampering them. Through a powerful scope, he traced their movement and took a deep breath when he saw some men advance and others succumbing to the force of the Channel. By then, he was familiar with amphibious operations and knew the risk and potential loss, fully aware that the U.S. had already experienced close to 100,000 casualties.

When Tony's unit assembled in the staging area prior to landing, they had a clear picture of the beach now saturated with the blood of war. Gone was the crystal-clear water that had gushed, unobstructed, to the shore in the past. Sunken landing craft and jagged metal shards rose out of the Channel defiling the curvature of its life and flow. Grease and mechanical fluids continued to bubble from below, clouding the clear blue water. Debris of different types, from personal effects to rounds of ammunition, shells, and rubbish debased the waterfront. The bodies of soldiers and numerous personal packs floated on the waterline.

Tony waited two full days in queue in the Channel, lamenting the destruction, the atmosphere it created, and the sounds of war he heard non-stop before seeing them firsthand. From his vantage point on the landing craft, he served as onlooker of the war rather than the participant he would become within minutes. Feeling divorced from the war, he studied it objectively through a critical lens as a journalist might. His method brought the reporter Luca to mind, and the fond memories of his reminiscences warmed Tony's thoughts, enabling him to stand strong and confront the reality of the battle he was about to enter.

Units in the division were dropping into the water quickly, their craft moving along to clear space for the next group. Tony was now in queue, and he could hear the call to "move along" from the vessel ahead. His boat was tossing and turning, rolling forward and back, and pulling sideways as it positioned for the drop. The speed with which the soldiers disembarked was swift, movement was ongoing and regimented. There was no room for hesitation, and when the space before Tony cleared, he jumped into the churning water. How different it was to experience rather than observe the drop. The weight of his wet gear surprised Tony yet again even though he had dropped many times. He felt a strong pull downward and surely could have faltered, had an appealing vision of his future not appeared before his eyes, causing him to refocus and surface. In the turbulent water, he alternated between swimming and striding. Close to the shoreline, he gasped and heaved himself forward, falling onto the sand and into his new war.

Tony was alive and alert, accounting for everything around him—the troops, the incoming vehicles, the injured soldiers, and enemy fire. He was confronted with a cacophony of competing sounds that would have caused anxiety a few years ago for his younger self, a farm boy from the hills east of Rome. Supine, he willed himself to stand upright and move while also dodging enemy forces. Unbeknown to him, he was crawling into a defining moment of his life.

The scene on land could have been logistically chaotic, yet the reverse occurred—a masterfully orchestrated undertaking exemplifying the dogged determination of the U.S. Army. Activity and movement were constant no matter where Tony turned, except for the injured awaiting treatment. The scene depicted a raw and realistic snapshot of war, one that would make any soldier wary.

Tony scanned his surroundings as he crouched and ran to wedge himself into the column of troops that was forming. Formation carried on non-stop. One completed column of soldiers was followed by another as soldiers continued to arrive. Others were already setting up a garrison, and more vehicles were filing in. Patton's 3rd Army was now positioning for the enduring battle against Axis Forces to liberate Western Europe. As the reality of their situation played out before them, a pressing question entered the minds of many, *Will we succeed?* While the question manifested, fear did not. They were ready to fight for the world as though they were fighting for their families and homes.

The enemy fire that greeted the July contingent of Allied Forces had been stalemated for over six weeks. It continued to rage, and the situation had become tense. Under the supervision of Lieutenant General Omar Bradley, the battle plan was rewritten, and Operation Cobra, a comprehensive long-term war plan that culminated in the fall of Berlin, was born. Etched in that plan, structurally and chronologically, was the blueprint for the 3rd Army's bold, brilliant, and feverish campaign for liberating Western Europe. A 271-day run of non-stop predominantly victorious combat, that massive field campaign advanced far and fast, penetrating enemy forces in less time than any other army in history. It signified the fulfillment of the vision for war born in the Louisiana Maneuvers and at The Desert Training Center that altered forever the conceptual framework for combat in the U.S. Army.

Patton's 3rd Army deployed immediately, first for construction work nearby and then moving on to France. Like most soldiers in the group, Tony was part of a re-constituted unit and was therefore surrounded by unfamiliar faces. Many of the troops were recent arrivals directly from the U.S., replacement personnel, or those coming by way of Italy or other international locations. That meant the group varied in age, experience, and place of origin. They traveled as a mass into France and would not learn their units and assignments until they were ready to disperse to different locations.

First, they traveled on foot to the cliffs, scaling them and then descending toward a field. There they shed some of their gear, received their weapons, and completed a two-day stint to level trees and clear land for road construction. Afterwards, they boarded the trucks of the Red Ball Express, the convoy system supporting the rapid movement of U.S. troops to the front. Along their route, they experienced firsthand more of the war's destruction. They saw people wandering around, seemingly lost amid rubble, but who reacted with excitement when they realized U.S. troops were arriving.

In time, the 3rd Army arrived in Le Mans, where they boarded a freight train. Tony stood in a coal car whose floors were covered with inches of grit. Thus far, on the day of their arrival, which had become a long day, the soldiers had waded to the shore, muddied themselves in the forest, sweat their way up the cliffs, and were now coated with black dust. Their "accommodations" were the best they had since leaving England for the staging area. Riding along, they continued to see the pattern of destruction. The ruins in the towns and cities they passed through told stories of charming historical places that a year or two ago would have been prosperous, thriving, and peaceful. To their surprise, they skirted the boulevards of Paris, something Tony did not expect, and despite his weariness and the smell of death on the outskirts of town, he was buoyed by his good fortune to see major European landmarks. He vowed to return to see the city and gave himself a few moments, a respite for the mind, to think about how his world had expanded since he left Italy.

His daydreaming went on to occupy his mind until they reached Nancy, France, a bustling city. On the other side of it they unloaded in a large field that had been fashioned into a camp. Massive Army tents consumed the grounds and informative signs in English dotted the land to direct the troops. The soldiers learned their assignments there through roll call. Those crossed several divisions and units, which meant the soldiers would once again split up and re-organize, an experience that had become all too common. Tony was assigned to an armored infantry battalion in the 6th Armored Division of Patton's 3rd Army. Since he had been involved in training as both trainer and trainee primarily in armor, he expected the classification.

The roll call and assignments concluded, the large contingent of soldiers re-organized by divisions into battalions, companies, and platoons departing the area through various modes, their individual war stories now following different paths. For the 6th Armored Division, which in time acquired the nickname "Super SIXth", the race across France to Germany had begun. Like most divisions participating in what became a nine-month operation, they advanced with breakneck speed and achieved great success. The Division's dizzying path began on July 25, 1944, as they traveled southeast to Le Mesnil, France, where Canadian and British forces had successfully secured bridges, making the 6$^{th's}$ passage through the 8th Infantry Division possible. From there, the 6th backtracked traveling a few hours to Northwest France, where they cleared the heights near Le Bingard to secure a foothold across the Seine River near Pont de la Roque on July 29. The division then continued to Avranches, France, their destination by way of Granville, a coveted port town in the northwestern part of the country. Throughout that thirty-four-mile trek, they dodged persistent enemy fire that involved convoluted detours. Their pace and the many distractions made for a hazardous two-day journey.

Just as the American troops sought the enemy, the enemy pursued the Americans. In the countryside and through the forests, the scale of the battle forced troops on both sides to separate into small groups or sometimes advance on their own. They experienced the risk of capture at those times, if not injury or death. That type of warfare increased as they continued the race. With casualties and imprisonment frequent, the size of the 6th and other divisions began to dwindle. Numerous impediments hindered their progress. The most frequent were incidents involving the escape of enemy prisoners of war. When in Avranches, the 6th learned about escapees from a prisoner of war camp in Granville. To avoid conflict and risk, they bypassed the village's port due to its proximity to the holding area and traveled through the city center instead. The tanks pounded the streets, and their passage was heard from a considerable distance though they were not pursued or harmed. They were in Allied territory, the port being an exception.

They returned to Avranches that night, to relieve the 4th Armored Division, and secured nearby bridges the next day.

In mid-August 1944, the 6th Armored Division moved approximately 125 miles west to Lorient and was relieved by the 94th Infantry Division in September. Concurrently, from August 7th to September 19th, sectors of the division participated in the Battle of Brest, France, a port city close to the western tip of the peninsula that transported tons of cargo for the Allies. Following the successful liberation of Brest and the clearing of the Brittany Peninsula, the 6th turned east, cutting across France and reaching the Saar River in the northeastern part of the country. In November 1944, they continued, crossing the Nied River on the 11th and 12th of the month fighting strong opposition forces. December brought the 6th to the German border, where they established and maintained defensive positions in the vicinity of Saarbrucken.

On December 23rd, the Division traveled forty-two miles west from Saarbrucken to Metz, France, to take part in the Battle of the Bulge, also known as the Ardennes Counteroffensive. That confrontation was a major operation on the part of the Germans, the bulge referring to the protrusion of German Troops into an area occupied by the U.S. Taking place from December 16, 1944, to January 25, 1945, the battle ensued in the vast densely forested Ardennes region of Belgium.[10]

During that assault, the Division became heavily engaged in the battle for Bastogne, taking on not only the enemy but the elements as well. Snow and ice blanketed the forest, impeding their progress whether on foot or in a vehicle of any type. U.S. troops were seriously outnumbered and further disadvantaged by the swath of land they covered.

---

10 Lone Sentry, Photos, Articles, & Research on the European Theater in World War II. Brest to Bastogne: The Story of the 6th Armored Division. https://www.lonesentry.com/gi_stories_booklets/6tharmored/index.html. Accessed February 16, 2021.

They battled on the move, covered by tanks. Their attrition was high, caused not only by injury and death, but capture and desertion as well. Though outnumbered ten to one at the onset of the engagement, U.S. troops eventually prevailed and drove the enemy back across the Our River into Germany by late January. The soldiers' lamentations following the assault mourned the dead and lost and reacted to the heart-wrenching destruction of the most beautiful forest they had ever seen.

Having pushed themselves beyond all limits in a confrontation that appeared lost before it began, the troops welcomed a short period of rehabilitation they were granted, but they became restless well before it ended. They had the fire in them to continue aggressively toward Germany, and they resumed with that goal in mind. They were close and realized their reprieve had served them well in providing the rest and renewal needed to press forward. A few days after resuming the assault, the 6th penetrated the Siegfried Line, also known as the Westwall, a defensive line the Germans had built in 1930. From there they passed through the village of Prum and reached the Rhine River at Worms, also in Germany, on March 21st. There they set up a counter reconnaissance screen along the town's west bank.

The Division's convoy continued into Germany, crossing the Rhine at Oppenheim on March 25th and rolling on to Frankfurt. While advancing, they simultaneously routed the enemy. Their travel was rarely direct. They navigated for their purposes, diverting, departing, and then returning from another direction to take on the enemy, going off road in pursuit. There was unspoken excitement in what they were doing and some guilt for their exhilaration. They continued by crossing the Main River and capturing Bad Nauheim to continue eastward to Muhlhausen. On April 4th and 5th, 1945, the Division captured that town after repelling a light counterattack. It then set off on a 60-mile trek across the Saale River to Buchenwald, the notorious

German Concentration Camp where Allied prisoners of war were also held. There the troops fulfilled their mission to free the prisoners. The Division raced on, taking Leipzig and crossing the Mulde River at Rochlitz on April 13th. The troops stopped there and awaited the arrival of the Russian Army. The two opposing forces, Russia and the Allies, then held their defensive positions along the Mulde River until the end of the hostilities in Europe.

Collectively in the race across France, the accomplishments of Patton's 3rd Army reverberated with the triumphs of a nine-month-long offensive sandwiched between the Invasion of Normandy and the arrival of the Russian Army. Fulfilling their mission in that abbreviated time frame, the troops crossed 24 major rivers and innumerable streams. They conquered more than 82,000 square miles of territory including 1,500 cities and towns and some 12,000 uninhabited places. In battle, they captured 956,000 enemy combatants and killed or wounded over 500,000 others.

Looking back, marshalling for the crossing had been flawless, an unparalleled exercise in logistics. Equally impressive were the landings along the coast, synchronized, executed in turn, troops fanning out to reach different destinations with the hope of punctuating the end of the war. U.S. Forces had come a long way since Operation Torch. Different countries in Europe—France, Belgium, Luxembourg, Germany, Austria, and Czechoslovakia—witnessed and attested to the accomplishments of Patton's 3rd Army, celebrating him as one of the U.S. Army's and America's greatest commanding Generals in the liberation of Europe.[11]

The pace of the 6th's race through France was dazed and frenetic. Fighting around the clock was the unit's tradition. The spirited troops

---

11   Lida Mayo. *United States Army in World War II, The Ordnance Department: On Beachhead and Battlefront*, Chapter 15. Center of Military History, United States Army, Washington DC, 1968.

embraced war as an all-day, everyday endeavor, which made for a unique and cohesive fighting force. They sacrificed their personal time, hope for free time, reveries, and lives for the race. They were recognized as one significant part of the larger relentless campaign to take down the enemy.

The exhilaration the soldiers experienced as they rushed forward, their buoyance at victory, and their overall youthful sense of adventure were offset by haunting moments on the battlefields and the brunt of the war in the countries they entered. Cities and towns lay in ruins from incessant bombing. They lacked running water, and food sources were scarce. Loss of life in communities and on the battlefield and the discovery of the camps represented unspeakable horrors that would never be forgotten. With each day and further advancement into occupied areas, the horrors of war had accumulated, yet the small amount of time off the battlefield limited the space soldiers had to sort through the events and outcomes of war. Only with the passage of time would they come to terms with what had occurred.

By 1945 the war was coming to a close for all soldiers but for those who would remain to participate in restoration and recovery. There was a feeling of unrest among the troops. Quite simply, they wanted to go home. By then the number of troops in Europe had increased significantly, and the efforts to repatriate them presented a herculean task. The soldiers had arrived in Europe in stages, staggered by the phasing of the war. In 1945, the scope of the required exodus made an abrupt return impossible. Departures lagged, leading soldiers to protest and demand their immediate return—a request that subsequently involved members of Congress speaking on behalf of their constituents. What developed from those activities was a point system for scheduling troop departures. For example, married men received more points and thus an earlier departure than those who were single and without a family.

The plan was well-received because it assured the troops that leadership was doing *something* to get them back to the U.S.

For Tony, one of the greatest lessons he learned off the field was that respect for authority comes with age and maturation. The positives of the long, drawn-out withdrawal from Europe outweighed the negatives. Tony thought of the strong sense of camaraderie that had quietly developed among members of the 6th during the nine months they fought side by side against the enemy. What he appreciated was that the bonding was sincere and came naturally as a product of time and circumstance. He and his fellow soldiers shadowed, looked out for, and saved one another. They acted not out of personal friendships, for their rotations were frequent and their interpersonal exchanges few as a result. Their relationships existed on a higher plane powered by loyalty, regard, and values. Many of them would not have made it to their separation from the military if one of their buddies had not moved them out of the line of fire, pulled them into a foxhole, or carried them to the final line.

Life on the battlefield was a matter of survival. And when a person had a face-to-face encounter with the enemy, they readily undertook an examination of self that gauged the level of goodness within them. In short, in their own way, according to age, disposition, life experience, and many other factors, each soldier in the 6th was transformed by their service and that experience bonded them to their fellow soldiers for life. No one knew the war as they did, fighting it together for their country, for Europe, and for the preservation of their own lives and way of life in the United States. Only with the passage of time would they come to understand how and why they changed. The family and friends who welcomed them home, though, immediately realized their loved ones had changed, some dramatically, as a result of their war-time experiences.

Chapter 28

Tony's War, The Stories of a War Hero

He ran under a sky of enemy fire. For a few moments, he felt as though he stood outside himself and could read his soul. An ordination transpired. Misgivings and self-doubt gave way to confidence and courage. The ridge in sight, he dropped to the ground and clawed his way to the summit.

During Tony's years in the U.S. Army from 1941-1945, the total number of troops grew from 1,500,000 to 8,300,000. History and life itself—at home, in the workplace, and in veterans' groups—have shown that though soldiers shared numerous experiences during the war, each of them returned with adventures, stories, and insights they regarded as exclusive to them and no other.

Tony's stories grew out of the limited casual moments he had. Those were simple occasions—an evening playing cards with his fellow soldiers or a respite when informal gatherings and conversation were possible. The soldiers' exchanges always gravitated to how the war was changing them. Many times, their discussions were light, and they acknowledged and joked about the habits they were forming, for better or for worse. Some of those were ironclad. For example, the soldiers were instructed to turn the radio in a vehicle off before the vehicle itself was switched off. That practice became locked in Tony's mind, and he brought it home with him. Another lifelong habit he adopted was to never have the gas level in a vehicle drop below the one-half mark. That, too, was a guideline for the soldiers that made sense given their circumstances. For the rest of his life, Tony lived by many of the rituals he acquired in the Army and even passed them on to family and friends.

There were also the unexpected golden moments when Tony crossed paths with his Italian cousins, brothers-in-law, friends from Connecticut, and others he met along the way who were also stationed in Europe, like Jack, who enjoyed the gatherings the first time he ventured into one and was considered an honorary Italian in the group, even though he had red hair. Those meetings occurred whenever the various divisions, battalions, and companies of the 3rd Army convened in a designated staging area to transact the business of war—logistics, re-organization, non-critical medical care, or the distribution of resources and information. During those dream-like encounters, the group enjoyed gatherings so warm and familiar that for a short while they all felt they were back in the U.S. in the comfort of their homes.

On those occasions, the men reunited for whatever time was granted to them—a few hours or even a day or two. One time they were together for four days. Family was family in the minds of the Italian immigrants fighting for America. Families could be trusted, and a person never held back in their discussions and conversations. Rather, they spoke heart-to-heart. When in each other's presence the young Italian American soldiers and their friends did just that. They started by peeling off the war's patina of violence and grit. They returned to their humble ways ready to confront the war's haunting nature as well as the challenges and fears each one of them faced—together. Often finding those unexpected gifts of time in the most unusual of places, like a farm or a playing field, they also shared family news, memories, and their hopes for the future.

Their stories about Italy's uniformed Youth Group gave them a unique perspective on the war and haunting feelings of a different nature. Throughout their growing-up years, they had discussed the organization, questioning its tactics in the training of boys and young men. Leadership was way too heavy-handed, especially with the youngest paramilitary "soldiers." Given the rigor of their training in the Youth Group, the Italian American men had never imagined that they would someday break their ties with the program and fight for the U.S. rather than Italy. During their time together on the battlefields of Europe, Tony, his family members, and friends had the unique and welcome experience of discussing the complicated differences between their paramilitary training in Italy and present service in the U.S. Army. They understood each other's views on those topics, especially the impact on children, as no one else could, neither their fellow soldiers nor their families in America. There was a strong sense of duality in their lives, eclipsed further by the participation in the Invasion of Sicily by some of them. The insights the soldiers gleaned from their experiences affected them psychologically and morally. Their principal means for sorting through their stories would always be the open and honest discussions they were able to have.

The group's stories lasted a lifetime and beyond. When they met by chance, they offset the seriousness by resorting to the quaint and goofy Italian humor of their childhood. The stories about those incidents were told repeatedly over decades to the point where every family member could recite them word for word. The story Tony recalled most often involved his brother-in-law Antonio who was also assigned to the 3rd Army though in a different division. They caught up with each other more often than expected. The most memorable "joke" from those occasions had Tony playing cards when Antonio arrived. Rather than walking up to Tony and greeting him, Antonio positioned himself to face Tony's back and approached quietly. When he reached Tony, Antonio tickled Tony's ear lightly. At first Tony thought an insect hovered by his ear and he attempted to brush it away. The touch occurred again, and Tony did the same. The third time, Tony turned his head to see the insect but saw his brother-in-law instead. The touch occurred again, the soldiers laughed, and Tony was overjoyed to see his good friend. In the end, the "fun" part of the war for Tony was that fraction of time when his cousins, brothers-in-law, and friends in Patton's 3rd Army gathered for any time granted to them. Post-war, they shared decades together, rehashing and reliving their war.

A different group of stories grew out of Tony's fascination with all facets of the army—the uniforms, protocols, logistics, equipment, training, and scope. He told grand stories of events unimaginable to family members at home, such as seeing the 4,500 ships positioned in the English Channel for the Invasion of Normandy, the experience of liberating Paris, hearing General Eisenhower speak to the troops, driving the lead Sherman tank in an invasion, barely surviving on a landing boat off the coast of Africa, and his arrival to Buchenwald. Tall tales that were real tales, exciting and grand because of the storyteller himself. Along with those were the magnificent drawings of war scenes crafted by his Italian hand that rivalled the sketches of Leonardo di Vinci.

Along with day-to-day activity on the battlefield, Tony collected a group of meaningful life-changing stories. Those involved joy, threatening scenarios, the thrill of victory, and the horrors of war. They truly belonged to Tony alone. The first took place in September 1944, when the 6th Armored Division's sizable convoy navigated the country roads in France on a carefully planned scouting mission shaped by intelligence reports. Reaching their destination meant handling or dodging the firefights their presence attracted. They wove their way to their destination, sometimes proceeding directly with boldness and purpose and other times pausing to strategize about re-directing the convoy's path. Through those daily ground missions, Tony developed the patience to deal with the war's fluidity. His circumstances were ever changing, and he learned soon enough that anything could happen. Such was the case when he was assigned a dangerous mission.

The day's objectives consisted of two intertwining goals, the first to drive the enemy from their positions and the other to scout for a large ammo supply that was said to be hidden in the area. With three men shadowing him and a full team behind them, Tony was to scale the steep hillside, reach and cross its crest, and then infiltrate one of the enemy's most deeply concealed hideaways. Well before Tony exited the convoy to undertake his mission, the division's combat units rolled toward the enemy's positions at a slight angle firing rapidly to drive them back toward the west. That movement aimed to open the area so that Tony could advance.

Firing continuously, the division pressed forward even though there was heavy return fire. While both sides were engaged in free fire and aggressive maneuvering, each following its own plan, the element of surprise the U.S. had planned for was achieved. Artillery flew in both directions, the exchanges continuous. The desired outcome unfolded slowly, the Germans shifting northwest rather than approaching directly. They hugged their side of the ridge, retreating from their hidden supplies as hoped. The Germans responded to the movement of U.S. troops as expected, opening a path for Tony's scouting mission.

Simultaneously, U.S. Forces continued shifting their movements to parallel their side of the ridge, pursue the German soldiers, and move equipment west and other supplies northwest to trap the enemy.

The path for achieving the mission appeared clear, and it was time to execute. What occurred from that point convinced Tony that no day during their 271-day trek across France to Germany would ever be routine. Adrenaline pumping, he moved rapidly, hopping out of the jeep, gaining his footing, and scooting toward the trees. Tony ran under a hail of enemy fire, so intently that he felt as though he stood outside himself and could read his soul. An ordination transpired. Misgivings and self-doubt gave way to confidence and courage. The ridge in sight, he dropped to the ground and crawled to the summit. He gained distance while also maintaining his movement as he made his way toward the ridge. The team followed behind while the onslaught beyond the ridge continued to drive the enemy back.

Tony wasted no time in getting to his destination. The trenches he encountered were more expansive than any report indicated. With care he negotiated the ditches watching his step and remaining outside any passageway. Using his binoculars, he scouted around the perimeter and realized he had found the weapons cache, which was larger than anticipated and could easily wipe out all Allied Forces in the region. The backup team arrived, assuming responsibility for the site. While they secured it, Tony awaited instructions for rejoining the larger group. A dizzying round of actions followed, all reflecting the chaos of war, sometimes seemingly well-orchestrated and other times completely spontaneous. Having received the coordinates for their return to the unit, Tony and the cover team dodged non-stop gunfire and artillery the entire way. Meanwhile, the unit continued the ground battle to distract the Germans, took prisoners, and prevented any enemy troops from returning to the munitions site. That cache of weapons became a busy work area, for the artillery company had arrived to examine, inventory, and dismantle the armaments as quickly as possible. In the meantime, the parallel team pursuing the Germans was positioned to capture them.

For the remainder of the day, Tony revisited his mission and his astonishment over what he had been ordered to do and succeeded in carrying out. Several days later, the story became real, a cornerstone in his Army experience. He received a commendation for bravery and was awarded the Silver Star, the 3rd highest award bestowed on a living soldier, one earned for valor and gallantry against an enemy of the United States of America.

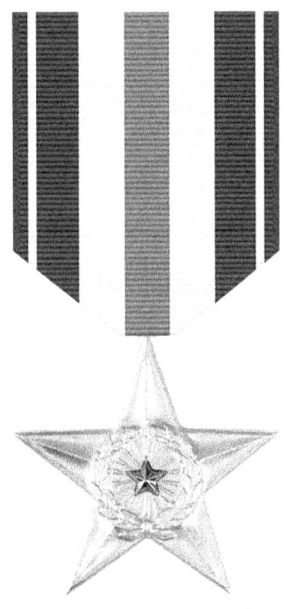

The U.S. Silver Star medal, awarded for valor and gallantry in combat

The complexity of the race manifested in the most powerful and unforgettable way in Spring 1945, in conjunction with the Division's general mission of advancing through Europe, combing the countryside for evidence of the enemy, and mopping up resistance while also taking on another special mission.

The war was winding down, the enemy was in disarray and erratic, and the Allies' mission began to evolve towards liberation and restoration. A facility of great importance lay ahead, but first the 6th needed to clear area roads to access the designated site. They removed debris and engaged with the enemy in the process, which was the essence of their daily routine. The division's destination that day was Buchenwald in the east central region of Germany, one of the first and largest concentration camps established in that country. Its internees were Jews, Slavs—predominantly Poles, the physically disabled, the mentally ill, freemasons, common criminals, political prisoners, and prisoners of war—to include U.S. troops. All prisoners were forced laborers assigned to the local arms factories. Conditions at the camp and the factories were said to be more brutal than those at other facilities. Prisoners were exposed to cold and ice inside and out without protection. The food supply was scant for the numbers held, sanitation was lacking, and executions were common.

On the day the camp was to be liberated, Tony's division secured the route to it. They ferreted out enemy forces, possible hiding places, traps, and prisoners. As the campaign ran its course, rooting the enemy out was becoming increasingly hazardous because German forces often occupied homes and used them to hide their presence. Along their route, they encountered and overcame enemy forces, taking many prisoners as well as freeing civilians. The division's medical units and military police traveled with them. Their mission was not only to reach Buchenwald safely but also to ensure the liberation of the prisoners, the imprisonment of the camp's staff, and the protection of the organizations providing vital support. Among those were neutral agents of the country of Switzerland and the transport it provided to resettle the prisoners and the Red Cross.

The 6th maintained its readiness as it continued toward the camp. It was on full alert, the latest communication about their mission describing the situation as chaotic because the enemy expected the arrival of U.S. Forces. The soldiers were riding into what would become the most emotional and extraordinary humanitarian effort any of them had experienced for the whole of the war. Realizing the unique nature of that mission, they plunged into it, at which point their story and that of the camp prisoners at Buchenwald intertwined.

What lay ahead in the distance, well before the camp itself, was at first barely recognizable. Debris lined the road leading to the facility. From afar the soldiers could not identify the objects obstructing the roadway. Binoculars came out immediately, and the convoy moved forward to obtain as clear an assessment as possible of the situation to formulate the best approach for handling it. The binoculars picked up surreal images, the lenses revealing horrific impressions of skeletal human figures moving about in a haze or lying in the road. They were not enemy combatants but rather exceptionally frail individuals. The rescue call was given, soldiers leapt from their vehicles and ran toward the figures, many of them deceased. The military police took charge of safeguarding the victims, weapons were deployed to secure the area, and the medics ran forward, equipment on their backs. Though the soldiers' minds froze momentarily in response to the images, their bodies did not. Amidst the haunting images, the troops checked for signs of life, covered the deceased, reached out to lift the living, and carried them to the medics. The prisoners had been released and they had tried to run to find safety. Some made it. Others did not.

The silence among the troops was deafening. They were engaged in the most intense life-saving effort of their war, attempting to save the true victims. They radioed headquarters, the Swiss nationals, and the Red Cross. They improvised, setting up two recovery sites, one roadside on the long winding street and the other in the camp where they were headed. A unit-wide effort was underway on the road, with more troops on site and soon to arrive. The convoy continued toward the camp, some soldiers running ahead instead. The imposing main structure confronted them, and they felt the chill of pure evil. Small barracks stood to the right side of the headquarters. There the prisoners lived without light, heat, or plumbing. The soldiers on the ground tread carefully toward the buildings, not knowing what they would find. It was not outside the realm of possibility to find themselves caught in a set-up, a ruse that could get them all killed. The closer they approached, the stronger the stench of illness and death hanging in the air.

The soldiers entered and met with a group of ghost-like figures with haunting eyes and fear written on their faces. The men pointed to the flags on their uniforms, and there was the desired burst of relief. The rescuers broke into teams—one group pursuing the staff in the facility, who were young, unprepared, and quickly captured. The other team fanned out in the main building and into the prisoner shacks, taking their time to walk through them. At all times they were ready to respond to attack, but their focus was the people. For the victims, the soldiers brought good will, distributed blankets and water, and offered the power of touch, albeit wincing within about the fragility of the prisoners. They came across children, handed them souvenirs, and assessed the situation, noting the location of the ill. The Swiss and Red Cross arrived to provide care. Their know-how and the order they gently imposed was as much a godsend as the liberation was.

That day, the 6th's mission presented the young troops with haunting inhumanity they were forced to process. The horrors of the camp became public following the liberation, and the soldiers felt vindicated as a result in a broader sense. They were granted additional time at the camp to pay respects at its hallowed grounds of suffering and death. At their next respite, their commanding officer lauded them, citing facts about the camp that had come to light. Between 1937 and 1945, 56,545 of the 280,000 prisoners who passed through the camp and its 139 subcamps died.[12] Following the report, the troops honored the dead a second time.

---

12   Buchenwald Concentration Camp. https://en.wikipedia.org/wiki/Buchenwald_concentration_camp, accessed March 19, 2021.

For close to two decades after the war, Tony mourned the atrocities at Buchenwald, questioning humanity and any possible justification for such heinous acts. His tortured thoughts were assuaged in an unexpected way in the early 60s when one of his children, a teenager, started reading a book required at school. Entitled *Night* and written by the distinguished author Elie Wiesel, who survived Buchenwald as a teenager though his father passed shortly before the liberation, the book drew Tony's attention. And he read it more than once. The story took him to that day in April 1945 and Wiesel's heartbreaking story about his father and him that was horrific and haunting to Tony while also instructive. Wiesel's compelling story heightened Tony's awareness of evil in a personal and relatable way, exposing Buchenwald for what it was. The intimacy of seeing and reading Wiesel's words and gaining full knowledge through them never allowed Tony to accept or forgive what occurred. Rather, connecting with a prisoner who was at the camp when the 6th liberated it transformed Tony. It gave him the peace and clarity to live his life in a manner that honored the souls of all the dead, injured, and abused that were mistreated or tortured by evil forces in the world.

The third threshold event in Tony's war involved a milestone of peace. It took place on July 4, 1945, though it would not have occurred without the three months' combat that took place beforehand and a hazardous march through ruins and rubble that presaged the war's end. The defining word for the celebration on that July 4th was *liberation*. Nothing soothed the souls of U.S. troops more than freeing places and people that had been occupied or captured during the war.

The ceremonial event followed the invasion of Germany, the Allied Victory, and the occupation of Berlin. Its purpose was to recognize the establishment of the city's American Sector under the leadership of General Omar Bradley. With fanfare and the presence of the U.S.

Forces who had raced across Europe to liberate countries and territories, the national anthem of the United States of America was performed, inspiring the troops at a time when they needed affirmation most. The people of Berlin cheered, exhibiting the will to look forward rather than dwell on the past. The uplifting day served the people and American Forces, creating an irrevocable bond between the soldiers and their war.

Whenever Tony revisited his war story, he also reflected on the war in an abstract sense —what he carried within and took from it, in addition to measurable accomplishments. He had strong feelings about how his military service broadened his perspective, directed his thinking, and informed his future. Since Tony developed the capacity to be objective as a soldier, he acquired a perspective on the military that enabled him to examine its worth as an outsider would. That ability manifested most frequently in his view on operations—how well units carried out their missions—and the quality of the leaders who directed the troops to that end. The latter shaped not only his path while in the service, but it also exhibited values and qualities Tony then cultivated to form what he thought to be the best version of himself.

As chance had it, Tony's war story coincided with the presence of two great military strategists of the time, Eisenhower and Patton. It was the case that either of the two generals, or both together, served in some capacity in every one of Tony's assignments but for Basic Training and his deployment to Curaçao. Tony was honored to serve under those masterminds in strategic warfare.

Tony learned from the two men because they were visible, they interacted with the troops, and in truth they exuded more warmth than his immediate commanding officers did. Tony was an avid observer of war, who entered the war keenly aware of its historical underpinnings.

He concentrated on military movements and tactics. He read everything that came his way about the war and was well informed. Getting to know war for what it was, he regarded Eisenhower and Patton as larger than life. They were *the figures* of the war whom he never forgot. Among the stories Tony told for the rest of his life were those in which he became close enough to the two men to appreciate their spirit, strategic minds, drive, and determination. That proximity occurred during briefings; through written correspondence that the men, especially Eisenhower, distributed; their hands-on involvement in training—Eisenhower in the Louisiana Maneuvers, where he shook the hand of every soldier in training, and Patton, who participated in the Desert War Games, lifting the soldiers' spirits and commitment, and refining their perspectives on war. The two generals were influential in what Tony regarded as his small existence for inspiring excellence and assimilation into American society. As an immigrant, Tony did indeed transform himself to become an American citizen one day, and he would always attribute his successes, in part, to the men he met in the military, placing Eisenhower and Patton at the top of his list as models of citizenship, duty, and loyalty.

During the 271 consecutive days of infantry and armored engagements through France and into Germany, which included the Liberation of Paris, Tony saw leadership in many forms and was inspired by his observations. His fellow soldiers hoisted the wounded, carrying them to a safe spot, sat with the dying, aggressively pursued the enemy, and performed armored maneuvers with precision. Underlying those and many other examples were the characteristics of leadership—know-how, initiative, strategy, implementation, courage, compassion, and humility. Having received the prestigious Silver Star, Tony forced himself to step out of his modest disposition and consider the actions that explained the recognition he received. Until he needed to carry out that mission for his Division, Tony had little understanding of his own capabilities. Only after the war could he begin to understand his response on the battlefield. He acted with expedience, precision, mental acuity, and courage. Never during those moments did he think about glory, winning, prestige, or distinction. His actions were not about him; they were about giving an advantage to his unit and saving lives in the long haul. For the rest of his life, Tony would reflect on how the war had impacted the trajectory of his life. What path would Tony's life have followed had he never left Italy and served in U.S. Forces?

One of the heartwarming insights Tony gleaned from his war-time experience was his realization that some aspects of life and living are the same around the world regardless of location, language, and cultural and religious practices. No matter where he traveled, he saw family and community as a strong bond. Families spent time together, though in circumstances different from what he knew and practiced. He felt the commonalities offered a means for people of different cultures to relate to one another. Another observation was the fear he saw in the eyes of many—families, soldiers, religious leaders—and that witness troubled him. While he was committed to his wartime service and felt he had proven himself, a question about the "why" of war haunted him and would for a long time. Why were the people of the world subjected to fear, loss, injury, dislocation, insult, and destruction? He would re-visit that question for the remainder of his life as one military conflict after another emerged somewhere in the world jeopardizing the lives of many.

Tony experienced different climates and standards of living in his deployments. When he arrived in Casablanca, he was surprised by the hues of the landscape in that sector of the world. He found the earth tones so beautifully calming and the warm dry air soothing. He saw little if any green, a shade that surrounded his life story, as he rode in a convoy across Morocco. Despite the differences in what Tony knew about the environment, atmosphere, wildlife, foods, and dwellings in places he visited, he saw a reverence toward nature and the land no matter where he went. That beautiful observation moved him, allowing him to sense a connection with everyone he met.

From village to town, in rural and urban areas in the three continents he visited, Tony saw joy, passion, generosity, warmth, and friendship in the eyes of the people he met unless they were under duress. He connected with the eyes of war—a woman bleeding on the streets of Paris, wounded on the cusp of the liberation, whom he gently lifted and carried to an ambulance. He peered into eyes like his—the eyes of Italian soldiers in Northern Africa and Sicily, many of whom he took into custody as the enemy though they were neighbors and compatriots. The haunting eyes on the gaunt faces of the starved, those in hiding, and those confined in Nazi camps. The plagued eyes of the emaciated, the vacant eyes of the soldier he carried over his shoulder, and eyes of fear that looked to him with a glimmer of hope when he entered the camp.

The faces of the war, the face-to-face encounters, transformed Tony, causing him to re-commit himself to the sense of goodness and kindness that characterized his nature and growing up years before the Youth Group, a precursor to his war experience. Looking back at what he achieved during the war, he would not have wanted his childhood and growing years to have played out any differently than they did. He realized he was meant to be in the U.S. and enlist in its Army. What he saw and learned during the war altered his life and person, making his heart larger than it was the day he enlisted.

Part VI
Forging an Identity

Chapter 29
Leaving Europe

The caravan was underway. The day was bright and beautiful, and a light crispness filled the air. Despite the sights and smells of war that traveled alongside them, the soldiers felt a sense of liberation. The convoy symbolized the first phase of their separation from warfare, their deliverance from the images that haunted them.

The soldiers were not idle while awaiting their orders. They reconfigured frequently to serve as task teams for the recovery effort. In short, for the war-weary soldiers, victory did not mean departure. By then, most soldiers had seen enough of the war. Tony, whose tour exceeded four years, was weary and troubled by what he had witnessed. The sights and scenes lingered in his mind, gnawing at him. His days in combat remained fresh in his mind, the faces of his lost brothers and the people he liberated lived within him.

His overwhelming need was to go home, but he allowed loyalty to the service to override his personal feelings. He was indebted to the U.S. Military for granting him the honor of a lifetime, aiding his maturation, showing him the world, teaching him skills and know-how, and, most important, enabling others around the world to realize the principles of freedom, humanity, and honor. There was no place he would rather have been during the past four years, despite the sacrifice and pain, than on the field watching historical events unfold as a member of the Allied Forces. He lifted himself up and carried on with his orders to re-position equipment and dismantle temporary structures in Germany.

Five months passed before Tony received his demobilization orders. During that period, he worked with people and teams that came and went with the flow of the dismantling process. The transience was as unsettling then as it was during the first year in the Army. It was an element of the military he never fully adjusted to, and he was disappointed that it would be one of the final memories he would take home with him.

Tony learned he was scheduled to depart Europe on September 9, 1945, from Le Havre, France to Boston on the U.S.S. Marine Angel. That information lifted his morale and freed his mind to think and dream about the future though he regretted he would leave the continent without seeing his family in Italy. They lived twelve hours away and were accessible by so many modes of transportation, but travel was forbidden. Tony sighed and summoned an image of his parents and siblings to mind as he knew them when he left in 1938. He willed them to think of him at that moment and to know they were in his heart as he prepared to return to the U.S.

On the day before his departure, Tony left formation after the roll call and spent the remainder of the day handling personnel matters and packing his belongings. He went about the latter slowly, using it to revisit his experiences and open the door for his exit. The images of war still played as a movie in his mind. It played and replayed, and he needed to harness its influence. To that end, packing was therapeutic. He had two pieces to carry home—his pack and his large duffle bag. The pack would hold his most precious belongings and the duffle everything else, from clothing to supplies, uniforms, and large objects.

Tony found himself reflecting on the war in a new way as he gathered the items he planned to carry home. Getting started, he recalled Mama's words about the stories baggage tells, "*il bagaglio ha storie da raccontare*," she always said. He scanned the items before him, surprised by how much he had. Noticing they all held sentimental value, he understood what Mama had meant. There he was sorting objects, cherished treasures that had something to say about his four and a half years in the U.S. Army. Studying the collection, he fingered his dog tags, realizing he would soon store them never to be worn again. The chain and tags signs of strength and courage, they elicited a strong emotional response. As the definitive means by which injured or deceased soldiers were identified, each set of tags represented the essence of a person. Tony was lucky to be alive and wearing his, but that was not the case for all his buddies and the men and women he'd never known. Killed in action, lying empty on the fields or in hospital beds, maimed, fighting for their lives. How many times had he rushed to check on a fallen soldier to be either overjoyed by the pulse of a heartbeat or destroyed by the image of a body that could not possibly be alive?

With deep thoughts threatening to distract him, Tony turned to his belongings, looking among them for an item of equal significance that was positive and uplifting. He touched the many letters he had received—from his Aunt, his parents, and his siblings, friends in both Italy and the U.S., and his wonderful fiancée, Helena and her family. He was astonished by how frequently others had thought of him during his lengthy deployment. He received numerous letters, often in large quantities at intervals due to field conditions, the ongoing movement of troops, and of course the screening of all mail. For Tony, receiving a bundle of mail was a richness more valuable than gold. The stories, encouragement, and loving words in the letters sustained him. Then there were the photographs, both those he brought with him and those he snapped during the latter part of his tour. They fell into two categories—pictures of the people in his life, his fiancée, parents, and relatives—the joyful moments. The other group his war-time photos, the uplifting ones depicting camaraderie among the troops and sights in Europe. Others portrayed a world at war—fallen buildings, fallen bridges, fallen people.

Also among his belongings was his Silver Star, a precious symbol of the war documenting his determination to attack and conquer the enemy, protecting his unit and potential victims in the process. He was proud of that accomplishment and still could not believe he was returning with such an honor. He eyed a gold chain that held a Medal of St. Anthony, his namesake and the saint to whom Helena prayed every day. She gifted the item to him a few days before he left, telling him he would come back to her. He kept it with him every day of the war, tucked away in a secure pocket on his uniform shirt. In times of great need, he placed his hand over that pocket, praying for strength. The day before, when sorting through the uniforms he would turn in, he removed the medal from his clothing and stored it in his wallet for safekeeping during the journey home. Tony touched his gold chain and horn, his *Cornicello Portafortuna*, not wanting to neglect it. He had worn it throughout the war and would wear on his return to the states.

What could Tony say about the German gun and the German camera? One was transferred to him legally as a war trophy for his valor in locating the huge munitions cache. The pistol lay among the more dangerous weaponry he discovered. After inventoried, it was gifted to him by the authorities along with certification of his legal ownership.

The German camera was a treasure he purchased during training for the Race through France to Germany. It fulfilled his dream to create artifacts that would help him remember as well as understand his war experience after separating from the service. His photos told stories, keeping his journal alive when the demands of the Race made it impossible for him to jot down more than a few notes here and there.

The camera also hinted at better days and the opportunity to take a completely different set of photographs—the beautiful pictures of his future. He looked to joyful days when he would use the camera to document his return and snap pictures of grand places in New York as well as its remarkable skyline. He dreamed, of course, of photographing the people in his life in the U.S. and the beautiful beaches a few miles from where he lived. One yearning he could not fulfill was to return to his Italian community, his camera in hand, to take pictures of his family, friends, and village to hold him through the years. To fill the gnawing gap those thoughts created, he returned again to the pictures he had set in his mind in 1938. They were still there and always available to him.

Many times, Tony merely held his camera in his hand, examining its mechanics while also imagining the stories it would tell over time. During those moments, pictures came to him. He saw himself with Helena, watching children playing in gardens and around trees. The scene filled his heart with hope and joy.

His keepsakes included a map of Paris that a Salvation Army volunteer handed him for reference during the Liberation. He held on to it for the rest of his life as a reminder of the worst of days of war and the need to create a better world. The map surprisingly brought Tony's attention to the present, rather than the war behind him, because he planned to shop for Helena in Paris during his short furlough and needed some ideas. He would consult the map when he headed out, for the bones of Paris remained intact despite the war and the map remained the best reference for getting around the city.

Finally, two journals packed with notes, stories, drawings, and inserts of memorabilia. Neither belonged to his transatlantic crossing and aftermath. That subject matter rested at home in the journal he left at this Aunt's house. The two beautiful journals with him were gifts from Helena, who understood his commitment to write for his parents and the peace he experienced when writing. He had penned his thoughts on and off during the war and often read selected pages from either journal to map the war's progress, revisit an important event, or soothe his spirit. At the least during the darkest and most taxing hours, Tony maintained a calendar and timeline of his whereabouts to map his war and preserve the big picture of his service. Working with that shell of information, Tony was able to flesh out the events of war with clarity and chronicle them as he had intended. Tony thought about the path of his life thus far, proud, looking forward to returning home, and weary from the war. He continued to pack, the remainder of his belongings functional and lacking the deep sentimentality of his personal treasures. His work went quickly, and he spent the afternoon and evening saying goodbye and socializing through dinner.

The next day, the first in a relatively long journey home, Tony reported to the command center, signed out from the post, hoisted his duffle and pack, and proceeded to the convoy as directed. The detail was sizable, including additional soldiers from other military installations in the region. Many more soldiers stationed in other countries would also assemble in Paris for the same sailing.

The caravan was underway on a bright and beautiful day when the air crisply hinted about the onset of fall. Tony thought about the number of soldiers traveling that morning, realizing from experience that no two soldiers would be thinking about the war in the same way as they rode along. Maybe they would discuss the war retrospectively at some point on the ship, but for now everyone seemed lost in their thoughts, and Tony did the same.

Despite the sights and smells of war Tony encountered that morning, he finally felt the current of his personal liberation from the battleground. The convoy served as a symbol for him that marked the first phase of his separation from the war, deliverance from the brutal images that haunted him. Riding through the countryside of Rhineland, Tony witnessed the cost of war—the crushing damage to structures—buildings, houses, roads—the destroyed power infrastructure, and the absence of drinking water despite the chlorination that U.S. Forces were providing. The war's aftermath presented a new set of images that troubled his soul in a different way. He realized recovery and restoration would be a sobering process of heartbreaking discoveries. There was also the reality that the complete withdrawal of U.S. troops would not take place for a long, long time.

Tony felt the enduring U.S. presence provided a silver lining for the Europeans, who grieved over the devastation that turned historic and grand structures into trod-upon ruins. U.S. convoys had already begun to flood the roadways of Western Europe in an early period of recovery, following newly-formed missions and traveling back into the war zone while others were finally escaping it. Wherever the soldiers passed, whatever direction they were traveling, they were welcomed as heroes and liberators. Horns honked, people waved, and the flag of the United States of America was held high with gratitude. That same fanfare occurred again and again as the convoy proceeded, and for Tony that reaction pointed to a new reality—he was driving by battlefields rather than fighting on them. That lens gave him perspective and objectivity. For the first time in years, he was observing the war from the outside looking in. And that moment did indeed mark the beginning of his healing.

While Tony was grateful for the time they were granted in Paris before sailing, the experience was bittersweet at first. Riding through the countryside and smaller cities to reach Paris, he felt the war pressing on him again, for he was witnessing the devastation in France. He could not ignore the destruction along their route, the rubble testifying, in part, to the 1,570 French cities destroyed and the fresh burial grounds marking some of the 68,778 people killed in bombings. During that interval of his journey home, Tony was unable to escape the war he was supposedly leaving. The aftertaste of strife surrounded him, tainting life. The smell of the bombings lingered. The rot sickened him. He felt as though he was being punished for serving and hoped he had now hit the lowest emotional threshold on the journey home.

Tony was just about ready, wrongly so, to claim shame, but then he noted the convoy was working its way out of the countryside. Paris lay ahead, and he knew the atmosphere there would be different. Life in the City of Light during the war had traveled a different path, one of hardship and duress rather than destruction and loss. The Parisians suffered through difficult years of rationing, restrictions and curfews, and mandated subordination to the Germans, who came first in all matters. As the convoy advanced toward the City, Tony felt its light. Unlike the days of the liberation of Paris, when inhabitants were hidden and filled with fear and the country's "joie de vivre" was lost, Paris was alive with color, activity, and vitality, offering a breath of fresh air for the troops. Along the Seine, by L'Arc de Triomphe, in the area surrounding the Eiffel Tower, people filled the streets. Shops were open on that beautiful September day, park benches were packed with people, and seating that lined café store fronts was at capacity. Bakeries and cafes dotted the City, emitting aromatic scents that sweetened the air in confined spaces, luring and soothing the populace. There was good reason for the people to gather, whether they came to mourn, celebrate, or balance both.

Tony's spirits lifted further as the convoy headed to the soldiers' accommodations, the U.S.O., and other services, and he sensed that many soldiers felt the same. They were billed in an upscale hotel levels above anything they had slept in for some time. That afternoon they were able to treat themselves to baths or showers and the heady experience of lying on luxurious mattresses. Re-fueling mentally and physically for a night on the town was not difficult.

Tony could not speak to everyone's plans while in Paris prior to sailing. All he could say was that they were out and about as he was with a few friends and acquaintances from the ship. On and off, Tony's friends gathered or headed on their own, their goals to enjoy themselves, celebrate their impending departure, and partake in all that Paris had to offer from food to art and everything in between. Tony had Notre Dame de Paris on his list to offer prayers of gratitude, take in the structure's beautiful architecture and adornments, and photograph it for Helena, who was devout and would be awed by the beauty of the historical edifice. Strolling along the Seine and stopping for coffee was something he did every afternoon, in the European tradition of coffee and cake after siesta yet well before the customary late dinner. He enjoyed learning about French pastries and comparing them to Italian confections. He always chose a waterside café because he loved the flowing river, its current symbolizing cleansing and renewal.

Although Tony was not a shopper, he planned to make some purchases, especially since he had received an accounting of his funds before leaving his final assignment. He had been paid regularly for over four years but was rarely able to check the balance of his funds. He knew his account covered some supplies and his uniforms, but the bulk of his earnings were largely unspent. When he learned during a respite that local vendors occasionally set up markets for troops in transition to acquire souvenirs from a specific region, he made it a point to always have cash with him. The situation, however, begged the question he explored frequently. Where and how would he find opportunities to spend money especially during his 271 consecutive days in the field as part of Patton's Third Army? But in Paris and for the remainder of his trip home, Tony realized he had amassed solid resources, a sum of money he never imagined having, now set aside for his future.

Each day, alone or with some of his fellow soldiers, Tony walked the boulevards of Paris enjoying the street life, window shopping, and options for meals. The break enabled him to relax and build on the idea of objectivity that was born during the convoy. He decompressed as a result and was feeling much better than he had in a long time in terms of keeping haunting thoughts at bay. With the luxury of time on his hands and money in his pocket, Tony decided he could no longer delay his shopping for Helena. How could he return after four and a half years without mementos for her?

A good starter for Tony's shopping was to find a beautiful Parisian hat because Helena loved hats. In most of his pictures of her, she was wearing some sort of a headpiece that went perfectly with the remainder of her outfit. Early on when he gave thought to her affinity for hats, he wondered where and how she acquired them, her means so modest. Thinking about it and her way of doing things, though, he imagined she routinely traded off hats with her sisters and friends, especially those who worked in the hat factory. He knew it was Helena's dream to learn how to make hats, and he had no doubt that she could be an exceptional milliner.

As he strolled, his eyes on the lookout for the perfect hat, he came across a small shop. Judging from the displays, the proprietor had an artful touch. Together, Camille, the shop owner, and Tony hobbled along in English with some reliance on Italian and French. Her enthusiasm for finding the perfect fetching chapeau for Helena warmed his heart and her assistance was more than he expected. Tony had no idea about how to proceed, yet Camille was forthcoming and to his surprise asked if he had photographs of his fiancée for her to study. Tony pulled out the nine photos he had with him. Viewing them, Camille smiled and was kind to acknowledge Helena's sense of style and obvious love of hats, for she was wearing a different one in each of the nine photos. Camille took charge and searched her inventory, determined to find *the* hat. She noticed some patterns that were helpful—how Helena's hats allowed her curls to show, all her hats were in lighter tones, and she tended to tilt them slightly to the side.

At that point, Tony regarded Camille as brilliant, and in good order she came up with a startling and delightful choice that he could see tilted on lovely Helena's head, showcasing not only her beautiful hair but her rosy skin as well. A pale, blush shade, the hat was sure to be a hit, especially in the U.S., where Helena was always told she looked like a million dollars! Camille added a detachable veil should Helena wish to wear the hat to church or some other dressy event. Packed in a glorious hatbox, the gift was elegant and romantic. Tony was pleased with the first purchase of the day and realized he had started with the most difficult item of all.

Next came a jewelry purchase. He wasn't sure about what to buy but knew with all the controversy about gold stolen during the war he would more likely find something suitable in silver. He strode from store front to store front, gazing at well-crafted, meaningful pieces, but had not yet found something that caught his heart. Continuing to walk, he crossed to the other side of the Seine. There in a shop's window he found something perfect, an etched pendant on a shiny silver chain that turned out to be a locket. Special indeed, he thought, though he found it difficult to turn a photo of him and Helena over to the shopkeeper and watch her cut it. But when Tony opened the pendant and saw the two images set side by side, his heart fluttered.

The final gift came easily. He had seen many samples of the item as he strolled the streets and merely needed to think of the style and pattern she would prefer. The gift would appeal to Helena the seamstress. What he had in mind was a gift set of lace-edged handkerchiefs in the fine handiwork of the French countryside. He wanted the finest linen and delicate designs. He thought through different options methodically. Helena favored flowers, so he chose an embroidered floral pattern. Spring was her favorite season, which meant bright pastels. Looking at a variety of samples, he decided on a crocheted rather than lace border because it was more practical and Helena herself loved to crochet. One final decision was not difficult. It was possible to have initials monogrammed on each handkerchief and he found that a nice touch.

Tony bought a few additional items and gifts. Though he was not a seasoned shopper by any means, he enjoyed his excursion through the shops, imagining Helena by his side and speculating about items she would find appealing. When he was sorting through different gift ideas, he sometimes felt as though she guided him to the item that would please her. He realized how helpful it was to focus on her and take another step to distance himself from the war.

Before heading out with his friends for the evening, Tony stopped at the Western Union Office to wire his Aunt about his impending departure with a reminder that the discharge process could be lengthy. He promised to contact her again when in the States. He knew her channels of communication would get his update to everyone, including his family in Italy where communications were in disarray and Tony was not able to connect with his parents before leaving.

As a farewell to Paris and the war, Tony and his friends enjoyed a night on the town, the beauty of the City, the music in the clubs, and fine dining. His small group of companions that evening included three men from Pennsylvania whom he'd known, on and off, for over two years by then. They lived in the Philadelphia area, which made reunions in New York City possible, and he was certain they would stay in touch. The others were soldiers from the 3rd Army they bumped into and invited to come along. Tony welcomed any solider to join in an adventure, a game of cards, or any other activity. He had come to realize that anyone serving in the Army would be a great companion and a good friend then and in the years ahead.

That next morning, all soldiers booked for departure to the U.S. from Le Havre gathered at the different quarters in town where segments of their convoy waited. The vehicles filled quickly, indicating the troops' enthusiasm. The convoys advanced to a waypoint where all vehicles on route to Le Havre formed an extensive convoy that proceeded to the Harbor, initiating the soldiers' return. They expected to reach the port in three hours or so, and that minor step away from Europe created an emotional moment. The ride north was refreshing, for the taste of the sea became apparent shortly after the convoy was underway. For the most part, the men slept, having been up late the night before enjoying the City and celebrating their imminent departure to America.

When they arrived at the port, Tony experienced a moment of déjà vu. The ship was the focus of their attention, for most of the soldiers stationed in Europe during World War II participated in at least one major amphibious offensive. There was also the obvious fact that troops arrived for duty in Europe by ship. The sea was part of the war, an enemy in combat and an ally in the business of war that transported millions of soldiers around the world. There had also been grand logistical seafaring feats involving four thousand ships or more that added a bold new chapter in man's story with the sea. Yet the one image of man, the war, and the sea that was most memorable was the sea convoy that formed between San Diego, the northeast coast of the U.S., and several points between the two. The majesty of the armada bearing U.S. flags would remain the most poignant and striking image of Tony's Military service.

His return to the U.S. placed him on his seventh ocean journey. Practicality aside, during each deployment by sea journey, Tony asked himself how many times in addition to his initial sailing to the U.S. had he boarded a ship for new destinations across seas and regions unknown to him. Part of him could not believe his war itinerary, the maneuvering for staging amphibious landings, and his exposure to so many countries and cultures. He never knew what to expect or where an operation would take him. But on that day as he boarded the ship destined for Boston, Tony knew with certainty where he was headed and what lay ahead, at least in terms of his personal life.

Between alighting from the bus and boarding the ship, Tony paused to breathe in the air of Europe. Difficult thoughts lingered in his mind as he savored a bittersweet moment. Walking up the gangway his pack on his back and his duffle over his shoulder, he boarded, allowing memories of his crossing to America eight years ago to flood his thoughts. At their center was Father boarding with him to get him settled. Sometimes he felt as though that day happened a lifetime ago. Other times, it seemed as though he and his father traced his route together a few days ago.

Chapter 30
Going Home

Early on the morning of September 17th, Tony stood on the deck of the Marine Angel, this time transfixed by the dazzling approach into The Boston Navy Yard. The scene was amazingly similar to what he remembered from his first crossing—the signs of dawn, the hovering mist, lights in the distance. First to greet him was the lighthouse in its charming island setting, a beacon to the seafaring. Symbolic, it brought other such landmarks to mind, the lighthouse at the edge of Gibraltar and, of course, the Statue of Liberty.

Tony had dreamed about his return to the U.S. and finally his departure was imminent. The emotional impact of war tempered his spirits though he was convinced his mood would lighten as Europe receded in the distance and the U.S. became more vivid in his mind. There was one fact he knew for sure. He would not pass on the opportunity to view and photograph the U.S. coastline and the ship's arrival in Boston. With that thought, his adventuresome spirit peeked through, and he sensed his soulful self. *What a complex matter life is*, Tony thought. *I was a boy when I left Italy. A boy on a journey, immature yet thoughtful and cautious. I left on what I perceived to be a grand adventure.*

A few years later, I eagerly engaged in another journey, that one born out of duty. I was on a mission then, too—my purpose critical and definitely not an adventure. I once regarded the war as the greatest mission in my life but now realize I was mistaken. Right now, on this warship destined for America, I am traveling on the most important mission, where the story of living life on my terms is about to begin. Tony sensed the light of all his tomorrows, and his inner joy began to rebound.

Tony settled on the ship, claiming a hammock in the communal quarters with familiar faces surrounding him. He was once again reminded of his first time at sea and the sailings that followed. Each was memorable, and he could recall vivid details about every one of them. What intrigued him was that as a poor immigrant he experienced a unique and elegant form of transportation before he entered the service and then traveled regularly aboard military ships. Both modes of transportation had their purposes, but for him the prize was that he had experienced and known the unique ambience of traveling on a commercial cruise liner. It was a memory he would hold onto with the hope that he would one day travel in that manner again to enjoy elegance on the seas with his family.

Reacquainting himself with a military vessel, Tony had to appreciate its transparency. Nothing was dressed up to be anything other than what it was. Information about the ship was forthcoming, and that detail brought a smile to his face. He remembered, with some amount of embarrassment, seeking time with the Captain on the S.S. Roma to ask his questions about the ship and tour it, relying on his friends Giovanni and Luca for assistance. On the military ships, information was posted up front and locations were clearly marked. The vessels had the military look, exuded mission, and there was no reason to tour the ship or poke around different sections of it. Thinking of a completely different location, Grand Central Station, which combined art and function, Tony realized the difference between the commercial ship and the war ship was not so much their look as it was a matter of function. What purpose did a vessel serve? A placard on the Marine Angel answered that question before it could be asked by providing a full overview of the ship's history, class, operational details, and missions. Like all other military carriers he traveled on, Tony knew each ship's entire story the day he stepped on to it and that gave him a sense of belonging and ownership of the ship's mission.

Now on his way home, Tony saw the environment on the ship as spare in terms of appointments and informal regarding atmosphere. It invited rest and the camaraderie characteristic of U.S. Forces. Together, the soldiers could decompress from their war-time experiences in that setting through ordinary activities—playing cards, reading, and writing, sharing anecdotes about their war experiences and their insecurities about the future, and spending endless hours telling elaborate tales about how they would spend their time when they arrived home. There were sad stories to share—some soldiers lost loved ones or received "Dear John" letters while deployed. For some, the laidback atmosphere was stressful, an abrupt departure from the rigor in the field. Many were in a rush to return home. They separated themselves from the war, were tired of it, and just wanted to go home. The return trip demanded patience, and one of Mama's adages came to mind, "*Tutte le cose al momento giusto*." [All things at the right time.]

The sea was calm as the U.S.S. Marine Angel set sail. The weather was excellent, and the days passed with ease, which meant the soldiers spent most of their time on the outer decks. Since the cooks on board were fellow soldiers, there were opportunities to ask for special dishes and desserts for a birthday celebration or other personal occasion. In a debriefing on the ship one day about life after the Army, Tony learned an interesting word from the officer leading the discussion. The word was "resilient," and the speaker's point focused on human resilience, the ability to bounce back after dealing with difficult situations. Tony was impressed with the session because the presenter went beyond the obvious—the nuts and bolts, the paperwork and logistics of being discharged from the Army. He spoke about humanity, dignity, and rising above— out of—trauma and pain. The instructor delivered a lesson on life that Tony never forgot.

On the other side of the ocean, millions and millions of households awaited the return of their loved ones, whose travel was lengthy and circuitous, depending on where they lived in the United States. Throughout the country, soldiers arrived in small groups at a time, via bus or train after departing their assigned posts, traveling to the designated point of departure, most likely crossing an ocean, completing all requirements for discharge, and then continuing to their destinations. For the waiting families who received telegraphs about return dates and approximate times, the arrivals seemed few and far between. Groups who left together did not return together, and as history tells us, many soldiers and civilians attached to the military, a combined total of 418,500 men and women, did not return alive. Until returning troops appeared in person, their families waited with cautious anticipation as well as worry and fear. It became common practice in cities and towns throughout the U.S. to have crowds at the bus and train stations *every day* awaiting *any* soldier's arrival. Emotions in the country were high, reflecting the might and accomplishments of U.S. forces, but they were also paired with anxiety for the families awaiting the arrival of their loved ones.

Circumstances were no different in Connecticut where the Italian American U.S. soldiers were returning home too slowly for everyone's taste. But the evening of September 16, 1945, was a time of heightened anticipation among Tony's family and friends. The Marine

Antonio's *Story* 335

Angel was scheduled to dock in Boston the next morning. The group awaiting his arrival would have been thrilled were they to learn of his safe arrival immediately, yet they would be in the dark until he contacted them or they read about the ship in the papers. A considerable amount of time would elapse before Tony returned to Stamford.

Early on the morning of September 17, Tony stood on the deck of the ship, this time transfixed by the dazzling approach into the Boston Navy Yard. The scene bore a striking similarity to his memories of his first crossing—the signs of dawn, the hovering mist, and lights in the distance. First to greet him was the lighthouse in its charming island setting, a beacon to the seafaring. Symbolic, it brought other such landmarks to mind, the lighthouse at the edge of Gibraltar and, of course, the Statue of Liberty. That day, Tony had his German camera with him, and he was prepared to take beautiful photographs of the city's skyline and landmarks. Those would be treasures to show his family and friends and hold within him as cherished memories.

The ship advanced, approaching its destination. Two expansive scenes stood out immediately—The Navy Yard and Historic Boston, both closely tied to the American Revolution. But what took Tony's breath away was the flag of the United States of America hoisted at the top center of the Yard's primary building. Firmly planted, waving in the soft breeze, the country's flag welcomed them home. In four and a half years' time, Tony had not experienced anything as filled with hope, aside from his brief furlough to the U.S. in 1943.

Wearing his dress uniform for the first time in more than a week, Tony was ready for arrival. His Silver Star, along with a few ribbons and commendations, adorned his jacket. Friends who saw him enter the mess hall earlier that morning felt their jaws drop when they noticed him wearing the prestigious medal for valor in combat. A war hero, they thought, something he had never mentioned. Indeed, Tony, who was pointedly humble, now came across as noble and distinguished in his decorated uniform. The moment captured his essence as a modest, hardworking man of integrity and honor from a small village in Italy. He had changed considerably during the war, but then he hadn't really changed at all.

Disembarkation was orderly as would be expected in a military exercise. Each soldier's papers were checked against the manifest. They had received medical exams prior to their departure from France and would have separation physicals finalized at their destination, Fort Devens in the Boston area. On arrival, Tony learned out-processing would be cumbersome. Though he had imagined getting home hours after the ship docked, he admitted to himself that a few days or so was probably a more accurate estimate.

They were to travel in a convoy to their destination. Exiting the Navy Yard, the soldiers found a large group of local residents gathered to welcome them home. During the jaunt to Devens, there was sustained attention to the troops with people gathered on streets and crossways in every village or town cheering their arrival with pride, patriotism, signs, music, chants, and flags. Tony found the attention heartwarming. The voices of the people spoke directly to him, and he felt affirmed as an Italian immigrant returning to his American home. Along with the charm of the local people, Tony reconnected with the familiar landscape of New England as they rode along. He studied the beautiful mature deciduous trees and rolling hills and submitted himself to the ambience of the seaport, knowing he was now hours away from home. He was refreshed by the clear air, the untouched land, green and thriving, as it contrasted the burnt, crumbling, dusty landscape of the post-war Europe he left behind.

Fort Devens was in sight. Its massive quadrangle could not be missed. As was the case in both Europe and Boston, there were grand gestures of appreciation—waves, salutes, horn-blowing—and those were gratifying. A large reception, an event planned by the community, welcomed the soldiers home that afternoon. There was fanfare, food, music, a welcome speech, and logistical information. For most of the soldiers traveling with Tony, the atmosphere was the home they knew from birth; for him it was an emotional reminder and realization that he was part of the American community as an adoptee. That understanding played with his mind a little, not because the situation and reality were unwelcome. Rather, it had to do with the breadth of his travel during the war and his renewed exposure to Europe, which reinforced his Italian roots and citizenship. He was welcomed back to the U.S. warmly, thankfully not feeling any of the discomfort or alienation reflecting the derogatory reports about Italian immigrants that circulated before he enlisted. Perhaps there was great wisdom in going off to war. And returning with a medal was not doing him any harm.

The welcome reception did not last long, and soldiers were free to leave for the barracks as they wished. Tony enjoyed interacting with military personnel and their families, the public, and local dignitaries and was also grateful for the refreshments. His family in the U.S. was front and center on his mind, though, and he hoped to get a telegram out to them as soon as he had some idea about when he might leave for Connecticut. Reaching the barracks, reporting in, and finding his assigned building, he perused the papers he received, finding a schedule of close to two weeks' separation activities. He would not arrive in Connecticut until the end of the month. The timeline was longer than he expected, but at least he had information to convey, so he headed to the communications room to send a telegram to his Aunt, deciding it was best to not be too specific. His final message estimated his return in two weeks or so.

Fort Devens offered a pleasant atmosphere. The post was in the country where the foliage was lush and the beautiful trees were beginning to hint about changing color. The amount of land on the reservation invited physical activity from hiking to baseball during open hours. The agenda was rigorous. Each soldier had a final thorough medical exam. The evaluations were a must because the Veterans Administration was responsible for injuries or conditions servicemen and women had sustained, and those had to be documented for benefits to be granted. If someone needed new glasses, they were provided, a cane it was provided. The goal was to send soldiers home with what they needed to re-establish themselves after the war. Attention to the soldiers' health included a broad focus on fitness that accounted for a wide range of conditions—evidence of excessive drinking or smoking, sleep patterns, nightmares, weight, hearing, the list went on. It soon became apparent that the exams they had previously completed narrowed the focus for each discharge physical to ensure the soldiers were healthy enough to travel, not carrying any contagious illness, and met the requirements for reentering the U.S.

The separation program also focused on the soldiers' lives after being discharged. There were, for example, information sessions on benefits to servicemen and women through the G.I. Bill. Guaranteed by legislation, those provided for a college education and were also applauded for democratizing education in the U.S. There were also programs and benefits for acquiring loans, such as home mortgages, at reduced rates. The soldiers learned about different organizations, like the American Legion, that held events and offered services for returning soldiers.

Debriefing sessions spent extended time on security issues since a good amount of war-time information the troops handled or knew firsthand was classified, and it was incumbent on the Army to advise soldiers separating from the service on their conduct and integrity in discussions about the war. The subject matter was abstract, yet Tony understood its point fully. As a recipient of a Silver Star, he had a citation with general reference to a battle and the type of circumstances in which he was involved. His location was not identified on any documentation, and sections of the citation were redacted. That personnel record remained unchanged and was never amended during his lifetime or thereafter, though Tony knew all details of the operation, including the region and town where it occurred. The debriefing underscored the responsibility of all troops, including those separated from the service, for protecting U.S. interests.

Tony's days in Massachusetts passed quickly. There was a good balance between debriefing, leisure time and recreation, fitness, and adjustment so that the young soldiers could begin to decompress. The one full weekend at Fort Devens allowed for time in the surrounding communities, including Boston, which was accessible by train. That weekend enabled the soldiers to reacquaint themselves with life in the U.S. outside the military, getting a taste of freedom and restoring their independence before reuniting with family. Tony and his friends chose to go to Boston for a day. There they had the chance to look at the sea in a different way, visit historic sites and museums, and begin their reentry to American life. Seafood was plentiful, and the soldiers ate well. After lunch, they sat on the pier for a while, separate but together, conversing but also sitting with their own thoughts.

The sea brought them peace and did indeed impress upon them that the day was real—they *were* back in the U.S. and would soon be on the final leg of their journeys home. Tony turned to the group and mentioned Boston's Little Italy, asking if anyone wanted to head there for dessert. Following a resounding yes, they stood up to go. As he strolled with the group along the sea, Tony's memories of his new hometown flooded his thoughts, shifting the war movies that had never ceased to replay in his mind to the background. The time to be joyful had begun and savoring Italian confections to celebrate his return was a good way to restart his life in America.

Chapter 31
Homecoming

When the train began to navigate a wide turn, Tony held his breath. He knew the bend well. There, beyond the curve, the ocean came into view. Helena and the sea, together they changed his life, turning turmoil and isolation into a future of hope. He threw the window open, listened to the gulls and reveled in the rush of the rolling waves. Finally, his return felt real.

When Tony's eyes opened on the morning of September 30th, he smiled, knowing his long-awaited return to Connecticut was a few hours away. Never in his life had he waited so long for something so special. He felt he had been teased along the way, waylaid by delays, his departure from the service always looming before him but never within reach. This day was real, not a dream. His spirits were high and his anticipation keen. He quickly dressed, ate, and met the convoy to Boston's South Station, where he boarded a direct train to his Stamford. The future lay before him and Helena, to be crafted by them.

The train from Boston fascinated Tony as much as the trains in the U.S. did his first day in the country. Since then, his experiences with modes of transportation had increased exponentially corresponding with the vast number of vehicles and equipment the Army utilized. He felt worldly but also his usual self. He wondered if he had changed more than expected or would he appear the same to everyone.

Tony was traveling with a handful of other soldiers. The train was not crowded, and each man was able to take a double seat and stretch out. They all appeared exhausted, more by emotion than physical fatigue, and kept to themselves. Tony's duffle was in the rack above and his pack alongside him. He had completed paperwork at Devens up to the moment he left, so his first order of business was to secure the loose material he was carrying. He pulled the pages from the sleeve in his pack and set out to arrange and store them. Looking down at his discharge papers, he saw his war story resting in his hands. Though he had planned to relax on the train, his mind could not.

The casual act of looking at his discharge papers brought the war back, causing him to drift to Casablanca, Sicily, points in France, Belgium and Germany, and the concentration camp. Now positioned outside the war, he looked in and confronted it. He considered facets of the war he never acknowledged—his loneliness, isolation, and identity. He formed questions about the how of war. *What political underpinnings drove the war? What did he learn about leadership during the war?* In his mind he ticked through the deployments delineated on the form. *What were the benefits and shortcomings of his military service?* He examined his separation papers again, amazed at what they laid out but sorrowful for what they did not capture. The words on his form could never adequately depict the war's scope, meaning, and impact as he knew them.

Lulled by the movement of the train, Tony's mind wandered. Images and emotions ran through his consciousness, often colliding. He revisited the operations that defined his war—the first amphibious assault, the invasion of Sicily, Normandy and the Race across France, and the liberation of Buchenwald. His war existed in cluttered fragments. There had never been the time to see it for what it was and how he was influenced by it. On occasion, when he had access to a mirror, Tony looked himself in the eye and could see the depth of his soldier self. He asked himself, "*Who is this person who feels fundamentally unchanged but different?*

Tony was experiencing the hunger to make sense of it all. He wanted to piece together the operations worldwide as they connected with one another to understand the war as a single entity, and he desired a better understanding of where he stood in a story of such scope. The information he sought would help him wade through the evocative questions he asked himself about his world before the war and how his world grew conceptually as a result of the war.

His ponderings caused him to consider what he took away from his time and experiences on the battlefields. He could imagine so many people asking him questions along those lines in the months and perhaps years ahead. He chased that thought, and more questions emerged. First, the fundamental question as to what lessons he learned from serving in the war. From that, several others flowed. *In what ways did his perspective change as a consequence of the war, given his background and story? What skills had he learned? What were the worst and best moments during his time in the service?* More questions came to the fore, telling Tony the war would be with him for the rest of his life. Rather than seeing himself at war in his dreams or thoughts as though he was watching someone play him in a movie, he would take the story on as his own and not let go of it until he understood it. One critical symbol of that process would be the day when he shed his modesty about his Silver Star while refraining from bragging about it though he need not worry about the latter. It was not his nature, but he had to push himself to loosen his humble self in that context.

Though the war was over, Tony could not deny that it sat in the forefront of his mind. He had lived and breathed it for over four and a half years. He thought about the war because he wanted to encapsulate it to avoid being consumed by it. There was so much he had to say about what he learned, but his thoughts were not organized. He surmised that in some ways his personal immigrant story blurred his thinking—the circumstances of his life in Italy conflicting with those of the war and vice versa. In short, Tony's life story was complex. It was not easy to separate Tony the immigrant from Tony the soldier. Although specific dates on paper seemed to define each for practical reasons, it really was not the case that he started and ended being an immigrant on the dates of his departure from Italy and his arrival in the U.S., nor did he start and stop being a soldier the day he reported for active duty and then the day he was discharged.

Tony accomplished something significant during that first hour or so on the train. He looked at the worst and the best of his tour in a stronger chronological sequence, clearing his mind sufficiently to turn to a new page in his life and return home less preoccupied and ready for what would come next. The thought of the new pages in his life allowed Tony's heart to overcome his mind and place a pleasant memory before him, 1943, when he won the lottery for a travel detail to the states. That recollection, a threshold event, had lingered in his consciousness day and night for the last year and a half. His good fortune made it firm that he and Helena would marry after his return. For Tony, the timing had been providential. During that visit to the U.S., Tony knew the worst on the battlefield was yet to come. But now he realized he was well beyond his greatest challenge during the war, the 271 consecutive days of warfare.

Tony's mood lightened, redirecting his thoughts to dreams. His daydreams began with an image of Helena front and center in his mind. Her lovely smile conjured stories and events they shared as well as exchanges by mail, always delayed by the war, about their wedding in eight months. He smiled and soon began to doze, Helena never leaving his thoughts. When his eyes opened next sometime later, they gazed on familiar land. The train had traveled beyond the quiet of northern Connecticut and was moving in the direction of the state's principal cities and towns. The stops were now frequent. When the train began to navigate a wide turn, Tony held his breath. He had his bearings, knew every inch of that bend, and he could pinpoint *the* spot where the ocean came into view. He was now traveling to Helena and the sea. Together, they had changed his life, transforming turmoil and isolation into a future of hope.

He threw the window open, listened to the gulls and reveled in the rush of the rolling waves. Finally, his return felt real. Tears filled his eyes. Now traveling through a dense urban area and its many stops, Tony sat through the repetitive cycle of the train moving and stopping, often dozing and waking with its rhythm. The shifting train rocked him much the way ships had, but the train's whistle and the movement of passengers always woke him. Each time his eyes opened, he was closer to his destination. Soon, every building he saw was recognizable, and his anticipation skyrocketed. He no longer dozed. Instead, he glued himself to the window, watching every familiar sight with care. He knew the moment when the station, a speck on the landscape from afar, would come into range. And there it was! The station, a pinpoint, grew steadily.

Tony was one of the few passengers who would exit the train in Stamford. A group of seventy-five people or so stood on the side of the track where his train was headed. For a while the figures were blurred, the train moving too slowly for his taste, much like the feeling he had in 1938, when time seemed to stand still and his arrival to the Port of New York appeared to have stalled. The train was slowing, the faces in the crowd became clearer—just about all of them recognizable to him. The scene that lay ahead was the work of Helena and her sisters. Oh, how they loved gatherings and parties! He had never seen a family so enthusiastic about birthdays and celebrations. And there she was in the front of the group with his Aunt, her parents, her sisters and brothers, and his friends from the deli, along with many other friends and neighbors. His beautiful Helena, just as he expected—wearing a stunning long beige coat with a fur collar for the cool fall afternoon, her curls covered in part by a lovely beige hat tilted slightly to the side. He looked out and his eyes found hers.

A reception for Tony began the minute he stepped off the train, and it continued through the evening at his Aunt's home. He enjoyed the ride from the station with Helena and her parents as reminiscent of his arrival years ago. The short drive seemed to take a long time, but Tony enjoyed taking in his surroundings, especially the signs of fall. He had been immersed in the process of arriving home for close to a month. Over the past two weeks, he experienced a slow return to the U.S., one paced by the program at Fort Devens. During that time, he began to re-settle in the states in a comfortable and unhurried manner.

When they arrived home, Tony sighed with great relief, his pointed exhalation surprising him. He was home. He had made it back. He was not one of the faceless soldiers slain on the battlefield, nor was he an unnamed soldier or one missing in action. His body was not one of the tens of thousands taken by the sea during the amphibious landings. There were many times when he thought he would not make it out of the battlefields. To have returned to seize his future was a momentous gift.

The collection of friends and family who had gathered at the train station came directly to the house after Tony's arrival. There had been a quality to the line of cars, a combination of pageantry and celebration. He smiled, thinking, *I have my own little parade today*. So many parallel scenes washed over his thoughts—the impromptu parade in New Orleans, the convoy perched high above San Diego Bay, and the memorable march into Berlin. Tony could not help but acknowledge the scope of his experience in the service—the rites and practices that transformed him into a better person. And now he returned to bring all that he learned and accomplished to life in America. His return, along with the others that had already occurred and those that would follow, made the day important for their community.

There was reason to celebrate, many reasons, for Tony quickly noticed that he was now another one of their own who had returned. Clustered by the door were those who had beat him back to the U.S.—his cousin Rocco, his brother-in-law Anthony, and his friends Paolo and Johnnie. When they all faced each other, their eyes spoke, showing the strains of war. They formed a circle and held on to each other, experiencing the relief of sharing something so horrific and personal with each other. They knew that discussing the war was for another day but embracing each other in camaraderie would sustain them until they gathered to talk.

For the next few hours, people arrived for the celebration, and Tony was pleased with the reception and the opportunity to visit with so many people. He wanted his friends and family around him, not to entertain him or share his stories, but to be with him to affirm the reality of his return. He wanted to learn how everyone was doing and how they had spent the last four and a half years. He was touched by the number of people who stopped by—from customers to distant relatives to the parish priest and a wonderful family who owned the local Italian restaurant. They came bearing mounds of food for that afternoon—all the traditional dishes Tony enjoyed, from pasta to veal, pizza, breads, and sweets. He felt like a kid again, the dark shadows retreating, and his memories of the Youth Group seemingly erased from his mind.

Lucia stole looks at him constantly as he greeted everyone, appraising his well-being as Mama had requested. No sooner after reliable information about Tony's return became available and was shared with Mama by telegram, Mama replied in turn demanding a complete report about her son on his arrival via the fastest means possible. Mama prayed that he was not haunted, gaunt, or damaged, and then she gave way to her tears. Since Mama had never seen her Antonio while he was stationed in Europe, she was heartbroken and felt he had left her twice.

Sometimes Lucia did not take her formidable sister-in-law's "orders" to heart, but she regarded the request an imperative and treated it as her life's mission. And though Tony was a bit thinner in one way, he was muscular, tanned, and healthy, and his clear green eyes were alive and not haunted at all. Mama would receive a wonderful report by telegram with letters to follow.

The conversations continued, refreshments were replenished, and Tony was gratified that life fell into place so effortlessly that afternoon. When he finally had a chance to talk with his Aunt, she gave him a gift he longed for—information about his family in the aftermath of the Nazi occupation. The family had re-established themselves in their home after their property and residence had been occupied, used, and then abandoned. There was no serious damage though they expected to lose a year's worth of crops. Their evacuation and exile had been harrowing—they boarded with a family in the lowland, and like everyone else in their situation, they struggled to obtain food and water because resources and mobility were limited. They were in good health and needed to revitalize their trod-upon land. Tony was grateful for the detailed information Lucia gathered though he could not erase the empty space in his heart that marked the absence of his family that afternoon. While he knew it was illogical and impossible, he would have loved to have his parents standing beside him along with everyone else present. Then he would be in the arms of his entire family.

Ever watchful, Helena noticed the brief slump in Tony's posture after he spoke with Lucia, and Helena walked toward him, delivering her good nature and caring disposition in a quiet way. She looped her arm around his, and they walked across the room to Luigi and Rosa. The four of them chatted, bringing Tony to the here and now. The warmth of the conversation soothed Tony, who moved on to ask about the wine press and wine production, which Luigi described as very successful with a vintage created for Tony's return.

As Luigi spoke and Tony listened to and enjoyed the story, Helena was gradually moving them toward the back of the parlor where a large window framed Lucia's lush backyard. Tony loved the outdoors and appreciated the light that was replacing the dark days of war. Standing near the window, he remembered looking out of it frequently to check his fig tree when it was taking root. Apprehensive at first because he had not seen the tree in more than four years since it had been covered during his visit in 1943, he peered outside, and his heart skipped a beat. There it was, his family tree grander and more splendid than he had left it. Luigi stood with pride for care of the tree—the pruning, fertilizing, and old-fashioned Italian watchfulness, including Rosa's prayers to her name saint. Tony was deeply grateful for their loving care, telling them briefly about his time in Italy. His story broke their hearts, and their compassion and love for young and courageous Tony, their future son-in-law, grew exponentially.

Figs from graftings of the fig tree Antonio brought from Italy

The house and hearts within its walls were full that day. The atmosphere celebratory and the company satisfying, yet Tony and Helena had eyes for each other only. Everyone expected Tony to talk about the war, and he graciously indulged them, knowing that they, too, needed to be soothed and comforted not only about his fate and that of other family members but those still residing in Italy as well. He did not need too much practice to develop a story line that was neither too much nor too little for fulfilling everyone's needs to hear stories from the battlefield firsthand.

Warmth and love permeated the afternoon and evening, enveloping everyone present. The mood was pleasant and joyful, urging Tony to follow Helena's family tradition for celebrations by giving her his gifts from Paris in public. He spoke briefly about her patient love and support throughout the war and his happiness over their upcoming wedding. That magical moment moved everyone in attendance, bringing light and happiness to the community. The gifts extended the good feeling, Tony's thoughtful mementos winning the hearts of everyone, sustaining the cheer. Piece by piece, Tony offered gifts to immediate family members—his Aunt and Helena and her parents and siblings. The gifts for Helena were the focal point, a sweet moment, during which the group applauded every item and then passed each of them around, one-by-one for a close look. Everyone, especially the women, loved the blush hat.

Tony's Silver Star did not go unnoticed that day. It caught the eyes of the men immediately, causing their regard for him to reach new heights. As for the women, some knew the medal for what it was, and others recognized it as something important. In their hearts, everyone present decided the evening was not about the war. It was about coming home, renewal, being in love, and the future, and they left discussion about the war as a matter for "domani" [tomorrow].

Chapter 32
Post World War II, A New Day

The fanfare, adulation, and spirit were exuberant. Sometimes the veterans felt they were riding a cloud, and other times as they looked into the distance, they saw images of war rather than the good will of the American people. For the most part, the boost of the parade outweighed the soldiers' haunting memories.

Throughout the war, Tony thought of the U.S. as a country consumed with fear and still lifting itself out of the Great Depression. Now back home, he looked for signs of change, yet what he observed was not what he had expected. A transformation had occurred during his absence— the nation was vibrant, invigorated by the war's outcome. He was not opposed to the revived character of the U.S., but the atmosphere was a stark change, one incompatible with the darkness of the battlefields on which he fought, and it was difficult for him to reconcile the past and the present. He wasn't prepared for the festive atmosphere and celebrations of the country as victorious. Instead, he yearned for time to adjust and sort through his war memories, feeling more comfortable about the U.S. he left rather than the one he returned to. Unlike him and the cadre of troops who had stood in the center of war, almost broken by it, the nation's people had participated from afar, living vicariously in its narrative from America's perspective as victor.

During the war, Americans placed their radios at the center of work and life while also immersing themselves in news from overseas and updates as they came in. Reported by American media, commentary tended to slant toward America, causing dizzying pride. The gravitas of the nightly news and updates broadcast throughout the day struck an unforgettable chord extolling the valor and heroism of U.S. troops, whose experiences, lives, losses, and victories became the people's stories. The war was widely discussed in homes, at work, and in casual social settings like the luncheonette where Tony had frequently enjoyed his morning coffee until leaving for active duty. In those venues, radios played non-stop offering the highly appealing programming that sometimes captured the jarring juxtaposition of Big Band songs and updates on military campaigns worldwide. Complementing the national programming was the conversation of everyday American citizens and residents, who dissected the war in a pitched feverish manner. The major figures in the United States Military, such as Eisenhower and Patton, became household names. Talk about them was familiar and casual as though they were family members. They were extolled and elevated to the highest levels of excellence in all discussions.

Life in the U.S. was saturated with details about the war, and most people wanted to hear more, especially the blow-by-blow details of combat on the battlefields. Yet the repetition of those stories most often overwhelmed the veterans. Their experiences were still too raw, an officer at Fort Devens had explained, to talk about the war without becoming emotional or depressed. The transition from being consumed by war around the clock and then not having any war or the change in identity to self rather than soldier was a process that took time, and the officer encouraged everyone to take that time. Tony understood the perspectives of those who had consumed the war from the homeland and appreciated their support and interest yet found interacting with the general community was not always easy.

Tony found his primary and essential support in family and fellow veterans, regardless of where and when the latter served. The war loomed over them. When a group of war buddies gathered, they discussed the war—their memories, questions, and nightmares—coming to terms with what had happened to each of them personally. Few outside those circles could understand or would want to imagine the war scenes the soldiers witnessed, the pain that followed and haunted them, and the difficulty they experienced with their return to an exultant U.S. They had stood face to face with the enemy and observed firsthand the destruction of Europe's landscapes, historic architecture, and art. Most soldiers found themselves reeling from the war's atrocities, sometimes perceiving themselves as complicit.

Though the country hungered for news about the war, it had longed even more for the soldiers' return. Unknowingly, those yearnings placed a burden on the veterans, asking for too much too soon when the newly discharged soldiers wanted to turn a corner and resettle in American society. Adjusting to life in general was also more complicated than the soldiers expected, for they returned to a new social context that was indirectly formed by the war. By virtue of circumstance, their generation was playing a critical role in the molding of a new period in the country's history.

One element of change, the shifting role of women, was a striking outcome of the war. As hundreds of thousands of young men left home to serve, the workforce, employment, and income were entrusted to women. Time quickly showed the ladies were up to the task and more than willing to do their share. That shift would persist, altering the structure of society in time. Another feature of change focused on regard for both male and female soldiers. Influenced by the media to a great degree, that phenomenon demanded respect for all returning soldiers, sowing seeds for further change in the years ahead. Social conventions also centered on respect for the military, a commitment to welcoming soldiers home, paying homage to their service, and helping them resettle. Those intentions and values translated into important tangible benefits that improved the veterans' lives, such as welcome home gifts, free meals at fancy restaurants, employment opportunities, assistance with housing, and tips on home ownership, which included obtaining mortgages.

For young couples like Tony and Helena, support and regard enabled them to advance socially and economically more rapidly than expected. They acknowledged the American Idealism that grew out of the war and also became its benefactors as it shaped the American Dream for the 20th Century. Within the context of war and the returning veterans, the Dream and regard for the troops had everyone operating under one perception about the soldiers who returned: they returned older and wiser than they had been before they left.

Whether they served two years or three or four and whether they enlisted early on or waited to be drafted into the service, most U.S. soldiers had stepped into the war unprepared for its scope and naïve about the responsibilities they would take on. But they trained well under the command of exceptional leaders, came to understand the nuances of the war, performed to please the leadership they admired, learned to navigate the pitfalls, and came of age in the least expected place—the battlefields of World War II. While the death toll surpassed anything ever expected, most of the soldiers survived, returning savvy, reliable, and disciplined.

The soldiers also returned home with their pockets full of money with the years of income they accumulated while deployed. The separation from home and the isolation on the battlefield made most of them yearn for relationships and stability, and they also returned with dreams. Together, the soldiers with their dreams and businesses with their resources intertwined to make the veterans' dreams come true and boost the economy on the business side for a huge step out of the Great Depression. That outcome reflected and acted on what many Americans had come to believe—that the country's honorable performance in the war was *the* factor enabling the U.S. to move beyond the Great Depression and erase the scars it left.

The buoyancy of life in America following the war carried a message for immigrants, both those who returned from the war and the immigrant population in general. Perhaps the outcome of the war, the moral imperatives of the U.S. during the war, and the contributions of immigrant soldiers played a role in improving attitudes toward the large number of immigrants who continued to arrive in the U.S. While that shift did not bring anyone closer to the citizenship they craved, it was the beginning of a movement toward a formal approach for addressing migration to the U.S. and immigrants' concerns about becoming citizens.

Against the background of a world changed by the war, the excitement about Tony's arrival, and the fanfare he and his fellow soldiers received, Helena and Tony reunited, deeply in love and looking forward to their wedding day. They were together as much as possible, under less watchful eyes now that they were engaged. They planned their wedding, and they dreamed, finding they were even more in sync with each other than when their friendship first began. When Tony showed Helena his bank statement from the military, she was overwhelmed and realized immediately that their possibilities for the future had increased considerably.

Although Tony knew he could work in his Aunt's laundry after returning home, she encouraged him to capitalize on his war record and aim for something that would elevate his opportunities over time. Tony and Helena discussed her suggestion, and even before Tony could set out to learn about employment in the area, the community hosted a job fair not only for veterans but for workers of all types, employed or unemployed. Tony, his cousins, and friends took the trolley to the vocational school the day the fair opened. Given the extensive promotion about the event, they were cautiously optimistic about their opportunities. What they wanted was exactly what the townspeople thought—solid employment that would enable them to care and provide for the families they hoped to have. The group separated shortly after arriving, Tony gravitated to his areas of interest—mechanics, fine handwork, micro detailed work on mechanisms with moving parts. Tony went through a few interviews yet spent most of his time with a supervisor from the lock factory and left the event as a Machinist 1 at the plant. That top-level floor position appealed to the essence of his skills, would hold his interest, and valued his time in service.

If Tony thought the reception at the train station was the sole recognition he would receive after returning, he was sorely mistaken. What occurred on his first day home barely scratched the surface of what would play out in the time ahead. In the United States, Fall 1945 was a time of renewal and formal celebrations honoring all veterans. The festivities, awards, and citations were many, and they took place in a variety of venues, especially city, county, state offices, and parades hosted by several organizations. The most significant of those was the city's Veterans Day Parade on November 11, 1945. For that occasion, the town's traditional parade route was extended and lavishly decorated. The event included social gatherings with refreshments both before and after the parade.

A ceremony for recognizing soldiers, awarding commendations, and issuing monetary awards donated by the community was another component of the parade. Military leaders from the state and region participated as did school bands. The parade's path included a pass by the site for the town's proposed World War II monument. Various professional and non-profit organizations, such as the Red Cross and the American Legion, participated as did the fire and police departments, and of course the military, which provided staff, flags, and vehicles, earning recognition for all branches of the service. All participating soldiers, and there were many, were uniformed traveling on military vehicles. The ceremony included benediction, speeches, and a period of silence for the 4,000 plus state residents who were killed in action during the war.

Emotions swelled during the event, oscillating across the full spectrum of responses, from euphoria to mourning. For the soldiers and veterans, all of whom wore dress uniforms, the images of war returned to their minds all too readily, catching them off guard and nearly uprooting them as a tornado would. The fanfare, adulation, and spirit were exuberant. Sometimes the veterans felt they were riding on a cloud, and other times as they peered into the distance, they saw images of war rather than the good will of the American people. For the most part, though, the parade lifted the soldiers' spirits, suppressing haunting memories.

The day's events cemented a transition, offered a portal that separated the war from the present moment, and served as a rite of passage for all those returning to civilian life. Most soldiers were so very young. They learned about the world during the war, but they needed support adjusting after returning. The seemingly extravagant parade celebrating their return suddenly seemed right as a means for honoring their service and redirecting their lives. When the parade began to form, Tony shied away from the elaborate undertaking at first, yet he couldn't help but engage and embrace the shift from the war to its aftermath.

For Tony's family, the parade and events that followed around Thanksgiving and Christmas gave them a new type of access to American society. Following the procession, different organizations, such as the Foreign Legion and the Veterans of Foreign Wars, held events for soldiers and their extended families. Participating in those, Tony no longer felt like a lone immigrant who had served in the war. Rather, he recognized himself among the thousands of immigrants in the state who also served, the majority of Italian descent due to trends in immigration since World War I. Given the absence of Tony's parents, Helena's parents and Tony's Aunt participated in veterans' events because they regarded his adjustment as their responsibility. In caring for Tony, the entire group, especially Luigi, Rosa, and Lucia, developed a better sense of place and belonging in the U.S., and in many ways they, as surrogates for his parents, became co-recipients of his Silver Star in the larger community.

The reaction to Tony's the medal, especially among friends and family, was on point about the value of his Silver Star and where it would take him. While Tony's courageous acts during the war were performed for reasons of duty and honor, people who met him understood the distinguishing characteristics of someone who earned such a medal. The award paved the way for Tony's acceptance and success in his new country. What formed in the back of most people's minds when they met him was a single question: Who would not grant citizenship to a man who risked his life for the United States of America and had to treat his own countrymen as the enemy in the process of doing so?

1945 had been a singular year for Tony and Helena with his safe return from the war and gainful employment. Yet another exciting year was underway, one filled with promise. May 25, 1946, their wedding date, rested on their calendars and minds as the day that would tilt their future. The country as a whole was settling into a new year that brought signs of prosperity. Those carried over to Helena and Tony, enriching their lives in a number of ways. She returned to the coat shop, where she worked with her friends in a less regimented and pleasant workplace. Together, she and Tony increased the size of their nest egg for the future. There was an added surprise in the new year, an unexpected wedding guest, someone Helena had never met, and that person's impending arrival caused spiraling excitement and emotion. Papa was the traveler. He was booked on a transatlantic crossing from Italy to New York that would arrive in mid-April. The journey would be his first visit to the continent but not his last. Mama, who wept over being unable to attend due to post-war financial constraints, remained at home with the children, waiting for information and photos that would enable her to share in the day.

Since the war and certainly as a result of it, Helena's and Tony's social circles expanded beyond the immigrant neighborhood, but never excluded their family members and neighbors, both Italian and American. At their church, they became friends with immigrants from other countries, predominantly Poland, they met veterans Tony did not know during the war, and they developed friendships with co-workers who befriended them in the workplace. Acting on the strong advice of his supervisor at work, Tony applied for U.S. citizenship and met a larger diverse population that both he and Helena got to know well through the citizenship classes Tony completed. More than acquaintances, those individuals, some without family in the U.S., became familiar faces at gatherings Tony's and Helena's families held.

Preparing for the wedding feast consumed more time than any other festivity since everything was made by hand over a lengthy period.

Even before Tony returned from the war, Luigi pushed the garden to produce more tomatoes than ever before and asked friends to plant extra for him. At the end of the summer, he, Rosa, and Lucia, along with Helena and siblings and a cast of friends and neighbors, spent days simmering and canning vats of marinara. Together, they cooked a record amount of amazing sauce with the aroma of the Old Country. The cooking team took a break after storing their sauce and did not resume until Tony returned. To his delight, they were moving on to another round of cooking, filling their houses and those of family and friends with his favorite handmade savory sausages. After storing the sausages in their earthen cellars, the cooks enjoyed another break during the winter though they planned for the next round—the cookies, vegetables, and pasta that they would prepare closer to the wedding day.

In April, they resumed work. The pasta and the wedding cookies involved delicate preparation, the women declared, especially the fig cookies and the anise knots. Both were tied to the homeland, the fig cookies Tony's favorite made from the paste of his own figs, and they required the hands and experience of the Old Country. The men had the task of adding to the pickled vegetables they had already stockpiled with fresh products and those from the late fall harvest that were also stored in the basement. The herculean effort was the pasta, which called for hundreds of eggs. Since they planned to dry it, they were able produce it in April, leaving their baking for the latest dates possible. The logistics demanded wizardry and the use of many households. Day after day during the month of April, the manual production of pasta was in progress.

Stopping by during lunch time one day, Tony felt the strongest touch of Italy in America as the women worked feverishly on the pasta. Out of the corner of his eye, he observed Rosa shape and flatten a sheet of dough the size of her kitchen table using her ancient four-foot Italian rolling pin. Petite as Mama also was, Rosa wielded the baton as a Samurai did his sword. Tony could see Mama standing there doing the same with Rosa, the two never competing but rather working together to get ready for the big day. Oh, how he wished Mama could attend the wedding too!

At intervals, the cooks moved on to the drying process to free their workspace for another round. Tony loved seeing the pasta drying racks every time he walked into either Rosa's house or Lucia's, where he still lived. Seeing homemade pasta draped on racks and surfaces to dry to perfection brought back memories. How fortunate he was to have so many wonderful women in the U.S. doing so much for him and Helena. His new community was a gift, and he knew at that moment that he would change their lives, care for them, in ways no one had yet imagined possible for an immigrant.

Chapter 33

Walking on Clouds

She alighted from the car along the side entrance where Luigi waited. Chords of music began, the procession formed, she and Luigi completed the line.

Papa was due to arrive during the throes of the industrial-grade food preparation. Tony reassured Helena about Papa's kindness, yet she was nervous about meeting him and how he would react to her. Both he and she were in the unusual situation of soon becoming one family without ever having met. She was fearful, too, about the rest of the family, especially Mama, whom she would not meet until sometime in the future when Tony's family would visit the U.S. or she and Tony would travel to Italy.

On the morning of Papa's arrival, Tony left Stamford on an early train. When he reached the terminal, the ship was in view, making its way to the pier....

Tony is waiting in anticipation for Papa to disembark from the ship at the Port of New York. Passengers are streaming off the vessel in droves, happy to be on land. At first sight, father and son rush through the crowd toward each other with excitement. The port is overflowing with people, but father sees only his son, and the son sees only his father.

As they make their way toward each other, with smiles on their faces and warm memories of their lives in Settefrati filling their hearts, the two men meet and are finally facing each other. Tony recalls that day eight years ago when Papa accompanied him to the ship for his departure to America.

As Tony's eyes tear up, Papa greets him, "*Figlio mio, figlio mio coraggioso, sono così orgoglioso di te e così felice di essere qui per il tuo matrimonio.*" [My son, My brave son, I am so proud of you, and so happy to be here for your wedding.]

"PAPA!!!! I am so happy to finally see you and thankful you are here for this special occasion." Tony is fondly recalling his original voyage to the United States to ask about Papa's. "You had a magnificent ship for your passage. Tell me about your trip, tell me all about the ship. I hope you had a pleasant journey"

Ahh, Antonio! *è stato meraviglioso, il sogno di una vita.*" [It was wonderful, the dream of a lifetime.] Tony remembers some of his challenges during his crossing to the U.S. and is anxious to know that Papa is fine. "I hope you had a pleasant journey. Did you eat well? What did you do for enjoyment? Did you make friends on the ship? Did you investigate the whole ship from front to back as I did on my first journey to the U.S.?" Tony is eager to hear everything about Papa's trip from start to finish.

Papa looks proudly at his son and smiles at his interest in his voyage and his well-being. "Antonio, you have changed but you have not changed at all. It was a grand trip, my son. The ocean was calm and soothing and a beautiful sight. I was well cared for and received much attention from the workers. The food was very good and there was plenty of it." And with a grin on his face Papa continues with "Mama will be very happy to hear that." Both men smile as they think the same thoughts about how lovingly Mama cares for them.

"It pleases me to know how happy you are my son, you have accomplished much in your young life. You are a war hero, and you honor our family with your service. You have a nice home, a beautiful bride, and are preparing for a new life. I am so thankful to be here and share in this joy. Come, let's go meet your bride."

"Papa, I can't wait for you to meet my Helena. You will admire her for sure."

Tony helps Papa retrieve his bags, which are filled with gifts from the townspeople as well as from Mama and Papa, delectable foods from home: prosciutto, provolone, sausage, all homemade, all Tony's favorites. And all prepared by and sent with love from Mama.

Tony continues questioning Papa about life in Settefrati, and Papa updates his son with all the goings on in the village; who has moved away; who has married and stayed in the town.

As the two men walk arm in arm towards the trolley heading for Tony's new life, they converse about how Mama, Salvatore, Mario, and Francesca are doing, and they reminisce about Settefrati and all its beauty and the people from the town who treat each other like family. They discuss the war, the day when Tony earned the Silver Star, and the people he met on his journey. There is one more topic Tony he needs to mention. "Papa, I need to tell you something important. Everyone calls me Tony now. It feels right in the United States. I hope you are not disappointed in me." "My son," Papa says, "Tony is a common abbreviation for Antonio. You were probably more comfortable as Tony during the war and also now with your new job. We are proud of you, Tony. Our prayers were for you to return to the United States healthy and whole and get on with your life, and our prayers were answered. You are an Italian American now. Mama and I are proud of you and very pleased that you did not change the family name. "I would never think of doing that, Papa," and they continued on their way.

Papa took to New York City as his son did. He now understood Tony's initial reaction and stories about the City. Like Tony, Papa admired the country's newness and found himself speechless when he entered Grand Central Station. He enjoyed the smooth train ride and the beautiful land. Everything Papa had heard about America did not give it full justice. When they were within range of the town of Port Chester, New York, Tony was anxious to point out the candy factory. Papa had a sweet tooth, and Tony had some of the candies with him as a treat for Papa after he saw the large candy display on the top of the company's headquarters. Just as Tony expected, Papa's sweet face, his joyful demeanor lit up when he saw the row of large plastic candies atop the building and received a small bag of the real candy for their trip. Father and son did love innovation, and Papa was mesmerized by the New World within hours of his arrival.

The ride to Stamford went quickly. It was déjà vu when Rocco appeared to drive Papa and Tony to Lucia's house. Papa entered the house admiring it and joyful to see his sister. A minute or two later, Helena exited the kitchen to greet Papa Angelo and found herself looking at the kindest face she had ever seen. Angelo's twinkling eyes emitted joy as did his smile. He was gentle and soft spoken, perceptive, and broke the ice by acknowledging how their meeting could have been awkward, yet he was so pleased to meet her. Sensing his warmth, Helena opened up, her smile bringing light to the room, and she told

Papa how delighted she was to meet him. Helena immediately took his jacket, prepared tea and refreshment for him, and sat beside him on the sofa asking about his journey.

During the conversation, Angelo reached for his bag and removed extraordinary gifts from not only him and Mama but from most people in the village. Clearly, Mama and Angelo had learned a great deal about Helena through Tony's letters, and they wished to pamper as well as please her. They showered her with beautiful fabrics from Italy that would enable her to create unique pieces for herself and the children they would have. The gifts also included kitchen staples, foods and linens, a gold chain that had belonged to Mama's mother, and a charming Italian hat to add to her collection.

After Papa relaxed for a while, Tony, Helena, and Lucia brought him to meet Luigi and Rosa. When Papa entered the house, he encountered familiar faces he had occasionally seen in passing in the district where they all lived. Papa knew of the family and was honored that Luigi and Rosa would be Tony's in-laws. As Papa took in the massive effort underway for the wedding, he was astounded by the generosity and authentic foods, and he, like Tony, saw Italy in the United States. *How fortunate Tony is so loved by all of them*, Angelo thought. He remembered what Mama had said from the start. She had been the force behind their son's immigration to the U.S. Her Angelo was shocked when she brought the subject up, wondering where the idea came from. How would that work he wondered, leaving Angelo to ask, "Are you thinking that we should all immigrate to the U.S.?"

When Mama replied "no," he was totally baffled, wondering how she could possibly consider sending her eldest child off to another country on his own. Who would care for him? But before he could ponder the thought, Mama said, "He is meant to be in the U.S." With those words, Papa understood that Mama had experienced a premonition. Her instincts did not come from stubbornness or desire. Rather, they were mystical. *She knew* a matter of destiny when she sensed one. In those situations, Angelo never resisted. Instead, he fulfilled his role by ensuring what Mama "saw" came to be. Now standing in his future daughter-in-law's home in the United States of America, seeing his son, a war hero, so happy, having met the woman of his dreams, someone whose heart was revealed to Angelo when they stood face to face, was an answer to Mama's prayers. How Mama will love Helena, Angelo thought. Within, Papa was filled with love and pride over the promise of Tony and Helena together.

As Tony had known for some time but was realizing once again after Papa's arrival, weddings center on the bride, and that was fine with him as it was for Papa. His precious time with Papa reassured Tony about his life in America during the critical period of his adjustment after the war and the joyful promise of his forthcoming marriage to Helena. Tony had not seen Papa since they spent time on the ship in Naples before its departure—eight years without any physical or direct contact with his parents and his siblings. Having Papa present to wish him and Helena well was the best gift he could imagine for the occasion. Theirs would be the perfect wedding, he thought, and it was.

A few days before the wedding, Tony joked about various logistical arrangements, claiming they rivaled those of World War II. He was referring to the mission to transport the largest food drop for the wedding to the church hall and store it for the friends and neighbors who would start preparing the meal early morning on the wedding day. The caravan carrying all the foods prepared except for the baked goods conjured the texture of a royal procession, which satisfied the drivers and their assistants who deemed their goods precious. Tony and his father provided oversight for the delivery, Angelo for seniority, and Tony because he was a war hero. Though the delivery team took the task seriously and worked hard, they were jubilant over completing their jobs with care and playing so important a role for Tony and Helena's wedding.

All other activity was otherwise calm, the bride and the groom considered older and perceived as mature. On their wedding day, May 25th, Tony was twenty-six and a half years old and Helena twenty-five. They were level-headed, did not lean toward excess, yet believed in a large and lively wedding reception that fed their guests well with traditional homemade dishes. Their modest approach reflected the immigrant way. It appealed to everyone and was respectful of both sets of parents and their modest means.

Helena was busier than Tony the days before the ceremony since she was placing the finishing touches on her gown and accessories while also checking on her bridesmaids. Tony and Angelo were free to spend time together while also getting Tony and Helena's apartment ready. As was customary with Italian families, the couple would get a head start in their married life with the goal of having their own home one day by living in one of the four apartments in her parents' relatively large home for a while. The couple was thrilled to have a place of their own close to her family.

Last minute details and getting the apartment in order consumed time the days before the wedding though the two families gathered every evening for dinner at least. Tony and Helena had no furniture of their own and selected some pieces from Rosa, Lucia, Helena's married siblings, and friends. Both Angelo and Tony cleaned and arranged everything, admiring the apartment in the process. Neither could get over its beautiful large windows and the lovely view of the gardens and small vineyard on the west side of the house.

The apartment's appealing features brought attention to an unusual contrast in living space between the northern part of the United States and the region in Italy where Tony was born. In the former, an urban area, private homes did not have acres of land, but the houses themselves were beautiful, offering interior space, high ceilings, and tall windows. Tony had always regarded himself as a person of light. He loved the sunshine and thrived outdoors. With its windows and high ceiling, the apartment pleased him for bringing the light of day inside. While there was so much sprawling land where Tony was born and raised in Italy, the houses were small, cave-like, and most often darkened to resist the warm Italian sun. It was rare to see a home in Italy with the small windows open and the sunlight pouring in as was the case in the apartment the day they were working. There was light and hope in the quarters Tony and Helena would occupy. It was the perfect nest for two shining people whose story together was about to begin.

⁓

Dawn broke on May 25th, the rosy sun giving way to a day of brilliant sunshine. Melodic birds sweetened the atmosphere, and the warmth of forevers permeated the air. Through the neighborhood and beyond, friends and family woke to the same rising beauty, their rousing thoughts turning to Helena and Tony—the promise of days to come.

Visions swirled and images formed. Forever snapshots of Tony and Helena at memorable places—the parks, beaches, and gardens that lined their story—warmed hearts, fueling excitement about the day.

The hours since sunrise were passing quickly. Guests appealed to time, asking it surrender to romance so that everyone could reach and rest on the pinnacle to watch the event unfold.

Fine clothing draped the chifforobe as the hour approached. Helena's gown and veil lay across the bed ready to crown the bride, the perfume from her gardenias scenting the room. Time stood still and then it rushed, a whirlwind surrounded the bride, yet she stood spellbound. Eight hands held the gown above her head and slowly lowered it onto her. The work of her hands fit her beautifully.

She knew herself, her look and style. Her maids stood amazed. She had succeeded in creating her dream gown. Silk satin with a sweeping twenty-inch train, a sweetheart neckline with a lace insert. Long sleeves falling below the cuff and a delicate heart-shaped crown with a detachable tulle veil met the length of the train.

Helena stood with her eyes closed feeling the rich fabric envelop her. Mother, her sisters, and a cousin touched up her hair and reached for the lipstick. "You're ready," they whispered, and she opened her eyes. Her gown, her image, her self.

Memories washed over her as they rode to the church. She saw Tony's face in her heart. The recollection of his arrival in 1938, his vivid green eyes that reached her soul.

The church stood peacefully. Ushers guarded the doors. She alighted from the car along the side entrance where Luigi waited. Chords of music began, the procession formed, she and Luigi completed the line.

Standing in the rear of the church, she saw little. As they proceeded, images came to life. She graced the walk by keeping her gaze forward. The scope of her vision widened, a cloud-like haze encapsulated Tony and her. Her eyes lit as she gazed into the penetrating joy in his eyes.

Chapter 34
There's No Going Back, Becoming American

When the shape of their charming cape cod house emerged, Tony and Helena's eyes teared up, they grasped their hands tightly and sighed, seeing themselves working side by side in the house to make it theirs. Against the backdrop of the lush back yard, the house was a palace in their eyes. They imagined their children on the grand porch on rainy days coloring, doing their schoolwork, and folding the laundry. Looking at their house from bottom to top, they felt elevated in society in a way that would benefit their family.

Tony and Helena traveled the familiar route from Connecticut to Grand Central Station after their wedding, basking in memories of their day. They talked about the special touches to their ceremony and reception, the importance of Papa's presence, and the circle dance, especially when the children joined in. They laughed about their story, Helena claiming that many of its chapters seemed to pass through the train station that had captured Tony's attention the day he arrived in the U.S.

When they reached Grand Central, they transferred to the Revolution Rail Co., a northern route that would take them to North Creek, New York, the town closest to Lake George. For a good portion of their trip, they rode along the Hudson River, another one of Tony's favorites for welcoming him to the United States. They passed from city to countryside, enjoying the river, the cliffs that rose from it, the historic mansions they passed, and the general ambience of a romantic train ride. Midway through their trip, there was a noticeable change in the landscape. It ascended and was deeply forested. That setting enhanced the dreamy fairy tale texture of the day. When they arrived at the station, they hired a taxi to take them to the Lake, where enchanting cottages of the past dotted the waterfront. There, they met Mrs. Marshall, the property owner who showed them to their charming cottage and oriented them to the grounds and surrounding area. Tony and Helena were besotted by their location. The atmosphere offered the perfect antidote to years of war and separation followed by eight months of frenetic activity after Tony's return, Papa's arrival, and preparing for the wedding.

Tony and Helena enjoyed idyllic days at the lake and in the small neighboring towns. They ferried the water on a steamboat, stopping in different locations for a meal or to visit a museum. They sat lakeside for many hours, savoring the protection of the mountains that wrapped around the water. The area was home to exquisite up and coming wineries that embodied the promise of fine wines from grapes grown in the U.S. The area's agricultural enterprises nestled between rolling hills and peaks exuded appeal since they evoked memories of Italy. Tony and Helena could understand why so many friends and family members recommended a visit to the Lake. When they arrived for what became the first of several trips to the area, they learned Italians often left New York City and made their way to the lake region to settle down and work the land. Though Tony understood the rationale

Antonio's *Story* 377

for living in a rural area, having grown up on a farm, he, and Helena too, genuinely enjoyed dynamic city life. But their love of the larger towns would never restrain them from returning to Lake George periodically during the hot city summers when the lake area was cool, refreshing, and relaxing.

The couple left Lake George one week after their arrival on a beautiful spring morning. While they thought there would a sameness to their ride, there was not. The vantage point differed, and the descent from the mountains was remarkable. Along the route, they reminisced about the week, starting with their wedding day and working their way to the present. They revisited Lake George in conversation, sharing their different views about what they favored about their stay and concluded there was still plenty to learn about the beautiful area. There was a matter Helena hoped to broach with Tony that morning, and she waited for the right time. As they traveled in the glow of the beautiful scenery and the past eventful weeks, she found the perfect moment for conversation.

∽

"Tony, don't you enjoy our car rides to visit the beautiful countryside and beaches in the Stamford area? We can stop whenever we want to explore lovely sights and take pictures."

Silence, as Tony is busy with wonder, observing the scenery from the train window.

"Tony, isn't it nice to go for a leisurely drive in the car to visit family and friends?"

"Helena, our rides are so enjoyable. It's a pleasure to explore Connecticut and go to New York City because the scenery is picturesque and always changing. We can take our time, relax, and enjoy ourselves."

"I agree, Tony. I love driving and was so proud when I got my license. Driving has brought a feeling of independence and has taken me so many places. But I was thinking it would be lovely to share in the fun of driving so I can take in the scenery from the passenger side too. If we take turns with driving, we can go on more rides than we do now. What do you think of that, Tony?"

Helena sees confusion in Tony's face, who says, "You know I love walking. My feet can take me anywhere I need to go. Trains are comfortable, too," he adds, and Helena realizes that Tony doesn't think of himself as a driver.

After speaking, it dawns on Tony that Helena may now be tired of always being the driver, but who will drive, he asks himself.

Several seconds pass with silence as Tony looks out the train window and the situation suddenly becomes clear. "Do you want me to learn to drive, Helena?" Tony now has terror in his face.

"I can see a strange look in your eyes," Helena says before she continues. "We need to think about when we have children. I will not be able to take care of the children in the car while I am driving. And we love our Sunday rides. I've been thinking of this for some time."

Brief silence follows, and a confused feelings float in the air.

"Well, yes, Helena, this is a great idea, something I never gave thought to do, but how would I learn?" This question is the cause for the concern on Tony's face.

"I will be your driving teacher!" Helena says. "I will teach you everything I know about driving."

Tony gives Helena a questioning look. "It would make sense for me to start driving too, and I'm sure you would be a great teacher, you have patience. But would I be a great student?"

"Well, Tony, let's give it a try and see how you do. We will take it step by step."

With a tentative smile, Tony responds, "This could be the experience of a lifetime and a great story to tell our children." And foremost in his mind, he is thinking about how overjoyed Mama will be when she finally meets his brave Helena.

Tony is now smiling happily, for he thinks of all the places he will drive his Helena.

Married life agreed with Tony and Helena. They created a warm and loving environment in their bright and airy apartment. The industry of work and homemaking served as the centerpiece of their lives, not in manufacturing terms but in the sense of building their nest, using the resources they had to create a welcoming atmosphere. They followed the Old World traditions of growing and canning vegetables and fruits, using Luigi and Rosa's gardens to increase plantings and then supplementing what they grew with the purchase of unique and hard to grow seedlings from local farms.

Though Tony and Helena were close to their Italian family, friends, and neighbors, they led their own lives. That could sound impossible, but they both held jobs and were out and about with other social groups a percentage of their time. They got along well with their family and friends but also realized differences in tastes and preferences. Tony and Helena never let go of the excitement of days at the beach, a show in New York City, traveling in the countryside, or taking a Sunday drive to learn about new neighborhoods being built. They were ambitious about their future, all in the interest of the family they hoped to have.

A little over a year after their wedding, Helena gave birth to their first child, a girl. Her arrival was the first in a succession of births, five total, four girls and a boy. With each child, the joy in their household increased to another level. The children became the center of their lives, the single most significant influence in every decision they made, and they began to dream about the opportunities their children would have. Two years later, when their second child was on the way, Tony and Helena started to think about more space and a place of their own. They explored different neighborhoods in their area looking for homes a comfortable walking distance from family, friends, and local schools. Neither of them wanted a house close to the center of town as those had limited property, nor did they find the construction of an entirely new neighborhood appealing as the properties lacked mature landscaping, identity, and character. They took their time searching. Eventually, their explorations guided them to an established neighborhood, where to their surprise a double lot with the option to build was on the market.

When Tony and Helena came upon the property during a walk, appreciating what they saw, a couple from the house next door joined them and introduced themselves as neighbors Helen and Howard, the lot's owners. The couple was friendly, a bit older than they, and childless, not by choice they lamented. Since Tony and Helena appeared interested, the four, along with the baby in a carriage, walked through the property, discussing the size of the lot and how a house might sit on the generous plot, which went uphill before it leveled to a huge and beautiful backyard where Tony already envisioned a lush garden. The property so appealing, they were interested yet concerned about new construction because they were not personally acquainted with any builders. When they mentioned their concern, Howard smiled and identified himself as the owner of a small construction company that built his house some time ago as a model. Helen graciously invited them in to look at the house and inspect Howard's work for reference. Their house was well maintained and well-constructed with several distinguishing features, such as large windows, a huge kitchen, elegant molding, a full basement, a pantry, and many other appealing touches. Tony could see the light in Helena's eyes. She loved the house and wanted one like it!

Tony took his time looking as they walked through the house, not that he was an expert but because he was certain he would notice major flaws if they existed. There was further discussion over coffee, which was a kind gesture, that delved into the type of house the couple might want. That topic was the exciting part for Tony and Helena. Since they had visited so many model and existing homes, they were clear about their dream house. Occasionally, the discussion shifted from the house to Tony, Helena, and their family. As was always the case, the conversation eventually included the war as well as where Tony worked and Helena's part-time work at home for the coat factory.

As the visit seemed to wind down, Howard reminded Tony that the price of the land was fixed, yet the overall cost would vary with their specifications for the house—its size and the features they chose, from the design of the front door to a porch or other external additions, number of floors, and types of windows. Tony asked about the general price range for a house like theirs and the land. The quote did not shock him. Tony and Helena emphasized they were interested, and before they could ask for time to think about the opportunity, Howard suggested they return the following week to discuss where they were in their thinking about the lot and a house and should feel free to visit the property any time. Helena sighed within, loving the property but not wanting to rush the decision. They exited the house receiving a warm good-bye. Helen looked down at the baby whose large dark eyes had opened and smiled lovingly, bringing warmth to everyone in the group.

Tony and Helena did not leave the neighborhood right away. They took their time walking through the lot again, and they began to vision their house. They could see themselves there whereas other houses or properties they viewed had pushed them away. Leaving in the direction of their apartment, they walked along most of the street, enjoying the children playing and the people smiling and waving to them. The couple talked about the land and a new house non-stop as they strolled. They were close to concluding that they were destined to live on that street.

Through the evening, they began the list of the features they'd like to see in their own home. They also talked about the neighborhood, especially Helen and Howard, who would be good neighbors. They looked at the property again on a weekday evening to learn more about the residents, the road that ran parallel, the streets, bus routes, and the location of schools. They also reviewed their finances. Neither felt they could pour everything they had into a house or have a mortgage payment they might not always be able to meet. They used a family member's car whenever they went places, but if they were no longer going to live with their family, a car would become a necessity and they had to budget for it. Thinking about a car, they thought of a garage, which introduced worry about spiraling costs, but they brushed their apprehension aside knowing they would have a house someday.

Tony and Helena were now feeling comfortable and excited about possibly striking a deal with Howard and Helen on the weekend. Howard was organized and knowledgeable when they met, explaining how costs were standardized, and it did not take long to for him to generate a fair contract. Tony left with a good feeling and the impression that Howard and Helen chose Tony and Helena as much as Tony and Helena chose their new neighbors and the beautiful lot.

The couple immersed themselves in the building of their home and relished following its construction. They appreciated how Howard managed the project and presented an overview of each phase before it began. His approach made it easy to adjust plans. They all worked well together and quickly became good friends as a prelude to being great neighbors to each other for decades. As they monitored the construction of their house, Tony and Helena met many neighbors and began receiving invitations to neighborhood events and activities. They were moving and starting their family during a time when the pace of life in America was calm and leisure time was enjoyed with family, friends, and neighbors. The vibrance of the neighborhoods and emphasis on socializing shaped the concept of the American lifestyle following the war. In the time ahead, families like Tony, Helena, and their children, who lived through that era, would look to the past as a time of innocence and good will.

Even before the house was completed, Tony and Helena began to cultivate the land. They added some of their favorites to the beautiful trees and bushes on the lot. Tony propagated and grew their trees, the most important one from the root of his fig tree at Lucia's house. As the days passed, the foliage of their existing trees became lush, and their vision became more vivid. Their back lawn had the look of a meadow and part of it was reserved for the picnic tables they would someday have. They talked about a traditional Italian outdoor brick oven, and Tony was sure he could build one with help of friends. Beyond the garden, they imagined a swing set for the children, and now they looked forward to two little girls on the swings as their second daughter was born while the house was under construction. The scenes they pictured and discussed caused their skin to prickle with excitement. Images became real in their minds, capturing the promise and richness of family life.

Shortly after the birth of their second child, Tony and Helena's family expanded in a completely unexpected way when Tony's cousin Antonio returned to the U.S. leaving his wife, Tony's sister, Francesca, and their child in Italy until she and the child were ready to enter the U.S. The day Francesca and her child joined the Buzzeo family in the U.S. was a celebratory occasion for the expanded the presence of Tony's family in America. Life with Lucia, Francesca and family, and Tony and Helena and family along with all of Helena's family was idyllic, yet it would get even better in time.

The frame for Tony and Helena's house was completed around the time of Francesca's arrival. The floor and wallboards followed, and excitement about the impeding completion intensified. Little by little, the family began to see the key features of their house— its structure, space, rooms, entries, attic, and basement. When the shape of their charming cape cod house emerged, Tony and Helena's eyes teared up, they grasped hands tightly and sighed, seeing themselves working side by side in the house to make it theirs. Against the backdrop of the lush back yard, the house was a palace in their eyes. They imagined their children on the grand porch on rainy days coloring, doing their schoolwork, and folding the laundry. Looking at the house from bottom to top, they felt elevated in society in a way that would benefit their family. Helena could see herself hanging the clothes on a clothesline that ran from the porch to the tree across the yard. She knew how she would enjoy every moment on that porch, especially looking over the property line in the back to the small pond and ducks. She could foresee her children's excitement over their presence. Dreams do come true, she thought, with gratitude for not one dream but for the bushel of dreams she was living then.

Eventually, their house was finished. Built with tender care and appointed well inside and out, it was another charm in a modest well-maintained neighborhood. The house rested at the top of the small hill in the front yard. It sat closer to the street than Howard and Helen's home did. The look was great, for the house appeared to be perched on its location and that gave it appeal. Situated as it was, the structure required ascending access to the front entry, and the resulting steps amplified the building's presence. Custom-made, the house met their needs and fulfilled a dream. The large kitchen suited Helena's love for cooking, baking, and hosting family dinners. She could enter the kitchen from the backside of the house, which was convenient for pulling the laundry off the clothesline and bringing fresh vegetables in from the garden. The entire interior was spacious, and all rooms were well lit with large windows. As the family grew with the addition of their third daughter, there was no problem with reconfiguring one bedroom to sleep all three girls, which was great fun and the source of forever memories for the children.

The couple was ambitious and put their energy toward transforming their house into a home. As a seamstress, Helena had a gift for working with fabrics to create atmosphere. She used the rich textiles Tony's parents gifted her to create elegant drapes for the living room and bedrooms. She also shopped at fabric sales, searching for discontinued materials and remnants to create a warm environment in the kitchen. Embroidery or trim in the ornate Italian tradition adorned all her handiwork though she shied away from bold colors, preferring light muted tones instead. Helena's bedspreads were works of art with subtle designs that were peaceful and restful. Her skills were the envy of many.

Tony's work addressed both indoor and outdoor improvements though he had an affinity for working outdoors. Inside, he set up the basement with tools and supplies, organized a storage area in the attic, painted accent trim in the kitchen, and hung family photos, religious images, and other adornments on the walls. His greatest contributions were seen outdoors, where he now had the wood-burning brick stove he dreamed of. He tended to their fig tree, which in time reached the height of those in Italy, bringing memories and their heritage to the New World while inspiring new dreams. He added to the backyard's country charm by planting peach and pear trees, growing red roses, and turning one half of the back yard into a vegetable garden.

The neighborhood they joined was a prize. It was not fully Italian American as the streets around Helena's parents' home was, yet it was a predominantly immigrant neighborhood with most residents first generation of European descent. Howard, their contractor, was also of European descent, second generation. The immediate community consisted of three streets, a total of fifty-six privately-owned homes off a wider and busier street filled with services—a deli, laundry, vacuum repair shop, and small grocery as well as bus service. Beyond that defined neighborhood came another larger community that ran west for close to two and a half miles. It was diverse in population and zones, whereby small manufacturing, businesses, and services were integrated with housing. All in all, the general location of Tony and Helena's new house reflected the essence of dynamic living. Diversity combined with access to transportation, services, and cultural as well as religious organizations shaped a robust community that enabled every family to thrive.

Through interactions at work, their church, and the school their oldest daughter now attended, Tony and Helena expanded their horizons naturally in their neighborhood, cultivating their interests and involvement. Their instincts led logically to concerns close to their hearts—the educational system, workers, and the immigrant community. Participating in the life of local schools was easy because they had a child in school already, and that meant participating in bake sales, helping in the classroom, attending bingo nights, going to PTA meetings, and voting for sound programs and services.

Their outside activities caused their circle of acquaintances and awareness of needs in the community to increase. Since Helena worked at home, her schedule was flexible, and she often spent time at school and played a special role with a few other mothers in supporting school plays by making costumes for the children. Her involvement led to knowledge about the schools that was otherwise difficult to obtain and also supported awareness about migration to foster wider acceptance and understanding of the needs of immigrant children.

There were parallels between Helena's civic activities and Tony's. His interests centered on the immigrant, grew out of his own experience, and were invigorated by the current movement to ensure fair compensation for unskilled laborers. Speaking from experience, Tony regarded labor as the backbone of the country's development. In the aftermath of the Great Depression, it seemed not only fair but a moral imperative to ensure adequate compensation and protection for workers. At the local level through his Catholic Church, Tony, by then a supervisor in a factory that manufactured meters, became a spokesperson for the rights of workers that helped introduce benefits plans in local plants.

In time, Tony was driven to do more than advocate. Initially, he and a few family members and friends organized a social club for Italian immigrants to establish casual connections and create a formal support system. Eventually, the group incorporated as the Settefratese Social Club, with Tony serving as one of the organization's founders. Within a year, the society constructed its own building, creating a meeting place where Italian families could socialize, hold wedding receptions, play bocce, and much more. It also provided a variety of social services.

Tony served as one of the club's officers for decades, experiencing the satisfaction of shepherding what became a non-profit entity to expand services beyond basic needs. Groundbreaking assistance supported by donations and dues introduced unprecedented aid, such as temporary financial support and medical care for members and their families provided by a group of dedicated Italian American physicians for a small fee. A model was born for other immigrant communities to follow, and the rise of the immigrant populations within the fabric of American society was underway.

Tony's and Helena's individual and joint contributions to their communities surprised their families and friends in the most pleasant of ways. The two could never adequately explain how their involvement evolved, but when the subject came to mind, it always returned to their children and the world they would enter. They were children of an immigrant, and Tony and Helena never wanted the status of or attitudes toward immigration to interfere with their children's opportunities and advancement.

The post-war period was a time for fulfilling dreams for Tony and Helena's generation. Opportunities to advance socioeconomically were playing out. Owning a home came first, and having a car followed. Other amenities regarded as frivolous in the past were now part of every household, items like electric kitchen tools, telephones, and a TV. American Idealism was functioning at its height spurring a generation to envision and fulfill their personal American Dreams in the wake of the Depression and World War II. The period offered the earliest signs of the prosperity within reach of post-war newlyweds, who had the luxury of following the dreams they wanted to pursue. In the case of Tony and Helena, there was such contentment with their own family and extended family that they never returned to any of the war-related dreams of traveling and seeing the world. Tony had never adjusted fully to the transience of military life and treasured the stability he had with Helena, their home, family, and community. One evening they talked about where their lives and family were headed, sharing contentment with their mutual plans and dreams. Together without prompting, they each stated simultaneously, "We are living our dreams," the greatest testament to their love and joy in life. But they had to ask themselves, will our family in Italy be comfortable with our long-term plans in the U.S.?

An unexpected event that could have been foreseen helped Tony and Helena answer their question. In 1953, Mama, Papa, and their youngest son, Mario, arrived in the U.S. after Angelo was recruited in Italy for long-term temporary work on the south tube of the Lincoln Tunnel, which would connect New Jersey to Mid-town Manhattan. The project ran through 1957, and the family remained in the U.S. for a few more years. Their decision to remain longer rested as much with giving Papa an opportunity to enjoy New York following completion of his temporary work as it did the arrival of Tony's brother Salvatore and his new bride while Angelo was still working. Since Tony had become a naturalized citizen of the U.S. almost a decade ago, he was able to sponsor his brother and sister-in-law, who arrived initially on a temporary basis and eventually became citizens. For some time then, Tony's entire family resided in the U.S., with Lucia, Tony, and his sister in Connecticut and his parents and two brothers in New York City. Those were golden years for the family. They lived fully during that remarkable period when they were all in America, enjoying time together, along with their Italian family and friends in both states.

For Tony and Helena's children, having two sets of grandparents in the U.S. was a thrilling experience, especially when they gathered in New York, which meant a train ride and arrival in the splendid Grand Central Station, their daddy always describing how he felt the first time he saw the opulent structure. As the decade continued and they moved toward the 1960s, their sense of financial security increased steadily, Tony and Helena welcomed two more children, a girl and a boy. The two children completed the family structure, and the couple continued to enjoy watching their children grow and their talents develop. School remained an important influence in their lives, more so than ever once all five children were in school and spreading their wings. The family's social circle expanded as a result, the children's friends bringing other cultures and faiths into their home. Together, the family learned "the American way of doings things."

Years had passed since Tony and Helena's first child entered school and the three of them attended open house, marveling over the bright school environment, the beautifully decorated classrooms, special programs like music and physical education, and a school nurse. Tony and Helena often reminisced about that meeting, for it set forth a rich portrait of the dreams they wished to follow. Welcome Night at school captured the essence of their character and love for their children. It showed the way they lived and what they honored, values they passed on to the next generation.

Time was kind to Tony and Helena, blessing them with love and joy though they never stopped working hard to fulfill their dreams. Family remained the focus of their lives, and they enjoyed the rhythm of their children's growing up years, their family story lively with the memory of decades of threshold events occurring at different intervals over time. More often alone at home as their children gained their independence, Tony and Helena frequently sat together and paused to look back at the yesterdays of their family life. They cherished each child as unique and special and celebrated their individuality and natures as distinct yet complementary to one another. Most often on those sometimes-lonely evenings, they took each other's hand and with tears in their eyes shared the realization that their children—their proudest achievement— represented the fulfillment of their lives together and the dreams that had begun to form when they first met on Tony's best-ever second day in the United States.

Epilogue, Part I

Mama

Kennedy Airport, New York
Summer 1966

Tony and his family stood on the tarmac, all five children in tow, sparkly clean and dressed in their Sunday best. They lined up by age, oldest to youngest, and eagerly awaited the plane's arrival. They could distinguish the aircraft easily from other planes due to its bright blue logo, and they watched it descend. The plane grew as it approached the runway. No one in the family, but for Tony, had ever been on a plane, so there was fear as well as amazement as the aircraft made its way to them, gliding along its path. Every now and then the plane was not visible, which scared the youngest children.

The view was clear when touchdown occurred, and the five children bounced when the plane did as though they, too, were landing. The aircraft taxied to the area where the family stood. They watched the commotion on the ground as the crew prepared for arrival by rolling the mobile gateway closer to the arrival point and then waiting. Slowly working its way to the gate, the massive plane grew larger and larger, commanding the scene. It arrived, the engines shut down, and they waited. When the means for exiting were in place, the door opened with a flourish. A gentleman, the airline's host for the flight, stepped out and then extended his left arm to a passenger ready to exit, someone important the children decided, and they waited for the famous person to appear.

The center of attention stepped over the threshold, turning back to wave to those in the doorway the way a Pope did, exited the plane, and then took the arm of the young man who would escort her down the stairs while holding the generations-old rolling pin as a gift for Helena in her other hand. The attendant and the woman proceeded down the steps in the style of Old World pageantry. The youngest child did not know the person. The oldest two knew and adored her, the middle two were confused.

Tony and Helena had to hold back their smiles in the likelihood that they would lead to laughter as Mama regally descended the steps, her entourage following with her two trunks and other belongings. Since Mama was exuberant and very social on the plane, no passenger or crew member mistook her for a religious sister although her attire suggested otherwise.

Mama was dressed in the traditional clothing of peasants from the hills beyond Rome—a long black dress to the ankle with a defined waistline and a very full skirt, a crisp white lace apron, and a white babushka covering her head. Though well-aware that she was in America, Mama honored her country and culture by wearing her region's traditional garb, pleasing the hearts of the predominantly Italian passengers on the plane. The oldest children versed the younger, telling them the woman was Nona and their eyes popped when learning the figure was grandma, their grandma, a fiercely loving grandma, they would soon learn.

Tony and Helena rushed to greet Mama, her son first with the others following in order. A dramatic, emotional, and endearing scene played out on the tarmac. Tony happened to look to his side, checking Mama's belongings, and found himself facing the pine treasure trunk he had carried to the U.S. in 1938. He was overwhelmed to see his traveling companion and even more overjoyed by Mama's arrival.

Epilogue, Part 2

Antonio

Rome Airport, Fiumicino, Italy
Summer 1972

When Tony stepped off the plane and into the airport, the dynamic environment, the aroma of baked goods and foods, and the rhythm of the Italian language reverberating from every corner of the building told him he was home. "*La mia Italia,*" Tony whispered. He managed to guide his family to the airport exit, his eyes searching for Bruno, who would take them to the village.

Bruno, a family friend who lived in Rome, waited in the carpark for Tony, Helena, and their two youngest children to arrive. It was not easy finding him at the crowded airport, but soon Bruno was running toward them, offering a warm welcome and shepherding them through the crowd and to his car. Their journey to the village was soon underway.

The initial segment of the route was not familiar to Tony since he had never traveled by car between Rome and his village, yet he was dazzled by the scenery. It was filled with lovely gardens, captured the contrast between ancient and modern architecture, and featured tall trees that carried a religious aura. The rings of Rome, the system of roads that spiraled out of the city, showed its outskirts, the residential, retail, business, and dining areas that bustled with life that morning.

When they traveled beyond the rings of Rome and headed to the hills, emotion washed over Tony because everything he saw was familiar and personal. The scenery pulled him in as though it had been waiting for his return. He breathed the fresh air and scent of the country, and it catapulted him to his past. Memories flooded his thoughts, and he was overcome by the vivid remembrances he had held onto for such a long time. They came alive as though they were born again that day.

Tony closed his eyes, his heart filling with emotion. He summoned images from his walk through the village the day before he left and toured the cemetery. Now, though, he saw Papa's name among the other Buzzeos.

Though Helena and the children were jet lagged, Tony was alive. He was returning to his childhood home for the first and only time since he left thirty-four years ago. He found himself glued to the window as he was the day he arrived in Connecticut. Though he knew every inch of the itinerary, he studied everything with razor-sharp attention as though it was brand new. He had never forgotten, could never forget, the road that climbed to the village though he now questioned whether he thought about it as much as he should have.

When Bruno navigated the final hairpin turn, Tony concentrated on its sharpest angle, seeing in it both his departure from Italy and, now, his return. He could see Mama and the villagers waiting for him in the distance, as Helena along with family and friends had when he returned from the war. Now approaching their heritage, he narrated here and there about points of importance. Mesmerized by the beautiful land, Italian architecture, gorgeous landscapes, and brilliant sun, Helena and the children surrendered to a connection that pulled them in. Italy was irresistible, and it was also their heritage. All five children were of one hundred percent Italian ancestry—children of the district where Papa and Mama and Luigi and Rosa had all been born.

They were now approaching the piazza, where a feast awaited. Mama, a beloved and generous figure in the community, stood at the head of the group. Italian music played, charming the children, who would be received lovingly by more people than they could ever imagine.

Arriving, the car stopped, and they stepped out. Now seventy-four years old and still thriving, Mama called out, "Antonio!" She ran to her son and through the line of her family who had come to visit, overcome with joy over their arrival. Everyone applauded. Helena and the children submitted themselves wholly to the welcome feast, joining in the revelry and applause of tears.

The villagers, Antonio, and his family wasted no time. They formed the traditional circle for a celebratory Italian folk dance, clutching each other's hands and dancing triumphant rounds that they reversed from time to time. They paused once to create an opening for Mama and Antonio to enter the circle, and mother and son danced in the town square as they did throughout his growing up years. The sweetest moment of a lifetime settled on Mama as she and Antonio swayed and twirled, bringing life to the medieval village.

A gentle breeze wafted from the valley as they danced, wrapping everyone in the exotic scents of the village that afternoon. The brilliant Italian sun was one of promise and life. For Antonio, the world shifted. He sensed Papa's presence in his mind and held the image of his hand tracing the ship's route in his heart. Antonio now understood his life story as Papa said he would. Everything he had undertaken and accomplished suddenly felt right and meant to be. As that thought crossed his mind, Antonio felt the comfort of Papa's arm across his shoulders.

Acknowledgements

Antonio's Story, Coming of Age on the Battlefields of WW II is the book I have longed to write for some time, and I am grateful to everyone who has helped me bring my dream to fruition. I am grateful to my husband, Laurence Best, for his interest, encouragement, and support from the start. His counsel, knowledge of military history, technical expertise, and willingness to read and discuss the entire manuscript enabled me to meet my expectations for the narrative and its appeal to readers. I am also deeply grateful to our children and their families not only for their interest but for the regard they have always shown for my passion to write.

Putting the pieces of the story together called for the daunting task of collecting family information and stories, interviewing elderly family members, translating my father's personal letters and writing, and drawing stories out of photographs. I would not have accomplished the aforementioned without the support and interest of an important segment of my audience, our children and grandchildren, along with my siblings, aunts and uncles, cousins, nieces and nephews and their families. For a decade, I tracked stories through them on holidays, during visits, and at weddings that enabled me to construct the storyline.

I must thank my sisters Louise, Rose, and Deb and my brother, Tony, for embracing my goal to re-create our father's story and recognize the contributions of my sister Deb, who read and commented on sections of the book, suggested ideas, shared stories, and provided much needed assistance with the authentic feel of Italian language and culture in the book.

Many friends have helped along the way. I appreciate the contributions of my long-time colleague and friend Sharon Haussmann for her critical reading of my first full draft of the manuscript. Her objective review led me to control or expand content as needed to achieve a stronger and more vivid narrative. My friend Tonya Belvin was enthusiastic from the start, always asking about the book's progress. Our discussions about it enriched my perspective on the subject matter through her eyes as a reader. Several groups of people who are part of my writing and reading life expressed genuine and generous interest in this book—the women in my LL Book Club, the women in my Prayer Group, the participants in my Memoir Writing Class, my writing clients, and my Community Writing Groups—the local in-person group and the vibrant international Writing Community on Twitter whose members have cheered me along, read excerpts of my manuscript, and provided the feedback enabling me to gauge the quality of my work.

From as early as first grade when I wrote a story entitled "The Magic Garden," I have found writing exciting for its power and voice. Eventually, I created a career around it. I have lived the writer's life as a Professor of English/Writing, a vocation made for me, and in that capacity, I expanded my knowledge of writing by learning ways of writing from colleagues and students. The latter including my current work totals at minimum 20,000 students/class participants who taught me as much as I instructed them. And I am grateful to every student I have interacted with for contributing to my growing awareness of writing's complex joy and revelation that inspired me to write *Antonio's Story*.

Lightning Source UK Ltd.
Milton Keynes UK
UKHW011823270622
405020UK00001B/33